A SONG AT TWILIGHT

BRYAN FORBES

A SONG AT TWILIGHT

COLLINS
8 Grafton Street, London W1
1989

William Collins Sons & Co. Ltd
London · Glasgow · Sydney · Auckland
Toronto · Johannesburg

BRITISH LIBRARY CATALOGUING IN PUBLICATION DATA
Forbes, Bryan
A song at twilight.
I. Title
823′.914[0]

ISBN 0-00-223442-4

First published 1989
Copyright © Bryan Forbes Limited 1989

Photoset in Linotron Times by
Rowland Phototypesetting Ltd
Bury St Edmunds, Suffolk
Printed and bound in Great Britain by
William Collins Sons & Co. Ltd, Glasgow

This book is for Sarah, John,
Emma and Graham

Every revolution evaporates and leaves behind only the slime of a new bureaucracy.

FRANZ KAFKA

MOST SECRET

HILLSDEN, Alec George Arthur, born 1926, educated West Ham Grammar School, married and subsequently divorced Margot Anne Willars no issue. No known political affiliations (see positive vetting records in restricted section). Served in Intelligence Corps 1944–5 obtaining war-substantive rank of Warrant Officer II. Seconded to MI6 upon demobilization and posted to Vienna station. Returned London 1950 attached D4 without special privileges. Posted to Cyprus 1952, Beirut 1954, then had spell as Military Attaché Toronto embassy with temporary rank of Major before transfer to Washington and later Bermuda. Rejoined Austrian station 1968 and remained there until 1978. During this second period formed adulterous liaison with Caroline Oates, GM (deceased/File 704/RT907 also File 709/RT/AZ re Nicolson). Returned to London (Ref: 8634/DF) until defection. Accused murder of Sir Charles Belfrage and implicated in Glanville affair. Present whereabouts USSR. Granted Soviet citizenship and given rank of Colonel in GRU. Case still open, refer any additional information DG only immediate. END.

Extract from entry in MI6 records

1

26 December

The Fat Boy had not spent that Christmas in London for pleasure. Unlike Baudelaire his eyes were not drawn upward to the stars when he walked the streets, and the festive season left him unmoved. Murder was the only gift he ever gave, death was the only gift he was likely to receive.

In order to meld into the landscape and prepare for his next assignation he had taken what the French call a *chambre de bonne* on the sixth floor of a building in the Brixton area, paying a month's rent in advance – just enough to satisfy the landlord's avarice. With his usual thoroughness he had assumed a new identity before entering England via the Harwich ferry at the beginning of December: his hair had been cropped and dyed a lighter colour, and for weeks before he embarked he had maintained a rigid diet, shedding some twenty pounds, for he was well aware that the facile nickname the Western press had pinned on him spelt danger. He was still big, but much of the grossness had gone from his face and gut, and he wore clothes a size too large which gave the illusion of less bulk. Several times since commencing his career he had endured plastic surgery, notably to reduce his tell-tale bee-stung lips; the Libyan surgeon had done a reasonable job, but the wound had turned septic, leaving a scar on the upper lip that stood out on his olive complexion. He had tried a moustache, but the hair had not grown on the scar and he had resorted to blotting it out with a feminine cosmetic cream.

He had no love for London, his accidental birthplace, or for the British for that matter. Born Rojas Jorge Rejano, he had suffered nine taunted years in a succession of English private schools until his obscenely rich and despised parents had returned home to Argentina; and it was there, suffocated by affluence, that he spent his formative years, indolent at university, only graduating in hatred. By the time he was seventeen he was a concealed member of Argentina's hard-line Moscow-orientated Communist Party. When he came of age he inherited a large trust fund set up by his grandfather and used the money to sever all filial ties, making his way to Moscow via East Germany. In Moscow he enrolled in the Patrice Lumumba University, a finishing school for subversives directed and largely staffed by the KGB. Regarded as promising material, his teachers sent him to Camp Matanzas in Cuba where he received further advanced training in urban guerrilla tactics, weaponry and killer-karate. As with many other youthful revolutionaries of that period, he lacked the historical justification of a deprived upbringing, so dedicated his life to the destruction of his own class. If, at the beginning, he had slavishly carried out Moscow's orders, he had long since exceeded them, disregarding individual causes, selling his lethal talents to the highest bidder and creating a unique terrorist currency to suit his own chilling philosophy. He was a whore for death, hawking his wares amongst a motley list of clients.

At precisely four o'clock that Boxing Day afternoon, after first donning a pair of fake pebble-lens spectacles, the Fat Boy left the room he would never return to. Outside, the city had started to come back to life. A light sprinkling of snow had fallen overnight, and the skies were still leaden. The streets had that air of quiet solemnity which always follows a day of celebration; for most people life was not quite normal but hung between the evening of pleasure and the morning when the struggle for survival recommenced.

He carried a plastic bag of groceries and walked unnoticed and anonymous to the Oval Underground station, occasionally grimacing to himself as he picked his way past scattered piles of refuse that would not be collected until the New Year. The station booking office was likewise fouled with discarded junk-food cartons. He purchased a ticket for a distant destination before boarding the first train to arrive. After travelling a few stops he switched platforms and doubled back, repeating this manoeuvre twice more before he was satisfied he was not being tailed. Only then did he board a train to a district in the East End of the city.

He emerged in an area of London that had once been a prime target for the Luftwaffe. Rebuilt by planners more concerned with redrafting the political map than with following the elementary dictates of architectural form, it had lost all identity, becoming with the passing of the years a faceless wasteland. The clusters of high-rise buildings gave the appearance of having been carelessly fashioned from children's toy bricks. Many were crumbling, and the hollow postwar promise of a better life for the underprivileged mocked from every broken window, every weather-soiled balcony.

Picking his way across an open piece of ground originally set aside as a children's playground, he skirted the defunct gallows-like swings, the twisted metal of a broken roundabout, and entered one of the tower-blocks. Inside the bare concrete hallway that stank of stale beer, an old man covered with cardboard lay sleeping off the night's excesses by the side of a lift that no longer functioned. The Fat Boy walked softly, approaching each graffiti-daubed landing with caution until he reached the fourth floor. A baby was crying behind one of the row of identical doors, and he heard a man shout an obscenity to silence it.

The scarred door he knocked on was opened immediately by a slatternly-looking girl in her twenties. She wore a T-shirt emblazoned with the face of a pop star who had long since died of a heroin overdose. She welcomed him with a seasonal greeting, but he made no response, walking past her and into the main room. Removing the bogus spectacles, he scanned the room with a practised eye, then moved to inspect the kitchen and small bedroom. Only then did he acknowledge the girl.

'You live like a pig,' he said.

She shrugged. 'When you live here you stay in character with your neighbours if you don't want to attract attention.' There was no resentment in her voice. 'You want coffee?'

11

He nodded and went to the window, looking down into the street without disturbing the frayed curtains. The girl watched him while boiling some water in a saucepan.

'Where is it?' the Fat Boy said.

'In the bathroom.'

He went there, and a cockroach scuttled across the lino at his approach. Ducking under a line of washing strung across the room, he stood on the toilet seat, lifted the lid of the old-fashioned water-tank and removed a small parcel wrapped in an oiled bag.

'It's clean,' the girl said when he returned. Now she spoke in French. 'It came in the diplomatic bag. Untraceable.'

The Fat Boy swept debris from the table and carefully unwrapped the parcel, revealing a further sealed plastic bag containing a revolver fitted with a silencer. He did not answer her, but dismantled the weapon and checked it thoroughly, examining every bullet, loading and reloading the magazine until satisfied that the bullets fed smoothly. Before finally replacing the magazine he tested the trigger pressure.

'OK? Satisfied?' She placed a cup of black coffee in front of him.

'What car did you get?'

'A small Ford.'

He grimaced as he took his first sip of coffee. 'This cup smells of disinfectant.' He turned the cup round and drank from the spot nearest the handle.

'Well, you wouldn't want to catch anything, would you?' she said, but the sarcasm was lost on him.

'Did you test it?'

'The cup or the car?' she answered with the same wasted irony. 'Course I tested the car. What d'you take me for? Here!' She dropped the ignition keys on the table. 'It's got a full tank of gas, the plates have been changed, and the engine and chassis serial numbers filed off.'

Removing some of her clothes from the only comfortable chair, the Fat Boy sat down and checked the gun yet again. 'I don't like this type. They're not a hundred per cent reliable.'

'It's what I was supplied with.' She stared at him. 'You've lost a lot of weight. I hope the clothes fit you. I went by the measurements I was given.'

'Where did you buy them?'

'In Northampton a month ago. Why a jogging outfit? What's that all about – you going in for a health cure?'

'Save the jokes.'

'What joke? Only trying to make conversation. I've been on my own in this bloody dump for six weeks.' She lit a cigarette and held out the packet for him, but he ignored the offer. 'Being on your own doesn't worry you, I suppose.'

'No.'

'Well, it makes me stir crazy. I hate this country.'

'All the more reason to be here. When you leave make sure you take everything with you.'

'Don't tell me my job,' she said. 'Anyway, you could die in this pit and nobody would know for weeks.' She stubbed out her cigarette on the table-top. 'Do you want to be entertained while you're waiting? I take it you're staying the night? Tell me and I'll try to oblige.'

He stared at her. 'Such as?'

'How about some jolly British Christmas cheer on the telly?'

'I'd rather watch paint dry.'

'A video, then? Fancy some porn?'

'That how you pass your time?'

'If you can't join them, watch them, is my philosophy.' She met his eyes without turning away.

'Don't tell me you went out and bought them?'

She got up and fed a tape into the machine. 'No, I didn't buy them. Santa left them for me. I found them here. Not great quality, pirated American stuff, third-generation. Some of it looks as though it was shot in a snowstorm.'

She fiddled with the rewind button. 'This one isn't bad, set in a girls' school, though the pupils are a bit long in the tooth to be wearing gymslips.'

The action commenced almost at once, with the school janitor giving a practical biology lesson in one of the class-rooms. A blonde student of indeterminate age immediately

13

succumbed to the janitor's advances. Quickly stripped and spreadeagled over a school desk, she resembled little more than a pink carcass being roughly manhandled. It was like watching a documentary on a meat market.

'Does it excite you?'

'Why would it?' he said.

'That's what they're made for. Does nothing turn you on?'

'Not when I'm working.'

'And after work?'

'You'll never know, will you?'

He got up from the chair and went to the window once more. It was dark now, and after scanning the street below he pulled the curtains closed. The girl stopped the video-tape and switched on a light.

'Well, I tried,' she said. 'How would you like to spend the rest of your time?'

'Let me see the clothes.'

She fetched them from the bedroom, and he examined every article carefully.

'If they need altering, I'll fix them.'

He stripped in front of her. 'Be all right with a belt,' he said, when he had tried on the trousers. The jogging-top also passed muster.

'Very fetching,' the girl said. 'I'm glad I did something right.'

As he took them off again and threw them to her she caught the scent of male sweat. It occurred to her that despite his act of studied calm he, too, was capable of fear. For the first time since he entered the flat he seemed human.

'Did you time the route for me?'

'Of course. Half a dozen times. Don't forget it's Christmas; this bloody country shuts down. At that hour there'll hardly be any goods traffic, but to be on the safe side I took the average. Give yourself forty minutes at the outside and you've got it made. You can park in Exhibition Road; plenty of empty spaces there.'

'You have something else to give me, don't you?'

The girl went into the kitchen, returning with a package.

14

'Composition C4,' she said, handing it to him. 'Semtex is too dangerous, now that they can trace it.'

'Make yourself useful and get me something to eat.'

While the girl prepared a meal he passed the time reading one of the Sunday tabloids, which featured such exclusives as 'Cheeseburger Kills Space Alien' and a report that Marilyn Monroe was alive and working as a nanny. Only once did he give a laugh.

'What?' the girl said.

'This story: "Human Mole Tunnels to France."''

'They make those up, if you ask me. Be interesting when they finally finish the real Channel Tunnel, won't it?'

'Yes. We already have plans for that. Once they've had their opening ceremony, we'll give them a closing ceremony.'

'At least they've got a workers' militia now, so maybe one revolution's under way.'

'Don't talk like a cretin. The British don't know how to spill their own blood.'

They watched the nine o'clock news bulletin while they ate, then the Fat Boy announced he was turning in. He took the only bed without asking, leaving the girl to sleep in the armchair.

The next morning he was up before she woke, dressed in the jogging suit and carrying his ordinary clothes in the plastic grocery bag. After listening for any sounds on the landing he left the room. The noise of the door closing roused her. She went to the window and watched as he walked to the parked Ford and drove away, her breath misting the view. 'Happy New Year,' she said softly, but it took an effort to believe that happiness existed for anybody, least of all for herself.

At six that morning Hyde Park seemed an unlikely setting for murder. It was near-deserted at that hour – only a troop of Household Cavalry from Knightsbridge Barracks exercising their horses in Rotten Row and a few overweight stalwarts grimly jogging round the perimeter track. Patches of overnight fog still clung close to the ground, and where the horses had passed piles of fresh dung steamed. Those plane trees that had not been plucked like healthy teeth in the 1987 hurricane presented drooped branches brittle with ice, and the grass beneath them was rigid with frost. Even so, despite the ravages of winter, it still looked lusher and less sinister than the black rocks and parched grass of Central Park.

Opposite in Kensington Road, two uniformed officers of Special Branch on diplomatic assignment waited for their relief shift to arrive. They stood shifting their numbed feet in the doorway of a Middle Eastern legation, a few steps from the building where once the SAS had performed live on television with spectacular effect to free a group of hostages. Their current duty was to guard a visiting emissary who had come to solicit an arms deal from the British government in order to sustain a subversive war. Since the man's enemies were thick on the ground in London (the British being crassly willing to provide a battleground for warring foreigners) twenty-four-hour protection had been provided at the public expense. It was not the most popular duty, certainly not to the elder of the two policemen, a married man with three sons named Langton, who had been known to voice views that conflicted with the recently strengthened Race Relations Act.

'Funny things, horses,' he said, staring across to the park as the Household Cavalry cantered by. 'Can't say I've ever taken to horses. Bovine creatures.'

'No. Cows are bovine,' his companion, Constable Jenkins, corrected.

'Well, you know what I mean. Nothing up top. Very little between the ears. And they're colour blind.'

'That a fact?'

Langton stared at him, irritated that his second statement should also be challenged. 'It's a *known* fact to most people. No, give me dogs any day. I was a handler before I was transferred. Had a wonderful bitch. Alsatian. That dog could have won Brain of the Year. She had more grey matter than half a dozen Chief Constables.'

16

'Still got her?'

'No. She copped a lump of brick up in Yorkshire during the coal strike. Cried my bloody eyes out, I did.'

His companion, Constable Jenkins, who looked absurdly young and sported a tentative moustache which he mistakenly believed gave him added maturity, let a hand rest on the bulge of his Smith & Wesson, which he had never fired in anger. The thought of Langton crying over the loss of a dog made him uneasy.

'That's the trouble with animals,' he said finally. 'They always die before we do. What time d'you make it?'

'Thirteen past.'

'Only another three-quarters of an hour, then.'

Both men lapsed into silence, willing the remaining minutes of their watch to go faster. A solitary jogger came into view wearing a woollen balaclava a size too large and pointed, giving him the appearance of a demented garden gnome. He crossed the road from the Alexandra Gate and disappeared down Exhibition Road.

'Easiest way to bring on a heart-attack,' Langton observed. 'Course, it's another Yank fad. The quest for eternal youth. Did you see that television programme the other night?'

'Which was that?'

'How they stay young in California. You wouldn't credit the lengths they go to. They had a plastic surgeon on who'd remade his wife. Literally reassembled her, like a human Lego kit. Took bits off her arse, had a go at the old hooter, siliconed her tits and as far as I made out sucked about a hundredweight of fat out of her thighs.'

Jenkins whistled through his teeth, impressed at last.

'Sucked?'

'Yeah, they Hoover it out apparently.'

'Bloody roll on.'

Jenkins's disbelief was cut short by the arrival of a squad car which did a Hendon Police School textbook U-turn and pulled up in front of them with blue lights flashing. But it didn't contain their expected relief team, merely a couple of the Traffic boys.

17

'You know anything about a body being found in the park?' the driver asked.

'No. Should we have?'

'Central had an anonymous phone call stating there's a stiff close to the Round Pond.'

'You'd better go look for it, then. Could be one of your lot lying down on the job. You'll probably find a woman under him.'

'Thanks. Very droll. You're a big help.'

The driver reversed the way he had come, activated his siren and gunned the car across the road and into the park. Shortly afterwards he and his companion walked past the bandstand towards the Round Pond. They spotted the body as they approached; it was a well-dressed male lying face down close to the water. Both policemen circled him at first, making no attempt to disturb him.

'D'you think he's dead, or just drunk?'

The driver considered the options. The CID boys threw a fit if anybody encroached on their sacred territory, especially if it was a homicide. On the other hand, he did not want to look foolish if all they were dealing with was a well-heeled alcoholic.

'You all right, chummy?' he said loudly. 'Come on, let's have you. Can't lie there; you'll catch your death this weather.'

There was no reaction.

'Have a look. Turn him over.'

His companion knelt by the body and pushed a hand under it to feel for a heartbeat.

'That's odd,' he started to say, but they were the last two words he ever uttered and the driver ever heard, for his hand touched something metal and the world around them disintegrated.

Half a mile away Langton and Jenkins heard the explosion. Acting on instinct, Langton immediately radioed for assistance, since memories of a past IRA outrage when soldiers and horses had been blown to pieces came quickly to mind. Ignoring orders, he left Jenkins on guard and ran through the early commuter traffic, hampered by the weight of his gun

18

and mobile radio and with the frozen grass crunching beneath his pounding feet. He slowed down as he neared the site of the explosion. Although familiar with the carnage of motorway accidents, nothing had prepared him for what he now found. The fact that he had been talking to the victims only minutes before gave the tragedy greater poignancy. At first glance he could have believed he was looking at a patch of poppies growing, but as he advanced closer he saw that they were bright fragments of human flesh. He went forward cautiously and had to fight not to gag as bile rose to his mouth. Dear God, he thought, what do we do it all for? Just a pension and the Queen's commendation for bravery if we last the course.

He sank to his knees a few yards from the centre of the explosion, but immediately scrambled up again: close to him was a man's hand standing upright, a wedding band on the ring finger – for all the world like the Victorian ornament his grandmother had kept on her dressing-table.

Two joggers approached, a girl and a young man, both beautifully kitted out in white, with headbands and Walkmans. Langton waved them to stay back.

'Can we help?' the young man shouted.

'No, thank you, sir. Just keep well away. Did you see anything?'

'We just heard the bang.'

The girl suddenly became aware of what she was looking at, and her face lost much of its rosiness.

'Oh, Jesus!' she said, crying.

'Did you notice anybody near here?'

'Only another jogger.' The young man was also ashen, but fascinated at being so close to death as an observer. 'Who was he?'

'Why d'you say "he"?' Langton challenged, ever the policeman.

'I just assumed . . .'

'What you see is all that's left of three bodies. Two of them were policemen, just doing a job.' Despite their innocence he could not keep the bitterness out of his voice.

He swung round at the sound of multiple sirens cutting through the distant traffic roar: the banshee screams of the American-type fitted to patrol cars and the deeper note of Fire Brigade klaxons. A few moments later a convoy of two police cars and a Heavy Rescue Unit entered the park and pulled up on Lancaster Walk. Half a dozen officers ran towards the scene. Langton met them halfway and told as much as he knew. Sobered by the death of colleagues, they stood in a bunch until members of the Bomb Squad arrived accompanied by a senior officer. Langton was closely questioned before anybody moved in.

Once the bomb experts had satisfied themselves there were no other booby traps, the area was cordoned off and all entrances to the park closed to traffic. Reinforcements were brought in and they began to scour the immediate vicinity for clues. The grisly remains were carefully collected, tabbed and taken away in plastic bags. A television newsreel crew and press photographers, quickly alerted, were kept at a distance and had to be content with a cursory statement from the incident officer. Beyond the park railings the usual clutch of onlookers that are always drawn to scenes of tragedy were kept moving, but the majority of commuters travelling past were unaware of the horror until the first bare details were given over the radio.

'Any trace on the anonymous tip-off?' Langton asked.

The incident officer shook his head.

'No clue at all?'

'Not so far.'

'And just telling us about a body? No warning of a booby trap?'

'That's right. You'd better get back to your post,' the officer said, dismissing him. 'File a report as soon as you go off duty.'

Langton returned to the steps of the legation where the relief pair had already taken over, though now he and Jenkins were in no hurry to depart.

'How bad is it?' one of the newcomers asked.

Langton took his time before answering. 'When they killed horses,' he said finally, 'it made the headlines all over the

20

world. But a couple of dead coppers will probably only rate the inside pages.'

His companions nodded, accepting, like Langton, the increasing isolation of their lot in a society where all the old values had been overturned.

The police were not the only ones uneasy about the changing pattern of their lives. There was evidence to suggest that the majority of ordinary citizens, young and old, black as well as white, had the same feeling that a corruption of the spirit had eroded society. For some, more privileged than most, the boom years of the eighties when the yuppies had celebrated the early run-up to Christmas by pouring Beaujolais Nouveau over their Porsches and girl-friends were now but a memory, looked back upon as an earlier generation had revered the sixties. Nobody quite knew how or why the bubble had burst. Was it the Big Bang, Black Monday, the fault of the Japanese, the Iranians, the American deficit or the show-business glitz foisted on the royal family by the tabloids? Had the greenhouse effect played a part? Was it lead poisoning, battery chickens, toxic additives to the staple diet, the spread of hard drugs, the atomic fallout contaminating the Sunday roast, or the sewage being dumped into the rivers which frightened many into using expensive bottled water for the sacred cup of tea? Theories abounded, blame was spread, there being no shortage of experts ready to claim their moment of glory on the television screens and contest for the Platitude of the Year award. Some felt the buck stopped right there: television was the root of all their evils; the nightly diet of soap operas, quiz games and lamentably puerile sitcoms had so dulled the general perception of traditional English life that it was small wonder half the school-leavers could neither read nor write. Was it the Pill, easy abortion, or the spread of AIDS? Was it plastic money, plastic food, the decaying inner cities? Violence stalked all streets, even in remote rural areas; child abuse and the abduction and murder of children sometimes appeared endemic; burglaries were an accepted hazard of everyday life and no longer confined to the

21

rich. Some blamed drink, some blamed God, others reviled trendy bishops who had forsaken God for the Mammon of politics. Others still charted the national decline from the moment when the England football team failed to qualify for the World Cup, while a section claimed that the display of topless models in certain of the national newspapers had irrevocably corrupted family life. Whatever the cause, few denied that the country, like the weather, was not what it had been, though exactly what it had been proved impossible to determine. It was said by many to be the worst of times while they struggled to recall what had been the best of times.

Perhaps those who had the greatest cause to be concerned were the least concerned. Denied office for well over a decade, the incumbent Labour government, now controlled by the hard Left and headed by the Right Honourable Toby Bayldon as Prime Minister, were keen to make up for lost time by blotting out all traces of the Thatcher years. There was nothing very surprising or new about this: every British government since the end of the war had followed the same dreary path – any advance made by the outgoing administration was automatically pronounced a disaster to be removed at the earliest opportunity, regardless of cost or practicability. Without benefit of a written constitution and a second house, British politicians subordinated themselves to party disciplines more draconian than in any other democratic legislature, frequently voting without having any conclusive grasp of what they were voting for, committed to election manifestos that were either fatuous or else swiftly rendered obsolete by events. Above all, the Prime Minister of the day exercised almost unlimited power, his immediate predecessors having succeeded in diminishing collective responsibility to the point where it was scarcely discernible.

Shortly after a hurried lunch taken at his club, Doctor Colin Hogg, CBE, the senior Home Office pathologist used by the security services, began his preliminary examination of the Hyde Park remains. It had been impressed upon him that his

22

most urgent task was to identify the third body and establish whether death had occurred prior to the triggering of the booby trap. But Hogg worked at his own pace: he was not a man to be hurried by civil servants.

His assistants had little enough to go on, and priority was given to separating the gruesome collection of human fragments. They were helped by the fact that the records revealed that both the dead policemen had the same blood group, and the hope was that the third man would prove to have a different group. While they carried out their tests, Hogg began his own methodical procedures, dictating his findings to an overhead microphone connected to a tape-recorder. He began by concentrating on two reasonably intact sections of lower jaw. He immediately noted that the first of these had some superb bridgework which suggested it was of American origin, or by a British dentist trained in American techniques. He photographed this using a macro lens, and then took X-rays. The second specimen had fewer fillings, and indentations on the incisors suggested that the owner had once worn a corrective brace. Hogg removed minute particles of food for further examination.

Surprisingly for someone who had spent a lifetime concentrating under artificial light, he still had 20/20 vision. The knuckles of his left hand were arthritic, but his right hand was steady with the scalpel and he dissected with all the delicacy of an etcher. One of his idiosyncrasies was to wear thick orange gloves of the kitchen-sink variety rather than the thin transparent ones issued by the department. 'I have no intention of catching AIDS at my time of life,' he remarked to his assistants. 'It would not only be unseemly but, as a bachelor, it would also give rise to a false diagnosis of my sexual proclivities. You can imagine what a field-day our tabloid press would have, given half the chance.'

It was now that he spotted something. Imbedded in a segment of flesh that he later confirmed came from the genital regions of a male in his late forties, was a piece of silk material barely larger than a postage stamp. He cleaned it carefully and examined it under a microscope. Woven into it were some

23

letters: *net Re*. They meant nothing to him, and he set the fragment aside, preserved in a plastic envelope.

'I think I've isolated the unknown victim, sir.'

'You *think*. You don't *think* about anything in my laboratory, Charles. You make tentative statements, or else voice positive conclusions. Which is it?'

'The test came up with AB, sir, distinct from the two policemen.'

'Then, say so. Good. That's a start. Wipe my forehead with a tissue.'

It was another four hours before they had every exhibit tabulated. The severed hand with the wedding ring on it gave them the only certain identification since it was engraved on the inside, *Liz and Bill, 22 July 1984*, which was later traced to one of the policemen. Having sent his assistants out for a quick meal, Hogg began to build up a mental picture of the third victim. He dictated into the mini-recorder.

'Preliminary findings as follows. Principal victim white Caucasian male. Blood group AB. Age estimated between thirty-five and forty. Of medium height, with a decent head of hair, colour auburn, possibly with traces of dye. One hand matched with blood group. Fingernails manicured, pointing to a sedentary occupation. Liver sample denotes upper levels of alcohol consumption, but lung tissue clear. Death estimated to have occurred prior to the explosion; actual cause of death as yet not ascertained. Further tests to be carried out on the viscera. Fragments of cloth fused to section of forearm analysed as pure wool, colour dark blue. Thus victim unlikely to have been a park derelict; evidence so far suggests somebody who enjoyed an above-average standard of living and could afford superior dentistry, which may prove to be of foreign origin. Positive identification impossible from the remains. Dental records most likely source of information. Examination continues. Timed at eighteen thirty-seven hours.'

'Play that back and give me your reactions, Charles,' he commanded when the two assistants returned. 'Yours, too, Graham, when you've emptied your mouth. What is that you're eating?'

24

'Chocolate, sir.'

'Excessive intake of refined sugar leads to early deterioration of brain cells, did you know that?'

'No, sir.'

'Well, you do now. Let's put it to the test. You start.'

Both young men concentrated. Graham, the younger of the two, and a regular recipient of Hogg's sarcasm on these occasions, prayed for inspiration.

'A banker, possibly, sir?'

'And by what tortuous thought process did you arrive at that instant deduction?'

'Sedentary occupation, sir, and the quality of the suit he was wearing.'

'You think only bankers wear decent suits, do you?'

'No, sir.'

'If you found me dead wearing a Marks and Spencer pullover, do I take it you'd immediately conclude I was a shop assistant?'

'No, sir.'

'Then, don't make ludicrous guesses. Let's have your two pennyworth, Charles.'

The second assistant hesitated, then began, 'Based on what you've told us, sir, there's a distinct possibility that the victim was American . . .' but he got no further.

'I told you no such thing.'

'Oh, I thought you said the dental work was almost certainly not done in this country, sir.'

'I said it was superior dental work, but people travel and often require treatment while abroad. If they're affluent enough or have taken the sensible precaution of insuring against such eventualities, they will avail themselves of the best.'

'I'm sure you're right, sir.'

'Of course I'm right. Is that the extent of your wisdom?'

When cornered, as he was now, Charles developed a slight stutter.

'I c-c-could make one other suggestion, sir.'

'Yes?'

25

'The label fragment you discovered.'

'What about it?'

'I might be able to fill in the missing letters. You see, sir, m-m-my girl-friend r-r-really supplied the clue.'

'How could you have discussed this with your girl-friend?'

'N-n-no, sir, you misunderstand . . . me. I haven't discussed it, n-n-naturally. You see, sir, she wears a c-c-certain type of underwear.'

'Charles, you know me to be a patient and tolerant man, especially when dealing with people of subnormal intelligence, but I have no wish to stand here and listen to the salacious details of your private life.'

By now Charles was sweating. He shot a desperate look at Graham, but no help was forthcoming. 'If I c-c-could f-f-finish, sir, the missing letters might be "JA" for the f-f-first word and "GER" for the second.' He waited, but Hogg merely stared at him.

'J-J-Janet Reger.'

'Janet Reger?'

'Yes, sir.'

'And what does that signify? The name means nothing to me.'

Only now did Graham take over, thereby hoping to claim some of the glory.

'It's a brand name, sir, for exotic ladies' lingerie.'

'And why would your hypothetical banker be wearing a garment produced by a purveyor of female undergarments?'

'Well, I have seen it reported, sir, that certain men do go in for that sort of thing.'

'Transvestites, you mean?'

'Not necessarily. I believe quite normal men get into them.'

'Your definition of "normal" is patently not mine; but, believe it or not, I'm always willing to broaden my horizons. Tell me more.'

'I don't know any more, sir. But I can assure you it does go on.'

'A further indication that our society is degenerating.' Hogg rounded on Charles. 'I stand corrected and amazed, Charles, by your extensive knowledge of the darker side of human nature.'

'There's n-n-no accounting for taste, is there, sir?'

'In matters sexual, no. But let's concentrate on these exotic female undergarments, since you have my undivided attention. What are we talking about – French knickers?'

'Could be, sir.'

'Well, they say one's education is never finished until one is in the grave.' Hogg stripped off his gloves with a flourish and cast them into a disposal bin. He next went to the washbasin, operating the taps with a foot pedal, and commenced scrubbing his hands. 'Assuming you both reduce your intake of sugar, it's possible that one day you might add something of value to the sum of human knowledge. Type up all my notes before you leave and make sure the dental records are immediately circulated. We'll continue first thing in the morning.'

'Excuse me, sir,' Graham said, 'but the Home Office were anxious for you to give them a report tonight.'

Hogg turned at the door to the washroom. 'Were they? Let me tell both of you something; and, if you learn nothing else while under my tender care, have this engraved in large letters above your beds: we were not put on this earth to be humbled by civil servants – that is not what God intended when He laboured for six days. If – *when* – they ring, tell them my report will be presented when I am ready to present it and not before. I am taking my niece to the theatre. She is the only member of my family I can tolerate for more than half an hour, and it happens to be her birthday. Tell them dead men take their time to tell tales.'

With this parting maxim he disappeared. The two assistants collapsed, laughing.

'French knickers!' Charles screamed. 'That brought a bloom to his cheeks. The silly old sod got quite excited.'

'You know what I felt like telling him?'

'No, what?'

'I wished I had the nerve to say: "Sir, I think we're piecing together the last hours of some old queen who trolled the

27

park in a suspender-belt and happened to die on top of an unexploded wartime bomb brought to the surface during the hurricane." '

'Christ! I'm glad you didn't.'

'Why does he have to be such a bloody know-it-all?'

'B-b-because he is,' Charles said. 'Because the old b-b-bugger just is.'

2

29 December

Bill Waddington was somebody who passed unnoticed in the Piccadilly lunch-time crowds; it was an attribute that had been useful to him in his previous career in the Firm. On this particular day he was breaking in a new pair of shoes and trod warily on the wet pavements; he had scratched the soles with a pair of scissors before setting out, but they still slipped. As he approached Langan's Brasserie he spotted the inevitable paparazzi cameramen waiting for celebrities, but after giving him a glance they turned their backs to the slanting rain. Not for the first time he thought what a boring existence they must have: keeping endless vigil in the hope of catching the transiently famous off-guard. It was a strange world they trapped with their lens – not the great or near-great, but teleprompter-readers, spent footballers and, favourite of all, those topless models afflicted with torpedo-like udders and their mentally shrivelled escorts.

Although ignored by the paparazzi, all unknowingly he was photographed entering Langan's from a fifth-storey window of an office-block on the opposite side of the road, the hidden observer using a 300-mm lens fitted to a motorized Nikon with a rifle mount.

Inside, the bar was crowded with a clutch of hopefuls who didn't have bookings. They nursed their drinks and forced smiles whenever the head waiter looked their way. Waddington deposited his raincoat and asked if his host had arrived.

'I'm lunching with Mr Keating.'

'Yes, sir. Mr Keating is through the bar.'

Waddington was not sure that he would be able to recognize

Keating. They had once both been in the Firm, but contact had been lost a decade ago. He had no idea why Keating had decided to seek him out, but these days a free meal was a free meal.

'Bill, how good of you to find time to see me,' Keating said, portly as Buck Mulligan and rising with some difficulty from an armchair. He had aged since they last met, but the changes in his appearance stemmed more from good living than from the advance of the years. Well groomed, florid of complexion, but still handsome – the sort of face that always graced the social pages of the glossy magazines: the rich, Waddington had noted, had a sameness about them. He gave the immediate impression that, like Fitzgerald's Gatsby, he never had to wear a shirt twice, and his immaculate single-breasted suit made Waddington feel shabby and out of place. Whatever experiences they had once shared were now separated by affluence.

'Hope this place was a good choice.'

'Splendid,' Waddington replied, and felt compelled to add: 'My expenses don't usually stretch to Langan's.'

Keating did not pick up on this. 'I use it because the food's good,' he said, 'and it's so noisy you can't be overheard. Most of the clientele's show-business – they're so busy talking about themselves they haven't got time to eavesdrop.'

'Are we going to be worth eavesdropping?'

Again, there was no reaction from Keating. 'D'you want to go straight in or have a drink here first? What is your tipple?'

'Oh, I'll just have a glass of wine with lunch. D'you mind if we eat straight away? I only have an hour, I'm afraid.'

'No problem.'

Keating deposited his half-smoked Davidoff in the nearest ashtray and took Waddington's arm, steering him through the crowded bar into the equally crowded restaurant. 'Driving you hard, are they?' He nodded to the *maître d'* with the assurance of somebody accustomed to favoured treatment, and they were immediately ushered to a table at the far end of the room.

'My boss demands his pound of flesh,' Waddington said. 'But it's a living.'

'Yes, I'd heard on the old grapevine you'd left the Firm. Without knowing the circumstances, I'm sure you were well out of it.' He waved away the proffered menu. 'I know exactly what I'm going to have. Give me some pâté and then a Dover sole, plain grilled with some *mange-tout*. And don't try to tempt me with French fries, because I seduce easily. What d'you fancy, Bill? Not on a diet like me, I hope?'

'Still looking at the moment. Is there a house speciality?'

'There used to be, but sadly he's no longer with us.' The in-joke was lost on Waddington. 'It's all good. Choose what you like. Bring us a bottle of the eight-six Chablis, Rico. Not too cold.'

Feeling under pressure, Waddington made a quick choice and immediately regretted it. Successful men like Keating intimidated him. He made small-talk until the wine arrived.

'Tell me about your present set-up.' Keating sampled the wine and pronounced it drinkable. There was an air of calculated sophistication to all his actions. At close range he gave off a strong scent of Cologne, and as he spread his pâté with the air of a man to whom the word *cholesterol* was anathema Waddington glimpsed a solid-gold Rolex, that mandatory symbol of captains of industry. It occurred to Waddington that he was dining with one of the unacceptable faces of capitalism. Once again he was conscious of his own shabbiness.

'My set-up? Nothing very spectacular. Bloody dull, in fact. After I showed my backside to the Firm I got a job with a small outfit, owned by a pompous little twit, that sells security installations to the well heeled. You know the type – still uses his army rank thirty years after the event.'

'Got him in one.'

'I'm there as a "consultant". What about yourself?'

'Can't complain, Bill. I've moved around, trying to keep one step ahead of the mob, dabbling in a number of things. Had a dip with property development at one point, but didn't like the company I had to keep. I finally found my spiritual home in the film industry.'

31

'How spiritual is it?'

'Somewhere between the Church of England and the Moonies.' Keating laughed at his own joke.

Waddington said: 'I've always heard film production is a very risky business.'

'Oh, I'm in at the right end, Bill. Nothing creative; I just supply the last third of the money and take the first share of the profits.'

'A far cry from the old days.'

'Thank God. Do you keep in touch with any of the gang? Mind you, quite a few have fallen off the perch, or committed social suicide by writing their boring memoirs. Still, that keeps the courts busy. Horses for courses.'

Waddington nodded in agreement. 'The answer is no, I haven't kept up with anybody.'

'Crossed them off the Christmas-card list, have you? Very wise. What is it they say? You can't revive old love-affairs. Which in turn asks the question, was it love for you and me? I mean, did any of it ever matter? Nothing matters very much, and most things do not matter at all. Our past lives were built on a myth.'

'People die and kill for myths.'

'Interested to know whether you departed with a bang or with a whimper,' Keating said, although the way he put it denoted a lack of interest.

'I was given the old heave-ho in the economy purge when this Labour government got in.'

Keating said: 'Somehow I can never quite believe they won the election. Such a third-rate shower. Not that I rated the previous mob. The Tories inevitably render themselves insufferable in power. The moment the votes are counted they switch over to cruise-control – no nuclear pun intended! They were competent, I suppose, and they tried to keep our defences up to scratch. Politics and politicians get up my nose. If you ask me, we Brits have always preferred to be governed by nonentities. Macmillan was the last Prime Minister I had any time for.' He broke a bread roll, buttered it, then put it to one side. 'Heard a good one in the club the other day.

32

Somebody described Bayldon and his cabinet as a black hole surrounded by a vacuum. Quite good, yes?'

Although Waddington laughed at this reference to the current Prime Minister, his mind was elsewhere; instinct told him that Keating had not tracked him down to swap political anecdotes. 'D'you ever miss the old days?'

'No way. The place fell apart for me when C retired.'

'Dinnsbury, you mean?'

'Yes. Couldn't stand the new *numero uno* at any price, never hit it off with him, so I got out while the going was good. God, we used to be the bloody elite, Bill, remember? The elite,' he repeated, as he quaffed his first glass of Chablis. 'But they threw it away, cut our balls off, shafted us, all those closet Reds in Whitehall. And you know why? Because we were on to them.'

Waddington let him talk, acting on the old principle that one should never commit too soon. Listen, observe, but don't unpin your hair before the money's on the table, as the whore said.

'God, the mandarins terrify me, and I had some eyeball-to-eyeball dealings while I was in property. You ever come across any of them?'

'No, I don't move in such exalted circles.'

'Don't go thinking I've mellowed into some sort of raving reactionary, but frankly I'm convinced we're on the downward slope the way this country's being run at the moment. We're going to finish up as a banana republic. The rot extends everywhere. We were the last bastion, Bill.'

'I suppose it could be argued that the Firm had its share of corruption.'

'Granted there were a few rotten eggs in our basket – no question of that, but they were all laid at a particular time in the same privileged nest if you think about it. Aren't I right? They all drank at the same trough, to mix my metaphors. Not the likes of you and me, but toffee-nosed degenerates who slipped the wool over most people's eyes. And don't tell me they weren't protected further up the scale. That's the ultimate closed shop: the old-boy network. The admission fees are

33

high but, once you're in, you're in for life. Christ, it went all the way to the Palace. Imagine if somebody put that into a novel, they'd be carted off to the funny farm. But it wasn't fiction; chummy there was lording it for years, touching his yellow forelock to the royals while good men were betrayed.'

'You're talking about Glanville, I take it?'

'Yes. I was one of the so-called Young Turks, remember? I took some of his early interrogations. We smelt him out; every time he opened his mouth he gave off guilt like halitosis – and he had a terminal case of it, by the way – but we got nowhere. A cold sanctimonious fish, camp as a row of tents as soon as he had a couple of gins inside him. The smug bastard knew he had us – there wasn't sufficient evidence to bring him to trial, so we were forced to strike a deal and give him immunity. It took that writer chap to bring it out in the open, otherwise he'd still be there. You study the photographs of him, look at all of them in that charmed fairy-ring and ask yourself why weren't they flushed years before. Any average village copper would have sussed them out, but yet they survived, travelling first class all the way. That's why I couldn't wait to quit.'

He paused momentarily and requested his grilled sole to be taken off the bone.

Waddington had the distinct feeling that the conversation was being steered away from the real purpose of the reunion. Keating had never been a close friend, and they had never worked together. At one time Keating had been earmarked for the top job; Dinnsbury, the then Director-General of MI6, had gone on record that he considered him the best and brightest hope. That had been enough to squash his chances the moment Dinnsbury was put out to pasture. The mandarins never liked to have court favourites promoted.

Keating continued to expound his theory of a calculated conspiracy as they ate their main course. Like many fat men he attacked food as though at any moment it might be snatched from him.

'If they believe Glanville was the last rotten egg in the basket, I'll go to the foot of our stairs, as my mother used to say . . . Funny expression that; don't know why it suddenly came to mind, haven't used it for years, and I'm not quite sure what it means.'

'My mother used it, too,' Waddington said, and for the first time during the meal he felt he had something in common with Keating.

'What are your views on the perennial supermole theory? I know it keeps a whole slew of ferreting journalists in business, but the possible cast-list gets longer every year.'

'Part of me goes along with it, and maybe there was some-body, some dedicated scalp-hunter, who's long since under the sod. It's the nature of the beast – there's a sneak in every classroom.'

At that point Keating's chauffeur appeared by the table to tell him he was being paged on his Answercall. Keating excused himself. As he walked through the restaurant several heads turned; he was a commanding figure, reminding Waddington of Orson Welles towards the end of his life. Through the window he watched Keating go to his Rolls Corniche and use a cellular phone.

'Sorry about that,' Keating said on his return, biting off the end of a fresh Davidoff. 'Do you use these things?'

'No, but I'm willing to be converted.' He accepted one from a leather case engraved with Keating's initials.

'I expect somebody will object. We smokers are pariahs now, they're out to make us an extinct species, but wait until they ban it altogether and see how their taxes rocket. The way the do-gooders prate you'd think every bloody non-smoker has been granted immortality.'

It wasn't until the coffee was served that Waddington got a positive intimation why he had been invited.

'Talking of corruption, I read an item the other day about our old friend Hillsden. Did you see it?'

'No. What was that?'

'There was a piece in the *Express*, just a paragraph, saying he'd been spotted being helped out of a Moscow restaurant. Pissed to the eyebrows, apparently.'

'I missed that,' Waddington said. He was taken off-guard.

35

The sudden mention of Hillsden disturbed all manner of memories, rolling back the years when their life together at the Firm had seemed full of purpose.

'Well, I imagine they all take to the bottle sooner or later. I know I would if I found myself incarcerated in that bloody city. I went there once and was slipped a Mickey Finn made from their *samogon*; lethal stuff that is, like drinking U-boat fuel. No, Moscow is a lonely corner of a very foreign field for the likes of you and me.' He switched back to the main topic behind a cloud of cigar smoke. 'You were very close to Hillsden at one time, weren't you?'

The question was patently rhetorical, and now Waddington was ready for it. 'As close as anybody, I suppose, excluding his wife. Or maybe even closer in one sense. The marriage crumbled. She never joined him over there.'

'Had more sense probably. Did you ever suspect he'd go over?'

Waddington took his time before answering. 'No. It was totally out of character.'

'But isn't that true of every defector? They're not suspected until it's too late.'

'Well, Alec doesn't fit in with your "rotten eggs" theory. He wasn't an Apostle, he didn't go to even a minor public school, he was an outsider.' Waddington hesitated before adding: 'For my money he was set up.'

'Really?'

'The whole business smelt.'

'But who would set him up?'

'Obviously, I don't know; it's just a strong hunch. In the first place I'll never believe he murdered that Foreign Office bod. What was his name? Bellridge?'

'Belfrage. Sir Charles.'

'Well, did *you* buy that?'

'I could believe quite a few people would want to do him in. I ran up against him on a couple of occasions. A career diplomat with all the built-in arrogance of that class. Had the roving eye for the ladies; though, mind you, having met his wife I could understand why. But you asked a question, did

36

I buy it? I suppose I did at the time. Interesting you don't think Hillsden was responsible; the evidence at the time seemed fairly conclusive.'

'There was no evidence, only conjecture. Alec never carried a gun to my knowledge. Whoever killed Belfrage was a professional hit-man. I've studied the papers. It was a text-book operation; the police never found a single lead. I admit it coincided with Alec's disappearance, but that's merely circumstantial . . . and very convenient. It took the heat off the lack of police progress. They were able to bury their failure.'

'Except he had done time, hadn't he, prior to his disappear-ance? A little smoke, maybe there was some fire?'

Waddington shook his head. 'Queer-bashing in pubs wasn't his style, any more than murder.'

'Desperate men often commit apparently irrational acts.'

'What makes you think Alec was desperate?'

'The net closing in?'

'OK, that was the popular view, but it didn't fit in with my reading of him.'

'Which was?'

'Right up to the moment he disappeared, I was convinced he was on to something big.'

'Did he ever let on what? Here, your cigar's gone out.' Keating offered a solid-gold Dunhill lighter, so heavy Waddington almost dropped it.

'Thank you. No.'

'That might have been part of his cover. If you were that close, he had to fool you more than the rest.'

'I like to think not. We discussed most things, and at that time, because he was obsessed with her murder, he was very forthcoming.'

'Whose murder? Who are we talking about now?'

'Caroline.'

Keating looked blank.

'Caroline Oates.'

'She was murdered?'

His surprise seemed genuine enough.

'You never heard that? Now, that's interesting, because you were around at the time. Presumably you heard the gossip about her and Alec?'

'Vaguely. Remind me.'

From the first mention of Hillsden he had detected a pattern to Keating's questions. He got the feeling that Keating knew the answers in advance, that somehow he was being used. Well, we can both play at that game, he thought. I still remember a trick or two.

'She was his mistress for a time. They became lovers when they were both in the Austrian station with Jock Calder. Alec got his marching orders because of their affair. Control read the Riot Act from his own version of the Old Testament: Thou shalt commit all manner of crimes in the name of the Firm, but thou shalt not have carnal knowledge of a fellow-operative. A curious kind of departmental morality, I always thought.'

'Yes, some of it comes back now you mention it.'

'Shortly after he was sent home, the whole network was blown. Everybody was wiped out. Caroline was taken in Berlin, and Jock . . . well, according to the official report he was drowned. Caroline was traded a few years later. What was left of her. She wasn't even walking wounded – a wheel-chair case. Moscow Centre did a really good job. Our grateful employers pinned a gong on her for services above and beyond and tucked her out of sight in a nursing home for incurables – where she was eventually murdered.'

Keating was silent for a while, nursing the ash on his cigar. 'Strange nothing came out,' he said finally.

'That's what riled Alec. He pressed hard for a full internal investigation, but was warned off. The reason Control gave was he didn't want to rock the boat. It was just after the Glanville scandal broke, the new government had just been elected, everybody was treading on eggs. Caroline was quickly cremated and the file closed.'

'You say she was a wheelchair case?'

Waddington nodded. 'I never saw her, but from all accounts she was virtually a vegetable. I remember Alec saying that to

38

me – "Why would anybody want to murder a burnt-out case?"
He was obsessed by it.'

'How was she murdered?'

'Injection. Old Hogg – did you ever come across him?
Home Office pathologist who did all our special cases – he
identified it as a shot of DS7, that instant way of shuffling off
life's mortal coil Adolf provided for the SS . . . Have you
ever put a dog down?'

'Not personally.'

'Nor me, but I saw it done once. We had a Yorkshire terrier
who came to the end of his time. Had cancer of the liver,
poor little sod. I held him while the vet put the needle in.
Worked like a charm – you couldn't count ten before he'd
gone.' Memory of the incident changed Waddington's face.
'We should all go as quickly. Well, I gather DS7 works just
as fast – complete respiratory failure in less than a minute.
Alec had such guilt about her, it destroyed him, altered his
whole personality. He might have faked many things, but I
know he didn't fake that. He was convinced that the reason
they killed her was that she still had something to tell.'

'Well, not to the Russians, presumably?' Keating observed.
'Somebody on our side, you mean? Somebody from the Firm's
dirty tricks department?'

'Who knows? Yes, why not? Why pretend our lot aren't
equally ruthless when it suits us?' Even as he agreed,
Waddington thought: Jesus! I'm getting careless, allowing
myself to be pumped like some rookie straight from Field
Security. Again it occurred to him that this might not be
just a school reunion. I've been away too long, he thought.
Absence has dulled me.

'Not a pretty story. Makes me glad I'm out of the game
earning an honest living – well, *almost* an honest living,'
Keating said, adding more sugar to his double espresso. He
waved a hand in the direction of their waiter and indicated
he wanted the bill. 'I wish I'd known Hillsden better in the
old days. Never know I might have been able to help . . . Too
late now. Burnt his boats,' he added from behind a cloud of
cigar smoke that provoked angry glances from the occupants

39

of nearby tables. 'The only thing that gives me private satisfaction is the thought that the Firm and Moscow Centre must be running around like blue-arsed flies, what with *glasnost*, *perestroika* and all that crap. Not welcome news for our old profession; threatens to put everybody on the breadline. You and I know that peace in our time is just window-dressing for the masses – the game will go on as before, because don't tell me that our buddies out at Langley are looking to go on welfare. All the players have a vested interest in keeping the pot boiling.'

Waddington nodded: 'I guess there won't be much call for secret services if everybody shakes hands and becomes friends.'

'Ah, but there's nothing like a friend when it comes to betrayal,' Keating said with a ghost of a smile. He signed the bill without looking at it and added a twenty-pound note as a tip. 'We should both be happy we're on the side-lines.'

'Except I can't pretend that flogging intruder alarms to exiled Iranians fulfils a lifelong ambition.'

'Pays well, presumably?'

'Just about enough to cover the alimony.'

'Oh, you've gone down that road, have you? I'm on my third. Did you have children?'

'No.'

'Well, be grateful for that. I'm supporting a whole brood of dropouts. I didn't spill my seed to any good effect. Not that I envy the young these days. It can't be much fun living with the spectre of AIDS. At least we didn't have that to contend with in our gilded youth. All we had to worry about was catching a dose of the clap or getting a girl in the pudding club. I heard an ugly rumour the other day. Apparently there's a very hush-hush project under way up north. According to my informant, the figures for AIDS victims have been heavily doctored. The real total could be anything up to five hundred per cent more than admitted. I was told they're building a sort of super leper colony – a self-extermination camp for terminal cases.'

'God! You think there's any truth in it?'

40

'I think it's bloody possible.'

'Political dynamite.'

Keating shook his head. 'No. They'll all close ranks if it's true. Nobody wants that hot potato.'

The whole conversation puzzled Waddington. Men like Keating who drove around in the latest Rolls costing three times his own annual salary didn't issue luncheon invitations out of the blue without good reason. Where's the catch? he thought. Or have I missed it? He made a show of looking at his wrist-watch, which in contrast to Keating's genuine article was a cheap Hong Kong imitation of a Cartier, just about to shake itself to bits.

'Well, this has been very pleasant,' Keating said. 'Thanks for finding the time. I hope I haven't made you late. Can I give you a lift anywhere?'

'No, it wouldn't do for me to arrive back in a Roller. The Captain would think I'd landed a new client.'

'Perhaps you have. You never know. We must do it again and sooner next time. It's good to go down Memory Lane occasionally.'

Waddington got to his feet, conscious that he hadn't managed to keep his cigar alight.

'Take my card,' Keating said. 'And let's keep in touch. Never know, I might be able to put something in your way. The film industry is a many-splendoured thing; there are always openings.'

To the regulars in Langan's it looked like a normal encounter: they assumed Waddington was an agent trying to hype a film deal with a producer and going away empty-handed. Few heads turned as he made his way to the cloakroom. As he waited for his coat he turned back to see that Keating had now been joined by a young woman. She had her back to him, but from the clothes she was wearing and the flow of her abundant hair he sensed she was the type that gravitated effortlessly to wealth – spoiled girls beyond his experience who never yielded their favours without a price-tag attached. It was none of his concern, but he wondered if, despite three marriages, Keating still played the field.

41

The rain had turned to drizzle during lunch but, slightly fogged with Chablis, he welcomed the dank air on his face. As he walked past Keating's Rolls to Piccadilly he was photographed again, the concealed observer securing three motorized shots before the angle of the building obscured him.

He bought a midday edition of the *Standard*, making a gift of the dead cigar to the newsvendor. The front page was given over to a report of the outrage in Hyde Park. Although so far nobody had claimed responsibility for the murders, the authorities were convinced it was the work of the Provisional IRA. It was the time of the terrorist cuckoo, planting lethal eggs in harmless nests.

Catching a bus to return to work, he studied the newspaper report. There were pictures of the two dead policemen under a headline which read: RIDDLE OF THE THIRD MAN. How odd, Waddington thought. At one time that headline would have meant something else, and for the second time that day he thought of old Alec Hillsden, a stranger in a country he had once professed to despise.

3

29 December

A long way from Piccadilly and the London he had once known with the familiarity of a taxi-driver, the man in Waddington's thoughts walked the streets of Leningrad with no purpose other than to kill time.

Alec Hillsden's appearance had changed from the last photograph on the Firm's file. His hair was greyer now, speckled white at the sides; in addition, he had grown a beard, giving his regular English features a coarser look. Boredom had increased his drinking habits, and the cheeks above the beard had become mottled. The strangers he walked amongst might well have taken him for a literary man, for he had acquired a Chekhovian look, the look of a man to whom the present is not quite real, his sights fixed on distant horizons.

Since being exiled from his native land he had become reasonably fluent in spoken Russian for his everyday needs, though he still had some difficulty reading it. More than anything else, the need to combat loneliness and keep up with events in the world he had left behind had speeded the learning process. As one of the privileged he was allowed certain Western newspapers and periodicals, but often they only served to intensify his sense of alienation.

There were new, untried freedoms in the Leningrad air, but Hillsden shared none of them, for his life had reverted to an old and familiar pattern; sometimes it seemed to him he had never known a day bright with promise. Often in the past, before joining their sparse ranks, he had wondered about the lives of defectors: Was the umbilical cord ever severed? Past experiences with the Firm, when he had spent long months debriefing those who had made the move to the West, had revealed few clues as to their real emotions. Now he knew why. And they had been the genuine article; unlike him, they had made a conscious choice, yet they were condemned to be eternal tourists carrying the luggage of regret. In his own situation he carried the added weight of bitterness – knowing that he had been tricked.

Leningrad was the third alien city to offer him a surrogate home. In relative terms he preferred it to Moscow where his last illusions had been buried. He had made an effort to blot out all memories except one of his stay in Moscow: the only good thing about those early days had been to discover a kind of loving with a girl named Inga, transient like everything else in his new life, something unexpected, enjoyed, then snatched away – the old cat-and-mouse technique both sides had long perfected. Later, when his defection had become public, closing the door for ever, his GRU mentor had permitted him to renew the liaison with this same girl and arranged for them both to occupy a Black Sea villa. Again, no illusions as to why: concessions were never granted without a purpose. In many ways Hillsden and the girl were birds of a feather, both carriers of the same secret from their first meeting in Moscow – an episode both would have preferred to forget, but couldn't. Hillsden was aware that Inga had been told not only to share his bed, but also to penetrate his thoughts. Knowing that she would have had no choice in the matter, he harboured no resentment. His GRU hosts had accepted him in their midst, and ostensibly he had passed their tests, but he remained an outsider.

Although he and Inga had originally been thrown together on a blind date, to his surprise (since there had been few casual affairs in his life) Hillsden had been immediately attracted: she had a gentle vulnerable personality, reminding him (he who always made literary comparisons) of Maugham's heroine in *Cakes and Ale*, one of life's losers. A peasant girl from Georgia, she had been working in Moscow as a hotel waitress when they met, and had a smattering of English he found as engaging as doubtless his stumbling attempts at colloquial Russian amused her. He had learnt that her soldier fiancé had been killed in Afghanistan, so equally they shared the loss of

44

a love. Totally unlike his ex-wife or Caroline, and younger than he had any right to claim, Inga proved to be a compliant uninhibited mistress, inclined to fat, but firm-breasted and voluptuous when naked. Through her he rediscovered a tenderness he once felt he had lost for ever.

'Why is it,' Hillsden once asked her, 'that women's breasts always feel as if they are weighted within, like mercury in a silk pouch.'

'I don't understand.'

'Know what mercury is? The stuff they put in thermometers.'

'You mean my breasts are hot?'

'No. Forget it. Just one of my fanciful flights, and translation is beyond me. You wouldn't know what "Bristols" means, either, would you?'

Whenever she failed to comprehend she invariably laughed.

'It's Cockney rhyming slang.'

'What is "Cockney"?'

'Argot. See, this' – touching her face – 'is your "Boat Race", face; "mince pies" equals eyes; "plates of meat" feet. "Trouble and Strife", wife, and so on.'

By now she was totally lost.

'Bristols are these beautiful objects.' He fondled the softness of her breasts. ' "Bristol City" – titty. Get it?'

She shook her head.

'Well, never mind. Took me an age to catch on, and I still used to get flummoxed.'

'Is very difficult, I think, English.'

'You think right. Plus we're the laziest nation on earth when it comes to speaking in a foreign tongue. Pure arrogance. We've always taken the line "To hell with it; the natives should speak our lingo". You speak better English than I'll ever speak Russian.'

'Am I the first foreign girl you ever went to bed with?'

'Let me think, he said, searching back over his hideous past. Second.'

'Who was she?'

'German.'

'Young?'

'Ish. But I was young then.'

'Rich?'

'No. Why d'you ask that?'

'I've always imagined girls in the West to be rich, wearing perfume and wonderful clothes.'

'Some, yes, but I guess I didn't happen to meet any of them.'

'Not even your wife?'

'She had nice clothes, nothing special, but nice. Rich women need rich husbands, and that wasn't yours truly.'

'What was she like?'

'Innocent,' Hillsden replied after a pause. 'Innocent of life and what I was. She deserved better from me . . . Like you.'

'For me, this is rich,' she said without guile.

He silenced further questions by making love to her, using the act to blot out a past he could not bear to recall. At other times, watching her clean the villa, he was consumed with a sense of loss. The differences between their manufactured intimacy and his failed marriage brought back too many memories of the life he had been tricked into leaving. It was tacitly understood between them that they were both puppets being manipulated; the rules had been laid down long ago – it was, after all, just one more layer of deception coating their day-to-day existence.

Once, when they were both agreeably in their cups, Inga broached the subject of a more permanent relationship.

'Alexi,' she said, using her chosen equivalent of his name that he found curiously affecting, 'how would you feel if I became your strife and trouble?'

He smiled at her attempt to remember the slang he had taught her. 'Is that a Russian proposal?'

'If you want it to be.'

'My dear, I'm too old for you.'

'But we suit each other. And we know each other for what we are. Most people don't have that. It takes them a lifetime to find out just a little. From the first time we are together we had to share secrets. Bad secrets.'

'Yes,' he said, not wishing to put her down.

'Old doesn't matter. What matters is affection, respect. When we first see each other you were so polite, so different from other men I meet, and you protected me. When I am told to come to that apartment I am expecting to be treated like a whore, but you gave me respect. I remember very much what you said when I did as I had been told and asked should we make love.'

'What did I say?'

'You told me I didn't have to do anything I did not want to do.'

'You mean I behaved well for once?'

'No, don't joke. It was nice. You weren't like your friend Jock.'

'Takes all sorts. Don't let's go back on that. Look, my sweet, naïve Inga, I'm very fond of you and in different circumstances I'd be lucky to marry you. But you don't want some old crock like me. You'll move on, you *should* move on. Either your youth will take you away or they'll move you on. I know that and you know that. Ships like us have to pass in the night.'

She began to cry.

'Is it you still miss England? Say it's that, please.'

'I miss what England once stood for,' Hillsden answered carefully.

'I shall miss you always if we part. My first Englishman.'

'Will you? Well, I'm glad you think you will.'

A few months later his prediction came true: Inga disappeared out of his life. He woke one morning to find her gone, all personal traces having been removed while he slept. She had not even left a note, just a small bunch of flowers by the bedside, a gesture he found unbearably moving. In the days that followed he discovered he was desolate without her, familiarity being sometimes more binding than passion. The villa soon lost the small feminine touches she had brought to it, and he quickly reverted to the disorganized life of a bachelor, cutting domestic chores to a minimum and neglecting to change his clothes regularly. For the first time in many years

47

he was, to all intents, a free man. The irony of his situation was not lost on him. He had lived a double life for so long that now he compared himself to an amputee who can still imagine feelings in a missing limb.

4

'Never underestimate human greed,' Commander George Pearson said darkly, sharing a philosophical mood with Alan Lloyd, his number two. 'Take me, for example. Why did I order a second helping of bread-and-butter pudding? I don't need it, but I took it, and now I expect I shall eat it.' He stroked the belt of fat round his middle. 'And I'll tell you something else: greed is stronger than the sexual urge.'

'You've got the hump today,' Lloyd observed.

'I'm disturbed, chum. Disturbed. In our well-regulated, seemingly civilized society, satanic forces are always at work. And at times like this the cloud sits right over me.' He ate with a fork, American-style.

As senior officer in the Metropolitan Police Anti-Terrorist Squad, Pearson was overworked and looked older than his forty-nine years. He lived with a grumbling duodenal ulcer which snatched meals and the police canteen food did little to placate. A married man with two teenage children he seldom saw and who were openly critical of the police in general, he could not be judged a completely happy man. Whereas at the beginning of his career the enemies of the State had been clearly defined, the threats now came from many directions, and the lines of demarcation were blurred. Like the weather, the climate of treason was difficult to predict from day to day.

'Have you studied old Hogg's report?' Pearson asked.

'Yes.'

'And? Any conclusions?'

'It's got some very curious aspects,' Lloyd said. 'Somebody, it seems, went to a great deal of trouble to remove a citizen.' Recently promoted, he was ambitious enough not to commit himself to hasty judgements. 'Have you definitely ruled out the IRA?'

'On the whole, yes. An isolated sectarian murder away from their own killing-grounds? No. Doesn't sit with me. Granted they are getting subtler and it was a particularly sophisticated operation, I still don't go for it. If we take it that their real aim was to attack the mainland security forces, then it seems an ill-considered affair, even for them. How could they be certain the booby-trap would be triggered by the police? Any curious good Samaritan could have disturbed the body. I think it was pure chance those two poor bloody coppers bought it.'

'Hogg reckons the unknown stiff was dead before the explosion.'

'And Hogg, we know, tells it like it is.'

'What really intrigued me', Lloyd said, 'was the bit about the female underwear. That's a new one. Very bizarre.'

'Oh, I don't know. When I first joined the force I had a station sergeant – tough as old boots, looked a bit like Wallace Beery, could drink most of us under the table – who took early retirement when they nabbed him wearing high-heels outside the Hammersmith Palais. Pathetic really, because even in drag he still looked like Wallace Beery. So don't mock it. Follow it through; it might be the only lead we've got. Who was he? That's the first thing we have to discover; then perhaps we might be on our way to finding out who took such elaborate pains to eliminate the poor bastard.'

He pushed the remains of the bread-and-butter pudding to one side and cadged a cigarette from Lloyd.

'Murder's also a form of greed, a greed for power,' he added, coughing at the first inhale. 'Whoever planted the bomb needed to prove something.'

'If we eliminate the IRA, how about the Middle East connection?'

Pearson shook his head. 'They go for straight assassinations. Nothing subtle about these bastards. I don't know why, but my ulcer's telling me that when we get lucky, *if* we get lucky, we're going to disturb a cesspit.'

50

'Are we on our own?'

'Yes and maybe no. Officially it's the CID's case, but a little bird whispered that the Century House mob are sniffing around. And that makes me particularly uneasy.'

Although new to the job, Lloyd was sufficiently aware of the power-play that existed between the various branches of the British security services to appreciate Pearson's concern.

Century House was a twenty-storey tower-block close to Waterloo Station on the South Bank of the Thames, one of a number of concrete monoliths erected post-war when the planners championed ugliness and size as a substitute for architectural taste. Anonymous as many of the surrounding buildings, its façade was stained by the elements like an ugly woman on whose face the mascara has run. Since the late 1960s it had housed the headquarters of MI6, known colloquially as 'the Firm' – the branch of the British secret service responsible for overseas espionage and counter-espionage. Until the aftermath of the prolonged fiasco of the *Spycatcher* trial, when the Thatcher administration introduced legislation to prevent further egg being sprayed on its face, a ponderous myth had been maintained denying the existence of the security forces in peacetime. Until then nothing about it was to be found on the statute-books, nor was it recognized by common law. There had even been a period when its operatives were only paid in untraceable gold sovereigns, since the budgets and operational finances were never openly debated in Parliament. Details of its past activities were zealously guarded, and there was never any public recognition of its successes – only major scandals occasionally forced attention to its failures. It necessarily followed that if the secret service officially did not exist, then the same twisted logic dictated that it had no staff or Director-General. This Alice-in-Wonderland scenario fooled nobody and achieved the reverse effect by ensuring the maximum speculation and media attention since the penetration of secrets, whether personal or public, is one of human nature's abiding attractions. The current Director-General was Sir Raymond Lockfield, commonly referred to within the Firm as 'Control'. Until the 1989 Act was passed

51

and he and his organization were afforded a quasi-legitimacy, his name and function were known to most of what used to be called Fleet Street and certainly to the KGB.

'Why particularly uneasy?' Lloyd asked.

'Put it this way: Why should Lockfield's truffle-hounds be trespassing on our territory? What do they know that we don't? And, if they know something, why aren't they sharing it?'

He forked a single raisin from the remains of his bread-and-butter pudding and popped it into his mouth. 'But two can play at their game. No reason for them to have a monopoly of dirty tricks, if you get my drift? Are you with me?'

'All the way,' Lloyd said, without quite knowing what he was letting himself in for.

The nominal master of MI6 was the Foreign Office. Control reported directly to Bayldon, the Prime Minister, and in theory was closely scrutinized by the Joint Intelligence Committee, on which body he served.

Born in Delhi, the only son of an Indian army officer, Lockfield had been sent back to England at the age of seven following the death from cholera of his mother. A War Office friend of his father had secured him a place in a decent prep school where he showed enough academic promise to gain an entrance to Westminster. From there he won an open scholarship to Trinity College, Cambridge, eventually taking the Classical Tripos and a First in Modern Languages. His scholastic triumphs were allied to a highly visible right-wing stance. His father's army pension allowed of few luxuries to flow to his son, and for most of his time at Cambridge Lockfield had been poor in comparison to his contemporaries. It was during this period when he was most susceptible to the persuasion that all men had not been created equal that he had been sounded out by one of his tutors, a placid old buffer most people took to be an amiable eccentric. Subtly, persuasively, applying no undue pressure, this man had guided the impressionable young Lockfield towards an understanding of what the future could be. It was in the quiet backwaters of

52

Cambridge that the definitive map of his life was drawn.

It had been generally accepted that he would either gravitate to the Foreign Office or else opt for a parliamentary career. He had in fact fought one by-election as a Conservative candidate, having been cynically selected for the thankless task of contesting a staunch Labour seat in the Welsh valleys, always a certain graveyard for the Tories, and predictably he lost his deposit. This brief flirtation served to instil in him a hidden contempt for the political machine and those who were wedded to it: he found most of them insufferably arrogant, woefully ill-informed about the world, blinkered to everything but their own self-advancement. What mattered, however, was that he had made the accepted gesture; afterwards new-found friends in Whitehall eased his passage into the Foreign Office. He worked his way through the ranks during the prewar years and when the war came swiftly gained a commission into the Intelligence Corps. By the end of hostilities he held the rank of Lieutenant-Colonel. Because of his special qualifications, his demobilization was delayed; he stayed on in Germany until mid-1946, working with the Allied Control Commission in Berlin, with direct responsibility for the repatriation of Russian prisoners of war.

Returning home, he joined MI5, and after the reorganization in 1953 he transferred to MI6 (Section V), heading the political subversion division during the height of the Cold War. In 1968 he was promoted to Assistant Director, finally becoming Director-General during the last Tory government. His credentials were sea-green, and both sides of the House expressed satisfaction that, at long last, the right choice had been made.

On the day Pearson and Lloyd were preoccupied with their own problems, Control was on a short fuse. It had begun with a particularly difficult meeting of the Joint Intelligence Committee arguing the Firm's budget requirements for the coming year. These would be handled under the Secret Vote, the annual sum allowed by Parliament without debate. Although Bayldon had assured him that it was only a question of going through the motions and what he had put in for would eventually be forthcoming, he had resented having to suffer a third-degree at the hands of the Committee's chairman, a black MP from Liverpool. Returning to his office, he had been greeted with the news that one of the Firm's secretaries had been caught in possession of a quantity of cocaine at Heathrow, and that the most scurrilous of the tabloids was poised to run the story, the girl having lost her nerve and revealed her place of employment. He immediately put in a scrambled call to the Commissioner of Police, who was sympathetic but stated that unfortunately the girl had already been charged and the law must take its course. Resigned to accept the inevitable furore and thoroughly disgruntled, he took lunch alone in his private dining-room, only to have this interrupted by Markham, his deputy.

'I hope it's important, Julian,' Control snapped.

'Well, it could well be. Apparently a character called Mitchell who works at GCHQ has failed to appear for the third day running.'

Control paused in the act of dissecting his smoked trout.

'What makes you think that piece of news is worth interrupting my lunch for?'

'Your recent memo, telling us to keep close tabs on GCHQ.'

Control grunted, extracting a fishbone as thin as a hair.

'Well, if it's three days old, why wasn't I told sooner? Didn't anybody check before?'

'I think it was assumed he might be ill. He was complaining he was coming down with flu the last time anybody saw him.'

'What does he do there?'

'He's a Grade One cryptologist, and head of his section.'

'Christ! That bloody place is a running sore. Well, have all the normal checks been carried out?'

'As far as I know; but of course, strictly speaking, it only becomes our concern if he's slipped the country. All the airports and ports are being watched.'

'What about his home?'

'He lived alone. There is a housekeeper, but she's Filipino, speaks very little English. All this is secondhand, but my sources are reliable.'

'Presumably she speaks enough to say whether he's in or out.'

'She hasn't seen him since he had dinner on Wednesday evening.'

'What about his desk? He was Grade One, you say? What were his special responsibilities?'

'His section monitors all GRU transmissions in and out of Moscow. As head of section he would have unrestricted access to anything that came in.'

Control got up from his lunch-table and went to the window. A seagull dipped out of the low clouds, passing like a shadow, but the noise of its cry did not penetrate the double-glazed windows. Markham winced as Control cracked three knuckles in succession; he recognized the danger signs. Without turning Control said: 'Keep on top of it. And don't worry about treading on MI5's toes. Put a couple of good men on it and tell them they have a free hand.'

'Right, sir.'

'Report back directly to me.' He stopped Markham by the door. 'You said your sources are reliable. How reliable?'

'The word I should have used is *impeccable*.'

When Markham had gone Control went to his desk and dialled a number on his scrambler. He waited but got no response. Leaving his lunch unfinished, he took his cashmere overcoat and bowler hat from the closet and left the building without telling any of the staff where he could be reached.

'Why me, Sergeant?' Constable Whiting asked. 'Why not one of the girls?'

'Because the experience will be good for you, lad. All part of life's rich pageant. Police work is a many-splendoured thing, as you will find out. In any case, don't argue. Get off and bring back the goods.'

Whiting left the desk reluctantly. 'And a receipt. Don't forget that,' the Station Sergeant shouted after him.

Heading along Regent Street in the direction of Oxford Circus, Whiting fingered the wad of twenty-pound notes he had been entrusted with. His temporary wealth troubled him almost as much as the reason for his mission, and the fact that he was in uniform was an added worry. Twenty-two, unmarried, very much the probationer with just over a year's service in the force, he was well aware of the ribbing he could expect on his return. The only time he had seen a comparable sum of money had been when a drug-pusher had attempted to bribe him, but at least that incident had been in the course of duty. His present assignment had never been covered in the police manual.

He made for Dickins & Jones in the Circus and wandered around the ground floor looking for a directory board that would point him in the right direction, eventually discovering that the department he wanted was on the first floor. On arrival he found it as daunting as he had expected – counter after counter of bras, panties, flimsy nightgowns, all the accoutrements his fevered imagination associated with the female mystique. A half-open changing-room revealed a glimpse of a middle-aged matron wriggling into a corset. As he hurriedly turned away he almost knocked over a lifelike dummy displaying a bra for the fuller figure.

His agony was relieved by an assistant, and to his dismay she was roughly his own age and pretty with it. His last hope had been to find some kindly old biddy who would have sympathized with his predicament; he was more at home with old people.

'Can I help you, Officer?' The last word was slightly accentuated.

'Yes, probably. I hope so; that's to say, I don't know,' Whiting replied, using his official voice that had only been tested twice in court. 'I'm looking for the . . . things . . . ladies' things . . . underwear.'

'Well, you've come to the right department.' The laugh-lines at the sides of the girl's eyes deepened although she kept a straight face. 'Anything in particular?'

'A selection.'

'Pushing the boat out, are you? Right. OK, you've got lots to choose from. What size is she?'

'Size?'

'Yes.'

'Oh, I don't think size matters. He didn't mention sizes.'

'You're buying for somebody else, are you?'

'That's right.'

The assistant gave him an old-fashioned look. If it hadn't been for his uniform, she would have passed him on to the manageress at that point. She was no stranger to oddballs.

'You have to have a size, you know. Is it for your . . . his . . . girl-friend?'

'Er, not exactly.'

'A mother or a sister, perhaps?'

'No, all I need is a selection, different pieces. Just a moment.' He fumbled in his top pocket and produced his notebook. 'Do you stock things made by Janet Reger?'

The girl brightened at this. 'Going for the best, are you?'

'To tell the truth, I don't know what I'm going for,' Whiting blurted, deciding his only chance was to make her an ally. 'I'm under instructions, you see. Official business. To buy specimens.' Sensing that this still wasn't a concise enough explanation, he glanced around to make sure they were not being overheard. 'To do with a crime.'

I bet, the girl thought. A crime not yet committed.

'Well, let's see what we can come up with. The Janet Reger range is over here. I must warn you it's not cheap. Very daring and super quality, but not cheap.'

She led him to another part of the department where he was confronted with a variety of articles he normally associated with the calendars stuck to the back of locker doors.

'You choose,' he said desperately. 'Here' – producing the wad of money – 'give me something for that lot.'

'All of it?'

'I don't care. Just choose and get me out of here.'

'The last of the big spenders, eh? I wish I had you for a boy-friend.'

'Well, that could be arranged,' Whiting said, gaining some confidence now that he had taken the plunge. 'Here's my number' – pointing to his shoulder. 'You can always find me at Savile Row.'

'I think I've got your number,' the girl said, but smiling. He chalked her up as a possibility and made a mental note of her name from the identification-tag on her well-filled blouse.

She chose three garments for him and wrapped them.

'Be sure and give me a receipt. I have to produce it for my sergeant.'

'You're sure you're not buying them for him?'

'Chance would be a good thing.'

'Well, any time, Number Eighty-Seven,' the girl said, handing him his parcel. 'I prefer serving men. Some of the old crows we get in here drive you round the bend. My half-day's on Wednesday and I've never been out with a policeman.'

'You're on, Isabel,' Whiting said. 'This was a first time for me, too.'

'There we are, Sarge,' he proclaimed on his return to the station. 'Piece of cake. When you want me to shop for you again, say the word. I enjoyed that.'

'Did you now?' the Sergeant replied, miffed. 'Well, now you can enjoy something else. Go to that takeaway Indian restaurant on the corner of Old Compton Street; there's a punch up to sort out. A waiter threw a plate of curry at one of the customers, who not unreasonably felt aggrieved. This the receipt?'

'Yes, Sarge. Can I ask you something? What do the CID want this gear for?'

'It's the Commissioner's birthday, and they're going to surprise him with a number from *A Chorus Line*. Don't ask questions, lad. Ours is not to reason why. They're all bent in that mob. Take my tip: stay young and innocent.'

Still puzzled as to exactly why the ubiquitous Keating had stood him lunch, Waddington found that old Alec was constantly in his thoughts – memories floating to the surface just as, long after the event, a still pool will suddenly give up clues to a crime. He had always hated unfinished business and he had felt strangely wounded by Alec's inexplicable flight; because of their relationship he had taken it as a personal betrayal – sudden withdrawal of friendship was never less than a blow to one's pride, and the passage of time had done little to lessen the feeling of loss. It was the absence of any rational explanation that rankled most; the fact that, despite all evidence to the contrary, he still did not believe his own judgement could have been so wrong. Old Alec might have been a different animal, treading paths in their jungle Waddington had never explored, but he had never been less than straight in his dealings with friends.

Even so, this loss of confidence in his own judgement, together with the fortuitous combination of two other major events in his life, had cast Waddington adrift. He and his wife had no sooner decided that they could not reconcile their long-standing differences than the main cause of their discontents was removed. Before the divorce became absolute Waddington had been informed he was being compulsorily retired from the Firm with a reduced pension. The grounds given were that it was now government policy to cut back on the security services in view of the improved relations between the West and the Soviet bloc.

After the statutory warning that any breach of the Official Secrets Act would bring down the full strictures of the law, he had shredded the contents of his desk and then shared a boozy and ultimately debauched farewell-party with several fellow-redundants before leaving the building for the last time. This departure, far more than the end of his marriage, had left him disorientated, though the divorce itself had been reasonably amicable. With no children to suffer traumas or confuse the issue, there had been few wrangles over the division of the spoils. Waddington had cashed in an insurance policy and given his wife the proceeds since she had expressed a wish to buy a barn in her native Yorkshire, while he kept their previous home in Beaconsfield and half the contents.

Although no stranger to loneliness, he found life as a floating bachelor presented an entirely new set of social problems. Life before the break had meant sustaining a bogus middle-class image of respectability with neighbours and his wife's circle of friends, the latter necessarily removed from any connection with the Firm. Many of these now cut him in the High Street –

the women generally assuming that he was the guilty party, the men not wishing to be tainted by association. Since his culinary skills were limited to heating tinned soup in the microwave, or scrambling eggs, he ate out most nights, often deliberately seeking out cheap and indifferent restaurants, choosing necessity rather than pleasure.

Job opportunities for his age group had proved to be sparse. He had been chary about revealing his past, since he had rightly surmised there was no advantage in describing himself as a former wine salesman, the cover he had used with the Firm. Although he had scoured the classified ads in both national and local papers, he had received few replies and at one point seriously considered emigrating to Australia, only to have his application turned down. Then, with his savings fast running out, he had chanced upon a technical magazine in his dentist's waiting-room which carried an article extolling the job opportunities in the growth industry of home security. He consulted the Yellow Pages and at the third try was given an interview with a company called Breakproof. The owner and Managing Director proved to be a weedy little snob who insisted on being addressed as 'Captain'. Judging his man correctly, Waddington conducted his interview with clipped precision, lying that he had just returned home from Canada following the death of his parents. He wore his old Intelligence Corps tie and sat to attention throughout the session.

'Let me put my false teeth on the table,' the Captain began, and for one ghastly moment Waddington thought he meant it literally. 'In the event I decide to take you on – and I'm considering a number of applicants – I must caution you that I run a very tight ship, to borrow a naval term. As an army man yourself you'll appreciate that when one is dealing with security matters everything has to be tickety-boo. We market and install the latest equipment to customers who want the very best. Your function, assuming you're offered the post, I can only describe as a technological padre, giving comfort to the many out there who feel that their lives are under threat. Do you follow my gist?'

'Oh, absolutely, sir. Very apt comparison, if I may say so.'

'Naturally the comfort we offer is material rather than spiritual, and of course you work on a basic salary plus commission. We preach the sort of faith people understand. Faith in the reliability of our product, which happens to be of Japanese origin – though we don't volunteer this information unless pressed – faith in our integrity as personified in the name of my company and, most of all, faith in the honesty of my employees. There are a host of cowboys out there, Waddington, taking the public for a ride.'

'I can quite believe it, sir.'

'*Cowboys* is a polite name for them. Did you know, for instance, that in the Greater London area a break-in takes place every thirteen minutes?'

'Unbelievable, sir!'

'We are living in violent times, brought about, I have no doubt, by the fact that National Service was recklessly abolished. What the youth of today needs is a taste of discipline. You benefited from it, and so did I. Six weeks' square-bashing at Pirbright Barracks would do most of these criminal layabouts a power of good.'

'I couldn't agree more, sir,' Waddington said, suppressing a rising desire to tell the old fool to go fuck himself. 'It's refreshing to hear somebody speaking common sense for a change. Having been out of touch, coming home I was appalled by the loutish behaviour and general lack of manners.' He had got the Captain's measure, and the lies came trippingly off his tongue.

'To be reactionary in these troubled times is to be progressive. My own view is that we should reintroduce capital punishment and the cat. I see here that you're not married,' the Captain continued in the same breath, consulting Waddington's application form.

'No, sir.'

'I prefer my employees to have a secure home life. Security in all things. No good locking other people's doors if your own is wide open.'

'I was married. I'm divorced.'

The Captain pursed his lips. 'Not a womanizer, I hope?'

61

'I don't think so, sir, though I prefer the company of women to that of men, given the choice.'

'What are your political views?'

'I'm uncommitted, sir.'

The Captain frowned. 'Can we afford such luxuries? I'll make no secret of the fact that I find our present administration regrettable.'

'You won't find me disagreeing, sir.'

After waiting a week, Waddington received word that he would be given a month's trial. The job proved to be boring rather than challenging, but at least he wasn't sitting at a desk from nine to five. Waddington swiftly discovered that the majority of Breakproof's clients seldom questioned the cost; all they wanted to be told was that their bodies and possessions would be protected twenty-four hours a day. As the Captain had indicated, much of the equipment was extremely sophisticated, ranging from passive intruder-beams to bullet-proof shutters, and was monitored from a central control-panel. The fine print of the contracts did not miss a trick and made it a condition that the installations could not be purchased outright, but only leased and subject to a maintenance agreement. This ensured a profit margin of some 500 per cent within the first year. 'Safety is never cheap,' was one of the Captain's favourite sayings.

The day Waddington returned to his office after the lunch with Keating he had exceeded the permitted hour by eleven minutes and was immediately accosted by his employer.

'I don't pay you to take extended lunches, Waddington. This outfit is run by the clock, as you well know. And why the hell don't you answer your bleeper?'

'I got held up in traffic and I'd no idea you'd been trying to get me, sir. The battery must be on the blink.'

'Nobody is indispensable, Waddington. There are legions of younger men out there, hungry for your job. I've made an appointment for you to see a Mrs van Norden in Cranley Gardens. Here's the indent. She's waiting for you, so get over there straight away. And suck a mint on the way. Your breath reeks of stale cigar smoke. I'm amazed you can afford cigars.'

'We bachelors, you know, sir, have nothing else to spend our money on.'

Cranley Gardens lay between Kensington and Chelsea in an area that had undergone extensive architectural plastic surgery in the previous decade; the rows of terraced turn-of-the-century town houses had been divided up into expensive apartments, sometimes twelve to a building. In many cases this had been tastefully done, with the original fireplaces and ornate ceilings preserved, and the conversions commanded high prices. It was considered a smart address, but the sight that greeted Waddington when he arrived at Mrs van Norden's house was not in keeping with the general air of affluence. A clapped-out American convertible, rusted and overdue for the knacker's yard, was parked directly in front of the porticoed entrance. Three Arab youths were bent over the open bonnet poking at an engine that looked as though it had been submerged in grease. Waddington stepped over their bag of tools and pressed the entryphone button alongside Mrs van Norden's name.

There was a pause, then a light over the machine shone on his face and a distorted female voice said: 'Yes? Who is it?'

'I'm the gentleman from Breakproof, madam.'

'Do you have any form of identification?'

'Yes. I don't know whether it will register on this camera.' He held up his identity-card to the lens.

'Not a very good likeness, I'm afraid.' He felt stupid talking to a machine and was aware that the Arabs at the kerbside were listening to every word.

There was another pause. 'Flat G, first floor,' the woman's voice said. A buzzer sounded, releasing the door-lock. The hallway was close-carpeted and tastefully decorated. When Waddington reached the first landing the door facing him was partially opened, but held secure on a chain.

'Show me your identity-card again,' the unseen woman said.

Waddington dutifully produced it.

'One can't be too sure these days.' Apparently satisfied at last, Mrs van Norden slid the chain and allowed him inside.

Waddington found himself in a large high-ceilinged room that he guessed had once formed part of the original drawing-room. The period fireplace had been left *in situ*, though it now housed an imitation log-fire. All the furnishings were in expensive good taste; anonymous, like an advertisement.

Mrs van Norden's disembodied voice had given him no clue as to her age or appearance, but now that they were face to face he was more than pleasantly surprised. Instead of the usual middle-aged matron ablaze with jewellery (known in the trade as 'Cartier mutton dressed as lamb') he was face to face with an extremely bedworthy woman in her early thirties, wearing an authentic Chanel suit (which Waddington recognized, since his ex-wife had once treated herself to a cheap copy in the sales), adorned with a single tear-shaped diamond on a gold chain that dipped between her cleavage. The face above the necklace was no hardship to behold. It was, in fact, a face that most men would willingly give diamonds to if allowed the chance. Her hair was shoulder-length and so carelessly immaculate it demanded to be ruffled.

'I'm sorry to be so cautious, Mr Waddington, but a woman living alone has to take precautions these days.'

'Absolutely, madam. Never take risks . . . So how can we help you?'

'Don't call me "madam". Makes me feel a hundred. This isn't my principal home, just a *pied-à-terre* I use when I come up to town to get my hair done or have lunch with a girl-friend.'

'And you'd like us to upgrade the security, I take it? I noticed you've got a decent lock on the door, and the chain, but of course any door can be jemmied. If you want extra protection, we could reinforce it with a steel surround and fit concealed bolts on the hinge side.'

'That sounds wonderful. I'm all for sleeping in a vault.'

Waddington walked to the large French windows looking out on to the street. 'At least the period shutters are still in place. Nobody's really improved on those. Do you close them at night?'

'When I remember.'

'You should, though as a general rule burglars are leery

about gaining entry from the front of a building – too exposed. What other rooms are there?'

'Just the kitchen, bedroom and bathroom. It's just a pokey little funk-hole really.'

She gave just the slightest emphasis to the word 'pokey'.

'May I?'

'Please. You'll find the bedroom a bit of a shambles.'

Waddington went through into the bedroom, which was mirrored on two walls. The bed itself was tented with a dozen pillows scattered on it, again looking as though it had been arranged to await the photographers. The curtains were drawn. He opened them and looked out.

'All you've got here is a simple window-lock.'

'No good?'

'Well, they're effective up to a point, but I wouldn't put too much faith in them.'

'What d'you suggest?'

'We've had great success recently fitting our exclusively designed steel shutters.'

'Would I like those? Wouldn't they completely bitch the décor?'

'No, they're mounted outside, and operated electrically by a small bedside switch.'

'I'd buy that. You're so full of ideas, Mr Waddington. Why didn't I find you before?'

Why didn't you? Waddington thought. Preferably when I was eighteen and raring to go. The bedroom was making him decidedly uneasy. He moved to the bathroom.

'This doesn't have a window, I see, just an extractor fan.'

'Oh, yes, they cram them in where they can when they do these chintzy conversions. I ripped out the original bath and put in a jacuzzi. Do you like jacuzzis?'

'Can't say I've ever tried one.'

'You haven't lived.'

They completed the tour with Waddington making other suggestions to improve the system. 'Would you like us to submit an estimate?'

'Just do it; it all sounds wonderful.' She led the way back

65

to the main room. 'How about a drink? I think you've earned one.'

'Only if you are.'

She returned from the small kitchen waving a bottle of white wine. 'Can you open this? I've got the curse of the weak wrists.'

While Waddington did the honours, Mrs van Norden produced two crystal glasses of a splendour he had previously only seen in glossy magazines.

'I can't tell you . . . what's your first name?'

'William . . . Bill.'

'Bill, you've no idea what a relief it is to find somebody who knows what he's doing. I had to call a plumber the other day, and some teenage dwarf turned up who completely bitched the bidet. And, believe me, life without a bidet is not worth living. He hadn't got a clue. Thought it was a foot-bath, can you believe? I mean, how do some people exist? There was a time when one could get hordes of those divine little Korean people who worked night and day for next to nothing, but not any longer. I suppose our new lords and masters have decreed that servants are counter-revolutionary. In the event, I had to trek back to my country place to get sane.'

She rattled off this monologue while pouring the white wine like pints of beer.

Waddington nodded sympathetically, thinking: She's the type they'll bring back the guillotine for. 'Where is that?'

'Where is what?'

'Your country home?'

'Just outside Amersham. Thank God I've still got some staff there. Cheers. Do you find staff a problem?'

'Not really, no. For the simple reason I don't have any.'

She gave him a blank look before continuing: 'Come to think of it, I could do with you taking a look at the situation down there. It's somewhat isolated, and my couple live in the cottage, and the system my husband put in is beyond me. It goes off if the cat farts, and of course the police get very beady – letters from the Chief Constable keep streaming in, saying next time it happens they won't respond.'

'It's probably one of those cowboy installations,' Waddington said, falling into his sales routine. 'Doesn't your husband understand it?'

'What husband?'

'I'm sorry, I thought you mentioned him.'

'Did I? That was a mistake. I gave him back to the world, and he gave me what he thought was a generous settlement. I live on my own; that's why I'm terrified at night.'

'Well, if that's the case, I'd be glad to take a look at what you've got and make suggestions to improve it.'

'Would you?'

'Only too happy.'

'Let me scribble down the address and telephone number.'

She went to a disorganized desk and wrote on embossed notepaper with a silver Tiffany pen. Waddington always noticed such small details. There's something about you, Mrs van Norden, he thought, that doesn't quite ring true. Why would a well-heeled piece of crumpet be spending time, to say nothing of vintage Chablis, to chat up next year's Willie Loman? A dyke, perhaps? Did the departed Mr van Norden find the heat turned off in the bedroom? No, I usually get strong vibes from dykes, and this one is giving off vibes of a different sort. But let's not be picky, Waddington old sport; trade isn't that good, and business is business.

'Can you read my writing?' she asked, handing him the address. 'When d'you think you could come? I mean, the sooner the better.'

'Let me take a look at my diary, then I'll ring and make an appointment.'

'Terrific.'

He finished his wine and left lighter of step, but halfway home it occurred to him that, although he might be able to safeguard Mrs van Norden against most eventualities, there was a strong possibility that he would need protection himself. He glanced up into his driving-mirror to check whether some alchemy had transformed him into Dorian Gray, but it was the same ordinary face that stared back.

5

1 January

It was a sullen start to the New Year; gales ravaged the south coast, much of Devon and Cornwall suffered floods, while in the north and in Scotland heavy falls of snow made many of the roads impassable and several outlying villages were cut off. Most of the population had cause to wonder why they had celebrated the night before.

Although the ports and airports were on special alert, the authorities had their hands full sorting out the havoc caused by the storm. In any event the police and security forces were on the lookout for the missing cryptologist, and the Fat Boy slipped out of the country without hindrance. The Ford he had parked in Exhibition Road was duly clamped and remained immobilized for three days before being towed away. It then remained in the police pound for a further month before it was examined, and only then was it discovered to have false number-plates and to be listed as a stolen vehicle. No connection was ever made.

The girl who had supplied the gun and plastic explosive device stayed put for a couple of weeks before she, too, went to earth. Acting on a prearranged plan, and with no shortage of funds, she first purchased some smart ski clothes, then checked into the Park Lane Hilton, had her hair permed, and booked a holiday in Switzerland. She travelled on a forged British passport until she landed in Zurich. There she was met by a middle-aged woman who, from all appearances, could have been her mother. An exchange of passports took place while they had coffee together in a café, and she travelled on to Frankfurt by train under her own name. There she made contact with her cell and was taken out of active service for six months, and obtained work as an au pair girl to an American family. They quickly thought the world of her.

Back in England the media finally got wind of Mitchell's disappearance. The Home Office issued a terse statement that was economical with the truth, playing down Mitchell's importance and stating that he only handled low-classification material. For a few days the story spawned the usual criticism of the lack of security in sensitive areas, before the headlines were taken over by one of those events which from time to time satisfy the morbid fascination of the British for sex scandals in high society. The most debased of the Sunday tabloids uncovered a ring of prominent citizens that included a High Court judge, a television personality, three members of the Stock Exchange and, predictably, a clergyman, who had all taken part in spanking orgies with young male prostitutes. A circulation war was created, with even the more staid national papers jumping on this lucrative bandwagon.

Although public attention was thus diverted Pearson and his team were still occupied with trying to identify the third corpse. The two policemen had been buried with full honours; the fragments of the unknown man had yet to be given a grave – nobody had come forward to claim or enquire about a missing father, son or husband. It was as if the remains in Hogg's plastic bags had no value whatsoever.

'Why can't these bloody cases ever be simple?' Pearson said, going over the facts yet again. His New Year resolution to give up smoking had lasted exactly three hours, and he wheezed as he spoke. 'I felt convinced that when Mitchell went walkabout we had it buttoned up.' He stubbed his cigarette out in his coffee-cup, a habit that had several times led to threats of divorce from his wife. 'What do we have? Precious little. A man is shot and then placed on top of a cunning little bomb designed to blow him and anybody else to pieces the moment it's disturbed. Therefore – what? Make an assumption, Alan.'

Lloyd stared down at the mass of paperwork on Pearson's desk. 'Obviously whoever shot the poor bastard wanted to dispose of the body in no uncertain terms.'

'And didn't give a toss who else got hurt in the process. To my way of thinking, that rules out your average murderer. By now I would have expected somebody to shout "Bingo!" and claim a holiday for two in sunny Belfast.' Pearson reached for another cigarette. 'But since the shamrock heroes haven't come forward and we've heard nothing from any of the Middle East mobs all we have is an unknown stiff who apparently liked tucking his family jewels into ladies' knickers. Not a lot to go on.'

'The only other break is the bullet fragment.' Lloyd picked up one of the reports. 'Our ballistics genius is ninety per cent sure it was fired from a modified French police revolver.'

'So?'

'Well, so far we've been assuming the victim was British. Perhaps he wasn't. Perhaps somebody followed him to London.'

'OK. Then, what was he doing in Hyde Park at that time of the morning? And who knew he'd be in Hyde Park at that time of the morning? We know the French order things differently, and if it wasn't for the bomb I might go along with the old *crime passionel* syndrome. A lovers' tiff. A couple of drag artists who fell out. But the bomb doesn't fit into that scenario. Jealous queens are not noted for being explosives experts. No, this is a professional hit-job.'

'Perhaps we'd be better off using a medium,' Lloyd said. 'That always produces results in the movies.'

'Oh, very helpful. All we've got to go on is a coincidence. Mitchell goes walkabout and the following day a man is blown up in Hyde Park.'

'Correction,' Lloyd interrupted. 'A *dead* man is blown up. Hogg reckoned he was shot before the bomb was triggered. Point is, was he shot in the park and then dumped, or was he brought there? If he was brought there, we ought to be looking for a vehicle.'

'Yes. Stupid of me to forget that. I haven't been sleeping well. What d'you do for that?'

'Not sleeping?'

'Yes.'

'Don't know that I'm ever bothered. Must have a clear conscience.'

'If we could somehow tie in Mitchell,' Pearson said, reverting to his original train of thought, 'I might get my head down on the pillow.' He studied the case-reports yet again. 'We seem to be tracking a non-person. An only son of deceased parents, no relatives – not in this country at any rate – mortgage paid up, secure job with an index-linked pension, on the face of it no worries.' Picking up Mitchell's passport, he compared the photograph to the one on the security-tag issued by GCHQ. Both showed the same bland, slightly jowly face of a man in his early forties. No distinguishing marks. He flicked through the passport; it contained an ordinary tourist visa for the United States with one entry for a trip to Miami and on succeeding pages rubber stamps showing he had visited Spain twice and Greece once.

'You've seen this?'

'Yes,' Lloyd said. 'Just holidays from the look of it. He probably went to Disneyworld on the Miami trip.'

'Disneyworld is right here, if you ask me. He belonged to no clubs, no political party. No known girl-friends. Or boy-friends for that matter. And I don't believe it – nobody lives that anonymously, especially in women's underwear. I think we should go back to the house and take a second look.'

They were let into Mitchell's house by his diminutive Filipino housekeeper. Pearson had often remarked that it was a characteristic of her race to conceal their fears by giving the impression they were giggling. While answering his questions, she kept both hands cupped over her mouth, and her pronunciation of English was so strange that she could have been talking in a totally different language. She had already been checked out, and her papers and work permit were in order.

'Did Mr Mitchell entertain friends here?'

'No, sar. No people not coming.'

'Never?'

'No, sar.'

'So you just cooked for him?'

71

'Yes, sar. I cook, clean house, do washing for him.'

'Did he ever have ladies call here?'

The cupped hands went across her mouth. 'No ladies, sar. Good man.'

Pearson was about to ask whether she had ever washed any female garments for Mitchell, but thought better of it. No such clothing had been found in previous searches. 'What I'm asking is – and don't be frightened, because nobody is going to harm you – whether you remember anybody who came to visit Mr Mitchell, ladies or gentlemen. Take your time, just try to think.'

'Mr Mitchell stay alone most nights. Play music.'

'He didn't stay home *every* night, did he?'

She began to cry. 'What become of me now?'

'You're not going to get anywhere,' Lloyd muttered.

'No, you're probably right.' Pearson tried her with a few more questions, talking quietly, but it was a waste of time; she was dismissed and went, tearfully, to her room. For the next hour the two men again searched the rest of the house. Nothing new was discovered, and at the end of the fruitless effort they sat in the kitchen cursing their luck.

'Call me old-fashioned if you like,' Pearson said, 'but I've always believed it's the small details that hang a man – a strand of hair, blood under a strangled girl's fingernail. You've always got to look for the needles in the haystack.'

It was only then that he noticed something.

'Let me ask you something, Alan. You ever read G. K. Chesterton?'

'G. K. who?'

'Chesterton. He wrote the Father Brown stories amongst other things.'

'That was on television, wasn't it?'

'I wouldn't know. Some of us don't get time to sit in front of the box.'

'Are we playing Trivia, or what?'

'I remembered a particular story about a postman who was a murderer. He took the body out of the house in his sack. Nobody suspected him for one simple reason. Know what

72

that was?' Alan shook his head. 'Everybody saw him, but *nobody* saw him, if you get my meaning. He was just a familiar object, so familiar that he didn't register.'

'What's that got to do with Mitchell? You think the postman did him in because he didn't get a Christmas box?'

'Turn round. Look behind you. What do you see?'

Lloyd swivelled. 'Dishwasher. Cupboards. Coffee machine. Last year's calendar.'

'Look on the floor.'

Lloyd stared where directed.

'A dog-bowl.'

'Exactly. But where is the dog? Nobody ever mentioned a bloody dog, did they? Everybody missed that, including me and you.' Pearson jumped to his feet and ran up the stairs to the housekeeper's room. He knocked on the door and waited until she unlocked it.

'I'm sorry to trouble you again, Rosa, but did Mr Mitchell have a dog?'

'Yes, sar. Nice dog. Good-behaved.'

'Where is the dog now?'

'Gone, sar.'

'Did the other policemen take him away?'

'No, sar. He went out with Mr Mitchell.' Tears began to course down her cheeks again.

'You mean that night? The night Mr Mitchell disappeared?'

'Yes, sar.'

'What kind of dog was it? A big dog?'

'Big, sar. Charlie.'

'Was that his name?' Her hands went to her mouth as though she had been caught out uttering some blasphemy. 'Charlie? That was his name, was it?'

She nodded. He questioned her further, but she was unable to identify the breed. All he could get from her was that it was a large brown dog. After calming her down he sent Lloyd out to buy an illustrated book on dogs, and when he returned they sat down with her and went through it page by page. Finally when they got to the section on Labradors she pointed to one of the illustrations.

73

'That one? You're quite certain?'

'Yes, sar. That like Charlie.'

'Did Charlie have a collar with his name on?' This seemed to confuse her further. Pearson ran a finger round his neck and spoke very slowly. 'A collar. With his name and address on it. Did he have one of those?'

She whispered her reply from behind her hands. 'Yes, sar.'

They left the house and sat in the squad car to talk things over.

'So what happened to good old Charlie?' Lloyd asked. 'Clever of you to spot the bowl, Chief.'

'That's because I'm an animal-lover as well as a pretty face.'

'Think it's a break?'

'Well, it's more than we had before. If we locate Charlie, it might give us a break. Right! The first move is to contact all the animal welfare services. You can get yourself down to the Battersea Dogs' Home. Ever been?'

'No.'

'You'll cry your bloody eyes out; that's why I'm not coming with you. Went there once when my little daughter lost her poodle. Nightmare! I couldn't take it. Let's go.'

Others were also perplexed, none more so than Control. He had good cause: Mitchell had been his own man; through Mitchell he had been kept fully informed of all GRU traffic passing between Moscow and London before anybody else. Mitchell had protected his rear and given him early warning of any change in Moscow's strategy.

Ever since the Thatcher government had removed union recognition GCHQ had been a breeding-ground for dissent, but Mitchell had not taken part in any of the demonstrations against the union ban and had been one of the first to accept the lump-sum compensation offered by the Government in return for signing a no-strike agreement. On the face of it, he had never put a foot wrong. That was why his disappearance was so inexplicable.

Twice in one week, taking a risk he had hitherto been careful to avoid, Control visited the dead-letter box set up for

74

Mitchell's drops, in the hope that contact would be re-established. Both times he came away empty-handed. As each day passed he became more anxious about being cut off from Moscow. Mitchell could not be replaced in a hurry: agents with his expertise and carefully placed did not grow on trees.

Coupled with this dilemma was an awareness that the Prime Minister was becoming increasingly intransigent. While it could not be said that Bayldon had absolute power, the process of absolute corruption had begun. Like others before him who had gained great office by deviousness rather than by ability, he had quickly fallen into the trap of believing the image created by the party's publicity machine. He had conveniently forgotten by which route he had been steered into Downing Street: in his own mind he was there by divine right. On several occasions he had deliberately flouted his side of the bargain, refusing to implement the agreed plans, so meticulously plotted prior to the coup. He had countered Control's displeasure by insisting that he was constrained by public opinion and his standing in the polls. The setting-up of the Militia had provoked fierce criticism from many quarters.

'In my judgement, I think we should let things quieten down for the time being,' Bayldon said at one of their meetings at Chequers in a room that had been made bug-proof and was regularly swept. 'I have a draconian Budget to get through the House, one that is hardly likely to be received with any enthusiasm. Taxes have to rise, savagely in certain instances, to pay for our new socialist paradise. Politics, Raymond, is the art of the possible.'

'A maxim first coined by a Tory,' Control observed. 'Rab Butler as a matter of fact. He used it as the title of his autobiography.'

Momentarily dented, Bayldon recovered with: 'One should always borrow the best from one's enemies. What I am trying to explain to you is only I can judge the pace of things. One can't rubber-stamp a revolution.'

'Can't one? I would have said history teaches it's the only way.'

'It's not the British way. I have my finger firmly on the

75

pulse of the British public. They can be led, but not forced.'

'Well, be that as it may, I can't conceal from you there is considerable irritation in another place regarding the lack of progress in dismantling our nuclear deterrent. You will recall that was high on the agreed agenda. I am being pressed to obtain some positive timetable.'

'The first stage will begin later this year.'

'That's already six months later than agreed. A further delay would be taken as a hostile act. Evidence that the dismantling has started is needed for the Moscow summit in July.'

Bayldon met his eyes. 'I want to be sure of the French attitude before taking a final decision.'

'The French are of no consequence.'

'Try telling them that.'

'The *Force de Frappe* does not enter into anybody's reckoning. I understand their farmers are more dangerous.'

'Please don't try to teach me my business,' Bayldon said at his most icy. 'The Cabinet has already approved my strategy.'

'So it's *your* strategy now?'

'Raymond, I happen to be the one in office.'

'It's up to you to manipulate the Cabinet. Why else d'you think you are there?'

The reminder was not to Bayldon's liking. 'Let's not open Pandora's box. The fact is, I'm in the job. You may have assisted along the way, but as far as I know you're not in a position to remove me. The boot is now on the other foot. It wouldn't take a great deal of effort for me to persuade the Cabinet that your entire department is now superfluous and a squalid waste of public money.'

'You don't think so?'

'I know so. Try to stitch me up and you'll stitch the only friend you've got.' He suddenly smiled, revealing teeth that had recently been capped since his wife had criticized his appearance on television. 'Raymond, Raymond, why are we having this conversation? I am here to preside over the orderly transition from a reactionary regime to a full-blooded radical state, always keeping in mind the fact that, historically, the

76

electorate of this country are creatures of habit. The majority have a built-in Luddite mentality, resistant to change. The changes must come about gradually, if we are to succeed in our joint aims. Our task is to sell the idea that what we impose upon them is what they have always wanted. It's a straight marketing exercise, like putting across a new brand of soft drink. You seem to forget that, unlike you, I am highly visible. Be good enough to leave politics to me. We still have an Opposition, you know.'

'Emasculated.'

'You wouldn't think so at Question Time.'

'But since you abolished broadcasting from the House who knows? What percentage of the public reads *The Times* or the *Telegraph*? And those who do are against you anyway. You're safe for another three years if you play your cards right. In three years you could re-invent the wheel.'

There was something in Control's delivery that caused Bayldon to backtrack. 'Don't get the wrong idea. I'm very conscious of the tasks I have to carry out. All I'm saying is that I'm constrained – "handicapped" would be a better word – by the permanent civil servants.'

'Purge them.'

'Not easy.'

'There are ways of skinning those cats. Give me names and let me take care of it. You have no idea how rewarding a few carefully planted rumours about their private lives can be. Of course you've denied yourself the traditional way of removing turbulent priests and the like.'

'How d'you mean?'

'Previously, you knighted them or sent them to the Upper House. Quick, cheap and effective.'

'I had to stand on the election manifesto.' Then he added: 'It didn't do much to alter *you*.'

'Ah, but I was a special case,' Control said evenly. 'And I was never a turbulent priest. Though I could be, if things don't go according to plan.'

'This is a stupid conversation. You know very well that I intend to honour my side of our arrangement. All I'm saying

77

is that in order to bring about the major changes we both know are necessary I have to play it by the existing rules.'

'You knew Moscow's rules going in.'

'I would remind you here we're still a democracy.'

'So I'm told,' Control said, 'so I'm told. But of course one must never believe everything we read in the papers. And of course, up until now, you've never had to test your popularity in a general election.'

'What you and . . . our friends . . . don't seem to realize is that there is only a certain amount of parliamentary time available in any day. They may be able to reverse policy overnight, but we have to comply with procedures. If I attempt too much too soon, somebody will smell a rat.'

'The agreed priorities have to be honoured.'

'Atomic submarines aren't Dinky toys with clockwork motors. One can't float them out to sea and sink them. Plus the fact that every week I get reports back from Washington that if we take unilateral action what they'll sink is the pound. You don't seem to appreciate that I have to juggle a dozen balls at once.'

'Well, you wanted the job,' Control said, and there was ice in his voice. 'You were hungry for it, as I recall, and that particular appetite is not yours exclusively; there will always be others anxious to feast at the same table.'

Bayldon's voice became more placatory. 'Raymond, you and I have always known we were playing for high stakes. Correction, the *highest* stakes. Equally, we could neither of us be under any misapprehension of the problems we would face. To bring this off in the way that we both want, to establish a true communist society – '

'Don't use that word, not even to me,' Control interrupted.

'This room is safe enough. You assured me.'

'Even so.'

'Very well, then, to "reverse centuries of reactionary rule" cannot be accomplished by the stroke of a pen. The committed Left has never achieved parliamentary power in England. Their real power has always been on the workshop floor, within the unions. We have to restore that, go back to our origins. Then, in the House, disguise the medicine, flavour it, a laxative masked with a nice taste, so that it slips down their throats unnoticed. I've got several surprises up my sleeve. The old parrot cry of "soaking the rich" isn't the answer. Everybody, including the brothers, wants to be rich. So our approach has to be more subtle. We have to instil fear, and the process has already begun. I've clipped the wings of the police. We could be in for a crimewave, and when that happens the public will scream for draconian measures, you mark my words. And I don't mean just letters to *The Times*; I'm talking about your average citizen, that great amorphous mass out there in suburbia who think that a takeaway Chinese meal is *haute cuisine*. That's where the Militia will come in. And, of course, I shall look to you to play your part and supply a few distinguished scapegoats. We shall need household names. You mustn't think that because I'm proceeding cautiously I'm not being diligent.' He smiled for the first time. 'So don't give me oblique threats, Raymond. Your advice and co-operation will always be welcome, but threats aren't on. I take exception when anybody positions tanks on my front lawn.'

'I'm glad you're quoting from an impeccable source,' Control said evenly. 'Wilson used that phrase, as I recall. He lost in the end, of course.'

Control left Chequers very disturbed. He had no special regard for Bayldon, either as a man or as a politician. Bayldon had been selected for one reason only: he was more corruptible than most; but now his conceits had become dangerous; too arrogant and ambitious to realize he was third-rate, goaded forward by an even more ambitious wife, the most potent of all human combinations.

As he drove back to London on treacherous icy roads, he began to think again: that which he and Moscow had joined together could as easily be cast asunder.

Sometimes life without Inga proved emptier than Hillsden could tolerate. There were nights when, stupefied with the Scotch he was allowed to buy, he considered pleading with

Abramov to bring her back. He was often drunk these days, shrinking his old personality, falling prey to self-pity as he contemplated the life-sentence ahead. Rare contacts with the outside world only intensified the need to bury himself. He roamed the empty villa, half-dressed, going from room to room, talking to himself like the shuffling inmate of an asylum. This period of hopelessness lasted several weeks until some inner resilience, a hangovered awareness of what he had become, pulled him back from the brink.

Almost casually, at first treating it as a necessary therapeutic exercise, he started to put his past life down on paper, hoping that by so doing he could somehow expunge those treacheries and lost loves that still consumed him. Much to his surprise, what began as an escape from oblivion gradually became something he felt he had abandoned for ever: the restoration of that old familiar – risk. As he scribbled, the bottle of Scotch forgotten, he found that he was writing not autobiography but an instrument of revenge, shaping his sentences into poisoned darts that could kill from afar. Once this realization had hit him, a more dangerous idea took hold. Destroying the score or so pages he had written, he began again, this time laboriously reducing his handwriting to minuscule proportions and filling both sides of each sheet. As the manuscript progressed he secreted the pages into the lining of the fur coat he had acquired during his original stay in Moscow.

Thus he passed the summer, putting in long hours at his desk during the nights and sleeping late into the hot afternoons. He omitted nothing, knowing that if the plan he had conceived was to work he had to make the material too explosive to ignore, albeit always conscious of the fact that if he succeeded he would be signing his own death warrant.

It wasn't until he reached the period he had spent in the old Austrian station that the momentum slowed. Memories of Caroline and Jock and the guilt he still retained for his neglect of her during those final years in the nursing home became almost too painful to record. It was now that a sense of total inadequacy overcame him – so common to all writers, regardless of talent, but in his inexperience shattering – a conviction that he had embarked upon an exercise in futility. For over a week he reverted to the bottle before finding the determination to continue.

The finished manuscript ran to the best part of fifty double-sided pages and he divided them into equal halves, then carefully stitched these inside both sides of the lining of the fur coat. It was only then, elated that he had reached the end, that he gave some thought to his next moves. He was forced to acknowledge that the effort which had cost him dear was of no consequence unless he could ensure it found its way back to England. He drew some comfort from the knowledge that he was following in illustrious footsteps: far greater risks had been taken with greater works than his; savagely painful documents written on hoarded scraps of paper in the bleakness of the Gulag that had somehow found their way into the free world.

In the subsequent weeks he thought of nothing else, devising, analysing and rejecting scheme after scheme before he decided on one that contained the germ of success. Even so, it depended on chance happenings coming in the right order, none of which he could predetermine. Yet anything was preferable – exposure, failure, death even – to the slow disintegration he had been condemned to before: that had been Caroline's end, and he needed to atone.

Major-General Abramov of the GRU, the Soviet army's elite security arm, recently promoted, had every reason to feel satisfied by the way in which his handling of Hillsden's defection had been received. His immediate superior, General Geichenko, who was not given to distributing casual bouquets, had singled him out for special mention, and hinted that he had a more exacting assignment in mind. But it was not in Abramov's nature, nor in the very nature of the career he had so resolutely pursued from the outset, ever to feel totally secure. That was for idiots; that was not the way of things. He was as careful in concealing his ambition as he was in hiding his true thoughts. Nobody penetrated his veneer of modest charm which, allied to his clean-cut looks, had always ensured sexual success. A Muscovite by birth, educated at the university, he spoke several languages fluently and had a firm grasp of world affairs. There was a certain fastidiousness about him – the way he wore his immaculately cut uniforms, the Western-style haircut he affected, his way of holding a wine-glass, the Dutch cheroots he smoked – which set him apart from his fellows. He treated the women he used with a remote courtesy, never allowing them to see any emotion, so that they departed from his bed satisfied but none the wiser.

There were ample historical reasons for his caution. Ever since the days of the Revolution there had always been bad blood between the two arms of the Soviet security forces, intensified during the Stalinist purges when the top ranks of the Army had been decimated. This hideous chapter had never been forgiven or forgotten by the Army, and it was during this period that the seeds of dissent were sown between the GRU and the KGB, for Stalin had used the KGB as the main instrument to carry out his perverted and (as the coming war was to prove) mistaken policy. Historically the KGB had always been closer to the Politburo than the GRU. During the years of mass executions, when nobody was safe and the merest suspicion was enough to denounce the innocent, be they man, woman or child, the rivalry between the two factions bordered on paranoia: it became part of the Russian consciousness to live in fear, for whole sections of the populace to be at the mercy of small-time bureaucrats strutting their meagre authority in every town and village, concealing their own fear of those immediately above them by acting with greater ruthlessness than the situation demanded. It mattered not that the guiltless died in their countless thousands, or else were deported to the living hells of the Gulag. What mattered was that the chain-links of fear, on which all despotic regimes depend, should not be broken.

Even when, after Stalin, the blood-letting dwindled to a comparative trickle, the KGB remained in the ascendant, culminating in the rise of Beria to the highest offices in the land, his stranglehold on the jugular of Soviet society seemingly unbreakable. Plots and counter-plots abounded within the Kremlin itself, the watchers in turn watched, their telephones tapped, their every movement tabulated, so that in order to survive they had to create secret organizations within secret organizations, never certain where or how the information they collected would be used.

Geichenko was a survivor with a long memory. His father, also a top-ranking officer, had perished during the Stalinist era, denounced by Beria for daring to criticize the performance of the second Five-Year Plan, and as a child Geichenko himself had been sentenced to ten years' exile in a labour-camp. Ironically, it was the war and the Army that saved him. His future shaped by those early experiences, once he had risen through the ranks to a position of power he had made it his business to surround himself with a hand-picked bevy of bright young officers who were his eyes and ears: he was a student of history and had noted that this was how Montgomery had operated to good effect. He demanded nothing less than total loyalty, and those who failed to live up to his exacting standards were swiftly culled. Abramov, a member of this inner group, was a favoured son who owed his rapid progress to Geichenko's paternalism.

The GRU's coup of landing Hillsden from under the KGB's nose, and indeed the way in which Geichenko had master-minded the entire British operation, meant that Abramov got his share of reflected glory. He had always been attracted to Western attitudes, and being in a position of privilege he had access to Western literature. During the many weeks when he had first interrogated and then debriefed Hillsden, their attitude towards each other had undergone subtle changes. He respected Hillsden, and their dialogues had often acquired a philosophical depth, straying from the strict business in hand to wider fields. It so happened that in the end he had been compelled to stretch Hillsden to the limits, and Hillsden had not failed him, passing all the tests set him, including the hardest of all. Because of this, and because Abramov had always admired a fellow-professional, their relationship had gradually deepened into a curious sort of friendship, though not to the extent that Abramov compromised his own future.

83

He always held something back even from those closest to him. It was his nature. He gave just enough of himself to inspire trust, a technique that had always served him well, for once trust had been established he had observed that friends and enemies alike dropped their guard, became careless – and carelessness was a tool he could always turn to his own advantage.

The girl, Inga, had served her purpose, placed in Hillsden's life as an extra insurance policy, for the confidences shared on the pillow were often those that made the vital difference. Since he never allowed his own life to be governed by a woman, he gave but passing consideration to Hillsden's feelings in the matter. Other girls could always be provided if the necessity arose, and he justified his action by convincing himself that in any case Inga was of inferior intellect to Hillsden, ignoring the fact that, in the sum total of human sexuality, intellect has not figured high.

Making one of his periodic visits to Hillsden he was, by his own standards, surprised and unprepared for the change of mood.

'I've never seen you like this, Alec. You seem depressed.'

'Not depressed so much as disenchanted. I'm becoming a hermit crab here.'

'I know your real problem. You want someone to share your bed. That can be arranged.'

'No, no more "arrangements", Victor. I'm too old for that game. It's just that I have an urge to see more of my adopted country. I'm a city boy, born and bred. I'm stagnating here. I want to sample some culture, theatres, museums.'

'But most people would envy you this situation.'

'Maybe, but I'm not most people. You should know that.'

'You prefer the cold to the seaside?'

'I prefer cities. Not Moscow. Moscow doesn't hold happy memories. But Leningrad for instance.'

'Well, I want you to be content, Alec. Your useful life isn't over yet. I will note your request and discuss it with General Geichenko.'

'Will it go with your blessing?'

'Alec, you insult me. When have I ever neglected your well-being?'

'There's always a first time, Victor, and time is not on my side.'

A month passed before word came back that permission had been granted. Within a further month Hillsden made the journey to Leningrad taking with him the few personal possessions he had acquired. He enjoyed settling into the drab, if roomy, apartment he had been allocated just off Leningrad's Arsenal Street and close to the Finland railway station: the two names gave him private satisfaction, reminding him as they did of a football team he had once supported and Edmund Wilson's erudite book. He set about making it more comfortable, and since his status allowed him luxuries denied the majority of Soviet citizens he gradually transformed it into a home.

Although the beauty of the city and its surroundings – the bright glitter of water everywhere (a revelation this), the four hundred bridges he solemnly counted during various excursions, the great flowering of baroque and classical architecture – astounded him, Hillsden never lost sight of the real objective behind the calculated move. He had chosen it as the city closest to the West, the one where he stood the best chance of making the vital contact he needed to set his plan into motion.

His first guest was naturally Abramov, who came in festive mood.

'I have been given good news, Alec, that I wish to share. Today I was told I am to be moved to the Second Directorate.'

'Congratulations.'

Hillsden was aware that the Second Directorate was the department of the GRU responsible for North and South America as well as for the United Kingdom.

'Yes, and I have come prepared to celebrate with you.'

He produced a bottle of fifteen-year-old malt Scotch.

'What is it you always say? "You will feel no pain when this passes your lips." '

'On the nail. We will drink superior Scotch in inferior

85

glasses. Sit you down.' He removed his fur coat from the back of a chair; it was part of his careful planning not to conceal the coat, but have it openly on display. 'Make yourself comfortable. It isn't much, as they say, but it's home.'

'I like to know you think that way.'

As the Scotch was poured Hillsden remarked: 'According to *Pravda*, excessive consumption of alcohol is now a social crime.'

'True. Everything in *Pravda* is true, as you and I know. But a drink between influential friends does not count.'

'I know *you're* influential, General, but are we friends?'

'How can you ask such a question after all we've been through together?'

'I like to have it confirmed regularly.'

'Then, I will do that.'

They toasted each other.

If only, Hillsden thought, we could accept each other for what we really are and admit that we have both been duped; admit how tawdry the whole game of spying is, how pointless in a world where the majority are starving. Who had sold the secrets of nutrition, who had microfilmed the cure for cancer or for AIDS? All we ever betray for is death. Nothing the Firm, the KGB, the GRU or the CIA did could ever help the child with the distended belly and the eyelids slowly eaten by flies. All we ever achieve, he thought as they swapped pleasantries and anecdotes of past encounters, is to prolong agony, extend the suspicions, multiply the betrayals. The only cause that was never short of funds was hatred. He saw in Abramov sacred and profane shades of his old self, and pitied him.

'There is the possibility', Abramov confided, 'that I might be posted to England.'

The news jolted Hillsden. He took on board the irony that whereas Abramov could move around the world, even visiting England, he was confined and trapped.

'Really? That's amazing. We should drink to that. Would you be posted to the embassy?'

'Yes, naturally.'

'Well, you realize if that happens you'll be living in Million-aires' Row.'

Abramov looked blank.

'Is that one of your great pieces of British humour? A joke in poor taste?' Humour, other than the coarsest variety, was not one of Abramov's strong points.

'No. Your London embassy is close to Kensington Palace in a private road locally known as "Millionaires' Row". From your bedroom window you'll be able to point a telephoto lens and observe members of the royal family going about their business. How about that? Maybe it is a joke of sorts.'

'Alec, I will have more serious duties to perform. In any case, I find the whole concept of monarchy to be a futile exercise in bourgeois sentimentality. How is it possible to still have such a thing? It is arcane.'

'I forgot. You go for regicide, don't you?'

'Don't say such things, even in fun, to anybody but me. Others might take such a remark as a sign that you are not yet fully converted.'

'I'm stating a historical fact. You can't rewrite history.'

'Why not? History is just another weapon to be used in the class struggle. Surely you must have grasped that by now? You are curiously naïve about certain things, my friend. Although you've come a long way since first we met, you still have some distance to travel. Learn our ways. Think our thoughts. History is what *we* decide. We plan, we wait, we allow others to make the mistakes . . . then, and only then, do we move in and pick up the spoils.'

'I'm sure that's good advice, and I'll remember it,' Hillsden said, thinking: I am learning your ways. Learning them to use them one day against you. 'May I?' He poured himself another generous measure of malt. 'You know the thing I've noticed most since coming to Leningrad? A new feeling in the air. A shiver of freedom.'

Abramov drained his glass, taking the malt like vodka. 'It was necessary for us to take a calculated step in that direction – what I believe the Americans call a "PR exercise". But freedom is like this excellent Scotch: give people too much of

87

it too quickly and they become overconfident and start believing in miracles . . . If I go to London, I shall miss our discussions, Alec. We have shared much together. We did, after all, share a moment of truth together without flinching. Together we wiped the slate clean.'

The oblique reference to the elimination of Jock took Hillsden off-guard: the subject had never been mentioned between them since the fateful night. And so much for honesty, he thought, his and mine. He can't bring himself to say it directly, and Jock's murder was the only thing I omitted from my hidden manuscript. There were so many Polaroids of memory that refused to be obliterated, the colours unfaded by time: Caroline alive, Caroline broken on Hogg's steel slab, a close-up of Jock's bleary face pleading justification.

'The ever-present past,' he said, looking away.

'The *necessary* past, Alec. There will always be difficult choices to be made in the life we both lead. It's what separates us from the rest.'

Again, Hillsden was taken back to Caroline. She had used more or less the same expression. He thought: The night before she went back into Berlin, the last time we made love, the last time I saw her alive, I asked her what made her the way she was and she answered: 'The life we lead.' How far removed and yet how close it seemed. So many journeys since, so many fresh betrayals, and now journey's end here, the mask in place, toasting a counterfeit friendship.

Abruptly changing the subject, he said: 'I shall want to know what you make of London, if you get there.'

'What tips can you give me? I want to arrive fully prepared.'

'When in doubt, talk about the weather,' Hillsden said, wishing he had a real friend to confide in, somebody familiar, and the only person who came to mind was Waddington.

Close to Abramov's possible London destination, Pearson confessed himself stymied. Despite intensive enquiries, there was no trace of the missing Labrador. The regular police had made house-to-house calls in the immediate vicinity of Mitchell's home, and reward notices had been placed in local shops. As Pearson had predicted, Lloyd found his visit to the Battersea Dogs' Home traumatic: every caged animal he looked at greeted him as a potential saviour and, although there were several Labradors, none of them could be positively identified as Charlie, nor did recent records show a dog answering to his description. Lloyd departed a shaken man, knowing that many of the abandoned pets would shortly have to be put down.

By a remote coincidence it was the hapless Constable Whiting of Janet Reger fame who stumbled upon the answer. He had been transferred from West End Central to Hampstead, a move which did not fill him with joy since it took him further away from Isabel with whom he was now enjoying a fruitful relationship.

'Here's a good one for you, Whiting,' his new station officer said one morning, 'your reputation having preceded you.'

'How's that, then, Sergeant?'

'I was told that at Central you were known as "La Bête Humaine". Shall I translate? "The Human Animal." So I thought this little problem would be right up your alley. Get yourself along to this flat in Lyndhurst Road and investigate a case of the barking dog. The neighbours have been complaining it's been driving them apeshit.'

Whiting duly found his way to the premises but failed to gain entry. The neighbour who had phoned the police, an old-age pensioner living in the flat below, was only too anxious to unburden herself. She and Whiting stood outside the door and listened to the dog; they could hear it scratching at the door, and it was obvious that the animal was desperate.

'The poor thing's been howling night and day. Terrible. I couldn't hear the television. Course these places are badly built. The walls are paper thin; you can hear everything that goes on, sometimes things you'd rather not hear, especially that young couple living below me. They're not much better than animals.'

'Whose dog is it?' Whiting asked, finally getting a word in.

'Well, that's the thing. Nobody seems to know.'

'They must know who lives there.'

'Nobody *lives* there, like I live here. I mean, it's not occupied full-time. There's a man what comes and goes, but we haven't seen him recently.'

'D'you have his name? Know where he works or anywhere we could contact him?'

The old woman shook her head. 'I know most of them here, because I take in the mail; not that I'm nosy – don't think that – but I'm usually around, you see. The others go to work during the day. But he never seems to get any letters.'

'So nobody's been in to feed it as far as you know?'

'No, the poor thing must be starving.'

'Isn't there a caretaker who could let us in?'

'With our landlord you're lucky if you get a dustbin.'

'And nobody's got a spare key?'

'No. Can't you break the door down?'

'Not without authority, I can't.'

'Oh, I thought you lot could get in anywhere. Not like "The Professionals",' she said, referring to a well-known television series. 'They don't seem to have any trouble.'

Whiting returned to the station and reported the situation. 'I'm not too keen to go in there alone, Sarge. Never know with dogs like that. Could have rabies.'

'Right, son. Leave it to me.'

Later that same day a member of the dog-handler unit, together with an inspector from the RSPCA who was armed with a tranquilliser gun, went to the house. There was no noise from the dog now. The door to the flat proved to have double security locks fitted and had to be forced.

The sight that greeted the two men once they had gained entry was sickening. The stench of animal faeces was overpowering, and they rushed to open windows. Much of the flat had been wrecked; in its frenzy the dog had chewed the furniture – the sofa was literally torn apart and there were deep scratch-marks on the walls and door panels. They found the emaciated animal lying in the bathroom where presumably it had gone to find water: the bowl of the water closet was dry. The RSPCA inspector immediately gave it an injection as a precaution before he examined it. The dog's jaws were flecked with foam and blood, and some of its teeth had been broken off during its ordeal. One back leg was twisted at an unnatural angle.

'Will you be able to save it?'

'Difficult to say. We'll have a try. He wouldn't have lasted much longer from the look of him. I'll get him away to our nearest depot and let the girls take care of him.'

'Poor bastard.'

'Yeah, the other bastard is the one who let him get this way. Come on, old fellow, let's get you to hospital. What's your name?' He felt for the collar, blood-stained like the dog's matted coat. 'Charlie, is it? All right, Charlie, easy now; no one's going to hurt you.'

He wrapped the dog in a blanket and carried him down to his van. Left alone, the police dog-handler radioed for assistance to secure the flat again. He remained by the open window, looking around at the wreckage. There was nothing to denote what was the lifestyle of the unknown occupant. The furniture was utilitarian, recognizable as coming from Habitat, the walls bare. It bore all the signs of being an occasional *pied-à-terre*. Resentment mixed with anger grew in the dog-handler, not only for the cruelty meted out to the pathetic Labrador, but also against those rich enough to afford two homes. He kicked at an upturned coffee-table, knocking it to one side. In so doing he revealed what to his experienced eye was a large bloodstain on the carpet. He bent down to examine it more closely. Although the dog had been bleeding from the mouth, it seemed to him unlikely that it could have haemorrhaged to that extent. He touched the patch: it was dry and darker in places where a clot had congealed. Straightening up, he returned to the window when he heard a police siren approaching. The patrol car drew up in the street below, and he shouted his whereabouts to the two occupants. It was only then that he noticed a bullet-hole in the wall close to the window-frame and the suspicion that he was concerned with something more than just cruelty to an animal began to take shape in his mind.

'Christ almighty!' the first patrolman said as he entered the

91

flat. 'Somebody been taken short after a curry dinner? What have we got here? Bloody roll on. Thanks for warning us.'

He and his companion held their noses as they advanced into the room.

'Well, it started out just saving a starving dog, but now I'm not so sure. What d'you make of that?'

The dog-handler pointed to the stain on the carpet.

'And this.'

Now he directed their attention to the bullet-hole.

'Out of our league, I think. Get on the blower and call CID.'

They waited downstairs in the fresh air until the plain-clothes crime squad arrived. 'It's all yours,' they said, 'and welcome to it.'

News of the discovery was quickly conveyed to Pearson, who immediately went to the flat. By the time he arrived it had been fumigated. The forensic team had established that the stain on the carpet had been formed by human blood; further tests proved it corresponded with the group of the Hyde Park victim. A photograph of Mitchell was shown to the old woman in the flat below, and she identified it as the man she had occasionally seen using the premises. A spent bullet was prised from the wall and sent away for a more detailed analysis. Pearson ordered the whole place to be taken apart. At around ten o'clock that same night one of his team got the break he was waiting for: concealed inside an inoperative VHS video-recorder was a powerful short-wave radio, a miniature camera and code-book.

6

Often Hillsden would wake in the middle of the night, his mind consumed with the same imponderables. He wished he had the sort of brain that could solve the *Times* crossword in ten minutes flat, or the mentality of an Agatha Christie – her Miss Marple or that fatuous Belgian would have the answer to his problem in a flash: they never failed to discover who killed the vicar in the locked room with the key on the inside.

More and more his thoughts turned to Waddington. Slightly stuffy, fixed-in-his-views-but-wholly-reliable Waddington. Once Control had brought him in from the cold to be a desk jockey, Waddington had been the only person in the Firm he had ever felt he could trust. The rest had been a dreary bunch, some of them halfway round the bend, deballed, treading water until pension-time, their minds ossified, terrified to take decisions unless one of the equally emasculated Standing Committees approved. Only Waddington stood out from the mob, a beacon of hope.

As an exercise of mind and body he took a series of long walks through the streets of Leningrad and set himself to recall the dialogues he had had with Waddington in the aftermath of Caroline's murder. Then he had used Waddington as a sounding-board for his own theories, Waddington arguing, sometimes agreeing, sometimes sceptical, though seldom dismissing anything out of hand. Memory often distorted past events, as most autobiographies proved, but Hillsden was certain that he had convinced Waddington of the existence of a conspiracy. There had been no opportunity for them to join forces and follow through; Control had seen to that. At the spider's beckoning, I walked straight into the parlour, he thought, spurred on by anguish over Caroline, accepting the reasons he sold me. Control had been one step ahead every inch of the way, baiting each succeeding trap – first warning me off any further interrogation of Glanville, knowing full well I would go against his orders, then making sure I would appear to be the last person to see Glanville alive. Afterwards, with my voice, my threats on tape, he had me cold. With Glanville and Caroline dead, I was the only one left to dispose of. *'I'm sending you back, Alec, to where it all began'* – making it sound like an enormous favour, and promising I'd be stepping across Checkpoint Charlie, traded, once it was over. All that remained was to shut one last door behind me the moment I was out of the country. It had to be something he could make public, so he pinned Belfrage's murder on me. How eagerly, blindly, I went along.

He walked the streets silently cursing his past gullibility. That was why he had to get the manuscript to Britain and in safe hands. The warts were all there on the pages: names, dates, the whole diabolical scenario. But maybe he attached too much faith to the credibility of others? Was it naïve to expect that anybody, even the most fervent anti-government critic, would swallow the proposition that the Prime Minister was being directly manipulated by Moscow? There was a spurious precedent: the groundswell of rumour that still surrounded Harold Wilson's sudden and unexplained resignation; at the time, on much scantier evidence, there had been numerous people prepared to accept the possibility of communist influences in Number 10. A group of past and discredited members of the Firm had been branded as the villains in that instance, but what if it had been tried before and failed? What if Wilson – wily, pragmatic old Harold in his raincoat and his uncanny political instincts – had seen through it in time and spiked their guns? Then a replacement Manchurian candidate would have been needed during the Thatcher years, groomed and kept on ice until the right moment.

The more he turned it over in his mind, the more he was persuaded towards Waddington as the only reliable recipient of his manuscript. If a way could be found to Waddington –

that was the next hurdle to overcome – and Waddington accepted it as genuine, he at least stood a chance. A president of the United States had been impeached on far less.

As he continued to wrestle with the problem he had no means of telling that the courier he would eventually use, a Grade Two supervisor in the Passport Office named Frampton, was at that moment making his own innocent plans for an appointment in Samarra.

Frampton could not remember a time when he had not felt ill at ease. He was only in his mid-thirties, but already worry had aged him, lightly foxing his skin so that it now had the texture of an antiquarian book bound in vellum. In contrast, his seventy-year-old widowed father had the complexion of a schoolboy, rubicund on the cheekbones where a lifetime's dedication to sherry of the cheapest variety had broken the small blood-vessels, but otherwise as clear as if freshly scrubbed.

The trail that led his son to Hillsden began on Christmas Day, which in the Frampton household was an annual nightmare. Frampton junior had always known he was different from the rest of the family, that he had nothing in common with the relatives who made the ritual pilgrimage – second cousins whose names he could not remember, aged, fully dentured aunts who talked of nothing but the dead and those about to die of some terminal condition, as though the marking of Christ's birth was the ideal occasion to recall all life's miseries. They arrived, locust-like, every Yuletide laden with unsuitable gifts.

When Christmas lunch finished that year he sat on the edge of his chair, poised ready to escape at the earliest opportunity. The qualities of the meal, which Frampton had found obscenely lavish, were being solemnly debated with much picking of false teeth and the occasional scarcely concealed belch. There was a slight lull while everybody watched the Monarch's speech on television, which took as its theme the need to vanquish the spectre of starvation in the Third World. Gluttony appeased, the audience around the table nodded in agreement. Once it was over some attacked the mince pies and lemon curd tarts again, for the mere mention of food had triggered off hunger pangs.

Leaving the debris behind, the whole tribe then migrated into the sitting-room. This had the look of a stage set in the process of being struck at the end of a long run: the furniture arranged in a haphazard pattern of his father's devising that ensured nobody could sit in comfort. If guests wished to use the sofa, they had first to navigate around armchairs isolated in the middle of the room, all facing away from the fireplace. Another television was placed at an angle in one corner, partially obscured for most of the viewers by a desk piled high with Frampton senior's hoarded correspondence. A grand-father clock with Westminster chimes vibrated the photo-graphs on the mantelpiece every quarter-hour while consistently showing the wrong time. Pride of place was given to a bird-cage housing a dispirited mute budgerigar that sat staring at its smeared reflection in a small mirror. If, as frequently happened when the room was crowded, somebody knocked over an ornament or stumbled against the three footstools positioned like land-mines for the unwary, the bird went into a spiralled frenzy, releasing a cloud of small feathers and millet husks into the air. It had never been known to talk and had one deformed hook-like claw. With a conviction nobody dared challenge, Frampton senior insisted it was a hen and had named it Elsie. He retained a curious love–hate relationship with it, cursing the mess it made, saddened that it would never come to his finger, yet bound to it in the way some men are bound to a loveless marriage.

Frampton made an effort to join in the conversation which, with nil spirit of goodwill, centred around an absent uncle who was apparently living in sin with his housekeeper. The strain of concentrating on this boring saga gave him a head-ache. He excused himself and went up to his room. There he took stock of his gifts: the usual hideous ties, gloves that did not fit, and the *pièce de résistance* this year, a musical beer-tankard that, when lifted, played a theme from *The Student Prince*.

He went to his record-player and selected a recording of Mahler's Fifth, a favourite ever since he had seen the film of *Death in Venice*. He was determined one day to visit the Lido. Throughout most of his life the family had taken their holidays together; even after his mother died the custom had continued, always to safe dull haunts in England, staying in boarding-houses or unlisted hotels, never abroad, for his father had an abiding dislike of foreigners. Frampton could never forget the humiliation of having to queue for the communal bathrooms and toilets that were characteristic of such humble establishments. Then, three years previously, in a rare show of defiance, he had booked himself a holiday in Russia – a deliberately contentious choice made in the certain knowledge that his father would never accompany him. The act of rebellion had never been forgiven, though it had provided Frampton senior with a new line in vituperation. 'See what your Red friends are up to now', or 'Amazed you don't go and live there permanently since you think the Bolshies are so bloody superior.'

Paradoxically, the freedom he had experienced away from the suffocating paternal presence in a country not noted for its freedoms had seemed to Frampton like beginning life all over again. Since it was novel to him he had scarcely noticed the petty restrictions; nor had the food served in his Moscow hotel seemed inferior to the boarding-house stodge he had endured in the past. He savoured every moment and went home enriched, determined to repeat the experience at the earliest opportunity.

Returning the following year, he had ventured further afield and explored Leningrad, going with even higher expectations and a certain smugness towards those in his party who solicited his advice, as an old hand, on how to behave; few before had ever asked his opinion on anything. Leningrad was preferred to Moscow; it appeared to him to be steeped in the mysteries of Imperial Russia, for this time he had prepared himself by reading the classic works of Tolstoy and Chekhov. His first visit to the ballet was an act of revelation, and the heady experience of discovering a purpose to his hitherto mundane life led him, all unsuspecting, to an awareness of his true self. Back in London the cult of the ballet had always seemed an elitist luxury, for the price of a good ticket at Covent Garden had always been beyond Frampton's means. Now, sitting in the old Maryinski Imperial Theatre, renamed the Kirov, confronted by the matchless precision of the Leningrad company, a sense of wasted years had gripped him. It did not escape his notice that he was not part of a privileged audience but was enjoying the enchantment with equals. When the lights went up at the first interval he found himself sharing his pleasure with a young Russian named Leonid Kiprenski in the adjoining seat. Speaking extremely good English, his new friend willingly explained the plot of the next ballet in the programme, and by the end of the evening they were on first-name terms.

'I would very much like you to visit my apartment, John. I have a wonderful collection of posters and ballet books.'

'How very kind of you. Is that allowed?'

'Allowed? What do you mean?'

'Well, we have a guide who plans everything for us. I don't know whether we're supposed to go off on our own.'

'Is permitted, believe me. Things have changed. I will speak to your guide and fix it. No problem. Which hotel are you in?'

Frampton gave him the details, and later that same evening the guide approached him as he collected his room key. 'Mr Kiprenski has spoken to me of your meeting. I think it would be pleasant for you to visit with him. We like our tourist guests to see how we live.'

The ease with which it was accomplished further strengthened Frampton's view that all he had heard about Russian bureaucracy was exaggerated. The following day he was driven to one of a group of apartment-blocks in the outer suburbs. An ancient concierge guarded the entrance, but the driver spoke to her and Frampton was allowed through without hindrance. Leonid's apartment was on the sixth floor; there was no lift, and Frampton was out of breath by the time he reached the door.

Leonid admitted him into a room some twelve feet square, comfortably furnished, though to his Western eyes the style reminded Frampton of the sixties. One wall was bookshelved from floor to ceiling; the others were hung with framed posters, most of them celebrating ballet and opera productions.

'I have prepared tea,' his host said. 'Just like England, I hope. What is it your poet wrote? "And is there honey still for tea?" I have learnt this poet by heart; he is very romantic, I think. You know his works better than me, no doubt.'

Frampton coloured, ashamed that his general ignorance of the arts should be so swiftly uncovered. 'I'm not a great poetry-reader, I'm sorry to say.'

'Oh, he was such a handsome young man, this Rupert Brooke. Like Byron in another age, and like Byron he died tragically. But then beauty is often tragic. I admire beauty, don't you?'

'Very much so.'

'I could not live without beauty.'

'Well, you certainly have a very beautiful apartment.'

'I am pleased you think so. I waited eleven years, you know, to get a place of my own.'

'Eleven years? Really?'

'Oh, yes, I am very fortunate.'

'Your posters,' Frampton said, trying to change the conversation since he was not sure how to react to the revelation about the apartment, 'quite a collection.'

'They remind me of what my life might have been,' Leonid replied, fussing with a small samovar. 'I trained as a ballet dancer, you see. Unfortunately, I was not good enough, and I had no wish to be second-rate. The ballet is for stars, not for in-betweens.'

'I have to confess I've only just started to take an interest in the ballet. What d'you do now?'

'Now I write criticism about people I envy. No, that is not true – a little joke in poor taste. I try to be fair about my old colleagues. I do that and I also translate for a publishing house. It's not the same as being the soloist in *The Sleeping*

Beauty, but there it is. What do you do, John?' He handed Frampton his tea in a glass.

'Oh, my life's very dull, compared to yours. I work in a government office. It's a responsible position, I suppose, but not very exciting. I attend to passports and visas.'

'Visas! But that must be an important post. And your wife, does she work also?'

'I'm not married.'

'Ah, we've both escaped that, eh?'

'I don't know that I escaped it; I just haven't met anybody who wanted to marry me. I live with my father; he's widowed – my mother died some years ago.'

They chatted amicably, and Leonid played some ballet music, explaining the intricacies required of the dancers during certain passages. At one point he gave a practical demonstration. 'I'm very rusty. Once you give up daily practice the muscles don't work as they should.'

'It must be a hard life, being a dancer.'

'The hardest.'

'But still you miss it?'

'There are other pleasures in life. And at least now I can stay up late at night without a conscience. The discipline of the ballet is stricter even than the army. Every single day of your life you are on parade; you must go to class no matter how you feel. Hour after hour, the same exercises until you are fit to drop. And always somebody better than you, watching, waiting for you to fail so that they can take your place.'

Frampton was fascinated by these inside glimpses of a world he had never known. It never occurred to him to question why Leonid had chosen him as a friend; he took it that Russians, contrary to what he had always been conditioned to believe, were naturally gregarious and sociable. When they parted company both promised to keep in touch by correspondence.

'I shall be back,' Frampton said, 'and perhaps one day you will visit London and I can return your hospitality.'

There was the slightest change of expression on Leonid's

face. 'That would be nice, but there are still certain obstacles.'

'Aren't you allowed to travel?'

Again a hesitation. 'Well, it is not encouraged, shall we say? When we apply for a visa we are asked, "Have you visited all of your own country yet?" and if, truthfully, we say "No" they tell us: "See Russia first and then think about travelling abroad." ' Then he quickly added: 'But things are changing. So maybe, one day, you will give me tea in London.'

Immediately on his return home Frampton sat down and wrote Leonid a long letter and, casting financial discretion to the winds, became a member of the Friends of Covent Garden. He was determined to enlarge his artistic education. He also purchased a Russian language course on cassette and attempted to master the rudiments, without great success, though he was careful to keep these activities from his father. Anticipating his parent's ridicule, he asked Leonid to reply to a post office box rather than to his home address. His own letters became more and more intimate, for like many lonely people he was best able to express his innermost thoughts on paper.

When his next holiday came around he booked his own passage rather than join a package tour. Arriving in Leningrad he took particular pleasure in greeting his friend with a few of his newly mastered Russian phrases. He had brought gifts from England: several books on the Royal Ballet, some Cologne from Penhaligan and a box of biscuits from Fortnum & Mason. In return he was treated to another visit to the Kirov and, after the performance, taken to a restaurant frequented by members of the company and introduced to them. The whole experience, coupled with too much unaccustomed vodka, proved so exhilarating that he almost passed out when gaining the fresh air. He therefore raised no objection when Leonid suggested he should not go back to the hotel but instead spend the night in his apartment.

They shared the only bed. Frampton fell asleep immediately and it wasn't until the small hours of the morning that he woke, sobered, to find Leonid caressing a part of his anatomy he had hitherto never considered an object of worship.

101

Despite the shock he found he could not prevent himself responding. He had known little passion in his life, and apart from occasional visits to prostitutes (which abruptly ended when the AIDS epidemic hit the headlines) his sexual experience had been arid. Even so, he was not so naïve as to be unaware that he was being led to the frontier of a secret and dangerous country. As if sensing this, Leonid stopped his expert ministrations. He stroked Frampton's face and spoke a colloquial endearment in Russian before reverting to English.

'Does what I do scare you? If so, I will stop. It's just that I am very attracted to you. You realized that, I am sure.'

'No.'

'Then, you are shocked?'

'Not shocked exactly.'

'You don't find me agreeable, perhaps?'

'No, I like you very much. It's just that nobody has ever said . . . done this to me before.'

'Forgive me, but I could not help myself. From your letters you wrote to me, I read between the lines and thought you shared my hopes.'

'I've heard . . . there are terrible risks,' Frampton said.

'Not if you go about it the right way. And there are no risks with me; I'm clean, I promise you. When I knew you were coming back, I took the test. So you don't have to worry on that account.' While he soothed with words, Leonid continued to manipulate Frampton, keeping him aroused. 'Just relax, give in to it; I know you want to . . . I'll make you happy.'

He pulled back the bedclothes and positioned himself between Frampton's legs. 'You'll find how exciting it is, what you've been missing.' To Frampton it was the twisted realization of many past fantasies, as though he was listening to a dialogue he had often rehearsed but never acted upon. In the barren aftermath of his occasional visits to a brothel he had often imagined scenes of love returned, when he would say such things to the unknown woman of his dreams. Fantasy had always been more successful than reality in satisfying his sexual hunger. With the help of pornographic magazines he had developed a complex system of stimulation to enliven his solitary pleasures. Now, as he surrendered to Leonid's experienced mouth, the slate of memory was wiped clean. New images swirled behind his closed lids while Leonid brought him to an unaccustomed fulfilment, and he knew he was powerless to alter anything that lay ahead.

During the rest of his holiday his sexual education was completed. Their relationship deepened, although Frampton still found it difficult to understand how it was that the younger man, somebody of superior culture and intellect, could possibly find him worthy of such affection. Leonid often pressed him for details of the homosexual scene in England, asking questions that Frampton could not answer with any accuracy; his knowledge, such as it was, had been gleaned secondhand – sexual innuendo was always being bandied about in the office where he worked. Now he gradually became introduced to the universal language of homosexuality, to its passwords and camp slang that so easily crossed frontiers that were otherwise impenetrable.

When the time came for him to return home their farewells took on an almost unbearable poignancy. Frampton could not contemplate the separation and during the flight locked himself in the toilet at one point to avoid being seen weeping.

Now, as he sat in his bedroom listening to the sounds of Christmas below, he made a decision. He had deliberately not taken a summer holiday that year but had accumulated the leave due him, a whole six weeks. He made up his mind to use it all on a prolonged reunion. His father would abuse him for callously neglecting his filial duties, but he would live with that. Knowing Leonid had given him new courage. There and then he began a letter telling Leonid of his plan, using the only Christmas gift that had given him pleasure: a new Parker pen he had bought for himself. As the smooth nib skimmed over the notepaper he wrote his glad tidings in the mistaken belief that soon he would be journeying towards a love that would never end.

7

Outwardly, there was little to suggest that Keating was ruffled. Yet at the time he made up his mind to seek out Waddington he was bitterly regretting his propensity for acquiring wives; wives moreover who followed a depressing pattern, periodically fouling the order of his life.

His first marriage had been a mistake such as anybody of tender years could make: a pubescent childhood sweetheart with an insatiable appetite for adolescent sex had seemed to fulfil a full-blooded young man's fevered prayers. A white wedding, a honeymoon in Bermuda, then home to a four-bedroomed detached in upwardly mobile suburban Weybridge, the gift of his wealthy parents. But in no time at all the delectable, ever-compliant, bikini-clad creature, pride of the pink Bermuda beaches, had become a surly and heavily pregnant shrew whose sole domestic skill was the ability to burn a boiled egg if cajoled into setting foot in the kitchen, and who eventually produced a male child which cried solidly for six months. Within two years Keating had walked out, though divorce before the permissive age was a protracted affair, and he was compelled to act the guilty partner, spending a long and boring night with 'a woman unknown' (as the law euphemistically then termed them) in a Brighton hotel. He considered her old enough to be his mother and, far from committing adultery, they played Scrabble until a paid private detective 'discovered' them in bed the following morning. Justice being hypocritically satisfied and the divorce granted, he played the field for a decade, kept clear of matrimony but caught two doses of the clap until, touching thirty, he became bored with the so-called thrill of the chase.

Throughout this period he worked as a partner in his father's stockbroking firm, and since in those days insider trading was considered a natural perk of the trade he made money and enjoyed spending it. He fell in love again during a cruise on *Queen Mary*, this time with an American fashion model, the only daughter of a Chicago meat baron ('Daddy made his pile from hogs' bellies,' as she put it). They lived in a variety of places while the marriage lasted, parting in Washington where the second Mrs Keating filibustered in the sack with at least three members of the Republican Party (Daddy didn't approve of Democrats) before finally running off with a West Coast type who promised to get her into movies.

As far as could be judged, it was around this time that Keating was recruited into MI6, though who made the first approach, or where, was never conclusively established. It was possible that Dinnsbury, the then Director-General, was personally responsible for netting him: the Washington office at that time was notably troublesome, and Dinnsbury might well have thought that somebody with Keating's personality, wealth and social contacts was a better bet than the usual languid Establishment types favoured by the Foreign Office. Dinnsbury never hunted with the pack, and was attracted to those of a like disposition, so Keating would have been a natural choice.

Certainly Keating stayed on in Washington for a further two years, dabbling in a variety of lucrative business deals and keeping his ear close to the ground. He was popular with the diplomatic set, and formed friendships with several CIA mavericks before returning home. There he married again, this time choosing a pleasant home-loving woman of his own age, who produced three children in five years and was quite content to lead a domestic life tucked away in their country home. Keating maintained a London pad, which she seldom visited unless the Harrods sales were on, while on the surface he acted the role of a successful entrepreneur, only going home to the bosom of the family at weekends. The three children proved a disappointing brood, and he was content to leave their upbringing to their mother – a mistake, as it happened, for they became hopelessly spoilt.

When Dinnsbury was put out to pasture and Lockfield took over, Keating made no secret of the fact that he was not enamoured of the new set-up. He clashed with Lockfield at an early stage, rumour having it that he had refused a posting to Cairo, as Lockfield decreed. Whatever the true story, shortly afterwards he vacated his desk at Century House and dropped out of circulation. Officially, he had never been on the payroll; at the time he was recruited he had apparently negotiated a special arrangement which again suggested Dinnsbury's method of operation, and was one of the prime reasons for his dismissal.

Now the equanimity of Keating's life was again threatened: with the children grown up and fled the coop, the current Mrs Keating, hot-flushed with the menopause, had announced that village life no longer held abiding attractions for her and that she intended to move back to London. She discovered organic food, plastic surgery and aromatherapy in quick order, had her hair dyed blonde and began to wear clothes more suited to a teenager. They had many acrimonious bouts on the subject which invariably ended in hysterics. Keating had no intention of surrendering his own lifestyle or his freedoms in order to accommodate the bizarre whims of a woman he no longer found attractive. Nor did it suit him to dispose of the country home at that particular moment; the housing market was depressed, especially for estates of any size, since the time had passed when the oil sheikhs arrived on the doorstep with suitcases full of banknotes prepared to buy anything with four walls that took their fancy.

In the end he was forced to call in the lawyers and hammer out a compromise: he would buy his wife a London house of her own, paying all outgoings plus a generous allowance in return for a trial separation to be tested over three years.

It was a particularly irritating and time-consuming episode he could have well done without, since he was poised to consummate a new business venture and could ill afford the aggravation. It meant that he would have to consider delegating some of the responsibility for his varied enterprises

106

– a course he had hitherto avoided, for he had always played his cards close to the chest. It needed careful thought.

'Do you like orgies?' the Italian Ambassador's wife asked when the conversation lapsed, addressing Charles Greening, junior minister for the arts, sitting on her left. Control, seated at her right hand, strained to hear the reply.

'No, I don't think I do really. I never know who to thank.'

Greening had cultivated a trendy personality following his appointment, but he had yet to put it across with conviction; most of the time he gave the impression that he was an actor in the first week of rehearsal trying to settle on a characterization that would see him through the run. Having delivered his response, he now laughed at his own wit, glancing across the dining-table to see if anybody else was joining in. Disappointed that nobody was, he made a note to try to plant it in one of the gossip columns; he needed all the publicity he could get – his speeches on the arts rarely commanded any media attention.

'What is your opinion, Sir Raymond?'

The Ambassador's wife leant towards Control, momentarily displaying even more of her ample bosom which constantly threatened to overflow from her Valentino gown. She was wearing an overpowering perfume that throughout the meal had made Control quite light-headed. She epitomized all that was most endearing about her race: excitable, indiscreet, given to broad gestures and a lack of inhibition.

'About orgies? I think any I attended in my gilded youth were fairly tame by modern standards. Public school life didn't present many opportunities for *la dolce vita*. I doubt if pillow fights in the dormitory could be counted as orgies. We were flogged, of course, and I believe there was one headmaster at Eton who was said to be more familiar with his pupils' behinds than with their faces.'

'How very droll! And so British. Tell me, what do you hear about Edwina and Henry? Are they splitting up?'

'I'm sorry?'

'Edwina and Henry. Don't you know them? The Maitlands. He seems to know everybody.'

'Except me. I'm afraid I don't keep up with society gossip.'

'But you should; it's one of life's few remaining pleasures.'

Conversation at the dinner-table had been a series of such *non sequiturs*, and the effort of keeping up with them had partially ruined Control's enjoyment of the superb food. He was always delighted to be invited to Winfield House, the London residence of the American Ambassador; dinners there were invariably superior to anything laid on by the Foreign Office. The present Ambassador, an engaging self-made man from Wisconsin, dispensed with pomp and protocol; speeches were kept strictly to a minimum, and the wine-glasses were constantly charged with the best Californian vintages. The moment guests stepped inside the elegant hallway they were wrapped in genuine American hospitality which, at this level, was unsurpassed; the Yanks, Control thought, have always had the art of enjoying themselves.

Few outsiders appreciated the extent to which the business of government was really conducted outside Whitehall. With the advance of technology many of the old smoke signals had disappeared. Who now remembered that lights burning in the Foreign Office after midnight had once betokened a crisis? Yet despite the computers, fax machines and satellites the human factor still played a major role: a discreet hint in the club, a nudge over the first gin and tonic of the day, the whispered confidence over dinner that could never be recorded and was always denied. Reputations were destroyed, advancements thwarted between courses; policies were decided upon far from Downing Street, in country houses, in back rooms on council estates, in closed cars parked in lay-bys, on holiday beaches, at the races. And always the manipulators acted without reference to the ballot-box.

Control used every means at his disposal to sift fact from rumour, to decipher the winks from the nods, the muted appraisals from the already-acted-upon. This particular evening at Winfield House, having had advance notice of the

guest-list – a mixed bag of politicians, business tycoons, television celebrities, together with members of the diplomatic
corps and the armed forces – he had been anxious not to miss
it. The Ambassador had been instructed to wave the flag ever
since Bayldon had announced his intention to remove the
American nuclear presence from British soil. This had provoked Congress into taking an increasingly isolationist stance
towards NATO: their land forces in Europe had been scaled
down, and the new President, anxious to sustain a popularity
rating in the polls, had introduced import tariffs on overseas
goods. Since taking up office Bayldon had made two trips
behind the Iron Curtain, but had so far boycotted Washington.
The once 'special relationship' between Britain and America
was under strain and the Ambassador, a committed Anglo-
phile, was under orders to rebuild bridges.

'The trouble with your opera', the Italian Ambassador's
wife said, turning her attention to Greening once again, 'is
that it's like your religion, dull; and the trouble with your
religion is that, like your opera, it lacks theatricality.'

'It's not *my* religion,' Greening said, trying to keep his end
up. 'I'm actually an atheist.'

'Darling, how can you sin if you're not religious?' She
suddenly switched. 'Tell me, who is that man sitting next to
the girl in that hideous orange dress?'

Greening looked and lowered his voice. 'Colin Deacon.'

'Should I know him? His face looks familiar.'

'He's a Member of Parliament. You've probably seen him
on television. He's never off – more's the pity.' Greening
could not keep the irritation out of his reply.

'Is he in the Government?'

'No, thank God!'

'How can you thank God if you're an atheist? Obviously,
you hate this man.'

'I wouldn't go as far as that.'

'Why not? Darling, one should always have people one
dislikes intensely. They're always so much more interesting
than one's friends. Of course if you can also dislike your
friends that's best of all. Is he one of yours?'

'My party, you mean? Yes, unfortunately. But an outsider. He doesn't accept the Whip.'

'What does this mean, "the whip"?'

'It's a . . . well, how can I explain it? An expression – no, not an expression. A ritual, I suppose, would be the best way of putting it. When the vote is taken, we have Whips that go around and make sure that the vote is carried.'

'And they do this with whips?'

'Not literally. It's more ceremonial.'

'Wonderful! I love it. In Italy they punch each other.'

Control declined to come to Greening's aid. Without knowing it, the Ambassador's wife had zeroed in on the very man Control was anxious to sound out after dinner. Deacon was the bogeyman of the Labour Party. Once spoken of as a possible leader, he had put himself out of the reckoning by his refusal to play by the rules but still commanded considerable grass-roots support and always scored heavily at the annual conferences, for he was a gifted demagogue, delivering the sort of speeches the rank and file wanted to hear. For as long as anybody could remember, in or out of office, the Labour Party had always been in the throes of a civil war. Deacon was always in the front line, spurring on the rebel troops and incurring the wrath of the party's hierarchy, for he consistently preached betrayal, taking his texts from those tablets that were, to some, written in stone. At one time a close ally, Deacon now made no secret of his loathing of Bayldon; his invective was a many-splendoured thing, eagerly seized upon and given prominence by the Tory press. He was interesting material for somebody like Control, for despite being out in the cold his political ambition was undiminished. Whenever he was written off as a spent force he somehow managed to bounce back and capture the headlines. Bayldon had attempted to buy him off when choosing his first cabinet, offering him a minor ministerial post, a ploy that Deacon rejected, preferring to remain on the back benches where he could inflict maximum damage on those he considered his inferiors.

At the end of the meal the ladies departed and the men

were left to sample some excellent port which Greening immediately passed in the wrong direction. Their host made a short tactful speech, expressing the hope that the two countries would not drift further apart, and there was a general discussion about the world situation. Control noted that Deacon made no contribution. It wasn't until they were invited to rejoin the ladies in one of the magnificent adjacent rooms that he made contact.

'Splendid dinner.'

'Yes,' Deacon said. 'Laid on for a purpose, of course.'

'Well, you'd understand that. Is anything in politics ever done for purely social reasons?'

If Deacon had a sense of humour, it very rarely surfaced. He did his best to give the impression that he was a man of destiny, and there was something slightly manic about him; even the way he carefully arranged his thinning hair was sinister rather than pathetic. He was a man who actively sought martyrdom; and the talents he possessed, which were not inconsiderable, had been diluted by spite.

'Actually, I'm glad to have the opportunity of bumping into you,' Control said. 'I'd like to pick your brains about something. Nothing urgent, but perhaps you'd find time in your busy schedule to have a meal one day?'

Deacon's reply was characteristically guarded. 'As long as you don't expect me to co-operate on any matters of security. You can't have overlooked my many speeches on the Official Secrets Act.'

'Oh, I wouldn't commit such a basic gaffe. Just there are one or two matters of mutual interest that are worth exploring.'

'Such as?'

'Why don't I give you a call and we'll try to find a convenient date to meet?'

'Well, you know where to find me. My phone number's in the book. Unlike your own.' Deacon walked away. Control lingered at the party for another hour, then paid his respects and left.

While waiting for one of the Marines to bring his car,

111

he was surprised to witness Keating's arrival, and further discomfited to be greeted in familiar fashion.

'Hello, Raymond. Leaving early to get your beauty sleep?'

'One might ask why you are arriving late.'

'One might, and the answer would be that I'm on a diet. I came for the really interesting part of the evening. Everybody will be slightly in their cups, I hope, and therefore indiscreet, whereas I shall be stone cold sober. One of Dinnsbury's ploys I've always been happy to emulate.'

The deliberate mention of Dinnsbury struck a particularly sour note with Control, but he was denied an opportunity to reply as Keating sailed past him and his car arrived. He drove off through the unlit park feeling extremely irritated by the encounter.

His home was a fifth-floor apartment in a modern block in Pimlico, close to Ebury Street where Mozart had once lived. He was not listed under his real name on the residents-panel; apartment 52 was apparently occupied by a Mr Purvis, generally thought to be a stockbroker by the other tenants. Before he had moved in, a team of the Firm's sweepers had sanitized every room.

That night he did not go straight home, but instead drove to a safe house on the outskirts of Hounslow. He let himself in with a duplicate key. In the heavily curtained living-room a young woman sat watching a late-night television programme.

'Apologies,' Control said. 'Sorry to be so late. Were you able to amuse yourself?'

'I've been watching a film about the happy new face of the Russian bear.'

'Sorry I missed it. I always enjoy good fiction. What're you smiling at?'

'I never realized you had such a sense of humour.'

'Ah, well. One learns something of interest every day. Did you give yourself a drink?'

'I couldn't find one.'

'Here.' He went to an antique corner cupboard which opened to reveal a small well-stocked bar. 'The Firm's house-keepers do sometimes live up to expectations. I'm going to

112

have a nightcap. Would you care to join me? I hate solitary drinking.'

'Just a small one. Whisky with water.'

As he prepared the drinks, taking a glass of port for himself, Control said: 'Are you pleased to be active again?'

'Yes. Yes, I am.'

'One must never rush these things. I thought a long sabbatical was a prudent move. Does it seem strange to be back in the field?'

'It's different.'

'Different from what?'

'The old days.'

'Ah, yes, the old days,' Control said, sipping his vintage Cockburn. 'Well, of course, we've moved on from then. Unless, of course, you were referring to your erstwhile partner. Pity about him. I don't usually take to Germans. But he had exceptional qualities. What was his name?'

'Gunther.'

Control nodded. 'I'm not very good at remembering pseudonyms. I was more at home when we only used numerals. Well, he was a considerable loss. Perhaps his enthusiasm for the craft of violence contributed to his last mistake. It's a German characteristic to act as though they are immune to error.'

'That's a strange word for it – *craft*. I've never heard it described that way before.'

'So,' Control said, abruptly switching to the business of the moment, 'have you made contact?'

'Yes. But, can I ask you something? Why is it necessary to keep tabs on him? I thought he was out of it.'

'One should never let sleeping dogs lie, especially those who left the fireside hearth with a grudge.'

'Is that how it was?'

'I fancy so. In any case, better to be safe than sorry. One can shred paper, pull the plug on computers, but the human memory . . . now, that's an altogether more complex proposition, unless of course one takes the final solution. Is that whisky too strong for you?'

113

'No, it's fine. He wasn't that well placed, was he? By that I mean I always understood he was small fry.'

'It's the little foxes, isn't it, who raid the vines?' Control said blandly. He sat behind his desk and picked up one of his lead soldier collection. It was half painted, and he examined it against the light. 'Attention to detail, that's the important thing. Take these. So beautifully made, but a slip of the brush, like the slip of a tongue, and one must start over again. Do you have a hobby?'

'Yes, I collect men. Isn't that why you use me?'

Beneath the moustache his mouth twitched into what she took to be a smile. For the first time in their relationship she had the feeling that in different circumstances she might have added him to her list of conquests.

Control carefully replaced the lead soldier. 'General Murat,' he said. 'Now, there was a ladies' man. When he faced the firing squad his last words were "Spare my face. Aim at my heart." '

'And did they?' Pamela van Norden asked.

'History doesn't record.' Control savoured the last mouthful of port. 'The reason I asked you to meet me here was to brief you on a number of developments. The process of changing the colour scheme in Downing Street is progressing, albeit at a leisurely pace. We still have a long way to go. The current assignment is really in the nature of a run-in for you, but now that you're back in harness I shall have other uses for you. Your ill-fated marriage proved useful – a legal change of name is always an excellent cover, and it's extremely unlikely that your quarry would make the connection with your old persona.'

'He's quite different from Hillsden,' Pamela said, 'though, of course, Hillsden was special.'

'Well, he certainly received special treatment. Even so, don't ever mention his name to anybody. Hillsden has to be buried, forgotten. We know he's out of sight. I want him out of mind.'

8

To counter his boredom Hillsden had become a frequent theatregoer. Given his privileged status, he never had any difficulty in obtaining tickets. Not only did it help pass the solitary evenings, but it also saved him from being forced to watch Russian television, prolonged exposure to which was more harmful than the local unfiltered Astra brand of cigarettes. Abramov had also permitted him to have a radio powerful enough to pick up the BBC World Service, but the sound of English voices made him too nostalgically depressed, and he had balked at Abramov's suggestion that he should make contact with some of his fellow-defectors. 'I could arrange for you to get together.'

Hillsden declined the offer. He was afraid he might not be able to conceal his hatred if he came face to face with some of the old gang he had once hunted. Equally, there was always the chance that, with their superior knowledge, they might find the chinks in his armour.

When his virtually monastic existence became unbearable, he resorted to casual sex with a woman he picked up in a restaurant. It was a barren one-night stand that he was in no hurry to repeat, and he confessed the incident to Abramov when next they met, just to be on the safe side, conscious that when, finally, he made his move he needed to know whether he was under continued surveillance.

'Yes, I was aware of it,' Abramov told him.

'I thought I'd passed your reliability test long ago.'

'Alec, if I didn't trust you, you'd be buried by now. Just a sensible precaution, mostly for your sake. I care for your welfare. Although they are few and far between, we do have certain minority elements in our society working against the best interests of the State. Mostly Jews, dissidents, religious fanatics and the like. They might try to use you. You're living a Russian life now; you have to make yourself think as we do.'

'I try; believe me, I try.'

'You're pleased with the housekeeper I found for you, aren't you? Say if you're not and I will change her. I want you to be content.'

'She's fine; it's just that passing the time of day with a *babushka* is not exactly stimulating. I don't have enough to occupy myself with.'

'How is your Russian coming along?'

'Slowly.'

'Why don't you enrol in the University and take a proper course?'

'Aren't I a bit long in the tooth to start being an undergraduate?'

'Age is not a drawback. I have an uncle who graduated in physics when he was sixty. Try it. You'd meet a different group, admittedly younger, but full of enthusiasm for the future. Perhaps what you really want is a more permanent relationship. At the University you might well find somebody more to your taste.'

'Would I be to their taste? That's the question.'

'You underestimate yourself, Alec.'

'I'm not looking for you to pimp for me.'

'Would I suggest anything so crude? I'm merely saying that by taking a course at the University you'd not only progress your Russian, you'd also meet people on your intellectual level.'

'What makes you think I've got an intellect?'

'Alec, don't insult me. We know your worth, your background; we've always known it. You're well read; one might almost say you have a literary bend.'

'*Bent.*'

'What?'

'The word is *bent.*'

'Thank you. I am always grateful when you correct my

English. If and when I get to London, it will be important for me to speak colloquially.'

'OK, assuming I agree to enrol, are you sure the other students won't think I'm a plant? My background, as you put it, is hardly likely to inspire instant friendship. They'll know who I am.'

'But you're regarded as a hero, Alec. One of the elite.'

After a further show of reluctance, Hillsden allowed himself to be persuaded and Abramov was as good as his word; the normal bureaucratic formalities were dispensed with and he found himself enrolled for taking the English language course, a choice which he felt gave him a slight edge over his fellow-students. They were not all in their late teens; some were much older, and he naturally gravitated to this group.

It was halfway through the term when he joined, and he found that they were taking two set books – *Oliver Twist* and Graham Greene's *The Heart of the Matter* – as well as a play of Shakespeare's. To his relief he was familiar with all three. His classmates were polite, but kept their distance during the first weeks. He had to demonstrate that he was amongst them to work before they gradually thawed. For his part, Hillsden scrupulously avoided any topic likely to arouse suspicion as to his motives, but answered their questions on the English texts while, in turn, they gave him assistance on the translations. It was a pleasant way in which to become more familiar with a language, and he made good progress. Although he had no yardstick by which to judge university life, he sensed that when it came down to it there was probably very little difference between Leningrad and Oxbridge. The girls were attractive, some of them stunningly so, with clear skins, well-groomed hairstyles and discreet make-up – there was none of the uniform dowdiness he remembered from Western news-reel footage. Equally, they did not flaunt their feminism, and their overt political attitudes were muted. *Glasnost* had lifted the lid, and students of both sexes sported bright clothes and exuded an infectious zest for life. Even so, Hillsden could detect the same scent of rebellion, common to students the world over, smouldering beneath the surface: the desire to

117

kick over the traces, the refusal to accept old values without question. Just as they sometimes surprised him by their frankness, he could equally amaze them when he refuted their misconceptions about the life he had left behind; and it was at such times, when forced to describe what now seemed a foreign country, that his desire to get even overwhelmed him. He never forgot the purpose of the manuscript in the lining of his overcoat.

He was in the library one day, struggling through a set paper, when he became aware that he was being closely observed by one of the older students in his class, called Galina. He guessed she might be thirty or so, and that she was a country girl. Ever the literary romantic, Hillsden compared her to those heroines Coppard always described in his short stories: enigmatic creatures, met by chance, who gave themselves to strangers in the dark bedrooms of English inns. She had a good figure which would one day thicken, but which now beckoned to be embraced. He had noticed her from the day he started the course and, although they had exchanged greetings in class, this was the first time they had been alone together.

'Are you having difficulties?' she asked. He had an arrangement whereby his fellow-students spoke to him in English and he attempted to reply in Russian.

'Yes. I find the grammar very difficult.'

'More so than your own language?'

'That I wouldn't know. You'd have to tell *me*.'

She came to him and looked over his shoulder.

'I seem to put everything back to front.'

Galina sat beside him and corrected a few of his mistakes. In turn Hillsden explained a passage from the Shakespeare they were studying. She wore no perfume, but the scent of her, clean and feminine, he found disturbing at close proximity.

That night they had a meal together; Galina took him to a restaurant close to the University patronized by many of the students. Hillsden had the feeling that she had deliberately chosen it in order to show them together. His first impressions of her proved wrong: she was not a country girl, but born and bred in Leningrad. Her father was a historian who, for the last seven years, had been researching and writing what was intended to be the definitive work on the siege of Stalingrad. Galina was concentrating on languages in the hope that one day she would be allowed to travel freely.

'Is it getting any easier to travel?'

'Perhaps, slowly,' she said. 'We have a lot of catching-up to do. You must have been to many countries?'

'Yes.'

'Tell me.'

'Oh, America, France, the Middle East . . . Austria.'

Mention of Austria brought a sudden intensity of feeling, his mind working on two levels at once.

'And now you are here,' she said, 'in Russia for the first time.'

'And my travelling days are over.'

It was the only time the subject had even been hinted at.

'We were all very curious about you when you arrived in class.'

'I can well imagine.'

'We knew who you were, of course. Are you able to talk about it?'

For the first time in years Hillsden felt no danger in the question. 'If you mean, do I *mind* talking about it, the answer is no. On the other hand, I don't want to compromise you by association.'

She stretched out a hand across the table and touched his. 'But it's all over now, isn't it, that part of your life? And you were working for *us*.'

Hillsden smiled and made no attempt to caress her hand. 'That's right.'

'So tell me what it was like.'

Old cautions surfaced, and it crossed his mind that once again Abramov had planted a companion on him.

'Well, the whole story would take too long, but if you want to know how I feel . . . I'll tell you a story about myself. When I was a schoolboy I once performed in a play. I was

119

given the role of a Nubian slave in *Antony and Cleopatra*.'

'We studied that last year,' she interjected.

'Then, you know I wasn't playing a leading role. We had a very enthusiastic English teacher who I suspect was a frustrated actor, and he insisted on realism. I had to stain my whole body. I dare say nowadays they have some easy way of doing this, but I was forced to sit in a bath of permanganate of potash which dyed me a sort of purplish brown. I literally changed colour.'

'Your face as well?'

'No, I wasn't required to go in for total immersion. My face was made up with sticks of make-up. Leichner's five and nine. That was the brand all the professional actors used.'

'What a memory!'

'It's been well trained,' Hillsden said. 'Anyway, to go on with the story, I happen to have a birthmark and, although the colour gradually faded from the rest of my body, the birthmark remained stained for life. You started by asking me whether that part of my life was over, and, yes, it is . . . except I'm stained by it. I was a spy, and you can't betray without it leaving a mark.'

Galina was silent for an appreciable time. 'Yes,' she said finally. 'Yes, I can see that.' She sipped her drink. 'Why did you?'

'Betray?'

'Yes.'

'You don't start out that way. At first it's just a job like any other. A fairly boring job, to tell the truth. There's no glamour in it. Well, take the Greene book we're studying. He says it like it is. Most of the time, you feel like Scobie – dirty, soiled. You enter other people's lives by the back door. Remember the scene where he finds the letter the captain of the boat has written to his daughter – I think it was his daughter – and he has to read it and confiscate it? A little act, nothing world-shattering, of no consequence to the progress of that war, but it destroys another man's life.'

'But aren't most' – she balked at saying the word *spies* – 'people in that position motivated by ideals?'

120

'I wouldn't know. Some of them perhaps.'

'You?'

'In the beginning maybe. It's like a continuous adultery. Who are you betraying in the end – yourself or others?'

She said nothing else, and they finished their meal and left. Hillsden walked with her to the student quarters where she lodged. At the entrance she turned and kissed him, as though on an impulse, but whether from affection or out of pity Hillsden could not tell. He returned the kiss on her cheek, rather as though he was seeing a daughter off to boarding school.

He had no further classes to attend that week and he found that he was dreading their next meeting in case what he had told her about his past put a stop to any closer relationship. Four days went by before they shared the same lecture, and she came and sat beside him.

'I missed seeing you,' she said openly. 'What have you been doing with yourself?'

'Swotting. And I went to the theatre.'

'I love the theatre. There's a new production of an English play you might know being performed by a group I belong to. It isn't a proper theatre. We use an old warehouse we've rigged up. If you'd like to come, we have a discussion afterwards in which everybody can join in and comment. Tomorrow night should be fun because we've invited a critic to give his views.'

'I'd love to join you.'

'It's on the outskirts of town, so we'll have to go by bus. I'll meet you in the main hall after work.'

They travelled during the busiest period of the day. 'So this is *chas pik*?' Hillsden said, airing his colloquial Russian for the rush hour. He was amazed how many people managed to cram themselves into the vehicle. Galina was pressed tightly against him, and their faces almost touched whenever the bus took a corner. 'I'm glad I know you, otherwise I might be arrested for indecent assault,' he whispered. 'This is rather like that scene in *Night at the Opera*.' Galina looked blank. 'Have you never seen the Marx Brothers?' Even as he asked

121

the question he wondered if mention of the word *Marx* might be misunderstood by those closest to them.

The converted warehouse was half a mile's walk from the nearest bus-stop, and they arrived just as the performance was about to begin. As Galina had described, it was theatre in the round; rough seating and, when the lights were up, devoid of atmosphere. A young and extremely talented cast gave their version of J. B. Priestley's *When We Are Married*. Hillsden had a vague memory of the plot, having seen it at least twice before when the British repertory system was in its heyday, and with occasional help from Galina he was able to follow most of it and enjoy the comedy. Priestley, he learnt, was a popular novelist in Russia where he was considered a true socialist. The audience, like the cast, was young and enthusiastic.

During the interval Hillsden was taken to meet the critic – predictably he found the man was one of those instantly recognizable poseurs who are always drawn to the arts, given to exaggerated gestures and obviously enjoying the opportunity to hold court. The male companion with him was never introduced.

'I didn't catch his name,' Hillsden said when they resumed their seats for the next act.

'Leonid Kiprenski.'

'Is he any good?'

'He mostly writes about the ballet. I think he was once a ballet dancer himself.'

At the end of the performance Kiprenski took the stage and delivered a gushing and condescending speech about the social significance of the play. 'Priestley was a minor playwright, who worked in watercolours rather than in oils, and this comedy of manners doesn't present a true picture of the British proletariat of the period,' was one of his most pretentious statements.

'Rubbish,' Hillsden commented under his breath, as Kiprenski went on to damn the cast with faint praise. A spirited question-and-answer session followed, with the actors giving as good as they had received when defending their interpretations.

'Did you find it interesting?' Galina asked, when the evening came to an end.

'I enjoyed the performances very much. Can't say that I agreed with most of what your critic said afterwards. After all, there's nothing wrong with working in watercolours. Turner didn't do so badly. I thought that a particularly pompous remark. But I guess it's difficult for foreigners really to understand a North Country comedy. I'm told we always make a hash of Chekhov.'

Just as they were leaving the critic approached Hillsden.

'My friend tells me I was very rude. I never introduced him to you, and you have something in common.'

'Oh?'

'You're both British. This is John Frampton. He's here on holiday.'

His companion came forward and shook hands. 'Alec Hillsden,' Hillsden said, 'and this is Galina Fedorenka. Are you enjoying your holiday?'

'Very much so. This isn't my first visit. I've been to Russia three times.'

'Well, you've certainly found your way off the usual tourist track.'

'That's thanks to Leonid.'

There was a pause.

'As I'm sure you know, I'm not on holiday,' Hillsden said.

The directness of the remark seemed to embarrass Frampton, and Hillsden felt compelled to make amends. 'You'll be able to go home and tell everybody you not only had a good time; you also met a notorious character . . . Where *is* home?'

'London. Forest Gate.'

'How is it these days?' Hillsden found himself prolonging the conversation for no reason other than that Frampton was the first Englishman he had talked to since his abduction.

'Oh, very much the same. The summer was a washout.'

'Of course. Where are you staying here?' he continued out of politeness.

'I got him into the Evopeiskaya,' Leonid said.

123

'Very elegant. What it is to be a critic and have influence. Well, very nice to meet you, Mr Frampton. Enjoy the rest of your stay.'

'Oh, I shall. This is home from home to me.'

They finally got away and caught a bus back to the centre of the town. The return journey was less crowded, and they were able to sit together.

'An odd twosome,' Hillsden remarked. 'Do you think we should draw the obvious conclusion?'

'I think so, don't you?'

'Amazing any of them still take the risk. Quite apart from the dreaded AIDS, it's forbidden, isn't it?'

'Yes, but like everything else in Russia it depends who you are and what influence you have in the right quarters. As you know everybody is equal here, but some are—'

'More equal than others,' Hillsden finished for her.

'Exactly.'

'Influence won't save anybody from the plague, though.'

Their first mention of matters sexual brought about a lull in the conversation. Hillsden thought: How subtly all our attitudes have changed; a tiny sliver of ice has been inserted into every relationship whether we like it or not. An atheist, he did not believe in divine retribution, but rather that Nature, the great leveller, was carrying out one of its periodic culls.

Because of this he was hesitant about inviting Galina back to his apartment for a nightcap and searched for the right words.

'I was going to suggest that we went to the Evopeiskaya for a drink, but I don't want to run into those two again . . . I have some perfectly good Scotch whisky in my apartment . . . or we could go somewhere you know of.' He felt like a schoolboy fumbling to secure a date.

'I'd ask you back to my place,' Galina said, 'except I share with two other girls. I'd love to sample your Scotch; I don't get many opportunities.'

When they arrived she stood amazed in the doorway. 'My! It's so big compared to most. You're very lucky.'

124

'Yes, I realize that. Make yourself comfortable while I fix the drinks.'

He sat some distance from her, still uncertain how to behave. He found her attractive, desirable, but was wary of any emotional involvement in his present circumstances. His thoughts went back to the night Jock had sealed his fate. They made small-talk, some of his unease communicating itself to Galina.

'Did you go to the theatre a lot in London?'

'No, I'm ashamed to say I didn't. No particular reason – I guess my old way of life was too erratic. My wife and I enjoyed films more . . .' He was suddenly compelled to add: 'I was married, by the way. I'm not any longer, so I'm told. Since I arrived here I have been informed that my wife divorced me in my absence.'

'She wouldn't come with you to Russia?'

'In fairness, she was never given the chance. But it had stopped being much of a marriage long ago. How about you? Why aren't you married? Or perhaps it would be more polite to say: Are you married? I would expect you to be.'

'No, I'm not. Like you, I was once. And, like you, it didn't work out.'

After a slight pause Hillsden said: 'The one thing I miss is my books. I had to leave them all behind. I've always been a great reader ever since I was a boy. I read everything I could get my hands on. When I first saw you, you reminded me of a favourite book, *Dusky Ruth*.' Seeing that the title meant nothing to her, he continued: 'It's a collection of short stories by an English writer long since dead, a master of the form called A. E. Coppard.'

'And why did this book remind you of me? Was it about Russia?'

'No, he was a very English writer who did his best work in the thirties . . . I thought of him when I saw you because his heroines were always mysteriously beautiful. I fell in love with them on the page.'

Galina coloured, staring down into her glass, then surprised him, as once before Inga had surprised him with her guileless honesty. 'Would you like to have a relationship?'

125

Hillsden took his time before he answered. 'You mustn't think I was using that to make a pass. I'm not that subtle.'

'If you did, I'm not offended.'

'My dear,' Hillsden said, 'didn't it ever occur to you that I'm not good news for somebody as nice as you?'

'Isn't that for me to decide?'

'Why don't we just go on as we are, remain good friends? I need a friend.'

'But that's stupid. If we like each other, friendship would never be enough.'

Hillsden moved to her and took her face between his hands. 'Look, don't think I'm not flattered. You took me unawares, that's all. I'm not used to people wanting to be with me. Of course I want you; I'd be a fool if I didn't.' He bent and kissed her on the lips.

'There's nothing wrong in being foolish sometimes,' she said, returning his kiss. 'One can't be wise all the time. And women always make the final choice.'

As she drew him down to her, Hillsden realized he was back in the territory of trust with no maps to guide him.

9

Slowly, painstakingly the dark corners of Mitchell's life were illuminated. On the surface, his existence had been a blank sheet of paper, but now his past, once written in invisible ink, responded to the heat of closer scrutiny.

After the barking dog had led the authorities to his secret *pied-à-terre* they began to strip away the layers of deception. Pearson's patience was finally vindicated: a subsequent search revealed a false compartment in one of the kitchen cabinets. In it they found articles of women's clothing – bras, suspender-belts and bikini pants – together with a quantity of bizarre literature mostly concerned with lesbian fetishes. Mitchell had also used a Polaroid camera to photograph himself dressed as a woman. He was always alone in these pictures, giving those who had the task of putting together the tawdry puzzle of his life glimpses of a sad misfit. There was some justification in assuming that, like many others drawn to the act of betrayal, he should also betray his own manhood in this manner. Sifting through the material, Pearson was less concerned with the Freudian aspects than with the other implications: anybody so consumed with the need to submerge his own personality was capable of a hundred other treacheries. A cassette of partially exposed, but undeveloped, microfilm found in the camera was developed and revealed that he had photographed a series of top-secret documents. These were later established as being transcripts of radio traffic originating from GRU headquarters in Moscow, much of it in code.

'It doesn't make sense,' Pearson said. 'Why photograph what you already have a right to see? He handled this stuff;

that was his job. It's like robbing your own piggy bank. Who did he steal it for?'

'Perhaps he needed the money to buy tights,' Lloyd remarked. 'Bloody things cost a fortune, according to my wife.'

Pearson chose to ignore this. 'Well, it isn't our headache. Special Branch and the MI5 mob can sort that one out. But it beats me how this joker passed through the nets. According to his file he was positively vetted on three occasions.'

'He obviously wasn't wearing high-heels when they interviewed him.'

'You're full of it today, aren't you? You should enter for "Opportunity Knocks".'

Despite Whitehall's strenuous efforts to suppress the story Mitchell's case received intense media coverage: the unmasking of a presumed spy who wore women's underwear was titillating enough, but the added fact that he had been murdered in such a hideous way and that, so far, the police had not been able to establish how or why the murder had taken place kept the story alive.

Nobody was more disturbed by the new developments than Control. Mitchell's disappearance and the subsequent confirmation that he was the Hyde Park victim left him as perplexed as anybody. By virtue of his position and the fact that within his closed circle Mitchell was assumed to have been in the pay of the Russians, he could openly demand access to all the available evidence: the matter was no longer the sole concern of MI5. He had an urgent need to find out as much as possible. Never the one to pass up an opportunity for intrigue, he planted the need for an official inquiry into MI5's vetting procedures.

Bayldon, heavily pressed by the Opposition, was forced to make a hasty and ill-judged statement to the House. Badly briefed, he allowed himself to be rattled when challenged, playing down Mitchell's importance, describing him as a misguided pervert who had only limited access to top-secret material. Since the newspapers had already uncovered Mitchell's rank and position this was howled down, one Tory backbencher being suspended by the Speaker when he called Bayldon a shabby liar and refused to retract. Even on his own side of the House it was generally thought that the Prime Minister had botched it, and the public interest continued unabated.

It was not Bayldon's week. More was to come. Attending the annual gathering of the Durham miners – historically a necessary pilgrimage to a depressed Mecca for all Labour leaders – Bayldon suffered what was described (and Bayldon himself did nothing to discourage being described) as an attempt on his life. All that actually happened was that a deeply disturbed local government official, angered that he had been cheated out of his expected accolade in the discarded honours-lists, had lunged at Bayldon armed with nothing more lethal than a letter-opener, and was swiftly overpowered. The incident gave Bayldon an excuse to intensify his criticism of the police. His Press Secretary announced that in future he would be accompanied by loyal members of the Workers' Militia when carrying out public engagements.

Why is it, a planted leader in one of the tabloids asked, *that not only can a spy be openly murdered in a London park, but it now seems that even the Prime Minister is at grave risk from those factions in our society who seek to overthrow our democratic way of life?*

It becomes increasingly obvious that our security services have failed to carry out the duties entrusted to them. Constantly compromised by an effete group of privileged men in the past three decades, answerable to no one, not even to Parliament, they now stand accused of further incompetence. The time has come when we must demand drastic changes. We can no longer tolerate a system which allows certain public servants, operating outside the law, to treat public life as an extension of the prefects' common room. Such a system attracts the unstable, the corrupt, the rogue moles who burrow under and into the very foundations of our most cherished citadels, fails to protect those it was brought into being to protect and by its incompetence threatens us all.

THE COUNTRY DEMANDS AN ANSWER. THE COUNTRY DEMANDS ACTION.

Naturally, ninety per cent of the country was not demanding and, in any case, did not get a true answer. Despite heading a government elected on the promise that it would introduce a Freedom of Information Act, Bayldon and his cabinet had swiftly been brought to their cynical senses: too much information, they decided, was injurious for the nation's health and their own survival. In point of fact, a majority of the electorate would have cheerfully voted for less information and a return of the death penalty if given the opportunity. Inner-city violence had spread outwards into hitherto quiet market-towns in Dorset, Somerset and even as far afield as Cornwall. Sporadic fights took place every Saturday night, work no longer being the curse of the drinking classes. Chief Constables remonstrated that their forces were undermanned and hampered by the increased powers of the Militia.

Still baffled by Mitchell's murder, Control thought it expedient to meet with his counterpart from MI5, Sir Oswald Leighton. Whenever brought into contact they circled each other warily, like two old alley cats.

'Curious business, this Mitchell affair,' Leighton said, with the fastidious smiling hauteur he reserved for those he considered his inferiors. 'I'm always miffed when two and two don't make four.' A Senior Wrangler with a double First in Applied Sciences, he had been recruited by Churchill during the war to join the team responsible for cracking the Enigma machine. On the eve of retirement, and one of the few active survivors of that elite group, he never questioned his own judgements. He liked to have the solutions to life's problems brought to him on a silver salver. 'What none of us here can fathom is whose payroll he was on. Certainly not ours.'

'Not ours, either.' Control just managed to keep the irritation out of his voice. He knew Leighton's technique in these matters.

'So who else would be interested in GRU traffic? We know there's no love lost between them and the KGB, but presumably if Moscow Centre wanted chapter and verse they could have achieved better results closer to home.'

'Unless . . .' Control began, then trailed off. Despite being

130

on his guard he found that Leighton's attitude discomfited him. He cracked the knuckles of his left hand.

'What?' Leighton tightened the knot on his Garrick tie.

'I was going to say unless we still have a mole and this was his way of keeping in contact.'

'Oh, God, I'm so sick of our lawns being dug up.'

'I agree; but, knowing our splendid press, it can only be a matter of time before one of the pundits resurrects the theory. I'm amazed it hasn't surfaced already. Has all the traffic been decoded?'

'Yes.'

'Anything startling?'

'Not really. Their stuff is as boring as ours, although there was one item that might interest you, Raymond. That chap of yours who defected, Hillsden, he got a mention.'

'Really? What was that?' Control registered the minimum interest.

'He's now in Leningrad, apparently, studying at the university there. They regard him as something of a prize, don't they?'

'I can't think why. He was very small fry compared to some that fouled and then fled your nest.'

Leighton took this in his usual bland manner. 'Yes, I suppose we've always produced a better class of defector. Seems odd they would put local gossip like that in day-to-day traffic, don't you agree? Stuck out like a sore thumb.'

'If we understood all their motives, we could retire.'

'Anyway, what we have to address ourselves to is the pervert Mitchell. There are so many curious aspects, not the least of which is: who took him out? A straightforward murder would have made life easier for all of us; it's the secondary factor that raises the big question-mark. Had it not been for the dog, we might never have made a positive identification. Since he wasn't working for you or for me, it presupposes there's a third party who bankrolled his exotic tastes.'

Control stared past Leighton, having just registered that a new Lowry had been installed above the fireplace. 'Could be the IRA, I suppose. They've moved up a notch from knee-capping recently – witness last month's barbaric lynching of that SAS man.'

'My dear Raymond, we've considered that exhaustively, but there's no mileage in it for them.'

'They killed two policemen.'

'Pure chance. Let me put a hypothesis to you, and bear with me for a moment: that it is the present government's intention to bring about a Marxist society.'

This took Control by surprise. 'Well, it's no secret that Bayldon's cabinet is predominantly left-wing, with more hard-liners than we've had before.'

'And?'

'Obviously they're keen to reverse as much of the previous Tory legislation as they can. 'Twas ever thus.'

'Nothing more than that? Just the mixture as before? What we've had ever since forty-five – yah-boo politics?'

'More concentrated perhaps.'

'You haven't really answered me. And I can't believe that you of all people, Ray, would fail to see the writing on the wall.'

Leighton's abbreviation of his Christian name nettled Control, but again he stifled his annoyance. 'I think we both know the score in our respective areas' – for a brief moment he was tempted to reciprocate and call him 'Ossie', except that would be descending to Leighton's level – 'but if you detect danger signs that have so far escaped me, then of course you are right to share them. What writing would I have missed?'

'The word *Militia* to start with. How did you read that?' He did not wait for Control's reply. 'Shades of the Blackshirts, would you say? Seems to me they're already being given too much rope. The Commissioner and I are not at all happy about the way they're developing.'

'Well, the PM was obviously shaken by that incident up at Durham, and I think those closest to him were looking for scapegoats. Who better than the police and the security forces?'

'Be a bad show', Leighton said in his usual understated way, 'if they got too powerful. Private armies are never good

132

news. Once they're let out of the pen they're difficult to fence in again.' He had a sheep farm in Monmouthshire and was inclined to introduce such metaphors. 'I think between us all we should watch it closely. There are enough loonies around without putting them into paramilitary uniforms. I'd certainly resist any suggestion that they should take over any aspect of security.'

'My own view is Bayldon is having a difficult job keeping the balance. He inherited a great many problems not of his making.'

'Exactly. That's my point. Bayldon's treading water in shark-infested seas. Somebody might burst his water-wings, and then where would we be? I thought we should put our heads together against such an eventuality, and have a contingency plan. Decide which arses to kick and which to kiss. We might need to help reclaim the middle ground.'

For some reason he's testing me, Control thought, immediately back on his guard. 'You're offering me guilt by conjecture. One shouldn't underestimate Bayldon's capacity to resist.'

'Aren't you forgetting that he only came to power second-hand? He could hardly claim to be there as the result of the popular vote. He didn't ride to Downing Street through cheering crowds; he came in through the side-entrance. Nor does he have to honour a manifesto. His elevation suggested a coup to some people. And don't misunderstand me; I'm playing devil's advocate. One can't ignore the fact that since moving into Downing Street he's packed, or been *made* to pack, the Cabinet with the far Left. I'm reading smoke signals that some of the older natives are getting decidedly restless – *uneasy* would be the better word.'

'Yes, but we have to stand aside from all that, do we not?' Control answered. There was no way he was going to give even a tacit blessing to Leighton's innuendo. 'We are not at the moment favourite sons. Once our masters detect a whiff of criticism, they can chop us off at the knees.'

'Don't I know it. Let me ask you this, then I'll shut up: What if the PM, despite his many and admired qualities, was

133

to be outmanoeuvred, outgunned, and had to relinquish the star part . . .? Where would that put us? Who d'you think would step into his shoes? And would they still fit?'

'I think you're just running around shouting "Fire" before there's any smoke.'

Leighton gave a thin smile, like a judge forced to teach a young barrister court etiquette. 'I like to know which part of the battlefield I might be fighting on. I've always acted on the principle that we have to protect our politicians from everything except their own excesses.'

There was a chill wind blowing as Control left the MI5 building, but the erratic winter sun was tempting enough to make him dismiss his car and walk to Whitehall through St James's Park; he felt the need for solitary contemplation while he mulled over Leighton's dialogue. Flocks of mallards huddled beneath the bare willows, deprived of their usual tourist pickings. The ice on the lake was still as thin as the sugar crust on toffee apples, and as Control skirted the perimeter a Canada goose made an ungainly landing, skidding and spinning as the shockwaves crackled the surface.

Despite the banked-up anger brought on by Leighton's infuriating air of superiority, he was not displeased at the way he had handled the meeting. You boxed cleverly, he told himself. He didn't get through your guard. Even so, he did not underestimate a professional like Leighton; they shared a past so complex that it was always a mistake to take things at their face value. That casual mention of Hillsden, for instance – had that been just an item of in-house gossip, a conversational gambit designed to push home old knives, or had Leighton been testing him, probing to see if any nerves were exposed? There were no rules of engagement in the long and cruel war they both waged; every truth was booby-trapped. But perhaps even Leighton was getting careless in his old age, making it slightly too obvious, presenting his convictions as hypotheses. Certainly even by Leighton's standards he had been remarkably indiscreet, handing me some useful ammunition, Control thought. The question now was how and when to make use of it. But that answer would come in the fullness of time; there was never any reason to hurry the inevitable.

After an interval of a week, Waddington fixed an appointment to survey Mrs van Norden's Amersham house. It turned out to be a listed Grade II authentic Georgian, with no trace of stockbroker-mock. Waddington was impressed. Although his current job often brought him into closer contact with the rich, most of his clients had appeared to have cornered the market in expensive kitsch. By contrast, the van Norden home epitomized discreet elegance. He had only the most rudimentary knowledge of art and period furniture, but as she showed him around the principal rooms it took little to convince him that he was looking at the genuine article. Early on in the tour he found himself thinking of Hillsden; old Alec always had some pertinent literary quote for these occasions. Alec would doubtless have reminded him of Hemingway's famous dictum on the rich.

'If I may say so, Mrs van Norden, you certainly have a lot of possessions worth protecting. I dread to think what your insurance premiums are.'

'Do call me "Pamela", otherwise it's too boring. I hate our British formality, don't you? This is the room I use most. As you can see, it gives the best view of my nightmare garden.'

'Why a nightmare?'

'Do you garden yourself?'

'I have been known to plant the odd window-box, but I have the opposite of green fingers. I only have to look at a flower and it withers.'

'Likewise. I don't know anything about Nature except you have to fork out all the time to keep it at bay. Despite what everyone says, God never intended the English to have gardens. The moment anything buds we get out-of-season frosts; as soon as the blossom arrives He sends gale-force winds; and during the three days laughingly known as the English summer the whole place is infested with bugs, wasps and other creepies and crawlies. The whole thing seems absolutely pointless to me, and I can't stand those intrepid

135

female neighbours of mine who are out in all weathers weeding and snipping; they must be demented. My gardener is always telling me I should plant more roses, so I forked out, but we had a monsoon and they all looked like anorexic débutantes. Last year the wasps got the plums, the squirrels – or was it the birds? – ate the apples, and the bloody lawn looked like Ethiopia. It costs me a fortune to create an annual desert.'

She delivered this monologue non-stop while Waddington examined the windows with a professional eye.

'Georgian windows are lovely, but they do present a problem.'

'Darling, everything I touch is a problem.' He noticed that she sometimes affected the exaggerated voice of an actress. 'Actually, I don't give a flying fart for material things. If I get ripped off and they steal the televisions, so what? But I hate the idea of being bound and gagged or worse. According to all reports, the average villain today would just as soon rape or kill you as look at you.'

'Do you have a panic button?'

'No.'

'I think that's essential.'

'Well, I'm sure you'll take care of me. Where would I have it?'

'Ideally, it should be by the side of your bed.'

'Why didn't anybody tell me these things? Well, let's go and look upstairs.'

She led him to the first floor, and he was taken into the principal bedroom. Everything was white: bleached white oak flooring covered with white scatter rugs, a white king-sized bed, white chaise-longue, white television, even a bookcase with every volume bound in white vellum. The only splash of colour was an enormous modern abstract hanging over the fireplace.

'I'd recommend a panic button here in easy reach,' Waddington said. 'It would be monitored twenty-four hours a day.'

'You mean if I pressed it you'd come running?'

136

'Somebody would. Our computer would alert the local police.'

'Big Brother would be watching me?'

'It's all technology, I'm afraid. But we at Breakproof like to feel that we still maintain the human touch . . . Talking of which, may I say I love the way you've done this room?'

'Well, after the divorce, I thought: Let's whitewash everything, Pamela.'

They continued the tour of the house with Waddington making further suggestions. 'If you decide to go along with any of this, I should warn you that our stuff doesn't come cheap.'

'Darling – sorry, I tend to call everybody darling – I'm not shopping for a chastity-belt in Oxfam. If you tell me I should have it, then that's good enough. I just want to sleep soundly.'

'Right . . . well, first thing in the morning I'll have my office type up a complete schedule of everything we've discussed. Then, if you OK it, we'll put the work in hand immediately. I'll mark it urgent. And thank you very much for the business.'

'Do you have to rush?'

'Now, you mean?'

'Yes. Do you have other appointments?'

'No.'

'Would you like to stay and have dinner?'

'That's very kind of you, Mrs van Norden, but I'm sure that's inconvenient.'

'I wouldn't ask you if it was. And do stop calling me that.'

'No, listen, I don't want to put you to any trouble.'

'Darling, I'm not going anywhere near the kitchen myself. I can only just find it, let alone use it. Bending over a hot stove is not one of my talents, thank God. The cook's Mexican, but we don't mention that because she hasn't got a work permit. Do you like spicy food?'

'Yes.'

'Then, that's all settled: you'll stay. After all, you've come all this way; I can't send you away hungry. Let's have a drink. Come into the games room and fix us both something. What's your poison?'

137

'Well, since we're eating Mexican, do you have any tequila to get in training?'

'Of course.'

He followed her into a room the furnishing of which appeared to have been lifted intact from a Ralph Lauren catalogue complete with an elaborate bar, pool-table and various pin-ball machines.

'You be the bartender,' Pamela said.

This is all very pleasant, but where is it leading? Waddington thought. There was something odd, something a shade too anxious, about the lady. Why would somebody like her want to spend an evening with the likes of me? It can't be that I've suddenly become the Sundance Kid in my middle age. In the space of a few short hours I seem to have travelled south of all previous borders. Why did I suggest tequila? It'll blow my head off on an empty stomach. Or have I become too jaded and cynical? Maybe she's just being polite and hospitable. Give her the benefit of the doubt, Waddington, and accept graciously.

As he fixed the drinks, Pamela picked up a house phone and gave instructions to the kitchen – speaking, he noted, in fluent Spanish. Then they sank into deep armchairs and chatted as the tequila swiftly reached his toes.

'Pity we have to live like this these days,' Waddington observed.

'How d'you mean?'

'Locks on all the windows, death rays, panic buttons. When I was a kid we never locked the front door. My mother used to keep the key on a string through the letter-box. If a neighbour wanted to borrow a cup of sugar, she just let herself in. Nobody got ripped off, as I remember.'

'Did people actually *borrow* cups of sugar?' Pamela seemed genuinely amazed by this social revelation.

'Oh, sure. Does that date me?'

'Where was this?'

'I was brought up in Birmingham, but I guess it was pretty general.'

'Sounds like another world.'

138

'It was.'

He wished she hadn't crossed her legs; that and the tequila gave him a sudden rush of blood to the head.

'Can I ask you something,' he blurted, 'if you don't think it's too personal? How come your ex let you divorce him? Didn't he go for these simple pleasures of everyday country-folk?'

'I wasn't his first, and I'm sure I won't be his last. Who knows why anybody really breaks up? Perhaps I wore him out,' she added, getting up to replenish their glasses. 'He caught me on the rebound, and I liked his aftershave. Let me ask you the same question. How did Mrs Waddington allow you to escape?'

'With relief, I think. All work and no play made me a very dull boy.'

'I can't believe that. Did you cheat on her?'

'I strayed once or twice.'

God! Waddington thought. Why did I get into the subject? He sipped at the second glass of tequila, like a bird taking water.

'I suppose in your line of work, getting to meet new people every day, temptation gets put in your way?'

'Not really. It isn't every day I walk into a set-up like this. Usually my sales-talk is directed at monosyllabic Arabs, or Jewish widows; and, if that sounds faintly prejudiced, I guess it is.'

'What made you choose this job?'

'A small detail known as staying alive. I wasn't always doing this.'

'What did you do before?'

'I was in communications, electronics,' he answered quickly, 'but, like a lot of us, the bottom dropped out of that – it was a British firm that didn't keep up with the times; those clever little Japanese cornered the market and I got shoved on to the rubbish-heap.'

Pamela stared at him in a manner he found increasingly disconcerting.

'Listen,' she said, 'don't think me rude, but I'm going

139

upstairs to have a bath and change. I've been in these clothes all day. Just make yourself at home. You play pin-ball?'

'Not for a long time.'

'My ex was obsessed, as you may have noticed. Come to think of it, that was another reason why we called it a day. He was always trying for the *Guinness Book of Records* and never came to bed.' She paused by the doorway, catching him putting his glass down. 'Would you like to freshen up, too? We do have more than one bathroom. Seven to be exact. How about trying a jacuzzi? You said you'd never had one.'

'You serious?'

'Of course.'

'Yes, OK, why not?'

She led him upstairs and into what had obviously been her ex-husband's wing, since the décor was decidedly masculine. The bathroom was vast, and the bath itself was big enough to take an entire football team.

'Christ!' Waddington exclaimed. 'Going back to my deprived childhood once again, they'd have called this a public bath.'

'Hans built everything big. Too bad he wasn't built that way himself. Look, this is how you work it. Make sure you fill it enough to cover all the jets, then press this. But don't soap yourself until it's switched off; otherwise the whole thing clogs up. Got it?'

'I think I can manage that.'

She collected an armful of towels and threw them down by the side of the bath.

'Enjoy,' she said in the manner of an American waitress, and left him to his own devices.

Waddington surveyed his coming destiny. Well, he thought, the Captain wouldn't approve – 'Fraternizing with the customers is off-limits' – but what the hell? He reached out and turned on the taps, which appeared to be made of solid gold. Piping-hot water gushed out, and he quickly added more cold, then fumbled for the plug. Shedding his clothes, he waited for the water to reach the required level; then, his head still fuzzy from the tequila, he dipped a toe in the water, found it

140

bearable, turned off the taps, and stepped in. He pressed the knob she had indicated and nearly slid under as half a dozen powerful jets hit him from as many angles. Any prior reservations he might have felt immediately left him; he lay back feeling decidedly hedonistic. The surging water had an alarmingly erotic effect, and he again wondered about Mrs van Norden. She was a one-off as far as he was concerned; he had never come across anybody like her. Either he had stumbled across a genuinely liberated woman, or else he was dealing with the genus nymphomaniac. In the old days with the Firm caution would have been needed; but, with the water soothing all muscles but one, caution was pushed to one side. Some time later – he lost track of time, for he had dozed off – Pamela's voice startled him. Opening his eyes, he found her standing by the side of the bath enveloped in a large towelling gown.

'How is it?'

'Terrific.' He rejected any coy gestures and just lay there, exposed.

'Dinner's going to be delayed at least another hour, because Cook insists on doing something special. Can you last out?'

'I think I can manage.'

'Would you like me to join you?'

'Join me?'

'That's what I said.'

There was no reasonable answer he could think of, but he attempted a feeble joke. 'Are you looking for a discount? I have to tell you my boss doesn't give any.'

She stared him straight in the eye while slipping out of her robe. Naked, she seemed totally unreal. She had that even, all-over tan that only the very young or the very rich seem to achieve.

'Look, I'm sure I'm being incredibly gauche for a man of my age, or maybe I'm hallucinating, but why me?'

Instead of replying she got into the bath and sat facing him. The turbulent water immediately clustered her breasts with bubbles.

'Don't you hate conventions?' Pamela said, sliding further

141

under the water. 'Most people waste half their lives wondering whether they are doing the right, the sensible thing. Such a bore. Relax. You look terrified. I'm not going to attack you.'

'What if *I* attack *you*?'

'I guess I'll have to take my chances. After all, you haven't installed a panic button yet. Haven't you done this before?'

'Yes, but not in these circumstances.'

'Didn't your nanny ever bath you? I've always been told that little boys get their first inkling of what it's all about from bath-time with Nanny. True or false?'

'I wouldn't know; I never had a nanny.' Even as he said it, Hillsden came into his mind. He remembered he and Alec had been discussing the results of Caroline's autopsy, and young Rotherby, always the one to flaunt his superior upbringing, had tried to score off Alec. He couldn't remember why the subject of nannies had come up, but he remembered Alec giving the same reply. It was too bloody incongruous to think of that now, yet somehow the memory sobered him.

'Does it bring back unhappy memories or something?' Pamela asked. She twined her legs round his.

'No, I wouldn't say that. It was just a smaller bath – in a Spanish hotel, if you must know – and we flooded the place.'

'"We" being the wife?'

'No.'

'She didn't go in for water sports?'

'Pamela, I think before this goes any further you and I ought to establish a few ground rules. I'm enjoying this – who wouldn't? – and I'm sure I'll enjoy dinner, but – call me old-fashioned – I still like the thrill of the chase. Not that I don't find you highly desirable; that much is staring you in the face, as you've doubtless observed. You might be sharing my bath, but you're out of my league. I don't earn enough to heat this jacuzzi. I live on a modest salary, plus commission, less alimony. I may not have had a nanny to guide my upbringing, but I did learn early on that men who live off women are known as pimps.'

'What's that got to do with it?'

'Everything.'

142

'Aren't we both free agents?'

'Yes, all right, up to a point. I came to sell you a burglar alarm, for Christ's sake! I didn't expect to end up sharing your ex-husband's oversized hot tub with his naked ex-wife. Curiously enough, that is not in our sales manual. Maybe I should switch jobs and start selling jacuzzis, maybe I've lost my true vocation, who knows? All I'm trying to say is, I'm astounded, amazed, flattered, and for the moment out of my depth.'

'Fine. No problem.'

'Now you're offended. I didn't mean it like that.'

'No, everything you say is very sensible.'

'You are offended, I can tell.'

'If I was really offended, you wouldn't get dinner.'

She switched off the jacuzzi and stepped out of the bath. Her wet body was even more dazzling. It occurred to him that if women didn't have breasts they would be less lethal.

'Come downstairs when you're ready.'

She left the bathroom. Who the hell would believe that scene? Waddington thought. What were you afraid of – hidden cameras, blackmail, all the paraphernalia that used to condition your every waking hour? Single-handed, you have just blown the entire *Playboy* ethic.

He remonstrated with himself all the time he was dressing, silently cursing his inability to shed the last skin of his old life.

Dinner was a muted affair, given what had gone before. They made conversation, even shared a few laughs when he told anecdotes about some of his more difficult customers, but he departed as he had arrived, the salesman, promising to put her requirements into effect, thanking her for her hospitality as though they had never shared anything more than a formal relationship.

'I'm sorry,' he said.

'What is there to be sorry about?'

'I guess I was pretty cross earlier on. If so, forgive me. I would like to see you again, but on my terms and my home ground. That is, if you still want to see me.'

'Then, I'll wait to hear from you out of office hours.'

143

Arriving home, he was greeted by the neighbour's cat proudly carrying a small rodent in its mouth.

'You evil bastard,' Waddington shouted, aiming a kick at it. The cat retreated slowly, staring at him with that superior air felines reserve for those who fail to appreciate their unique qualities.

The moment he entered the house he was conscious that something was different. There was nothing out of place yet a sixth sense convinced him the house had been violated in his absence. Searching every room, he found nothing untoward. He had two telephones, one in the kitchen, the extension in his bedroom. Knowing what to look for, he took both instruments apart, but again drew a blank. Then he turned his attention to the answering machine and it was there that he located the bug. He left it in position and carefully replaced the casing, then poured himself a drink and sat down to consider the implications. Imperceptibly, mementoes of his old existence were creeping back. He had never set much store by coincidence, but pondering this latest development he sensed a pattern emerging. For some reason, someone was tracking him, and he needed to find out why.

10

From time to time and in return for various privileges accorded him, Hillsden was expected to give his analysis of intelligence reports originating from Soviet agents in the West – a task he readily embraced since it gave him an inside track enabling him to keep abreast with what was happening in England. He was often compelled to conceal his surprise at the extent of Soviet penetration into every corner of Western political and commercial circles; their thoroughness was impressive, and he began to appreciate how often the Firm had been duped in the past, how skilfully they had been deflected into concentrating their efforts away from the main danger areas. He now began to suspect that some of the major spy scandals had been deliberately engineered in order to divert attention from a more potent army of subverters, carefully positioned and concealed – self-styled 'moderate' general secretaries of trade unions, organizers of minority pressure groups, citizens of irreproachable character who were nevertheless ideally placed to foment trouble and dissent. Historically the KGB had abandoned a frontal attack on the British Parliament; card-carrying members of the British Communist Party seldom stood for election, for Moscow had long since concluded that the real power lay outside Parliament, taking their lead from the civil service, which had always controlled the pace of events no matter which of the two main political parties held office. Even so, various backbenchers on both sides of the House frequently cropped up in the reports – fellow-travellers who were usually to be found in trade missions visiting Eastern-bloc countries.

His memory having been well schooled over the years, Hillsden was able to store and cross-index certain items from the reports, building a composite picture of who was in place and where. The true identities were hidden in most cases for operational reasons, but he was able to establish that there were sleepers in many of the major seats of learning and communication, in the BBC and ITV companies, in provincial universities as well as Oxbridge, and of course firmly based in a multitude of local authorities. Recruitment was an ongoing priority, any failures being ruthlessly weeded out; on at least two occasions he saw evidence of actual eliminations. Gradually he formed a mental map of an England networked with cells operating outside the democratic process, but always using democratic means to subvert the majority will. There were gaps in the network, for he was unable to detect any signs of corruption in the higher echelons of the armed forces or the police, though several Police Watch Committees were shown to be controlled by political activists. He derived a certain cynical amusement from the fact that Moscow made little use of the old guard of the Labour Party, regarding them as useless reactionaries. These revelations brought home the urgency of his own situation, convincing him that he must put his plan into operation as soon as possible.

In offering his interpretations to his GRU masters he was always careful never to reveal he knew the full extent of the role being played by Control. Because Control's duplicity had never formed part of his original debriefing, nor had it been broached since, he was confident that Abramov had no inkling that Jock Calder had told all before his death. He had gone over the whole sequence of events many times in the intervening two years, but even now he found it difficult to come to terms with the fact that he had only bought his alien brand of freedom by killing a man. In the country he inhabited there were convenient phrases for what he had done: Moscow Centre called it 'wet business', the Firm's vocabulary had it down as 'expedient demise', abbreviated to three innocuous letters, XPD, but there was nothing innocuous about the recurring nightmares that left him drained and sweating. Hillsden knew he would never expunge that memory: killing Jock had avenged Caroline's murder, but had brought no peace of mind, nor had it removed the architect of his present situation. Control was still in power.

He used these sessions with Abramov to exercise old skills, searching for any chinks in the armour of Soviet penetration that he could use for his own ends, updating his manuscript whenever he could positively identify individuals. Not surprisingly, none of the traffic ever mentioned Bayldon; his name only surfaced once during a light-hearted exchange about British television programmes. It was standard GRU and KGB practice to monitor Western television output, particularly programmes with political content, or newsreel material critical of Soviet policy or intentions. Abramov confessed that he was baffled by a popular BBC television series called 'Yes, Prime Minister'. The tapes were sent over in the diplomatic pouch and screened, but the humour did not travel well.

'How can they show your Government in such a poor light, Alec? The man who plays the Prime Minister is humiliated every week by this civil servant character.'

'That's the whole idea. It's a comedy.'

'But subversive.'

'Yes, thank God.'

'But it must surely have a profoundly negative effect on the population.'

'I don't think so. They lap it up.'

'But there are even physical similarities with Bayldon.'

'Yes, I suppose there are, now you point it out.'

'They are quite happy to be shown that a Prime Minister can be manipulated in this fashion?'

'Oh, yes, we like to have our cynicism about politicians confirmed. It's what keeps the British vaguely sane.'

'A dangerous game. Once people cease to fear their leaders, the rot sets in.'

'But you have your own brands of humour. You Russians are not prudish; you have sex jokes, political jokes. I've seen examples in your underground press.'

'Exactly! It is not *official* humour. It doesn't go out on state television. Nor do we allow pornography to be openly shown.'

'Oh, come off it!' Hillsden remonstrated. 'Don't tell me

147

you're still living in the same Russia as the merchant's daughter in Chekhov's story. If you recall, she refused to look out of the window because there were naked horses in the streets.'

'No, this is not so. Pornography is a manifestation of Western bourgeois degeneracy.'

'Then, why do you have a name for it? *Samizdat*, isn't that right?'

'That is only used to describe foreign material smuggled into our country by subversive elements.'

It was during one of these relaxed sessions when the vodka had mellowed them both that Hillsden felt confident enough to test Abramov's reaction to the next stage of his plan. He approached the subject circumspectly, hoping that he could plant the idea in such a way that Abramov would believe it was his own.

'What impresses me, Victor,' he began, 'and I was never really conscious of it until I arrived here, is the way in which you go about things.'

'Things? What things?' Abramov's speech was slurred; his capacity for vodka was impressive, but Hillsden felt he had the edge.

'Your capacity for planning long-term strategy and sitting it out until exactly the right moment.'

'Yes, we're good at that. When the revolution started we used to have five-year plans, but they were never long enough to achieve anything, so we learnt to be more patient.'

'We don't have that sort of mentality.'

'No?'

'No. But let's be fair; British intelligence can be very good. It was very good during the war, better than yours; and, although we shared it when we became allies, Stalin ignored most of what we told you, which proved costly on several occasions.'

'Is that the truth?'

'Sure. The difference is that you have an overall world plan, whereas we don't. It's hit and miss most of the time. Our Foreign Office needs firecrackers up its arse. Since the war it's reverted to its old sloth; the FO doesn't rate us professionals

– we don't have the right accents and we didn't go to the right
schools. That television programme you don't understand –
believe me, it's very accurate. The permanent civil servants
call the tune; they can run rings round the average minister,
and the reason we get up their noses and they do their best
to fuck us is that they can't control us. So they do the next
best thing: they sit on our advice until it's too late. Even when
the evidence is staring them in the face they deliberately
misread it – witness the Falklands. We told them what was
going to happen weeks ahead of the invasion. Did they listen?
Did they bollocks.'

Hillsden poured more vodka. He had Abramov's full attention now. Abramov liked nothing better than stories about
Western incompetence and Soviet superiority.

'The truth is, Victor, today you are the masters, the origin-
ators; we are late-reactors. It's the human factor: we don't
breed people like you, we still recruit from the old-boy network – a friend of a friend of a friend, regardless of whether
they have any real feel for the job in hand – fourth-division
material playing in the top league. During the war, yes, things
were better. Because of the need to survive, the class barriers
were lowered, we had proles working alongside university
types as equals. But that didn't last. Come VJ-Day and the
old guard started to close ranks again.'

'But they did recruit you, Alec.'

'I was in the game from the start, learning our trade the
hard way, in the Army, like you. They must have been
delighted I came over – it proved their point, don't you see?
I wasn't one of them.'

'And now you are one of us, the best, among the elite.
And, if we're talking about perfection, there is only one
perfect spy, and that is the spy who is never caught. How
good it is to have these talks, to speak the same language . . .
How are your studies, by the way?'

'Coming along.'

'Being at the University has made life more interesting,
yes?'

'Definitely.'

'I was right to take care of that, to push you. What of your little Galina?'

'She's fine.'

'Your type, I think. Better than the one I chose for you before?'

'You sly bastard! What don't you know?'

'Very little.'

Hillsden saw his chance: by now Abramov was well tanked and relaxed. 'OK, let me test you. What d'you know about a man called Kiprenski?'

Abramov squinted over his vodka-glass. 'Kiprenski? The name strikes a bell.'

'He's a ballet critic.'

'Ah, yes, I recall now.'

'And a homosexual.'

Abramov waved his glass. 'No, it's not allowed to be a homosexual in Russia, Alec. You know that.'

'How stupid of me! I should have remembered. Forgive me.'

'That only happens in the degenerate West.'

'I sit corrected.'

'What d'you want to know about him?'

'The other night Galina and I went to the theatre and I met him. He was with a "friend", a British tourist.'

'So?'

'A somewhat odd couple.'

'Explain.'

'Well, this critic, who obviously is not gay, since he's an upright Soviet citizen, seemed to be very familiar with this tourist – who could well be gay, since the degenerate British have a lower standard of morals. And it occurred to me that possibly we could make use of him.'

'How?'

'Didn't you tell me to think as you do? So I found out which hotel he's at and I made a point of bumping into him there.'

'That could be dangerous, to be seen with a man like that. Did he know who you are?'

'I think so. I think the penny dropped. But I had good

150

reason for taking the risk. I discovered he works in the London Passport Office, quite a senior rank, with particular responsibility for vetting applications from aliens. Now, assuming I'm right, assuming he and this Kiprenski are a twosome – despite it being forbidden – then he might be suitable material for blackmail. It would be very useful, would it not, for us to run somebody in such a position?'

'What gives you the idea we would ever blackmail innocent tourists?'

Hillsden returned his grin. 'No, obviously that's just a wicked lie invented by our gutter press.'

'Which hotel is he staying at?'

'The Evopeiskaya.'

'For how long?'

'Until the end of the week. So if we move fast, and you provide me with the necessary, I could work on him. It would have more impact coming from me and give me a chance to dust off my old technique.'

Abramov considered the proposition for a few moments, then nodded.

'Yes. Why not?'

Two days later Hillsden was summoned to GRU head-quarters.

'That matter you mentioned the other day . . . I hate to admit it, but you were right. It appears that there are Russian citizens who still indulge in forbidden practices. Very regret-table.' He pushed half a dozen photographs across the desk. They showed Frampton and Kiprenski engaged in sexual intercourse and had obviously been taken by a hidden camera. Hillsden did not linger over them.

'I think maybe you should test his reactions to these. It's surprising how such photographs concentrate the mind. Tried and trusted methods are still the quickest, and since we don't have unlimited time I suggest you contact him today. He is in the hotel right now. I have had him kept there on a pretext, though he is unaware of the true reason. When you get there just produce your GRU identity-card to the man at the desk. He has already been told to co-operate.'

151

On the way to the Evopeiskaya Hillsden thought: I wonder if I can go through with this. Do I have the resolve to intimidate an innocent? He found the unfortunate Frampton in the lobby trying to sort out disputed items on his bill.

Hillsden approached him. 'Can I be of any help?'

'Oh, thank you. I don't understand what is wrong. Something to do with my traveller's cheques. My Russian isn't good enough, I'm afraid.'

'Let me try.'

Hillsden palmed his identity-card and flashed it at the hotel official without Frampton being aware of the action. In colloquial Russian he said: 'I'll deal with this now. There is no further need for you to be involved.'

The official bowed out. Hillsden walked Frampton away from the desk.

'I told him I will take care of everything. They always make a fuss when hard currency is involved.'

'Thank you. I was getting worried. Lucky you came along when you did.'

'Ah, well, I have a little influence. Do you have time for a chat?'

'That would be nice,' Frampton said, 'but I couldn't make it today. I have things planned. Unless you'd like to have a drink here?'

'I don't think that would be a good idea. As you realize, I have certain privileges, which give me access to confidential information. You see, I didn't come to your rescue by accident. You seem to have run foul of the authorities, and I thought I would like to help.'

'I thought everything was sorted out?'

'Not that. I wasn't referring to what just happened, but to something more important.'

Frampton's expression changed. 'How d'you mean?'

'You've apparently broken some of their laws.'

'But I've done nothing, not that I know of anyway.'

His attempt at defiance carried no conviction.

'You formed a certain relationship, I believe. One has to be extra careful about one's choice of friends in this country.

152

Believe me, you need my help. Better to deal with me than with the secret police.'

'Police? Why would the police be interested in me?'

'Don't raise your voice. Just be calm. We can't discuss it here. Just trust me, and come with me.'

'To do that I have to cancel an appointment.'

'Then, cancel it. I'll wait here for you.'

Frampton stared at him with a bloodless pinched face, then went to telephone. On his return Hillsden obtained a taxi and they drove to his apartment but did not go inside. Instead, Hillsden suggested they walked in the nearby park.

'Just to be on the safe side. They have a habit of bugging rooms.'

'Why would they bug your room?'

'Because they leave nothing to chance.'

'Tell me what I've done. I've been on holiday, that's all.'

'And how have you spent your time?' Hillsden asked.

'Sightseeing, visiting museums, the theatre.'

'With the friend I met the other evening?'

'Yes.'

They stopped and sat on a park bench. Hillsden produced the packet of photographs. 'Perhaps your choice of a friend was not a wise decision.' He handed the packet to Frampton. 'I think you should see these, John,' deliberately using his given name for the first time.

Frampton withdrew the photographs slowly. He stared down at them, his face suddenly transformed.

'Oh, God!' he whispered. 'Oh, dear God!'

'Now do you see what I mean?' Hillsden took back the envelope.

'What will happen to me?'

'That depends. The reason I wanted to have this talk was to put a suggestion to you. Because you're a fellow-countryman, I interceded on your behalf and persuaded the secret police to let me deal with the matter. Obviously if these photographs got back to England and found their way into the wrong hands, you would lose your job – and worse. Equally, should you not go along with what I am going to

153

suggest, your Russian friend will be punished.' Even as he pushed fear into Frampton, Hillsden thought how easy it was to descend to this level, employing the same techniques blackmailers had always used. Yet the distaste he felt for what he was doing was stifled by his own needs; oppressors could always justify the means. 'On the other hand, there is an escape route for both of you. In return for you performing a few minor tasks when you get home, I can guarantee that neither of you will be exposed. But debts of this nature always have to be repaid, don't they?'

Frampton nodded.

'You have a responsible position, a sensitive position in a government office, one you've worked hard for with a good pension at the end of it . . . It would be a pity to jeopardize all that.' He paused, studying Frampton's face; the man seemed close to tears, and again Hillsden forced himself to elbow aside conscience. Softening his voice, he continued: 'It's possible that in the future somebody may contact you and ask you to do certain favours in return for keeping your escapades here secret.'

'What sort of favours?'

'I've no idea. You may never be called upon, for all I know. But they want to take out an insurance policy on you.' Hillsden waited, letting this sink in. 'For the moment all that will be required is for you to relay a message when you get back.'

'A message?'

'Yes. Nothing complicated. Something you can easily learn by heart. That's not much to ask, is it?'

'Why should I trust them to keep their side of the bargain?'

'I don't know why. Perhaps because you have no choice.'

'What happens to the photographs?'

'This particular set? Nothing. You can have them for all I care. The negatives are another matter. They are the insurance policy.' He offered the packet again, and Frampton accepted it. 'So the choice is up to you. Take a message or else face the probability of public disgrace. Do you have a family?'

Frampton nodded.

'You wouldn't want to bring that on them, surely?'

'It wasn't what you think,' Frampton blurted, fingering the packet. 'These only show one side of it.' Now that he knew the price he had to pay there was a hint of defiance in his voice. 'But I don't suppose you understand my kind of love.'

'You could be right at that,' Hillsden said, rising from the park bench. 'It's a dangerous game, love, whichever way you play it. Most of us are betrayed in the end.'

11

Had it not been for the telephone call, Waddington would have thought it a normal Easter-holiday weekend: the yearly carnage on the motorways, air-traffic controllers on a go-slow throughout Europe, the cross-Channel ferries on strike (with the usual protestations that the timing and inconvenience to the public were purely coincidental) and of course riots and killings in the birthplace of Christ.

He walked back from his local pub on Good Friday, having enjoyed a ploughman's lunch and a pint or two of draught beer. His mood was reflective; days like this made him strangely disorientated – they felt like Sundays, which he had always loathed, being non-religious. When at home on Sundays during his marriage it had been his habit to get breakfast and take it to his wife in bed. Now he found it curious that he remembered those lazy occasions – when more often than not they had made love – with greater clarity than the rest of the time they had spent together. It was difficult to apportion blame, or pinpoint the exact moment when any relationship failed, but in his own case he had no doubt that the Firm had been the cause and the effect. As with Alec's marriage, the deceits that were part and parcel of the job had rotted the very fabric of his marriage, just as termites burrowed unseen in the foundations of a house. Perhaps ordinary adultery would have been easier to conceal. He thought of their early years together with something approaching pain, punishing himself in retrospect for acts of indifference. And, inevitably, the predatory male mind being what it was, side by side with remembered regrets came thoughts of more recent events. Did he want to repeat the whole process over again, entering into another person's life just because the old phallus dictated the momentary pleasure? He was aware of the sexual threat that Pamela posed and, although he had so far resisted contacting her again, he carried an image of her like emotional excess luggage. Alone at night he tried to analyse why he had not succumbed to her obvious charms at first bidding. After all, her body was the stuff that chauvinistic dreams were made on, so what had held him back? Was it just a reluctance to become involved again, or had darker instincts surfaced?

These inconclusive thoughts occupied him as he walked home along old Beaconsfield High Street, an oasis of architectural calm that so far had escaped the ravages of the property speculators, and which never failed to reveal new pleasures. For once the weather had exceeded seasonal expectations; a profusion of early cherry blossom topped mellow brick walls, window-boxed daffodils and narcissus graced the Georgian façades, and with the absence of traffic the whole street had a picture-postcard quality.

The mood was shattered when once again he was greeted on his doorstep by the neighbour's cat, this time proudly carrying a half-eaten thrush and uttering those curious little cries that advertise a kill.

'You murdering sod! Don't you know it's a holy day?' Waddington said.

Inside the house he took a can of beer from the fridge, then switched on the television, flicking through the channels in a search for something to hold his interest. He found an old black and white Katharine Hepburn movie, and settled down in an armchair. Only then did he notice the warning light blinking on his telephone answering machine. It was the first time it had been activated since his discovery of the bug. Waddington stared at it over the rim of his beer-glass. Whoever was keeping tabs on him would presumably be ahead of the game. There was always the chance that the bug had been installed on the Captain's instructions; Waddington wouldn't put it past him since the machine was the property of Breakproof, every employee having one on loan, the Captain insisting they be on call twenty-four hours. The crafty old bugger

157

was manic enough to have thought up something like that.

Waddington finished his beer before going to the machine. He switched the control to the answer-play mode and waited for the tape to rewind. After a pause, 'You don't know me,' a male voice said, 'but I've just returned from a holiday abroad and I have a message for you from a friend.' The words were blurted out as though the caller was under stress. 'I was told not to trust it to the post, but give it to you in person. So can you meet me? I will be in Harrods food-hall on Tuesday at twelve-thirty. Look for somebody carrying the current issue of *Country Life*.' The line went dead.

Waddington rewound the tape and played the message again. He could not place the voice, although he detected remains of a Cockney accent in some of the vowels. What friends do I have living abroad? he thought, pouring himself a second beer. And in any case why contact me in such mysterious fashion? He eliminated the possibility of some elaborate joke – April Fool's Day had passed, and in any case none of the Captain's staff possessed that sort of imagination, their humour being confined to schoolboy smut and tiresome anecdotes about their Sloane Ranger girl-friends. Equally, it was hardly the sort of joke the Captain would play; he was too strait-laced for that. Could it be merely a boring hoax in the same category as an obscene phone call, some anonymous twit passing the time over the holiday weekend? He sipped his drink and pondered the mystery. A certain unease seeped into his consciousness. Various strands were looping together. Were they all unrelated, a series of coincidences, or did they add up to something yet to be revealed? He thought back to the luncheon with Keating, coming as it had out of the blue, yet forcing him back into the past. Then the discovery that the house was bugged, and now this. Even the entry of the randy Pamela into his life now seemed loosely connected, or was he becoming paranoid? One thing was for sure: he was not the only recipient of the anonymous message. Whoever was monitoring his calls would have the same information. In turn that could mean that the device was a plant to trap him. But trap him for what?

158

Katharine Hepburn and Cary Grant were struggling with a leopard as he took the problem back to his armchair. Who from his past would want to go to such complicated lengths? *I have just returned from a holiday abroad*, the voice had said, *and I have a message for you from a friend.* Who fitted that description? Life in the Firm had never been conducive to normal friendships, and since the break-up of his marriage he had not formed any new relationships, nor had he kept up with the old. Keating had been his only recent contact with that past shadowy world. He continued drinking while he searched for a plausible answer, reviewing faces he had imagined he would never see again. Once again he concentrated on the operative word *abroad*, but the solution still eluded him. By now his thoughts were blurred and he sat in the darkening room with a sense of foreboding. It seemed to him then, just before the effect of the beer closed his eyes, that possibly the only certainty left in the world was Hepburn's ageless beauty.

As Waddington pondered what to do next, an American Airlines flight from New York was just landing in Antigua, West Indies. Amongst the horde of white-faced tourists making their way across the hot tarmac towards the Arrivals building was a man whose fame had been recorded in the deathless prose of the *Hollywood Reporter* over the past three decades. Born Mischa Rabonovich in Warsaw, he changed his name to Mike Raven shortly after emigrating to the United States. He spent the first ten years in Chicago, establishing himself within the large Polish community there, and gaining employment in the Marshall Field store. Diligent, he quickly embraced the American work ethic and was promoted from the shop-floor to the position of head buyer for the shoe department, and used the experience to build his own contacts. When he had saved enough capital he gave notice and opened his own shop, selling a range of cheap imported footwear that undercut the competition. Within three years he had a chain of ten shops scattered around the poorer districts of Chicago. Never the one to neglect any opportunity

159

for social advancement, he joined the local tent of Variety Club on the introduction of one of his major suppliers. It was in such company that he first became aware of the richer pickings to be made in the film industry. He listened and learnt fast. For a comparatively modest sum he bought the film rights of a wildly salacious novel prior to publication, and the gamble paid off: it got into the bestseller-lists and three of the major studios were in the running to buy him out. Raven hired a lawyer and only parted with the rights on the condition that he was hired as Executive Producer on the film – a title originally invented by Hollywood to pacify the egos of those who had money but no talent. Raven's lawyer also secured him a percentage of the profits. Since the subsequent film turned the basic dross into glossy dross, Raven found himself not only rich, but also accepted as a man who could pick a winner. He was given a three-picture deal, a suite of offices on the studio lot, purchased the obligatory mansion in Bel Air, was quickly trapped into marrying his secretary, a girl of headstrong qualities, and went from strength to strength, having learnt the first time around that messages are strictly for Western Union.

Four marriages and some score of films later, he was now a member of the Hollywood establishment, not on the A List, but nevertheless a player. He had a true instinct for corporate necrophilia and knew where the important bodies were buried.

His last wife had been the pick of the quartet. Sadly, she had died on the operating-table a few months before his trip to Antigua. The purpose of his visit was to meet up with two tax lawyers who needed to wash one of their clients' undisclosed funds.

Disgruntled that he had not been given VIP treatment on the crowded flight and suffering from dyspepsia and dehydration, he made slow progress through the wall of heat. A long queue had already formed at the two passport-desks and the local Immigration Officers performed their duties in slow motion. When, after a delay of some twenty minutes, he obtained his luggage he was then required to open his suitcase.

160

'Nothing. I got nothing to declare. No liquor, no cigarettes, no gifts, zilch.'

'Open,' the Customs Officer said, unimpressed.

Sweat dripped from Raven's brow on to his clean shirts as he complied. The Customs man made a thorough examination and came up with a small white phial.

'Be careful with that,' Raven said.

The cap was unscrewed, revealing that the phial was filled with a greyish dust. The Customs man sniffed at it.

'What is this?'

'Well, it ain't drugs, if that's what you're thinking.' Raven glanced around, then lowered his voice. 'If you must know, it's my late wife's ashes. We used to come to these islands for our holidays, and she expressed a wish that I scatter her ashes here – a sort of sentimental gesture, you might say.'

The Customs man looked dubious and seemed about to tip the ashes into his palm.

'If you lose any, I'm gonna sue you,' Raven barked. 'Have some respect for the dead.'

Raven's tone, and the fact that the Customs man was out of his depth, persuaded him to give Raven the benefit of the doubt. The cap was screwed back on the phial and returned to him.

Outside the heat pushed against him like an angry restraining hand. After an argument about the price he secured a taxi and was driven off to his hotel.

In contrast to many of the hotels dotted around the island, Curtain Bluff had been an oasis of luxurious calm for the best part of twenty-five years, and Raven was greeted as an old friend by the long-serving staff. He was quickly shown to his suite, where high ceilings and revolving fans cooled the marble floors.

'I'm meant to be meeting a couple of guys here. D'you know if they've arrived?'

'What names, Mr Raven?'

Raven consulted his bulging Filofax. 'Ruddock and Grunwald.'

'Oh, yes, they got in last night. I dare say they're on the

161

beach. I'll have them paged and tell them you're here. Can I get you anything?'

'A Jack Daniels on the rocks, and make it a double.'

Raven unpacked his suitcase, putting aside several copies of the screenplay he hoped to hype. The phial containing his wife's ashes he placed in the room safe.

Having changed into casual clothes, he sat on the balcony and waited for his drink to arrive. All the suites overlooked the east beach where the surf continuously pounded. As though alerted of his occupancy by some mysterious radar, small cheeky birds fluttered fearlessly across his balcony in their quest for titbits. Far out to sea a four-master made stately progress. Raven nursed his drink, grateful for a chance to relax and collect his thoughts. The sweat dried on him in the sea-breeze and, as often happened when away from Hollywood, he wondered why he did not give up the rat race. The castaway syndrome of island living always beckoned on the first day, but he knew himself too well. Cut off from his battery of phones, denied the trade papers, left out of the day-to-day in-fighting, he would soon be stir crazy.

When eventually the two lawyers showed up, Raven was disconcerted to find they were both in their twenties: youth in general made him ill at ease; youth allied to business deals positively alarmed him.

They were equally thrown by the fact that he immediately launched into a somewhat maudlin account of his wife's recent demise.

'My late bride and I used to come here every year. A sort of annual honeymoon.'

They winced.

'Matter of fact, I've got a duty to perform this trip. I brought her ashes with me. She always wanted this to be her last port of call.'

'Gee, that's really nice,' Ruddock said.

Grunwald said: 'Where are you going to . . .?' He searched for the appropriate words. 'That is, how d'you go about that, sir?'

'I thought down there on the beach,' Raven said, unaware

162

that the two young men were having difficulty keeping a straight face. 'Perhaps you'd both care to witness the ceremony? I thought I'd do it tomorrow morning before breakfast.'

'Our privilege,' Ruddock replied after the briefest of pauses. 'Right, Bob?'

'Wouldn't miss it.'

'I appreciate that,' Raven said. 'OK, let's get down to business. Have you two done your homework?'

Ruddock assumed the role of spokesman. 'We've prepared this memo for you to look over. Basically there are certain advantages for our client setting up a corporation on this island. No income tax and a ten-year honeymoon on profits. But naturally he would want certain safeguards built in.'

'What line of business is he in?'

'He'd prefer to keep that confidential, sir, but I can assure you he's a man of substance and that the necessary funds are available.'

'Do you have a budget figure yet?' Grunwald interjected.

'I've got a guesstimate,' Raven said, using the normal film-industry parlance to denote that he was keeping all options open. 'I can give you the below-the-line, but the above-the-line depends on which stars we eventually cast.'

'You have a director, though?'

'Yeah. I've got Zev Winter on hold.'

'You'll have to forgive me,' Ruddock said. 'I'm not a great film buff. He's good, is he?'

'He made *Terminal Rider*,' Raven said, as though that settled the matter. The two lawyers looked blank. 'Took nearly thirty-eight million in rentals.'

'It was a profit-maker, in other words?'

'You bet your ass. Only cost seven.' Raven went to the spare twin bed where the scripts were laid out and gave them one each. 'This is the latest draft of the screenplay. Still wants a dialogue polish, but I got somebody lined up for that. No point in wasting money until we cast it. Like, when we cast it, whoever plays the lead is going to want changes. Or his fucking analyst is going to want changes. We're getting

163

screwed by talent. Suddenly they're all Warren Beattys.'

'As far as our client's concerned,' Ruddock said, 'you could shoot the New York telephone directory. All he's interested in is the bottom line. In return for providing the finance, subject to normal guarantees naturally, he wants to come out in first position on the gross until double negative, then he'll split seventy-thirty in his favour. You make the deals to fit in with that. No creative book-keeping and we counter-sign all cheques.'

'Oh, and by the way,' Grunwald chimed in, 'once the final budget's been agreed, that's it. Any overage comes out of your fee.'

Raven made no comment, but his brain was already working like a calculator. The terms were tougher than he had anticipated, but he could work round them. If he had to wait for double negative before he saw any piece of the gross, he would pad his own fee up front, and steal from a dozen different items in the budget. These two guys might think themselves smart, but they would have to get up very early in the morning to put one across on him. He knew fifty-eight ways of skinning any cat.

'How does that sit with you, sir?' Ruddock asked.

'I can live with it. It ain't chopped chicken liver, but I'm a realist, gentlemen. One thing you should know, whether you read the script or not: we've got a sequence in there which has to be shot in Russia. How does that grab you?'

'I don't see any problem. I take it the script isn't anti-Russian?'

'No, just a love-story. Do yourselves a favour – read it.'

After another short discussion about what casting Raven had in mind, the meeting broke up. Arrangements were made for them to meet on the beach the following morning. Before turning in, Raven checked that the ashes were still in the room safe, took a laxative, and put in an alarm call. A cool sea-breeze penetrated the mosquito netting, but it was still too hot for sleep and he lay naked on top of the bed and studied the memo they had left with him, his eyes going straight to the fine print: it took a con man to know one.

164

Whoever had drawn up the document had done his home-work, but Raven spotted a couple of loopholes he could covertly exploit. He read it twice before fatigue and the sound of the surf closed his eyes.

He met the two lawyers on the empty beach as arranged, though he was irritated that they were both wearing tennis clothes – it seemed irreverent for the occasion. They all walked barefoot across the damp sand to the water's edge, while crabs scuttled for the safety of their overnight holes. Blackened coconuts, looking from a distance like severed human heads, rolled backwards and forwards in the spumed waves. All too late in the day it occurred to Raven that perhaps he should have prepared a few words to mark the occasion. He dimly remembered snatches of dialogue from a funeral scene in one of his films, but felt incapable of quoting them. The phial of ashes clutched in his hand, he hesitated at the water's edge, then was forced to retreat as a large wave crashed on the beach. Stumbling, he lost his footing and dropped the phial. Grunwald rushed forward and retrieved it before it was washed out to sea, and the scene took on some of the elements of farce.

Ruddock helped Raven to his feet and brushed the wet sand off his back. 'We both had a look at the script,' he said in desperation, 'and we enjoyed it, didn't we, Bob?'

'Yeah, got some good stuff in it. I'm no expert on these things, of course, but I liked it.' After wiping the phial dry, he handed it back to Raven.

'My late bride was my best critic,' Raven said, 'and that script was the last thing she read. She said: "Daddy, you've got to go with this one. Run with it." '

'Well, a woman's instinct is not to be ignored.'

'She was a lovely lady.' He unscrewed the phial and ap-proached closer to the water's edge. 'I wish I had the right words for this occasion, gentlemen; but, not being a religious man, you'll have to excuse me.'

'I'm sure your bride would understand,' Ruddock said helpfully.

Raven poured the ashes into his cupped palm and prepared

to do the deed, but his pudgy arms hardly extended over the tideline, and it was obvious to Ruddock and Grunwald that the symbolic event was courting tragedy.

'Perhaps if you stood on those rocks,' Ruddock suggested. But he was too late. Raven's pitching arm had not been put to any major test since his Junior League days, and as he made a feeble gesture skywards a sudden gust of wind blew off the sea and returned the ashes back at him. He staggered drunkenly as the gritty remains of Mrs Raven filmed his face and clothes.

'Jesus!' he shouted, turning in agony. 'I got 'em in my eye.'

'Don't rub it,' Ruddock said. 'Let's go back to your room and get some drops.' Grunwald, whose powers of resistance were minimal, fought a losing battle with hysteria. He produced a handkerchief as though about to offer it to the stricken Raven, but instead clapped it over his mouth. Neither of them could look at each other as they helped Raven up the sandy incline.

The damage repaired, Raven recovered some of his customary chutzpah over breakfast, even to the extent of making a mild joke at his dead wife's expense. 'She was always the clinging type, my bride.'

'I wouldn't feel too badly,' Ruddock said. 'It's the thought that counts.'

'You're right. So let's put our false teeth on the table. I've done all my deals on a handshake; that's the way I operate. You legal boys usually want to make a meal of it, but I'm ready to sign a heads of agreement and get the show rolling. Just give me your top figure and I'll work to it.'

It was a ploy he had often used in the past: get the other side to commit to a price, then ensure he padded the budget so that it came out just under their maximum.

'I think', Ruddock said, spooning an over-ripe papaya, 'our client would prefer to have sight of your budget first, then decide whether it's too rich for him. That's how we've been briefed.'

His first bluff called, Raven tried his alternative. 'Well, tell him he's gonna lose it if he pussyfoots around. I got Warner hungry for this script, but I've been holding them off. Can't you give me his name?'

'No disrespect, sir, but our instructions preclude that.'

They're fronting for Mafia money, Raven thought, having over the years learnt to smell out laundry deals. So what? Everybody had an obligation to screw the IRS if they could get away with it; it was virtually written into the Constitution.

'When you think you can come up with a final budget?' Grunwald asked.

'I got my people standing by. Soon as we get through here, I'll get them working on it. Too bad we can't finalize it now.'

'Yes,' Ruddock said, 'but we neither of us want to make a mistake, do we?'

They left immediately after breakfast, but before catching a flight to New York they called London from the airport to give a progress report to the client.

'I wouldn't say our Hollywood friend is somebody I'd buy a secondhand Chevrolet from; but when he agrees your terms, as I'm certain he will, I think we've built in sufficient safe-guards to protect you all the way, sir.'

'Fine. Sounds like you did a good job. Keep me posted.'

'Rely on it, Mr Keating,' Ruddock said.

Adopting a fatalistic attitude, Waddington made no attempt to cover his tracks when he set out for Harrods on the appointed day; he calculated that whoever else was aware of the arrangement would be in position inside the food-halls before he arrived and that any complicated subterfuge on his part would be a waste of time. He entered Harrods well before half-past twelve, choosing the side doors nearest to the cosmetics department. A demonstration of the latest rejuvenating cream was in progress, and he edged his way past a crowd of blue-rinsed matrons intent on sampling an elixir that promised to retard the ravages of time.

The plan he had decided upon was not to make immediate contact with the messenger, but merely to observe him at a distance in the first instance. He made a couple of small purchases for appearances' sake, noting any faces that he saw

167

more than once, then began a casual circuit of the various food-halls, cursing the stupidity of his unknown caller for choosing such a non-specific rendezvous. The lunch-hour had brought in hordes of shoppers from neighbouring offices, and in places the crush made his task impossible. After ten minutes he had failed to spot any likely suspect and he was inclined to the belief that it was a hoax after all. It was then, through a gap in the crowd, he caught sight of an anxious face standing by the bread-counter. At first glance there was nothing out of the ordinary about the man; in fact the very reverse. He seemed to epitomize the average: average height and build, average two-piece suit, neat collar and tie, suggesting some-body in a sedentary occupation. Before the crowds obscured him again Waddington saw that he was holding a copy of *Country Life*. Even at a distance he could make out the cover photograph – a large hare – which he had already checked was the one on the current issue. Convinced by this and by the fact that the face above the magazine was pinched and anxious, Waddington make no abrupt move but, keeping the man in view, eased his way to another vantage-point. He had to assume that both of them were under surveillance. Now he changed direction again, this time walking straight for the man to give the impression that he was about to make contact, all the time watching for any untoward movement in the crowd. At the last moment he veered to one side, and his efforts were rewarded: two men suddenly elbowed a passage through the shoppers and with obvious intent bore down on the scared messenger. Then things happened very quickly. The two men were impeded by a stout old party laden with parcels. They sent her crashing to the floor, scattering her groceries. A bowler-hatted type of military bearing reacted, blocking their progress and remonstrating with them for their loutish behaviour. The two men attempted to push him aside, but he was made of sterner stuff and a scuffle started. Two security guards appeared and helped tackle the assailants; in the struggle several glass stands were overturned and jagged shards of glass flew in all directions. Displays of tinned biscuits and iced cakes collapsed, and to his horror Waddington saw one of the security guards stagger backwards and fall, a sudden spurt of blood staining a large wedding cake with the word 'Congratulations' piped on it. Women shoppers were screaming and fighting to reach the nearest exit as alarm bells were activated. In the mêlée the panicked Frampton made good his escape, pushing through the crush close to Waddington, close enough for Waddington to grab at his arm as he passed, spinning him round. Frampton struck out blindly, hitting not Waddington, but an elderly man in the face, smashing his John Lennon spectacles. The copy of *Country Life* dropped at Waddington's feet and, involuntarily, he bent to retrieve it. Off-balance, he was knocked to one side, rolling over several times to avoid being trampled on. When he picked himself up Frampton had disappeared and the food-hall was emptying. The security guard lay in a pool of blood and white cake, for all the world like a seal killed on the ice. The fight with the two hit men seemed to be continuing in another part of the hall, for he could hear shouting in the distance. Two policemen now ran in, one pausing by the fallen guard, the other going towards the noise of the fracas. Waddington made his own escape, still clutching the magazine.

He left by the Brompton Road exit, scanning the street in both directions, but the pavements were crowded with the curious and the scared – word of trouble always travelled fast – and he could not spot any trace of Frampton. A police car screamed to a halt bringing reinforcements, and Waddington took advantage of the stalled traffic to dodge across the road and into a café. He selected an empty table nearest to the window so that he could observe any developments.

'What's happening over there?' his waitress asked as she took his order.

'Seems to be something going on at Harrods.'

'Lot of police. Hope it's not another bomb. D'you want a pastry with your coffee?'

'No, thank you.'

'You can't have coffee on its own.'

'Right . . . well, bring me a croissant.'

'We're out of croissants.' Even the possibility of a bomb

169

could not keep a note of satisfaction out of her voice as she imparted this news.

'OK . . . well, *you* choose something – a Danish, anything.'

He watched other police cars arriving, then realized he was still holding the magazine. Flicking through it, he came across a single sheet of lined notepaper tucked inside the centre pages. Written on it in neat script were some seemingly unrelated words, suggesting a list of reminders.

> *Lenin*
> *James/Aspern Papers*
> *Imperative*
> *No contact wine*

Waddington stared at the list while eating his Danish, totally baffled; nothing made immediate sense. A flake of fresh pastry fell on to the note, staining one corner. The only certainties were that he now knew that the call had been genuine, that his telephone calls were being monitored and that somebody had been anxious to get to the courier before he did. The man had obviously been scared off and was unlikely to contact him again. Sipping his espresso, he studied the list again, trying to decide whether the words represented a code. He jotted down all the capitals – L-J-A-I-N – but could make nothing out of them: the solving of acrostics had never been his strong point. The only item that seemed to be intelligible was the reference to *The Aspern Papers*. Although his literary education had been nothing like as catholic as Alec's, he had studied the Henry James novel as part of an English course at college, but the intervening years had dimmed his memory of the plot. He lingered over his coffee until, in the best tradition of British café society, his waitress made it obvious he was outstaying his welcome. A bunch of suburban matrons were already queuing for lunch, all chattering like linnets about the Harrods incident. Waddington waited in the doorway of the café until he spotted a passing taxi, then dashed out to flag it down. As an extra precaution he did not go back to the Breakproof offices, but instead had the taxi drop him off in Kensington High Street. From there he went into the

Royal Garden Hotel and called his secretary from one of the public phones.

'If our fearless Captain asks where I am, tell him I'm chasing new business out of town.'

That done he took another taxi and retrieved his car from the underground carpark at Marble Arch, but before going home he made a second detour and stopped at the local bookshop.

'*The Aspern Papers*? You should find it in the Penguin rack, under "classics".'

Waddington searched as directed. 'No, doesn't seem to be here.'

'Oh dear, has she gone again?' the proprietor said. He was a middle-aged queen, sometimes given to fits of temperament and very choosy as to who he was nice to. 'Can't keep everything in stock all the time. Very popular these days, our Mrs James. She's having quite a little surge. Shall I order it for you?'

'Yes, if you would. How long will that take?'

'I don't write horoscopes, dear. Depends whether I've paid my fucking wholesaler's bill this month. I'll try for the end of the week, but I can't promise.'

'I don't suppose you remember the plot, do you?' Waddington asked.

'Can't read her, dear, never could. Boring as watching paint dry.'

Waddington knew better than to pursue the subject. 'Well, do your best.'

The chewed head of a mouse greeted him on the doorstep when he arrived home. He kicked it into a flowerbed before examining the front door: he had used the old trick of a fixing a hair in place before leaving that morning. It was still intact.

Once inside he searched his own bookshelves on the chance that he might have a copy. He found a dog-eared paperback of *Washington Square*, but no *Aspern Papers*. Frustrated, he poured himself a large malt whisky and drank it neat while waiting for the bath to fill. Immersed, he soaked until his skin started to wrinkle, trying to fathom the significance of the

171

note and recall the plot of the elusive novel. He could vaguely recall that it was concerned with a missing manuscript. Michael Redgrave had once dramatized it and, although he had seen the production, he could remember little except Redgrave's performance and the fact that it was set in Venice. Was that a clue? Venice. Do I know anybody living there? Somebody called James, perhaps? Nobody that came readily to mind. I knew a Jim Bishop once, but he fell off the perch years ago. What else was there? Lenin. Try word association. Russia, revolution, Highgate cemetery – no, wrong, it is Karl Marx who is buried there – Moscow, Red Square, the tomb? What was the last line on the note? *No contact wine.* What the fuck did that signify? Why doesn't my brain work any more? he thought. He said the three words aloud as he reached for a towel and stepped out of the now tepid bath. He said them again, staring at his reflection in the mirror, willing something to prompt his memory. Of course there was always the chance that the note had no connection with the telephone call. Perhaps it was just an innocent shopping-list, left in the magazine by accident. Except for the word *Lenin*, which touched a chord.

Clad in a dressing-gown he went downstairs and started to prepare some spaghetti (his only accomplishment in the culinary arts), opened a bottle of reasonable Chablis and was reminded of the time when the Firm had used the wine trade as a front. They had only stocked plonk, but at least he and Alec had managed to help themselves to a few crates before the bloody stuff reverted to vinegar. He poured a tin of ready-made tomato sauce over the slightly overcooked spaghetti and recalled with nostalgia the meals his ex-wife had put before him. Twisting his fork into the sticky concoction, he wondered how she was finding the rural life, and this train of thought led him back to Pamela. Maybe, since the house is bugged, I ought to reconsider her offer to move in, he mused. It would have definite advantages in many ways, and I'd certainly eat better.

Looking up at a slight sound, he found next door's cat staring in at the kitchen window. The animal's mouth opened as it gave a plaintive unheard cry. 'Piss off, you murderer,' Waddington shouted. His cooking suddenly revolted him and he scraped the remains into the sink, before retiring into the sitting-room to draw the curtains and switch on the television. He looked for that day's newspaper to see if there was anything worth watching, and it was then that his eye went to the copy of *Country Life* again. For the first time he noticed there was a small white subscription-label pasted on the back cover. He picked it up; the label, although torn at one corner, had a name and an address printed on it which were still legible: *J. H. Frampton, 194 Cranmer Road, Forest Gate, London E7G 4QP.*

Waddington stared at it, unable to believe his luck. Nobody but an amateur would have overlooked such a damning clue. Wait, though, he cautioned himself. Don't get elated too soon. What if by finding this you are drawn further into a trap? Think it through before you jump.

He sat down to consider new options while, outside, the cat hunted smaller prey.

12

'Now, there's a funny thing,' Pearson said, munching on a takeaway pizza crust, then wincing: he had bitten on a dodgy filling, and the pain shot up his cheek to behind his right eye. He had already cancelled two dental appointments to have it attended to; there never seemed time for body maintenance and, as the years advanced, he frequently chided himself for the neglect. If it was my car, he often thought, I wouldn't hesitate to have a rebore and anti-rust treatment.

'I've got to get this bloody tooth fixed,' he said to Lloyd.

'How about trying a cotton tied to the doorknob? My granny used to swear by that. Of course, she wrecked a number of doors.'

'Yes, and Sexton Blake solved all his murders with a magnifying glass.'

'What did you start to say, Chief?' Lloyd asked. 'You said something was funny.'

'Did I?' Pearson tossed the rest of the pizza towards a trash-basket. It fell short, and as he bent to retrieve it his kneecap creaked. 'And don't get me any more of those. Inedible frisbees. I think I've been chewing on the wrong tooth where Mitchell's concerned – sorry, I've got dentists on the brain at the moment. We took it as read, did we not, that he must have been a KGB plant: a classic case of infiltration into a very sensitive area that always presents an attractive target to them? A strange little character, given to some quirky ways of self-amusement, if not self-abuse – witness Exhibit A, certain items of women's underwear – who suddenly gets himself blown apart by a sophisticated bomb in Hyde Park.'

'But not before he's been shot,' Lloyd interjected.

'Exactly. No discernible motive and no trace of the killer. Subsequently, and purely by luck, we discover his hideaway, which gives us a little more to go on. Exhibit B, a radio, miniature camera and a code-book – the Reader's Digest do-it-yourself kit for spies. Right?'

Lloyd nodded.

'Now, then, you would think, would you not, given the hysteria that normally surfaces whenever GCHQ is involved, and given the fact that Mitchell was patently not a boy scout spotting train numbers, but had to be collecting highly secret information for somebody, that our friends in MI5 – and, indeed, in MI6, for that matter – would be shitting themselves? Instead, it could be eleven o'clock on Armistice Day. Nobody is shitting himself that I can discern. Apart from you and me, not a mouse is stirring. All is quiet. That's the funny thing that puzzles me.'

He gently moved his tongue against the offending tooth, masochistically testing his tolerance while staring at Lloyd.

'How come the awkward questions have stopped being asked in Parliament? By rights, it should be obvious cannon fodder for a dispirited Opposition. Why no embarrassing documentaries on television, no investigative journalists sniffing around? Mr Mitchell has somehow become a non-event. Why?' He suddenly picked up a phone and buzzed somebody in the outer office. 'Sarah? Oh, Lucy, sorry, do me a favour. Get hold of the Yellow Pages, look up D for Dentists and pick one, any one, within half a mile of here. Tell them it's an emergency and get me an appointment. Now, soon as possible. Ring me back when you've fixed it.'

Lloyd said: 'It's certainly odd.'

'Odd it certainly is, my dear Watson. Didn't Holmes suffer from toothache?'

'He played the violin and took opium, that's all I remember.'

'I'm beginning to detect the whiff of corruption in high places. What makes me think that?' Lloyd was silent. 'Ask me.'

'What makes you think that?'

175

'Pain has a way of concentrating the mind, and I was up all night with this bloody tooth. If – and notice I stress the word *if* – Moscow planted him, why did they use somebody handling their own traffic? Doesn't add up – not much mileage in stealing from yourself, is there? *Unless* you need to know how that material is being interpreted at this end. Perhaps the whole exercise was to feed *dis*information. How does that strike you?'

'Plausible.'

'But not watertight. If that had been the case, then all he had to do was decode it and pass it over. No need to smuggle anything out. He could go home at night, feed the dog, put on his bra and panties with nobody the wiser. But that isn't what he did. He took elaborate precautions to conceal his true persona. It was only by chance that man's best friend led him to us. So that must lead us to the conclusion that he was also feeding the same information to somebody else, presumably somebody who didn't normally have access to it, *or didn't want to reveal that he had access to it.* Subtle difference. And if you take it one step further, take it to a logical end, Mitchell's secret task was to translate coded phoney information but give his unknown contact the real gen.'

'You should have toothache more often,' Lloyd said, impressed.

Pearson massaged his reddened cheek with the back of his hand. 'Oh, I'm not there yet. But I've got a gut instinct I'm on the right track. And I act on the principle never trust anybody.'

'Not even me?' Lloyd sounded hurt.

'Never trust anybody who has the power to alter your life. You shouldn't trust me blindly.'

Lloyd was bewildered now. 'How d'you mean?'

'Because we've never been put to the test. Would I save you in a burning building, or would I save myself? We don't know, do we? I'm kidding. I'd probably throw you a fire-extinguisher. What I'm really saying is the human mind is capable of being bent every which way, so never take anything for granted. Give you an example of how the criminal mind

176

really works. Way back when I was in the CID we were after a forger. He was passing brilliant ten-pound notes – the old large variety, you wouldn't have seen any, before your time. The genuine articles were beautifully engraved on top-quality paper, real works of art, not the Monopoly money we handle these days. The counterfeits were works of art, too, needed a real expert to detect them. They kept turning up for about two years, always in the same area, one at a time. We finally nabbed him, by chance. His house caught fire and we found all the gear. Know what? He was a master engraver in his own right, and it turned out it took him a week to forge a single tenner. If he'd been legit and followed his trade, he could have made fifty quid a week, but instead he made just ten. That's the criminal mind.'

'Yeah, fascinating,' Lloyd said, 'but what's that got to do with trusting you? You've worried me now. I thought we were talking about Mitchell.'

'We are, we are! But all we've done so far is skim the surface. We know a bit more about him than when he first landed on Hogg's table, but we don't know what made him tick. Or who he was ticking for.' He broke off and clapped a hand to his cheek. 'Christ! This sodding tooth.' He turned away from Lloyd until the pain streaking towards his eye subsided. 'Terrorism isn't just bombs, Lloyd old son. Not just blowing innocents to pieces, or opening their skulls with a sniper's dum-dum bullet. There's another variety, perhaps the worst kind, whereby you don't kill them outright, you kill them slowly, take away their power to think and act for themselves. Ever been behind the Iron Curtain? I have. Of course that's not a term used much these days. Not fashionable. We have to go along with the pretence that things are getting better in Warsaw, Prague, Hungary. We're meant to forget things like the Gulag. It's give-them-the-benefit-of-the-doubt time. Just like there was once a fan club for Mussolini because he made the trains run. And it's all bollocks, a bit of mind-bending.'

'You've never come out with that before.'

'Haven't I? Well, maybe I'm getting more bloody-minded

177

and reactionary in my old age. You think it couldn't happen here? It already has. Because we British are so slow on the uptake. Both of our glorious political parties have been playing dirty for years. Turn up any carpet in Whitehall and you'll find hidden Tory dirt, hidden Labour dirt mixed together. Indistinguishable.'

The phone rang at that moment. Pearson picked it up. 'Good girl. Remind me to climb through your bedroom window with a box of Milk Tray one of these nights. Give me his name and address.' He wrote the details on a pad, tore off the page and replaced the receiver.

'I've got an appointment round the corner in ten minutes' time. Walk with me.'

They left the office together, but Pearson remained silent until they were out in the street.

'Who do I think killed Mitchell? My guess is somebody on our side arranged it, some dirty tricks operation, hence the deathly silence. I can smell it.'

'When you say "somebody on our side" who are you thinking of?'

'Could be any one of ten outfits. There are wheels within wheels within wheels in the espionage game. What was it that joker wrote?'

'Which joker?'

'That old-age pensioner who lives in Tasmania and wrote his memoirs. He admitted that in his day they burgled and bugged their way across London. He should have added "buggered" for some of them.'

'But casual bugging was made illegal. The Secretary of State has to give his authority now.'

Pearson gave him a pitying look. 'Providing the Secretary isn't looking to get even with somebody who's crossed him. Going back to Mitchell, quite a few people would be interested in a cipher clerk at GCHQ handling Russia traffic while he was alive. What we have to find out is who wanted him dead. What secret died with him? So, in the interests of pushing things along faster, I'm inclined to think we should start looking for another mole burrowed in high places. Dirty

178

opponents require dirty tactics. Time we committed a few professional fouls ourselves.'

He glanced at the address on the piece of paper as they turned the corner. 'I have a conspiracy theory for most things that happen to and around us. I believe in Manchurian candidates.'

They arrived outside the dentist's surgery. Pearson studied the name-plate by the door. 'I want Dr Amid. Yes, here we are.'

'Sure you don't want me to come in and hold your hand?'

'I'm past cowardice. I'll see you back at the office. Mull it over and pick holes in it.'

Pearson went inside. The receptionist showed him into the waiting-room where the only other occupants were a woman and a small boy fighting back tears. Pearson smiled sympathetically, but got no response from the child.

'This lady has very kindly said you can go ahead of her son. Dr Amid will be ready in a minute.'

'Thank you.'

'Are you having your treatment done on the National Health?'

'I can never remember my number; but don't worry, I'll pay cash. Right now, the way I feel, I might make over the deeds of my house.'

Pearson sat down opposite the small boy and winked encouragement, again drawing no response. 'Very kind of you to let me go first. And don't worry: dentists don't hurt these days.' Tears formed in the boy's eyes as he looked away.

A moment later Pearson was called into the surgery. He sat in the chair, rinsed his mouth, and leant back. Dr Amid was a slight man of indeterminate age, assisted by a young Asian nurse.

'Now, then, Mr Pearson, isn't it? What seems to be the trouble, sir?'

'I would like you to take a gun and remove this tooth.'

'Oh, we don't go in for such drastic measures. Let us have a look.'

Dr Amid probed around the sensitive area. Pearson bore

179

the examination with fortitude. 'Yes, yes. Well, Mr Pearson, we don't seem to have taken great care with our teeth, do we? It is a shocking sight, your mouth. How long since you last paid a visit to a dentist?'

'My work keeps me very busy.'

'Not a good excuse, sir, if you don't mind me saying. But I think we can do something. This is painful, yes?'

'Yes.'

Dr Amid spoke softly to the nurse, and she prepared an injection.

'What is your work, sir?'

'I'm a security officer.'

'A valuable contribution, I am sure, to our troubled society, but you should be more secure about your teeth. This won't hurt; you will just feel a little sting.'

He gave the injection expertly. 'Now, what I am doing is to remove the old filling and see what is under. It might be that what we find is not happiness. It might mean that I must ask you to come again and I will have to perform a root canal. This is a dying tooth, oh yes. We must work quickly.'

He had the high-speed drill in his hand and once the injection had taken hold he commenced the exploratory work. Pearson braced himself for pain that never arrived. He gradually relaxed his grip on the arms of the chair; and it was then, while Dr Amid worked with delicate skill, that his thoughts returned to Mitchell. If he was right, he would need to extract the truth with the same delicate touch, working perilously close to the nerve ends of the corrupt world it was his duty to protect.

Corruption was second nature to General Geichenko: throughout his early life he had been conditioned to find it in every aspect of human behaviour, and without it the system would have collapsed. Now he was in a position to root it out and get even. He never missed an opportunity to pay off old scores, reserving his special energies for acts of revenge against the KGB. Just as the German High Command had always despised the SS, so Geichenko, as an army man, nurtured a hatred of his father's executioners. Nothing gave him greater pleasure than to sabotage their efforts in the operational field. That was why he derived such satisfaction from the way in which their British plan, once their brightest achievement, was now floundering.

'The arrogant bastards can't make it out,' he boasted to Abramov, whom he treated as a confidant. 'They thought they had it made there. All sewn up. Very soon, if they don't get results, heads will begin to roll. We are going to see a few exiles leaving Moscow.'

In appearance he was not unlike that fine Austrian actor Oscar Homolka who always portrayed Russians in Hollywood spy dramas, but he had none of Homolka's natural charm. Some men emerge from long years of deprivation and the constant nearness of death with their character changed; some achieve a kind of saintliness; others stumble from the darkness with their sense of reality forever distorted; others still are mad with much heart. Some, like Geichenko, remain sane and survive on the adrenalin of hatred, spending the rest of their scarred and truncated lives hunting down those they consider responsible.

Abramov knew some of this, but was astute enough never to probe his superior. The General did not welcome enquiries about his past; nor, unless roaring drunk, did he ever volunteer such information, though Abramov retained scant recollection of such occasions for the simple reason that he had usually passed out, being no match for the General's capacity to absorb alcohol.

By skilful manoeuvring Geichenko had brought Hillsden within GRU control, knowing full well that those in Moscow Centre responsible for running London would suffer as a result. The Centre had always considered London their exclusive territory and felt that Hillsden's past connection with the woman Caroline Oates gave them a prior claim to him. Geichenko had proved them wrong. Likewise he was entirely satisfied with his protégé's handling of the final episode in the Hillsden affair. Abramov had displayed a positively Machiavellian skill in the way he had disposed of the man

181

known as 'Jock' Calder. Geichenko could not have done better himself, which was the highest praise he could bestow. To have convinced Hillsden that he would be justified in killing Calder was a masterstroke. And the beauty of it was, should at some later date questions be asked, the department would be in the clear: the liability of Calder removed, Hillsden bound for ever by guilt and their own hands spotless.

Now, and again due to Abramov's skills, they were poised to bring off an even bigger coup.

It took Waddington the best part of a week to decide on his next move. Since the episode in Harrods, he had taken certain basic precautions: varying his normal routine by leaving the car in the garage and travelling to work by train; at lunchtimes making a point of joining some of the other salesmen (previously he had avoided social contacts); on two occasions, instead of returning home, checking into cheap commercial hotels. When in his own house he slept in the spare bedroom, the entry to which he booby-trapped. Renewing an old underworld connection, he obtained a gun which he kept loaded by his bed. On the pretext that his nonexistent wife was receiving obscene phone calls he had his telephone number changed. Now, as far as he knew, only the Breakproof switchboard had the new one, which narrowed the field. He felt he was in harness again as he began to shape more subtle plans. Calling on a favour still owed from his time in the Firm, he contacted a friend, Commander Pearson, and had Frampton checked out: the word came back swiftly – no previous form, nothing known.

His bookseller duly produced a copy of *The Aspern Papers*, and he reread it, confirming that the plot concerned a missing manuscript, and gradually the scrambled clues in Frampton's note began to assume a shape. He tried them in a different order. If *Lenin* equalled Russia equalled the location, and the James novel established the existence of a manuscript, then the next word, *imperative*, could either denote urgency or be linked to the final clue, *no contact wine*. Was it 'imperative do not contact wine'? The inclusion of *wine* stymied him for a long time, though later he reviled himself for being so dim. He woke one morning after a long wounding dream about the old days, and the possible answer was miraculously there. He could not believe his own stupidity. When he and Alec had been together, their cover had been a bogus wine company. It was only now that the possible truth entered his consciousness. More than anything else it was the literary association that convinced him he was on the right track. It would be typical of Alec to have included the Henry James gambit.

In all probability the four clues had merely been set down to remind Frampton what he had been charged to deliver in more detail. Taking it step by step: (*a*) Alec was in Lenin's homeland; (*b*) there was a manuscript in existence; and (*c*) it was *imperative that nobody in the Firm be contacted*. Well, I'm no longer in the Firm, Waddington thought, and I'm certainly not about to contact anybody there. How and why the as yet unknown Frampton had been chosen as the messenger boy remained to be discovered. Somehow, despite the risks (and it was obvious from what had taken place in Harrods that risks were present) Frampton had to be tracked down and made to give the full story. Waddington considered the options, then made a decision.

He rang Pamela.

'I want to apologize for my previous crass behaviour. Either I'm going through the male menopause, or else I'm deficient in vitamin E, but I really feel very badly about the other night.'

'Apology accepted.' Her voice still had a chill in it.

'Can I make belated amends and give you dinner? I promise I'll only eat humble pie. How are you fixed this week?'

'I might have an evening free.'

'How about Friday?'

'Let me check.' It was fully three minutes before she returned to the phone and it was obvious that she was extracting her full pound of flesh.

'That seems OK,' she said without undue enthusiasm. 'I'm coming up to town on Friday to have my hair done.'

'Friday it is, then. Where would you like me to pick you up?'

'Why don't you meet me in the Ritz bar at around seven-thirty?'

'The Ritz at seven-thirty. Terrific. You'll recognize me again,' Waddington said, trying to thaw her. 'I'll be the one wearing sackcloth and ashes.'

He had taken the first calculated risk. Despite his previous misgivings about becoming involved with somebody of Pamela's undoubted wealth, weighing the alternatives he had convinced himself that her set-up in the country gave him a greater degree of day-to-day security. Always assuming that she allowed him to move in and become involved. That crack about vitamin E wasn't too far from the truth, he thought. He had the feeling that Pamela was out of his league, sexually as well as financially. Brush up on your charm, he told himself as he mapped out the next moves.

On the Friday evening he made sure he arrived at the Ritz ahead of time, ordered a Perrier and lime and had a bottle of Montrachet put on ice. Pamela proved reasonably punctual for a woman entitled to score Brownie points. Rising to greet her, Waddington had to admit that she had more to offer than a secure haven of rest. Recalling the body beneath the smooth lines of her expensive silk dress, he wondered why he had ever hesitated.

'I like the old Ritz,' she said as a waiter greeted her as a familiar. 'It's never lowered its standards, unlike some places. As a matter of fact I lost my virginity within these gilded walls.'

Well, we're off to a good start, Waddington thought, raising his glass to her.

'Is that something you want to elaborate on?'

'Not really. It was a friend of my father's. I suppose I made the running; I was bored not knowing what one had to expect and thought I'd get it over with with somebody who knew the ropes. He didn't as a matter of fact; the whole thing was a disaster.' She surveyed the bar while she talked, never looking straight at him, giving the impression that if something better

184

came into her eye-line she might dump him. 'Where are you taking me to eat?'

'I've made a booking at a little place I like called Veronica's near Notting Hill Gate.'

'Good food?'

'I think so. Sort of superior French bistro, and very intimate.'

'Is "intimate" going to be the operative word?'

'The choice is yours,' Waddington said, playing her game, but feeling foolish as he did so. It was a long time since he had seriously set out to charm. I sound like Caesar Romero in a late-night movie, he thought. One half of his mind was concentrated on the real reason for dating Pamela, the other was wondering how good she would be in bed. Some outwardly sexy women proved a disappointment, only too content to let the man lavish his attentions on a statue.

'So that's the name of the game tonight, is it?' she said. 'An intimate dinner, followed by what – jolly romps in the jacuzzi?'

'Again, up to you. I'm here to be forgiven or rejected. Either way I'll try to give you a pleasant evening.'

'I'm not often put down like that.'

'I can believe it.'

'Nor do I go in for one-night stands.'

'Not my style, either.'

'So, if we're going to start over again, it's as well to know the house rules.'

'My feelings exactly. There is one thing in my favour,' Waddington grinned since the atmosphere was now less tense. 'I may not be able to keep you in caviare, but I'll make sure the security system works.'

They had a second glass of wine before leaving for the restaurant. Waddington was about to ask for a taxi when the doorman handed him the keys to a Jaguar XJS V12 parked on a double yellow line outside the entrance.

'That's why I always choose here to meet people,' Pamela said as they headed down Piccadilly towards Hyde Park

185

Corner. 'They always take care of me. I think if I ever got clamped I would just lie down in the gutter and die.'

The smell of new leather combined with her perfume had an erotic effect on Waddington; he was beginning to relax and enjoy himself. Once out of the park and finding a clear stretch of the Bayswater Road, he put his foot down.

'Ever driven one of these before?'

'Sadly no.'

'Perhaps you should start getting used to it,' she said enigmatically.

To his relief she immediately warmed to the atmosphere at Veronica's. As usual, apart from their own reserved table, the small restaurant was full; it was one of those places that commanded a faithful clientele.

It wasn't until halfway through the meal that Waddington angled the conversation away from the mundane to the particular.

'You mentioned house rules earlier. Are there a whole bunch of them?'

She shook her head. 'No lifelong vows, no cheating while it lasts, and no smoking in the bedroom. I pay all the household bills, which I'd do anyway, so that shouldn't make you feel like a pimp, and you spend as much of your hard-earned money as you please bringing me flowers. How does that sound?'

'OK. Assuming you don't change your mind by the end of dinner, let me ask you one thing. Why me?'

'Oh, come on, let's not be too modest.'

'I'm serious. Girls like you haven't crossed my path too often, and certainly not for a long time.'

'Let's just say I've had it with rich men.'

'Does that mean you want to try slumming?'

'God! What did your ex do to you?'

'I guess she didn't exactly do much to boost my confidence, and you have to believe I've never had a very good line in chat.'

'I intimidate you?'

'I wouldn't put it quite as strong as that, but you certainly take . . . took . . . me by surprise.'

186

'Well, that adds to the excitement, doesn't it? Maybe *you'll* surprise *me*. Would you rather I came straight out with it and talked like a character in one of those raunchy novels? I can if you want – anything that turns you on. Most of them are written by women these days, wouldn't you know?'

The dialogue was interrupted by the proprietor enquiring whether they'd enjoyed their meal.

'Couldn't be bettered,' Waddington said.

'Would you like to see the desserts?'

'Just coffee,' Pamela said. 'Black, please.'

'How about you, sir?'

'The same, thank you.'

When Veronica was out of earshot Waddington said: 'Does coffee keep you awake?'

'I hope so.'

The die was cast now, and it was curious to think that if all his conjectures were correct it was Alec who, indirectly, had provided the fillip to get him into Pamela's bed. Was it fortuitous, was it kismet, that so many new elements had entered his life at roughly the same time, and all of them seeming to have connections with the Firm? First the lunch with Keating, then Frampton's message and, swimming tantalizingly in the middle, the slightly alarming Pamela. There were still questions to be answered, his own safety to take care of and problems to be solved, but for the moment the one uppermost in his thoughts was sitting opposite him.

'It's not you,' Hillsden said. 'Please don't think that. I'm just going through a bad patch. Never happened before.'

Although common sense dictated it was stupid to expect an early response to the message entrusted to Frampton, he had become increasingly uneasy, and his disquiet carried over into the relationship with Galina. He found himself impotent for the first time in his life.

'Then, it must be me.'

'No, I promise. I couldn't wish for anybody more attractive.'

'Except . . .'

Humiliation made him reply more sharply than he intended.

187

'I've told you, it's not you. Just be patient with me. It'll pass.'

'I don't mind.'

'But *I* mind.'

'What I meant was, it isn't the end of the world. Why do you attach so much importance to it?'

'Because it's insulting to you.'

'Only if I take it that way, and I don't.'

'No. Well, you're very special.'

'Tell me what's worrying you. Perhaps I can help.'

Hillsden stroked her bare back, tracing a pattern to the base of her spine. 'Probably just a wave of remorse for a misspent life.'

He swung his legs over the side of the bed. How could he confess the real reasons? Already, even at this early stage, the spirochaete of deceit had burrowed into their affair, following the old pattern. And it was all his own doing. In recent weeks he had alternated between states of moroseness and irritability – moods that reminded him of those times in his life when he had attempted to give up smoking.

'I know how difficult it must be for you,' Galina said. 'Don't think I don't.'

'Do you? How d'you know that?'

'Because. Why don't you talk more about it? Don't you trust me? I love you.'

He looked at her open guileless face; it was like receiving a declaration of love from a stranger. 'I've got out of the habit of trusting people.'

'That's not very kind.'

'No, and I didn't mean to say it like that.' He kissed her. 'Am I worth the effort to love?'

'I think so.'

'Why can't the whole business of living be simpler? I wish I had a belief in something. I know a man . . .' He stopped and corrected himself, suddenly recalling that Belfrage was dead, murdered. 'I knew a man in England who asked me just that. "What d'you believe in?" he said. And I remember how I answered. I said I believed in evil, good old-fashioned evil.'

188

Galina stared back at him.

'That isn't much to write home about, is it, after over fifty years?'

'I don't think you mean it.'

'Well, I dare say it's difficult for you to understand.' Not for the first time he had to stifle a desperate need to confide in her, to lay himself bare, destroy her innocence. He wished he had an old diary that he could point to and say: 'That was the day when I committed my first betrayal. That's when peace of mind ended.' But there was no one date to point to: deceit covered a lifetime, fogging the day-to-day incidentals. He had drifted into betrayal, just as some men drift into adultery or alcoholism. It had been just a way of earning a living in the beginning, not unlike being in a bank, taking home a regular salary, routine stuff, a means of paying off the mortgage. One did not sit any exams for a career in MI6; indeed, it was with the benefit of hindsight that he still stood amazed how casually his recruitment had come about. He remembered his first meeting with his past boss, old Dinnsbury – owl-faced, short-sighted Dinnsbury, who had brought to mind memories of a childhood literary hero, Billy Bunter. The way in which that initial interview had been conducted was not unlike a vicar asking a prospective bridegroom whether he had the right mental attitude towards holy matrimony. So oblique had it been that for the most part he had little inkling of what Dinnsbury was talking about. It gradually became apparent that he was being asked to join a club, the rules and workings of which had never been set down on paper, the membership of which would remain largely unknown. How could one explain such a beginning to any outsider? Would any innocent such as Galina readily accept that you could live in the closest married intimacy, share the same toilet and bed year in and year out, and yet remain a stranger? Women could sometimes excuse and forgive physical betrayal, but what salve could they use to heal the wounds brought about by an unknown adversary? Spying left no tell-tale lipstick-smears on the adulterous face across the breakfast-table.

189

'Is the reason you don't confide in me you're still not sure I wouldn't betray you?' Galina said.

Hillsden shook his head. 'There's nothing left to betray.' Lying to her yet again. 'I'm safe now,' he said, as though one could ever be safe in the world he inhabited.

'Why the sudden change of heart?' Control asked.

'I've no idea, unless of course he found my charms irresistible. There's always that vague possibility,' Pamela replied with just a hint of resentment.

'My dear girl, that goes without saying. Well, I'm delighted; it makes our task that much easier.'

'You mean *my* task, don't you, since I'm the one sleeping with him?'

'Don't pick me up on words. I have a lot on my plate at the moment. These are trying times. One of your earlier conquests is not proving as pliable as I had hoped. Plus other matters.'

'Such as?'

'Nothing you can help with.'

He prevented her pressing him further by abruptly reverting to the original subject. 'Do you think one of the reasons why he decided to move in was because he discovered his phone was bugged? He spotted it and changed his number, you know.'

'No, he's never mentioned it, and it's hardly something I'd ask him.'

'All calls from your house are being monitored, naturally. He was a smart operator. Don't underestimate him.'

'Perhaps he still is. You've never fully explained why you got rid of him,' Pamela said.

'Surely it's obvious. He and Hillsden were very close, too close for comfort, and he was never convinced about Hillsden's sudden defection. For a time, until I blocked it, he tried to follow the trail. We know he contacted Hillsden's wife. The main reason I sicked you on to him was I want to be doubly sure he isn't still nosing around.'

'You have such a charming way of putting things.'

'Don't be so touchy, my dear; it's just an expression.'

190

Control walked to the shuttered and curtained window as though listening for something. He's uneasy tonight, it's out of character, Pamela thought.

'There is another reason why I wanted to see you,' he said finally. 'I may have to ask you to take a trip abroad.'

'Where?'

'At the moment it looks like Prague. I'm awaiting confirmation.'

'Why Prague?'

'To meet somebody.'

'Who?'

'It's better you don't know in advance. But when I've finalized the arrangements you'll be contacted on arrival and be given certain verbal instructions to bring back to me. I can't use the regular channel. Make sure you go a roundabout route, not direct – Paris never arouses suspicion where women are concerned, does it?'

'Doesn't it?'

'Don't women like you go there to buy the latest fashions, frocks and the like? Why are you smiling?'

'I never knew you were such a student of feminine wiles. But, if you don't mind me correcting you, nobody talks about "frocks" these days; that's practically Victorian.'

Control's mouth tightened; he did not like to be caught out on details. 'Well, I'm sure you can concoct some plausible story for your new boy-friend, using the right terminology.'

'Question: Why send me now? I thought my current assignment was urgent.'

There was a slight pause, then Control said: 'Because you're one of the few people I can rely on absolutely.'

It was the first time he had ever allowed her to see his scheme of things had cracks in it. He suddenly seemed normal. Men who played with toy soldiers, like those who kept tattered teddy bears on their beds, had always made her uneasy.

A week later she had cause to respect the way he worked. Her morning post contained an invitation to attend the Yves Saint Laurent collection in Paris the following Tuesday,

191

together with a slip confirming a reservation for a suite at the George V.

'Darling,' she said to Waddington over breakfast in bed, 'do you think you can live without me for a few days?'

'If forced to. Why?'

'Well, not that you'd understand, but I can't pass this up.' She waved the invitation in front of his bleary eyes. 'These are gold dust, like front-row seats for the finals at Wimbledon.'

Waddington peered at the embossed card. 'Wonderful.'

'Can you read it? I know you can't focus in the mornings.'

'Yes, it's an invitation to spend a lot of money on something you don't need.'

'One has to keep up with fashion. Skirts are going to be much higher next season.'

'Ah, I'm all for that.'

'Will you miss me?'

'As an egg would miss its shell – I shall fall apart.'

'No, seriously.'

'Seriously, I shall miss you, but bear the loss with fortitude. No, I'll be fine. I have a lot on in the next week.'

'Just tell Maria what you want to eat every day and she'll fix it.'

'Leave a phrase-book, then, because I can't understand a word she says.'

'And use the Jaguar. I've had it insured for you to drive.'

'God! Greater love hath no woman in that she laid down her Jaguar.'

While shaving that morning with the gold-plated razor Pamela had given to him, Waddington began to think how he could now advance his own plans: during Pamela's absence in Paris he would move to track down Frampton. He had been waiting for just such an opportunity. Even so, he had not been idle, but had already carefully pinpointed Frampton's address on the map, and examined a variety of routes before deciding which one he would take.

On the day Pamela departed he kept to his normal schedule, driving to the railway station and parking in the station car park. On his return that evening he telephoned Pamela at the

George V and told her he thought he was coming down with flu and would be taking a couple of stiff whiskies and aspirin.

'Not only to stave off the cold but also to make sure I get a good night's sleep without you, darling. Otherwise I shall be rattling around in our enormous bed.'

'It's nice to be missed,' she said. 'Take care of yourself and sleep late. Can you take the day off from work?'

'What a good idea.'

He had dinner and before retiring told Maria that he was not to be disturbed in the morning. Once in the bedroom he did not undress, but instead watched television. When the late news finished he waited another hour, then switched off the newly installed burglar alarm and let himself out through the kitchen. In addition to the Jaguar, Pamela also possessed a small Fiat Uno, and this was the vehicle he had elected to use. He drove on the orbital M25 motorway, leaving it at Waltham Abbey on the north-east outskirts of London. There he checked into a small motel, paying cash in advance for his room and putting in a wake-up call.

The following morning he was on the road again before seven, dodging most of the commuter traffic by taking a back route through Epping Forest until he reached Wanstead. From there he had everything committed to memory.

Cranmer Road, the destination he sought, had been named after one of the martyred bishops burnt at the stake during the reign of Bloody Mary. The roads that ran parallel to it were likewise terraced memorials to the victims of that past religious persecution: Latimer, Lorne, Tilney, Ridley. They all opened at the north end on to the scrub wasteland of Wanstead Flats, an expanse of grass, neither park nor pasture, dotted with a few sparse plantations of dying trees. In prewar days there had been a bandstand where on Sundays brass bands played to genteel audiences sitting in hired deck-chairs; there had also been a pond on which paddle-boats plied. Generations of small boys had played cricket and football there, and it had also served as a trysting-place for desperate precursors of the permissive age for, after dark, the plantations had provided cold sanctuary. The Flats had

193

seen violence, too, during the thirties, when Sir Oswald Mosley marched his blackshirted legions through the East End to confront the Jewish community. Pitched battles had taken place, only broken up by charges from mounted police armed with long staves who bloodied anybody in their path.

These days the thin grass was trampled by different feet. A second generation of postwar immigrants now claimed it as their own; turbaned Sikhs played hockey, and sad veiled women, far from home and sunshine, took solitary walks over the urban desert of the gravel dunes.

As Waddington drove round the perimeter of the Flats he saw a detachment of the Workers' Militia drilling. They had cropped heads and wore paramilitary uniforms. This glimpse of an Orwellian scenario contrasted sharply with the orderly row of terraced houses as he reached Ridley Road where some residences abutted the walls of a cemetery harbouring the crumbling mausoleums of Victorian aldermen. He selected a local pub, noted the name and location, then parked his car close to a sub-post office where he felt he could be reasonably sure to find a set of telephone directories and an unvandalized public phone.

He was in luck. There was only a single Frampton listed, and the address tallied with the one he had memorized. The telephone was an up-to-date model requiring a plastic phonecard to operate it rather than coins. He purchased one and inserted it.

Again his luck was in: Frampton answered after a couple of rings.

'Mr Frampton?'

'Yes?'

'I'm a *Country Life* reader who frequents Harrods. I'm close by and I think it would be useful if you and I met.'

Waddington heard the sound of a man's voice shouting in the background.

'Nothing, Father,' he heard Frampton say. 'It's a call for me.' He spoke softly into the receiver: 'I can't see you now.'

194

'You have to. I know where you live, and if you don't agree to meet me I'll come calling at your house.'

'No, please,' Frampton whispered. 'Don't do that. I can't see you today; I was just about to leave for work.'

'You just got sick, didn't you? Too sick to go to work today. You can think of some excuse. I shall wait for you in the saloon bar of the George at opening-time. If you don't turn up, expect a visit. Understood? Just be there if you know what's good for you.' He hung up before Frampton could make any further protest.

Needing to kill time until the pub opened, he returned to his car and drove to Cranmer Road. There were signs of urban decay: in the front garden of one house a rusting motorbike with both wheels missing propped against a bow window; moth-eaten privet hedges, graffiti on a blank wall, plastic garbage-bags spilling their contents on to the pavement. He slowed down as he approached Frampton's house. A National Front poster was pasted inside the downstairs front window; the paintwork was in better condition than its immediate neighbour, and the garden was tidier, but otherwise it was indistinguishable from the others in the row. He noticed a metal sign attached to the gate which read NO HAWKERS, NO CIRCULARS. Driving on, he found the sad high street which, like so many others, was devoid of any individual character, just a series of garish shop-fronts plastered with sale notices; a plethora of junk-food establishments, and uninviting ethnic restaurants, cut-price chemists and betting shops.

He drove on, depressed, until he found a sandwich bar where he could get a snack and what passed in England for a cup of coffee, served in a plastic cup too hot to hold.

He arrived at the George ten minutes before the doors opened, and positioned himself in the car park so that he had a good view of the entrance. It was another twenty minutes before Frampton appeared and entered the saloon bar.

He found Frampton sitting in one of the booths. Now that Waddington had a closer look at him, he saw it was a face

195

that had fear etched into it as surely as coal dust impregnates a miner's features. A noisy darts match was already in progress; this and the deafening sounds of a juke-box and a pin-ball machine ensured that their conversation could not be overheard.

'I'm glad you decided to show up. Can I get you a drink?'

'I don't want a drink. I'm not stopping.'

'You'll go when I let you go. Have a drink; it will calm you. What's your tipple – beer or something stronger?'

'A small whisky, then,' Frampton said, sinking back defeated on the ripped-leather seat of the booth.

'Good. That's better.'

As Waddington returned from the bar with their drinks, one of the darts hit the wire and flew off the board, landing close to their table. Frampton jumped, spilling some of his whisky.

'My, my, we *are* jumpy.' Waddington retrieved the dart and handed it back to the player. 'What are we nervous about?'

'I don't want to be involved in this.'

'It's a bit late to say that.'

'Who are you?'

'I'm the one you phoned. Why else would I be here?'

'Who were those other two men in Harrods?'

'Your guess is as good as mine. Not friends of either of us, that's for sure. But let's not worry about them for the moment. Give me the message you were to deliver.'

'I do worry about them. Can't you understand? I don't want to be involved.'

Waddington ignored the plea. 'First of all, who gave you the message?'

'How do I know you're not the police? You could be a blackmailer for all I know.'

'Let's just say I'm another sort of policeman, one who doesn't have to account for his actions. And don't raise your voice. Just keep calm. Take it step by step. You met somebody abroad. Where?'

'I was just on holiday.'

196

'Where?'

'Leningrad.'

How dim of me, Waddington thought. Of course *Lenin* in the message had been used as an abbreviation. 'Good. And you met somebody?'

Frampton nodded. He could hardly hold his whisky glass.

'Who did you meet?'

'A stranger.'

'Did you get his name?'

'All I had to do was contact you and give you a message from him. He promised I would be left alone after that. He made a definite promise.'

'Well, I can't be responsible for other people's promises. Who was he – a Russian?'

Frampton shook his head.

'Who, then? Come on, let's get this over quickly.'

'I've never been in trouble before.'

'What makes you think you're in trouble now?'

'Those men. They scared me. Why were they there?'

'That's a mystery I haven't solved yet,' Waddington said, easing the pressure now, using the gentler voice of the experienced interrogator. 'I'm the only one you have to worry about. I'm on your side if you tell me the truth. I'm here to protect you.'

'Protect me from whom?'

'Other interested parties. But so far I'm the only one who could have traced you. Just get to the point, give me the message and tell me who sent it.'

Frampton put his glass down and gripped the edge of the beer-stained table. He leant closer to Waddington as the darts game reached a climax.

'Will I be left alone when I've told you?'

'I'll leave you alone. I can't vouch for anybody else.'

'And you swear you're not one of them?'

'Them?' Waddington said, and the irritation at the delays hardened his voice again.

Frampton's face was close to him as he whispered the word, and Waddington caught his bad breath. 'A spy.'

197

'No, I'm not. Let me make it easier for you. This stranger, did his name begin with "H"?'

Frampton nodded.

'Good. We're making progress at last. Now, what message did he give you for me?'

'That he had a manuscript he had to get to you, but he couldn't risk sending it by any normal route.'

'What sort of manuscript? Did you see it?'

'No. Something he'd written himself. He said it was for your eyes only because it told the truth and you'd know what use to make of it.'

'Is that all?'

'No. There was one other thing. He said to tell you everything was out of control.'

'Out of control?'

'Yes.'

'You're sure those were the exact words he used?'

'Yes, I swear.'

'And how was I to contact him? Did he give you an address?'

'Yes, but you were not to write to him.'

'Understood. Give it to me.'

'Flat Eighteen, Ninety-eight Ligovsky Prospect.'

'Ninety-eight Ligovsky.' Waddington committed it to memory. 'Leningrad, I take it?'

Frampton nodded and swallowed the remainder of his whisky.

'Well, that wasn't too painful, was it?' Waddington got to his feet. 'I meant what I said. As long as you don't tell any of that to another living soul, you won't be bothered by me any more.'

Some colour had come back to Frampton's cheeks, but whether it was caused by the whisky or by relief that the ordeal was over there was no means of telling.

'What about my friend?' Frampton asked.

Waddington had started to leave, and turned back, puzzled. 'Your friend?'

'Yes, will he be safe, too, now that I've kept my side of the bargain?'

Since Waddington had no idea what this referred to, he answered: 'Neither of you will be bothered as far as I'm concerned. Just forget you ever saw me.'

As he left the bar one of the darts players shouted, 'Go for a treble six, Mike, and you've got him!' as though most problems in life could be solved by one well-placed arrow in the dark.

13

On her second day in Paris, Pamela still waited for the
expected contact to be made. Then shortly after breakfast the
front desk informed her that an envelope had been delivered.
She had it brought up to her suite and did not open it until
she was alone. Inside was an unsigned typewritten note on a
plain sheet of paper. The note said:

> *Change of plan. Leave today for Marseille. A room is
> reserved for you at the Sofitel Vieux Port. Again wait there
> until contacted. Ring your lodger and say some old friends
> have invited you to drive down to the South with them for
> a few days.*

She burnt the note, flushing the ashes down the lavatory,
then asked the concierge to book her on the three o'clock Air
Inter. When this had been confirmed she rang Waddington,
but he had already gone to work. Rather than leave a message
at his office, she scribbled a contrite letter on hotel stationery,
using the names of some dead friends of her parents, to
explain the new arrangements, posting this Express Delivery
when she checked out. Before having an early lunch she took
the added precaution of going to the Yves St-Laurent salon
and making a purchase.

The Air Inter flight was short but alarmingly turbulent; she
was relieved to be on firm ground again smelling the distinctive
scent of Provence – that strange heady mixture of petrol,
ozone and the fragrance of flowers. Marseille was a city she
only knew from films. The hotel selected for her was well
situated, and from the windows of her penthouse suite she
had a bird's-eye view of the old port bristling with the masts
of yachts and fishing boats. There was no message waiting for

her so she took a shower and ordered a bottle of *blanc de blanc* from room service. It all seemed a far cry from Amersham, and she realized how much she had missed the adrenalin of the old days when she and Gunther had moved across the world leaving havoc in their wake. She had a sense of the past pressing in upon her.

It was dark before the call came: a message from the front desk to say that a car was waiting outside. As she walked through the crowded lobby she was again reminded of the past; it was at times like this, setting out towards the unknown, that she came alive.

The driver of the Citroën waiting for her had a vaguely Slavic appearance. He greeted her in French but made no reply to her enquiry about their destination. Had she been more familiar with her surroundings, she would have recognized that she was being taken a complicated route which eventually led them to the immigrant areas around the Porte d'Aix and the rue St-Barbe. The car pulled up outside a small shuttered *tabac*. The driver got out and opened the passenger-door for her, indicating an unlit alleyway to one side of the shop. She took a few steps towards it, then turned back to ask, in French, 'Will you wait for me?' but the car was already making a U-turn.

Walking slowly down the middle of the alley, she was convinced that she had been led into a trap and silently cursed her own stupidity. What had Gunther always told her? Never go anywhere without making sure you have an escape route. At any moment she expected to hear the sound, like a cushion being punched, of a silenced revolver. But it didn't come. She had only taken a few steps when a door in the wall on her left opened and a man's voice said in softly accented English: 'Please come in.'

It wasn't until the door closed behind her that a light was switched on and she saw the man for the first time. He was tall and good-looking and, unlike some tall men, made no attempt to reduce his height, but held himself with military bearing.

'I hope', the stranger said, 'that the sudden change of venue did not inconvenience you?'

201

'No. I do what I'm told.'

'Of course. Don't we all? We travel too far, too quickly and too often,' he added cryptically. Then: 'Excuse me, but I have to search you.'

She remained passive while he carried out a body search, clinically, with an expertise she recognized from her own past.

While his hands probed her body she took stock of her surroundings. She was in what appeared a storeroom; boxes of Gauloise and Badois were stacked against two of the walls.

'Thank you,' the man said when he finished the search.

'Do I get to do the same to you?'

He smiled thinly. 'I'll save you the trouble. I am armed. Come this way, please.' He led the way through another door to an all-purpose room she assumed was the living-quarters of whoever owned the shop. It was poorly furnished and divided up into three areas: kitchen, bedroom and shower. The air was stale, a sour combination of cigarette smoke and garlic.

'I apologize for the surroundings,' the man said. 'Take the best chair.'

There was only one overhead bare bulb to provide illumination, and as the man moved to offer her a battered armchair his head brushed against the bulb causing it to swing to and fro. His features seemed to come and go, now fully exposed, now half in shadow.

'Are we going to be introduced?' Pamela asked. 'You presumably know who I am. How about telling me who you are?'

The man smiled. 'You're quite right. I do know who you are.' He drew up a kitchen chair and sat opposite her at the table. Now that she got a better look at him, it seemed to Pamela he was too pale to be a native of Marseille. She found the glacial quality of his smile disconcerting.

'I know, for example,' the man continued, 'that you have recently been reactivated, and that you come with excellent credentials. So let's leave the question of who I am, and just say that we are both professionals working for the same end result. What we have to discuss tonight concerns your people

202

and mine. An unfortunate gap in communications has come about between those I work for and London. It is a situation we are here to rectify.'

As he spoke Pamela tried to place his accent.

'Certain decisions have been taken at a level far beyond your and my humble status.'

'I don't believe your status is humble,' Pamela interrupted. 'Nor does Control deal with juniors. That's why I'm here.'

'May I continue?' he said without change of expression. 'It is our job to make sure these decisions are set in motion. We are to co-ordinate the process of discrediting someone, doing it in such a way that the evidence we plant can never be traced back, and that it has irrevocable effect.'

'Who?'

'Somebody you once knew intimately, I believe.'

For some reason Pamela blurted: 'Hillsden?'

The man shook his head. 'Now, that's interesting. Why would you think it was him of all people?'

Flushing, embarrassed at her involuntary reaction, Pamela said: 'I don't know. Perhaps he's been in my mind in recent weeks.' That'll get back to Control, she thought, and what did he impress upon me? Forget Hillsden. Don't mention his name. I blurted that out like a novice.

'I must ask him if his ears have been burning,' the man said. 'I'm sure he'd be flattered . . . No, you're a long way off the mark. The person concerned is your current Prime Minister.' He paused to let this sink in. 'Does that surprise you?'

'Yes. Yes, it does. Everybody went to a lot of trouble to put him where he is. I thought he was – '

'Firmly in place? Oh, we would all do well to remember that nobody is secure when the stakes are that high. He hasn't been keeping his side of the bargain, and we can't afford to wait for ever. The cloak of *glasnost* is just that – a chance for us to catch up lost ground. Diplomatically, certain cosmetic advances have been made, but there is no military version of *glasnost*. We still have to continue the invisible war, the only important war.'

203

Pamela nodded, only now recovering from the double shock of her own mistake and the revelation that Bayldon was the target.

'And the reason you are here to take back the first stage of the scenario we have devised is that a vital link in the chain between Moscow and London was recently broken when Mitchell was eliminated.'

She looked blank. 'Mitchell?'

'Ah! Well, if that means nothing to you, don't worry about it. My mistake for assuming you know more than you do. I'm sure Control had a reason for withholding his identity from you. I would prefer you not to repeat my reference to him.'

Pamela felt they were even now: his mention of this Mitchell cancelled out her gaffe about Hillsden.

'Because of Bayldon's position we have to be exceedingly clever. Since we are not dealing with small fry, we have to fox him into a corner from which there is no escape.'

'You mean *box* him in, I think,' Pamela said.

'Do I? Thank you. We must discredit him not only in the eyes of his party, but also in the eyes of the great British public. It needs a great deal of ingenuity, since we'll only have one chance.'

'A Watergate operation?'

'Something like that. Except in this case it won't be by his own hand like Nixon, though it has been decided to use the Americans in the first instance. As you know they have such an absurd mania for revealing all.'

'Isn't that true of your country now? Aren't you all for truth now?'

'And what is my country?'

Pamela suddenly flared. 'Look, if you want to play games, fine. I know you're Russian, otherwise I wouldn't have been sent here. You said you were going to treat me as an equal. So don't insult me, and don't feel you have to charm me. We're both here to do a job of work.'

'Good. Very good. You have spirit.'

'And don't patronize me, either.'

'My apologies. May I continue? The initial rumours will be

204

leaked at the United Nations. We'll let others do most of our work for us, so that our hands stay clean. Such a useful organization, the United Nations, for disseminating lies; there's nothing our friends in the Third World like better than a chance to besmirch the hands that feed them.' Again the smile without warmth. 'Such a corrupt society, America, and yet so obvious about it. One must protect corruption more carefully than innocence.' He broke off. 'They were supposed to leave some liquid refreshment for us. Can you see any?'

They both looked around. 'Perhaps in the kitchen,' Pamela said.

The man got up to search and produced an opened bottle of *vin ordinaire*. 'This seems to be it.' He rinsed two coffee-bowls under the cold tap and poured the wine. 'I'm sure we're both used to better, but cheers. Did I say that with the correct British intonation?'

'Perfect,' Pamela said. 'If you ever get to England, you should apply for an Equity ticket.' They both drank. The man grimaced and smacked his lips.

'Where did you learn your English?'

'At university.'

'Which one?'

'What an inquisitive girl you are,' he said in a way that dismissed the question. 'If we can stay with the main topic . . . The plan, then, is to make the first plant in America. I have no doubt it will find its way back across the Atlantic quicker than your Concorde. Bayldon was put into Downing Street to implement a timetable, but rashly he has not kept to it. Now, although certain cosmetic improvements have taken place between the two big power-blocks, we need to accelerate the pace of change in your backward country. So he must be replaced by somebody more reliable.'

'Why not assassinate him? I doubt whether the entire nation would go into mourning.'

'Too crude. It was considered, but rejected. It might have the reverse effect. No, the plan is more subtle. You know of course that he is married to an American, a rich American, and as I am sure you are aware the British have never forgotten

that another ambitious American woman toppled their be-
loved King Edward VIII. We thought it would be amusing to
use his wife as the means of destroying him. A variation on
the campaign directed against Madame Pompidou in sixty-
eight, but which failed, like the French Revolution. A number
of scurrilous stories will be put into circulation about the rich
Mrs Bayldon, all of them without foundation but sufficiently
titillating to ensure they are widely repeated. There seems
nothing your fellow-countrymen like better than the destruction of a reputation, especially if it is brought about by
some sexual aberration – is that the right word, *aberration*?'

'Yes.'

'We have some excellent rumour-mongers in all the right
places. That is why America is the obvious ground in which
to sow the seeds – the freedom of their press and their greasy
legal system combine to make the perfect compost-heap for
germinating lies. And once they have flowered they will
condition public opinion to accept what comes after.'

'And what does come after?'

'She is, you recall, second-generation Irish American. It
will come out that she has covertly donated considerable sums
to the IRA through Noraid. These funds will be shown to
have originated from a secret bank account she keeps in the
Cayman Islands.'

'Does she have such an account?'

The naïveté of her question made the man smile. 'She will
have. She will have,' he repeated. 'Photostats of the cheques,
bearing her genuine signature, will find their way to Fleet
Street – '

'Wapping,' Pamela interjected.

'What does that mean?'

'Fleet Street has moved.'

'This is so? Well, once again I thank you for correcting my
ignorance. So the British newspapers will come into possession of these photostats. Other copies will be sent to certain
members of the Opposition parties. But, in addition, we will
also make sure that sufficient supplies of arms and explosives
reach the IRA to enable them to mount a new campaign on

the British mainland. Sleeper units are already in position and will be activated when we judge the time is ripe. The main target on this occasion will be one of the royal residences.' He paused and finished his wine to let his words sink in. 'I think, don't you, that the revelation of Mrs Bayldon's criminal duplicity combined with such a terrorist outrage will ensure that her husband is removed from office. And the beauty of it is we don't get the blame. Our Irish friends can have all the credit. We're not greedy.'

'Very ingenious.'

'It appeals to you, yes?'

'Oh, I like it. You say her signature will be genuine? How will that be done?'

'Don't worry; that's the least of our problems.'

'But she'll deny all knowledge.'

'Of course. Who wouldn't? We are talking about half a million dollars. Anybody who conceals such a sum from the tax authorities is unlikely to plead guilty. But who will believe her? I promise you the mud will stick, and coupled with the parallel IRA campaign your Right Honourable Mr Bayldon will be finished, never to rise again. Then he can be replaced with somebody more amenable to our wishes.'

'Has the replacement been selected in advance?' Pamela asked.

'Oh, yes.'

'Who?'

'All in good time. Your immediate job is to report this to your Control. Describe the plan and confirm it has already been set in motion: the phoney bank account has been opened, and the first rumours will be in circulation this week.'

'That's it? Nothing else?'

'Well, if you like, you can also tell him I am impressed with you. And I am not always impressed with the way your people operate.' He pushed charm across the table like a croupier awarding a winner. 'Perhaps, next time we meet, we can get to know each other better?'

When Pamela made no response, he produced a small bleeper from his pocket and pressed it three times. 'The car

207

will be here shortly to take you back to your hotel. Fly home tomorrow on the first available plane.'

'Where do you return to?'

'Home, like you. We're both going home.'

'You don't take chances, do you? The strong silent type,' she added with a touch of bitchiness.

'Not the first time around, no. Shall we finish the wine while we wait?'

She shook her head, and he drained the bottle into his bowl.

'Funny you mentioned Hillsden earlier,' he said casually. 'I know him well. Perhaps not as intimately as you, naturally, but well enough. If you wish, I could give him a message from you.'

Pamela thought quickly, again remembering Control's warning and scenting a trap. 'I don't think he ever knew my name.'

'But I'm sure he remembers your face, or even more than your face.' The obvious sexual innuendo again annoyed her.

'Does he enjoy his new surroundings?'

'No complaints that I know of. He has a girl now, who he lives with.'

'Good for him. And you're pleased with him?'

'Oh, yes. An honourable spy. He's rendered excellent service to us.'

His bleeper sounded, and he rose to his feet. 'Until the pleasure of our next meeting,' he said, taking one of her hands and brushing his lips against it. 'Let me go first and make sure it's all clear.' He switched the light off, and she followed him through the storeroom to the alleyway door. The same car and driver were waiting outside. She got in and was driven away.

Abramov watched the car out of sight, then closed the door and walked off in the opposite direction.

14

Major Hugh Woodley, DSO, was up and about at his usual early hour before the rest of his household was stirring, showering and shaving in the cold water he preferred. In his middle forties, he kept himself in good trim and was often taken for somebody ten years younger. Women thought him attractive, but studying his early-morning face in the bathroom mirror he wished he had more definite features, a touch of grey at the temples, anything to get away from the nickname 'Young' Woodley that had stuck with him ever since prep school when he had been cast in the title role of the play of the same name. He had tried a moustache, but it had proved a sparse comic affair, like something stuck on for amateur theatricals, and hated by his wife. He had entered the army straight from university, and had been commissioned in the Grenadiers, following family tradition. After serving several tours in Germany and Northern Ireland he had applied for a transfer into the Special Air Service. He now commanded an operational troop of the Counter Revolutionary Warfare Squadron. This was the term normally used by the press, but within the SAS they were referred to as the Special Projects Team.

It was common knowledge in army circles that the existence of the SAS was now viewed with a jaundiced eye by many of Bayldon's Cabinet, and shortly after becoming Prime Minister Bayldon had ordered a committee of inquiry to investigate its methods of operation with a view to bringing in stricter controls, using an incident which took place during the previous administration's time in office as justification.

'We cannot allow this highly specialized section of the armed forces to operate with disregard for the normal rules of engagement. I refer, of course, to the "shoot to kill" policy that has been applied in the past and which my government is determined shall never be applied again. We want no repetition of Gibraltar.'

There were cries of 'Traitor!' and 'Shame!' from the Tory benches, but Bayldon shouted down his opponents since he was playing to his own gallery. The mention of Gibraltar was a reference to an incident that had provoked violent and prolonged debate at the time; members of an SAS unit had shot and killed three unarmed IRA terrorists on active service. Bayldon had used it more to appease certain of his ministers than from personal convictions. The recommendations of the committee, which were never made public, were not implemented, since Bayldon was cynically conscious that any restrictions put upon such a highly trained force might one day work against his own safety needs. He never lost sight of the fact that in reaching for power one had constantly to guard against the enemies within. Fortuitously, shortly after the committee handed in its findings, the SAS had successfully taken out a Libyan terrorist squad attempting to assassinate the Israeli Ambassador in London. Woodley had been in command of the troop involved, and the ensuing international approbation had given Bayldon the excuse he needed to shelve the report.

For all that, Woodley was first and foremost a soldier prepared to serve the national interest regardless of whoever occupied 10 Downing Street, somebody who relished the role assigned to him. Like many of his colleagues he was increasingly disturbed by certain developments, in particular the setting-up of the Workers' Militia. The SAS had always enjoyed close collaboration with the regular police, but the emergence of a second force with paramilitary ambitions seemed to him a dangerous experiment.

That morning, after he had completed his toilet and activated his bowels with two cups of strong espresso, he dressed in civilian clothes but did not neglect to wear a concealed shoulder-holster in which he placed a loaded Browning Hi-power. Then, after exercising his two Dobermanns, he

210

drove away in a specially strengthened Range Rover that, amongst other refinements, had bullet-proof glass and tyres.

His destination was Chobham Common, a long way from his Cotswold home. This barren piece of the Green Belt lies between stockbroker Woking and stockbroker Wentworth, bisected by the M3 motorway. In spring the gorse blossoms and bracken fronds push upwards through the acid soil, but most summers the landscape blackens, scarred by fires started by careless picnickers, giving whole sections the look of a petrified forest. Certain parts of it are used by the army as a tank-testing ground, and at night it is a lonely, even sinister area only frequented by lovers with something to conceal who satisfy their passions in locked cars parked off the roadway to the distant accompaniment of gunfire from the army range. From its high points on a clear day one can see planes rising every few minutes from Heathrow.

Woodley's route took him past the old Denham film studios, long since demolished and now a shopping complex, then on through the outskirts of Slough, where groups of small immigrant children were being shepherded to school, coming to Datchet and the boundaries of Windsor Castle, then following the road that ran alongside the Thames until he branched off up the hill to the small hamlet of Englefield Green. There he picked up the main road into Virginia Water, passing close to Fort Belvedere, the last British home of Edward VIII, until he reached Sunningdale. He was forced to slow down by a tailback of commuter traffic waiting at the railway level crossing. As soon as he could, he took a left on to a secondary road and accelerated through the undulating countryside. Early-morning mist still clung in pockets over the Common, and he narrowly avoided an urbanized fox loping home to its lair.

Reaching the midway high point, he swung the Range Rover off the road into one of the parking areas that afforded him a clear view of the road in both directions. He could hear the continuous roar from the nearby motorway and counted himself lucky that he did not belong to the nine-to-five rat race. Despite the traffic he had still made good time. Taking advantage of this, he rolled a crude cigarette from a packet of rice paper and loose tobacco – his concession to a habit he refused to break and which filled his children with despair. All around him were the charred remains of small conifers and birches, stark memorials to past conflagrations and reminding him of First World War photographs of no-man's-land. A large crow flapped away as he struck a match to light the ragged end of his home-made cigarette.

A few minutes later he saw another car approaching. It slowed down as it neared the parking-lot, then drove straight past and disappeared. Woodley waited. Then the same car returned from the opposite direction and this time bumped over the uneven ground to park a short distance from him. Commander Pearson got out and looked around before walking to the Range Rover.

'You make me feel like I'm back in the Vice Squad, Hugh,' arranging to meet here,' was his opening remark after they had greeted each other warmly.

'Really?'

'This is prime country for a bit of you know what. There was a famous case some years ago when two young coppers spotted something naughty going on in a closed car. Oral sex, I believe it's called now, though we had another name for it. Turned out to be an engaged couple, and they pleaded not guilty. The newspapers had a field-day reporting the trial, because they brought the car into the court and the defence counsel made the two coppers assume the same position as the prosecution alleged the accused had taken up on the back seat. Then the defence proved the cops could not have seen what they said they had seen because the windows were misted up. Case dismissed with costs. Made legal history that one, to say nothing of what it did to the two young policemen. Had a sad ending, though. The couple never got married after all that.'

He breathed in the air. 'God, it's a relief to get out of the office once in a while and take in some pure lead poisoning from the motorway. You're looking good, Hugh.'

'I don't want to hear that. Just tell me I've aged.'

212

'Were you surprised to hear from me again?'

'Pleasantly surprised.'

They had first met in Belfast on a clandestine operation during one of Woodley's tours and had hit it off from the word go. It was one of those friendships that did not depend on everyday contact.

'Good of you to see me at such short notice,' Pearson said.

'I was glad of your call. I get bored as hell when I'm on leave. Seeing as you didn't invite me to lunch at the Ritz on your generous expenses, I take it whatever you wanted to talk about is off the record.'

'What expenses? Yes, I've got a problem. And excuse me if I occasionally dribble; not senility, not quite anyway – the canteen tea has finally done my teeth in. I've been spending most of my spare time at the dentist lately, and last week he fitted a temporary bridge – a bridge too far in my case. Now, where shall I begin? How long have you got, by the way?'

'I'm all yours. The only thing I'm missing, happily, is a shopping expedition with Mary.'

'Do you rate coincidences?' Pearson asked, jumping straight in.

'I don't ignore them.'

'Me neither. Hunches, they say, have hanged more men than fingerprints. Just recently two or three apparently unrelated incidents seem to share a common factor when examined more closely. Do you remember the case of a man called Hillsden a few years back? He was MI6 and linked to the murder of a Foreign Office bod. Subsequently he defected and surfaced in Moscow.'

'Rings a bell, yes.'

'Well, a couple of days ago I was contacted by another ex-MI6 officer who I've known on and off. Always struck me as straight and reliable, otherwise I wouldn't waste your time. Name of Waddington. Ever come across him?'

Woodley shook his head.

'He bent my ear with a bizarre story that this Hillsden, who's in Leningrad now, had got a coded message to him via a tourist – who Waddington believes was an innocent carrier.

213

The message, when decoded, apparently revealed that our chum Hillsden has written his memoirs and wants to smuggle them back here.'

'Ah! another *Spycatcher*?'

'Maybe. Waddington once worked alongside Hillsden and is convinced that his defection was a frame-up. Now, in the ordinary course of events I'd take that with a double dose of salts, except that I'm currently trying to solve the death of a cipher clerk from GCHQ, and there are aspects of the case that point to the possibility he was murdered by or on the orders of our own security boys. I'm talking about the Hyde Park do at Christmas, when two policemen bought it as well.'

'Oh, that. Yes, very nasty.'

'Somebody went to a lot of trouble to try to destroy the evidence, and we only got a break by pure chance.'

'Remind me.'

Pearson sketched in the salient details of Mitchell's sad life and untimely end. 'I'm convinced he wasn't killed by the IRA or by any of the known terrorist groups, nor do I believe it was a KGB job. That leaves us with somebody closer to home. Now, then, if you tag on Waddington's story, that Hillsden was stitched up by a dirty tricks operation, perhaps certain pieces start to dovetail.'

'Go back on something,' Woodley said. 'This tourist, the one who brought the message, is he kosher or a plant?'

'Waddington is convinced he's clean – shit-scared, but clean.'

'And Waddington's also convinced he's right about Hillsden?'

'He swears that Hillsden was well and truly fucked because he'd stumbled on the existence of a supermole.'

'Oh, we're back to that, are we?'

'It doesn't go away.'

'Did he say who his money's on?'

'No. But he believes Hillsden knows, hence the memoirs.'

'That's strong beer, and a lot of people have tried to swallow it without success.'

'Hugh, nothing in this game surprises me any more. Look,

I don't have to remind you that for years now, ever since the Cambridge four hit the headlines, a whole cottage industry has sprung up – at least a dozen books have appeared, some from so-called experts, some from ambitious journalists with no particular qualifications, and some from ex-members of the Firm – all jumping on the supermole bandwagon. Conflicting views in nearly every case, and no real evidence produced, but somewhere along the line there could be buried truth which so far nobody has disinterred. Why pretend that the Establishment live and abide by the Queensberry Rules? They don't. The number of files that disappear whenever one tries to follow through would make a scrap-paper merchant rich overnight.'

'So what's your bottom line?'

'I can't discount it entirely. Stranger things have happened. After all, if I had come to you today and said that one of the Cambridge spies, probably the most lethal, had been a respected member of society, working in Windsor Castle and Buckingham Palace as Keeper of the Queen's Pictures, you'd drive away convinced you'd been dealing with a lunatic. Maybe the only person who might have settled the issue one way or the other was Philby, but if he knew the secret he took it with him to the grave. And don't forget the KGB had Philby lined up to take over the top job – if it hadn't been for Maclean and Burgess panicking, they'd have succeeded. They came bloody close.'

'What if the whole thing is a KGB sting?'

'Yes, that was my immediate reaction, but Waddington argued that if that was the case the Russians could publish it themselves. There'd be no need for Hillsden to go to such lengths.'

'Unless they wanted to make it look more authentic.'

'Except, if they do have a supermole still in place, they're hardly likely to make us a gift of him.'

'True,' Woodley said. 'I'm just being devil's advocate. Have you thought what you'd do with it in the event it passes the tests?'

'No.'

Woodley rolled another of his highly combustible cigarettes. 'Can I make you one?'

'Why not? I'm already living dangerously.'

'Why is Waddington ex-MI6?'

'Made redundant in the Bayldon economy purge.'

'Except those boys never retire, do they?'

'Any more than your mob ever fade away. Where would the letters column in *The Times* be without regular contributions from "Disgusted Brigadier of Harrow"? You'll be writing them one day.'

'Thanks a lot. Sorry to press you, but you're not the type to buy gossip off the streets. What's his present occupation?'

'He works for a private security outfit.'

'That's suspect for a start.'

'Yes, he admitted as much. But not in the way you mean. He said it was a rip-off operation. The main reason why I believe him is that I knew Hillsden.'

'Ah! Now you're getting to me. Why didn't you say that sooner?'

'Like Waddington, I never reckoned Hillsden to be what they said he was. For one thing he came from a different background, there were no public-school connections, he certainly wasn't gay and he never hunted with the pack.'

'Neither did George Blake. That proves damn all. Next question. Why was he singled out for redundancy?'

'You'd have made a good policeman, Hugh. I've given you the official reason, but maybe he probed too deeply into sensitive areas, like Hillsden.'

'Got a chip on his shoulder, then?'

'Yes, probably. Who hasn't?'

'So, if he has an axe to grind, maybe he's set the whole thing up just to get even.'

Both men glanced up as a helicopter crossed the sky.

'Again, can't be ruled out; it's a murky old world he once inhabited.'

'Records can be doctored.'

'Well, I'm not infallible when it comes to judging character,' Pearson said, 'but I'd give him a clean bill of health. See,

216

from the moment Hillsden disappeared he smelt a rat and tried to follow it through, but was told to lay off by Lockfield himself. Subsequently he got the chop. His contention is that the two things were not coincidental. He's convinced Hillsden was on to something big. Even so, I wouldn't be wasting your time or mine with hearsay, if it wasn't for the fact that both Hillsden and the dead cipher clerk point me in the same direction. That's the hunch, and I'm going along with it.'

Woodley handed him the manufactured cigarette. 'Careful how you light it. Sometimes the end drops off. I've burnt at least six pairs of trousers.'

Pearson took a drag and choked. 'God! What do you put in these things?'

'State secret.'

'You have to admit there have been some odd developments since Bayldon came to power. Curious, don't you agree, that the only outfit to be given an increased budget in the last review was Lockfield's. Why single him out?'

'Jesus!' Woodley said. 'Are you really telling me you think Downing Street is directly involved?' He glanced up as the helicopter returned, this time making a lower approach above them. 'A lot of overhead activity – must be a golf tournament on at Wentworth. They shuttle in the top brass to avoid the traffic.'

'Yes,' Pearson said, 'except he's been circling, not landing. My teeth may be rotting, but I've still got twenty-twenty vision . . . Not that it's much good when you're fumbling around in the dark. Have you still got a purpose in life, Hugh?'

Woodley was still shielding his eyes and staring up at the helicopter.

'Purpose?'

'Yes. What keeps you going? What stops you taking a nice well-paid directorship in the City? With your record and background they'd jump at you. Why do you stay in the firing-line?'

'Why do *you*? Because we don't know any different.'

'I used to enjoy it. Always wanted to be a copper, solving crimes. Once upon a time it was cut and dried. You knew who the villains were, what they'd done, what they might do, even how they'd do it. Breaking and entering, loitering with intent, a bit of assault and battery, a murder now and then, usually a family job, all nice clean stuff, uncomplicated, never too difficult to solve. The ones we caught were all little men, pathetic cases most of them, nothing special, just lost causes. I've known some of them throw a brick through a window on Christmas Eve, then stand there and wait for the Black Maria to turn up and take them in. They couldn't wait to get back inside – three meals a day, a bed, four walls around them and the company of their own kind. It was life. Now . . . it's all different. Now the real murderers are amongst us, and I don't enjoy it any more. Sometimes I get the feeling that I'm peeling off layer after layer of a dung-heap, and I'm never going to get to the bottom.' He stopped, suddenly conscious that he was pontificating. 'Hey, thanks for listening. I didn't mean to waste your time.'

'Don't be a cunt – you haven't. I wish I could be of more help.'

'Just talking it out helped. If you come across anything, you know where to reach me. Give my regards to Mary.'

As they left the helicopter drifted sideways across the grey sky, like a watchful buzzard.

15

Few people at Marseille airport paid any undue attention to the elderly Arab woman slowly wandering round the departure lounge. She was dressed in a billowing black gown that denied her femininity, and her features were two-thirds obscured by a head-dress made of the same black material. A keen observer might have spotted she was wearing a pair of modern sneakers instead of the traditional sandals, but otherwise there was nothing unusual about her and she blended in with a variety of other ethnic types: Algerians, returning Anglo-Saxon holidaymakers florid and peeling from over-exposure to the Mediterranean sun, the odd priest, a party of German hikers, native French students, a boisterous group of young Scandinavians loaded down with knapsacks and carrying home the radiance of summer, seasoned businessmen easily distinguished by their briefcases and air of studied superiority.

As with the majority of air travellers they circled restlessly as though some collective inner fear compelled them to savour their last moments on firm ground. Having passed the perfunctory security checks, they were now privileged captives, compelled, until their planes departed, to live in limbo, for they had crossed the frontier that separated them from everyday existence. In these last moments many were also infected with the urge to spend their remaining currency in the duty-free shops, buying expensive trinkets that, in the ordinary course of events, they would have hesitated to acquire.

There being no direct flight to London until the afternoon, Pamela had booked herself on the first Swissair to Geneva after confirming that she would arrive in time to make a connecting flight to Heathrow. Now, having purchased a glossy fashion magazine, she sat observing her fellow-passengers. Through the sound-baffled windows glinting with the rising Midi sun she heard the muted roar of jet engines. She, too, had a spasmodic fear of flying. Not for the first time the thought struck her that they were all too conscious that, once in the air, they would have no further control over their lives, that for the duration of the flight their destinies would rest with a pilot they would never meet face to face, handling many tons of complicated metal and machinery that mysteriously defied the laws of gravity. Pamela had always been a keen reader of horoscopes; she invariably turned to the relevant page whenever she purchased a new magazine, but it had occurred to her that what mattered when flying was not one's own horoscope, but the pilot's.

The elderly Arab woman passed in front of her several times, making a tour of the duty-free shops. She walked with measured steps, lingering before a window full of cameras, transistors and other electronic toys before finally deciding to enter the perfume shop. Despite their outward drabness the Westernized Arabs were now the *nouveau riche*, Pamela thought, travelling first class with the excess baggage of their affluence, monopolizing the gambling-tables, visiting the smart clinics in Harley Street, raping the showcases at Asprey's and Harrods, or colonizing the Home Counties on a prodigious scale as they reversed the role history had previously allotted to them. Choosing to ignore her own wealth and the fact that she had been brought up by doting well-heeled parents, Pamela had little time for the oil-rich expatriates: at such times she felt an even greater affinity with the PLO; wealth allied to vulgarity offended her, no matter where it had been acquired. On a non-selective non-racist basis she also had an equal loathing of the *Tatler* types who peacocked around in the Royal Enclosure at Ascot.

The elderly Arab woman did not emerge from the perfume shop until the second call for boarding. She came out carrying a plastic shopping-bag and with head lowered surrendered her ticket at the departure door and walked across the tarmac to the waiting plane. She was travelling on an economy ticket

220

and once on board was directed to the last row of seats at the rear of the aircraft close to the toilets. She refused the stewardess's offer to stow her shopping-bag in the overhead racks, but clutched it to her bosom.

Pamela had been assigned a window-seat in the front, first-class cabin. Ignoring the businessman next to her, she fastened her seat-belt and settled down to read a copy of French *Vogue*. Engrossed in the latest dictates of Chanel and Valentino, she did not look up from her magazine when a final passenger boarded. This was a bulky young man in a well-cut suit who took the only remaining first-class seat two rows ahead of her.

The doors were secured and the aircraft taxied out to the runway. After a short wait it was cleared for take-off and rose towards the morning sun, its initial course taking it out over the sea, climbing to a third of its cruising height before turning back on a heading for its destination.

As soon as the seat-belt sign had been extinguished, the young man got up and made for the toilets at the rear of the aircraft. There he allowed the elderly Arab woman to precede him. She still carried her shopping-bag. While the steward-esses began to take the orders for complimentary drinks he stood waiting in a position that effectively blocked the view of the toilet door.

A few minutes later the elderly Arab woman emerged. Except that she was no longer elderly. Minus the black gown, stripped of her grey wig and dressed in jeans and a leather jacket, she was revealed as a young woman in her twenties. She stood with her back to the cabin and handed the young man a mini Uzi automatic with spare magazines and an H & K P7 9 mm revolver from the shopping-bag. She was armed with a Beretta 92F, and the pockets of her jacket were stuffed with plastic explosive and the necessary detonators. The weapons and explosives had been given to her by an ac-complice in the duty-free shop after she had passed through the security check.

The young man walked to the front of the aircraft, holding the Uzi straight down and close to his right leg, the P7 in his

221

pocket. There was a priest sitting in one of the aisle seats, and as the young man passed he dropped the P7 into the priest's lap. The girl remained where she was. At this point none of the other passengers had noted her changed appearance. The young man edged past the stewardess serving drinks, excusing himself politely, and continued through the first-class cabin to the cockpit door, his movements so casual that none of the passengers paid any attention. The cockpit door was unlocked, and he went straight through, bringing the Uzi up as he entered and pushing it against the pilot's neck.

'From now onwards do exactly as I tell you,' he said in French. 'Inform air-traffic control that your aircraft has been taken over by Action Direct and that you are changing course and proceeding to Cyprus. When you have done that, tell the passengers of this development and warn them not to make any stupid moves. They and the cabin staff are to remain seated with their seat-belts fastened. I am not alone. I have two comrades in the cabin, like me fully armed, and explosive charges have already been placed and primed in the rear toilet. If you or anybody else attempts to disobey my orders, we will blow up the aircraft. Later you will relay our demands to your government. For the moment that is all. Plug me in a set of phones.' While adjusting them he kept the gun against the pilot's neck.

The pilot gave his call sign to air-traffic control and alerted the authorities of the hijack. He was asked to repeat the message. After a pause the controller accepted it as authentic and gave him a fresh course heading and permission to climb to 12,000 feet. The co-pilot punched the new headings into the computer.

'You will now maintain radio silence.'

'I can't do that,' the pilot said flatly. Both he and his co-pilot were Swiss nationals and had done their compulsory military service. The pilot had also been trained in anti-terrorist psychology and was fully aware it was vital to give rational replies to all the hijackers' demands, especially at the outset when the adrenalin was pumping. 'I have to stay in contact to receive regular clearances. This is very congested airspace, and I'm sure you don't want a mid-air collision.'

'OK,' the young man replied. 'But don't try anything clever. What is the flight-time to Cyprus?'

'Just under two hours in normal conditions.'

'Do you have enough fuel?'

'Yes. But you realize we shall have to get permission to land there? They might refuse permission. We can't stay up for ever.'

'How long?'

'Three and a half hours maximum.'

The controller's voice crackled in the headphones giving a further change of course and a new height. When this had been acknowledged the voice asked: 'What else can you tell us?'

The young man pushed the barrel of the Uzi into the back of the pilot's neck.

'Nothing else.'

'How many are they?' the voice asked.

'I am not able to tell you that. Have you alerted Cyprus?'

'That is under way. Are there any casualties?'

'Not that I know of.'

'Good. We are keeping this channel open; all other aircraft have been told to change frequencies.'

'Roger.'

'Good luck.'

'Thank you.'

'You did that very well,' the young man said. 'Just keep it that way. Now inform the passengers.'

In the cabin Pamela looked up from her magazine as the pilot's calm voice made the announcement. Listening to the news, she shared the common shock. The man sitting next to her gripped her arm and moaned 'Oh, God, no!' Further down the cabin a woman screamed in disbelief and a child cried out, but for the most part the news was received in silence.

When the announcement finished, the bogus priest, gun in hand, came to the front of the cabin and addressed them.

223

'Everybody will remain in their seats with their seat-belts fastened. That includes the cabin staff. If you do what we say, no one will get hurt. Keep quiet, don't make any sudden movements, do nothing. Explosive charges have already been placed on the aircraft. We will collect all the passports.' He spoke in English first, then repeated the warning in German and French, but it was difficult to pinpoint his true nationality.

Now the girl worked her way through the aircraft taking the passports.

'Mine is in my briefcase in the overhead rack,' the business-man whispered to Pamela. 'What do I do?'

The bogus priest immediately stepped up to him and pistol-whipped him across the head. Blood from the wound spattered Pamela's skirt.

'You weren't listening, were you? I told you not to speak.'

That's a bad sign, so early in the game, Pamela thought. He's jumpy. He's the one to watch. She remembered how tense she had always been when she and Gunther went out on a mission. The first moments were always the worst. Even so, the bogus priest's reaction betrayed that he was on a short fuse. Moving cautiously, the businessman's head lolling on her shoulder, she carefully opened her handbag and took out her own passport. When the girl reached her she handed it across the injured man. She met the girl's eyes. Pamela took a chance: 'His is in his briefcase in the rack,' she said softly.

The girl made no reply, but opened the rack and took down the briefcase. Opening it, she held it upside down and emptied it on to the floor, then bent to extract the passport from amongst the scattered contents: a bulging Filofax, traveller's cheques, a copy of a raunchy magazine, an electric razor, pens and pencils and a leather photoframe containing a coloured snapshot of two small children. She kicked these to one side and moved on. Blood from the businessman's wound dripped steadily on to the central arm-rest. As the aircraft climbed to the permitted cruising height he became a dead weight on Pamela's shoulder, but for the moment she judged it unwise to make any move to help or comfort him.

She sensed the plane had changed course, and twisting her

head slowly, one eye always on the bogus priest, she glanced out of the window, but it was difficult to guess where they were heading. Through a break in the clouds she saw the sea below and the thin glinting wake, like a snail's trail, of a steamer. Then as the plane's shadow travelled across thick cloud she judged their direction to be south-east. Her feeling of shock and disbelief was receding, to be replaced by anger. How can this happen to me? she thought, and the irony of the situation was not lost on her. She had long been familiar with the techniques of hijacking – at one time she and Gunther had been trained for a unit of the Red Army Faction targeted on a Lufthansa Jumbo carrying several top-ranking NATO officers. At the last moment, with the unit in position at Rome airport, the plane had been diverted because of fog and the operation had been aborted. Even so, she well remembered what they had been taught. It was important to disorientate the victims as quickly as possible: separate the men from the women, break up family groups, commit one violent act very quickly after the seizure of the plane, give no information, show no emotion, if necessary be prepared to kill at random. Thus, alone amongst the hundred or so other passengers, she was in a position to gauge the future sequence of events. Pamela knew the routine where the passports were concerned. They would be sorted into nationalities, then, depending on the terrorists' aims, certain groups would be isolated. Holders of American and Israeli papers were usually the prime targets, assuming that the hijackers were from one of the Arab organizations, although in this case the fact that they had selected a Swiss aircraft puzzled her. The Swiss were an odd choice. Unless there was somebody on the passenger-roster they were particularly interested in. The fact that she was a woman, gentile, and had British papers meant the odds were minimally in her favour. The vital thing was to keep a low profile, do nothing to draw attention to herself. She hoped to God nobody would attempt heroics at this stage, setting off a chain reaction that could only bring disaster.

While she was pondering these and other aspects of the situation, the door to the cockpit opened. From where she was sitting the angle was too acute for her to see the third terrorist, who Pamela presumed must be the leader. Unseen, he issued a command in German to the priest, ordering him to take over in the cockpit. They crossed in the narrow space between the toilet and the galley, and it was only now, as the young man came into her view and stood surveying the sea of frightened faces, that the shock of recognition was shared between them. Although he was slimmer than the last time they had met, and both age and artifice had worked subtle changes on his features, there was no mistaking the face that stared at her. Irrationally, another image from the past flashed into her mind – she was suddenly reminded of the classic introduction to Harry Lime in the film *The Third Man*. Perhaps the comparison was justified, for there was more than a passing resemblance between the remembered screen image of the actor and the terrorist now confronting her. Fate had reunited her at 29,000 feet with the Fat Boy.

16

Whoever they were, Pearson was to say afterwards, they did a messy job, almost as if they didn't care.

'Very messy,' he remarked to Lloyd. 'Like you and me squashing a cockroach. Casual and messy. I've handled a few of these in my time, and pleasant they are not.'

Frampton's house had been entered from the rear, a downstairs toilet window having been smashed. None of the neighbours reported hearing any sound of the break-in, though this was not unusual. There was no local Crimewatch organized, and Frampton senior was anything but popular, having made no secret of his political and racist views. The crime was only discovered when young Frampton's office reported his phone out of order, after making repeated attempts to find out why he had been absent from work for five days. Getting no answer, the telephone engineers who made the service call raised the alarm having discovered the broken window. The overworked local police had responded an hour later, and the first grisly sight of what was inside the house fell to two officers of a mobile patrol car, one of whom was a policewoman.

They found Frampton senior in the living-room with most of his brains splattered over the screen of the television set. It was still on, and the cabinet was hot to the touch. He had been shot at point-blank range in the back of the head, and the force of the impact had thrown him into the fireplace. Soot and ashes were mixed to a paste with his blood. There were no other signs of disturbance, though the budgerigar was stiff at the bottom of its cage.

Making a preliminary search of the rest of the house they came upon the real horror. As they mounted the stairs to the upper floor they were aware of the stench of death. Their noses led them into the younger Frampton's bedroom, and nothing in the policewoman's training had prepared her for the sight that greeted her. Frampton's partially clothed body was lying face upwards on the blood-soaked bed, with both arms tied to the brass bedstead. His bare chest was a mass of small burns such as could have been made by a lighted cigarette. One ear had been completely severed. It was subsequently discovered that he had been emasculated.

The room itself had been totally wrecked. Papers, ornaments, pictures, his record collection and books lay smashed and thrown to one side. The clothes from his wardrobe had been taken apart; even the heels of his shoes had been removed. The sides of the mattress had been slashed, and the cheap horse-hair stuffing, stiffened in places with his congealed blood, bulged from the gashes as though the material formed part of his own mutilated body. It was as if a maniac had been let loose in a toy shop, and that what lay on the bed was not human, but a broken doll.

The policewoman retreated to vomit on the landing. Her partner took her downstairs into the fresh air, and she sagged against the bonnet of the patrol car while he radioed for assistance. By now a small group of curious onlookers had gathered, some of the faces bright with morbid expectation. In quick response to the urgent summons, other police quickly arrived, and by nightfall a mobile incident-room had been set up in the street and the murder house isolated. A forensic team made a detailed examination of the bodies before they were bagged and taken away for autopsy. The front and rear gardens were combed for clues and every resident of the street questioned. Apart from conjecture, nothing of substance came to light. Newspaper reporters and television crews swarmed into the area and, although kept at a distance and given nothing but the bare facts by the Detective Chief Superintendent in charge of the investigation, treated their readers and viewers to lurid hearsay descriptions of the crime. Having gleaned from all-too-willing neighbours that there had always been bad blood between father and son, some of the reports concentrated on this aspect, one even going so far as to quote a 'reliable source'. CRAZED FATHER KILLS SON IN FAMILY BLOODBATH, screamed the headline the next morning.

Domestic murders, however hideous, seldom involved Pearson, and in the ordinary course of events it is doubtful whether he would have done more than glance at the story. But the name of the two victims nudged something in his memory. Being in all things methodical he followed up.

On the afternoon of the day after the discovery Waddington was in the office typing up an estimate when his employer sent for him.

'What's going on, Waddington?' was the Captain's opening remark.

'Going on, sir?'

'Yes. Don't play the innocent with me. I've just had a call from a Commander Pearson at Scotland Yard who's anxious to interview you. What's it all about?'

'I've no idea.'

'My relations with the police have always been top-hole. I deal with them direct at the highest level, as one would expect with a firm of this standing. I have a reputation to maintain which I do not want sullied by underlings. Why would a Commander Pearson wish to see you?'

'I've already told you, I've no idea.'

'I hope you're not lying, Waddington. Lying is something that I will not tolerate. If subsequently I find your denial is false, it will be instant dismissal.'

'When does he want to see me?' Waddington said, cutting through the threats.

'As soon as possible.'

'Then, am I allowed to go?'

'Provided you make up the lost time, yes.'

'Did the gentleman say where I was to meet him?'

'New Scotland Yard, of course. And I shall expect a full explanation on your return.'

'Thank you, sir.'

Waddington took a taxi to the Yard. A pass had already been left for him at the door, and he was shown up to Pearson's office.

'You dropped me in it,' Waddington said the moment he entered the room.

'Oh, sorry about that. Couldn't think of any other way to contact you, and something's come up that I felt merited urgency. I also thought it vital we met on safe ground. I'm told my office is safe, as far as anything is safe these days.'

'Was it something about Hillsden?'

'Yes and no. Tell me again – what was the name of the courier, the one you had to meet in Harrods?'

'Frampton.'

'You're quite sure?'

'Yes.'

'Have you seen the papers?'

'Not today. I had to keep an appointment early this morning before they arrived.'

Pearson picked up a copy of the *Sun* from his desk and swivelled it round so that Waddington could see the headline. 'Read that. Is that our man?'

Waddington studied the story, taking in the salient details.

'Jesus!' he said. 'Yes, yes, it is.'

'Positive?'

'No question. Same address.' His mouth had suddenly gone dry, and he found it difficult to speak.

'They don't have the full story. Just as well because the true facts will turn your stomach. Whoever did him in didn't do it neatly. He was tortured before they killed him. Tortured in a very nasty way. He got the Abelard treatment.'

'Abelard?'

'And Héloïse. Didn't you ever read that story?' Waddington shook his head. 'They cut his balls off, to say nothing of his ear. The young policewoman who was first on the scene is on sick leave seeing a shrink. People imagine we're all hard-boiled Philip Marlowe types. We're not. We're just garbage men these days, picking up every kind of human debris. Ever seen a motorway crash? When you've taken your first dead child out of a family hatchback squashed to the thickness of a plank, you don't need to hire horror videos.'

He walked to the window while getting that speech off his

230

chest as though anxious not to let Waddington see his face.

'Could it have been the father as this report hints?'

'Not from our evidence,' Pearson said, turning back, composed again. 'The old man had the back of his head blown off, but since they didn't find any trace of a weapon it doesn't suggest a self-inflicted wound. They'd both been dead five days. Did you see him again after that first visit?'

'No.'

'No contact whatsoever?'

'None.'

'When you met him in the pub, could you have been recognized?'

'It's always possible.'

'The two men who tailed you to Harrods that day, did you get a good look at them?'

'No. It all happened too quickly.'

'Well, adding it all up, it sure as hell doesn't suggest coincidence, does it? What you have to worry about is how much they got out of him before they killed him. From what they did to him he must have talked, poor bleeder.'

'How d'you know there was more than one?'

'I don't. Just a guess on my part. Has the look of a team job. How safe are you these days?'

'Safe?'

'Yes, where d'you live?'

'I'm staying with a friend right now.'

'In London?'

'No, in the country.'

'Look,' Pearson said, 'you're in the middle of something whether you like it or not. Maybe Frampton told his killers more than he told you, or maybe there was no more to tell. Either way, you have to be next on the list. Now, if it was me, I'd want to do more than just change the locks on the doors. These characters are not your average housebreakers. I might be able to arrange for you to go to one of our safe houses. Unofficially, of course. And I can't promise. You married?'

231

'Divorced.'

'Children?'

'No.'

'That's a plus. Any current attachments?'

'I'm living with a woman.'

'Serious?'

'I don't know yet. It's early days.'

'Does she know any of this?'

'No way. She'd find it odd if I suddenly disappeared, that's for sure.'

'She'd find it even odder if you ended up like Frampton. If you want my advice, I wouldn't be too visible right now. Do you have any friends you can trust? What about ex-colleagues? For all we know, given your Hillsden connection, it could be in-house. Did you think of that?'

'Yes.' He glanced down at the newspaper again. 'Listen, I'm grateful for the offer, but I think I'll take my chances elsewhere for the moment. You mentioned Hillsden. Does that mean you believe my original story?'

Pearson did not answer at once. He seemed to be choosing his response with care. 'Put it this way. You came to me, and I listened. I went further, discussed it with somebody just to talk things out, test the water so to speak. Levelling with you, until this happened I was in two minds. It's not my usual line of country. What little I knew of Alec Hillsden I liked. You worked with him, and you liked him, too – enough to go out on a limb for him against all the evidence. Now this, a definite connection. It adds up. So as and when you can count me in. In what way I don't rightly know. But let's not make it public, eh? We both have to do a lot more thinking before we make the next move. Let me know where you hole up and use this number' – he scribbled it down on a piece of scrap paper – 'that's my direct private line. Not even the wife has that, so don't abuse it. If I don't answer, keep trying until I do. And don't speak to anybody else in this building. One last thing: don't walk out of here. I'll get you a Q car, have them drop you off somewhere.'

He was as good as his word, and Waddington left from the

232

rear of the Yard in an unmarked police car. He had no intention of returning to face the Captain; that reunion would have to wait. He asked the police driver to take him to Euston Station. There he joined the crush of commuters and dived into the Underground, catching the first train that came in and strap-hanging his way through a dozen stops before alighting. Above ground again he went into the first pub he came to. He ordered a double Scotch and sat with his back to the wall in a corner concealed from the doorway. Downing his drink, he attempted to sort out his thoughts, relieved that her current absence meant he could delay having to deal with the Pamela situation. The first name that had come to mind in Pearson's office when asked to think of a funk-hole had been Keating. Keating answered most of the basic criteria: out of the game, but not entirely divorced from it, somebody who knew the ropes – the luncheon had established that much. But how much should he tell Keating, if anything? He would need to concoct some plausible reason to justify turning up out of the blue.

He left the pub and went in search of a phone-booth. Keating's butler answered, and after a pause he was put through.

'Bill, how goes it? Glad you rang. Coincidence, because I was going to give you a bell tomorrow. Must be mental telepathy.'

The warmth of his greeting surprised and fazed Waddington momentarily.

'Really? How odd.'

'So when can we meet? Got your diary handy?'

'Not with me . . . In actual fact, the reason I'm ringing is to ask a favour,' he said, plunging.

'Go ahead.'

'I'm in a spot of bother and I need somewhere to go.'

'Like here, you mean?'

'That was the idea, but I'd quite understand if that's impossible.'

'Got the wife's lawyers on your tail?'

'Something like that.'

'No problem. We've got spare rooms. Ten to be exact. You want to come now?'

'In a word, yes.'

'See you in a little while, then. I'll be here, and we can go into it then.'

Walking away from the phone-booth in search of a taxi, Waddington felt he had made the right choice. The beauty of somebody like Keating, somebody from the Firm, was that they knew how to live with the unexpected.

17

While Waddington was on his way to Keating, the first sparse details of the hijack were released, including a statement from the Swiss government that so far the terrorists' demands were not known. This was a deliberate piece of misinformation since the authorities were already in possession of the Fat Boy's conditions, namely the release of three members of the French Red Brigade currently being held in Swiss gaols, together with a ransom of 10 million Swiss francs. Urgent negotiations were under way between the Swiss and the Cypriots, who were currently refusing to allow the plane to land.

The Swiss already had their own premier HRU force – the Zurich 'Enzian' unit – airborne. Also on board were trained negotiators, a full medical team including surgeons, together with government officials carrying the ransom sum. In addition, requests for back-up forces had been made to the British, Israeli and Turkish governments, and these had immediately put HRU teams on full alert. Within an hour of receiving the request, the Turkish unit, known as the Jandara Suicide Commandos, were on their way to the island. Intelligence forces throughout Europe were monitoring all radio traffic to and from the jet, feeding everything back to Komissar, the West German computer system used to keep track of all terrorist activity. Constantly updated, the computer analysed the options, dealing out poker hands. The three gaoled terrorists had been taken under armed guard to Zurich airport, and a jet was standing by to transport them should the situation demand it.

Back in England, SAS Headquarters at Hereford had kept MI6 fully posted as a matter of routine, and when Control returned to his office that afternoon the reports were on his desk. Included amongst them was the passenger-indent for the Swiss airliner. He scanned it to see how many British nationals were on board. As he went down the list the name *van Norden, Mrs P.* leapt out at him from the page. He checked where the flight had originated just in case the name was coincidental, but the combination of Marseille and her name left no room for doubt: somehow the unthinkable had happened.

Using his hot line, he immediately contacted Hereford for the latest information and was told that the plane had still not landed. The Swiss were putting pressure on the Cypriot authorities to relent, but time was running out.

'The last report from the cockpit was that there was only fuel enough for a further twenty minutes' flying-time.'

'When was that logged?'

'Seven minutes ago.'

'How many terrorists on board – has that been established?'

'Not definitely. It's believed there are three.'

'What's the Swiss attitude?'

'Wait and see. The Turks have got an HRU team on the island and the airborne Swiss unit now have the plane in sight, plus the Yanks have scrambled three fighters from the Sixth Fleet. You've got the passenger-list, I take it?'

'Yes,' Control said.

'We make it there are eighteen British subjects on board. Anybody of particular interest to you?'

'No,' Control answered quickly, 'but keep me fully posted.'

'Will do.'

'Has your help been asked for?'

'We've got a troop ready to go if needed.'

'Have the French come up with anything, seeing as Action Direct are responsible?'

'Nothing that we know of so far.'

'Curious choice, Marseille.'

'Yes. Still, share and share alike. Makes a change. Things have been too quiet recently.'

'It can never be too quiet,' Control said acidly, finishing the call. Incredible, he thought. The odds of Pamela choosing to fly on that one plane were equivalent to winning the Irish Sweepstake lottery outright. And from Marseille of all places! It just went to prove that in the world he inhabited it was not the obvious one had to guard against, but the long arm of chance. And there was nothing he could do about it; like the Swiss he could only wait and see. Would Moscow pick up on it? he wondered. Not that they could influence matters; the only people in control for the time being were the actual hijackers.

He ran his finger down the list of passengers again rather like a disappointed beneficiary studying a will in the hope that he has misread it the first time.

'It's no use you threatening me,' the Captain said to the Fat Boy. They had been stacked and circling for the last ten minutes while the Captain made repeated and increasingly urgent calls to the control tower. 'I happen to be on your side right now. You heard me: they've got the runway blocked off, and we only have another eleven minutes' fuel.'

'Do we have any other options?'

'One. There is a military airport in the Turkish sector we could just make, but I doubt if they'll help us down. I'll have to fly clean, go straight in first time on a visual approach. It's now or never, so make up your mind.'

The Fat Boy hesitated a second. 'Do it. Go in.'

'You'd better strap yourself in the spare seat. It's likely to be a dodgy landing. And please don't say anything else until we're down; that is, *if* we get down.'

As the Fat Boy harnessed himself into the third seat, the Captain was already altering course, taking the plane into a gentle banking turn as he began the descent. The escorting American fighters tucked themselves in behind him, above and below. The voice of one of the American pilots crackled in his headphones, asking his intentions, but the Captain ignored him, concentrating on giving concise orders to the First Officer.

'Give me twenty flap.'

'Twenty flap on.'

237

'Igniters.'

'Igniters on.'

'Tell the cabin crew and passengers to take up positions for an emergency landing.'

The First Officer made the announcement.

'Call it out,' the Captain said.

'Three thousand. Speed two six zero.'

The First Officer's knuckles whitened over the throttles. The plane levelled out, the engines biting into a layer of cloud.

'Two thousand. Speed two ten zero.'

'If I've got it right, when we get through this cloud it should be straight ahead. Reduce throttle.'

'Fifteen hundred. Steady at one eight zero.'

The Fat Boy twisted in his seat to see past the Captain as the cloud finally thinned out and they were once again in clear sky. He could make nothing of the terrain ahead.

'One sixty, one fifty-five at one thousand. Still at twenty flap.'

'Landing gear.'

The First Officer activated the switch. There was a whine of hydraulics as the undercarriage locked into position. Then the aircraft began to drop at a faster rate as the Captain lined it up on the distant runway.

'Speed one forty. Three degrees nose up.'

The Fat Boy could now make out figures on the ground, and cars like Dinky toys. There were some swimming-pools, scattered squares of bright blue amongst the counterpane of brown and green. Every now and again the sun reflected back from a greenhouse, as though someone was flashing danger signals.

'Six hundred.'

They were on the final approach now, and the engines took on a different note.

'Five . . . four . . . three.'

Through the narrow windscreen the Fat Boy could see activity ahead: half a dozen vehicles streaming out from the main cluster of buildings towards the runway; figures running; and the ground rushing up to meet them, the last half-mile eaten at an alarming speed, the aircraft rocking in the currents of hot air as the Captain made subtle movements with the stick. Tensed in the cabin, bracing herself and the injured businessman against the landing impact, Pamela prayed for the first time in years.

'One hundred . . . fifty . . .'

The first yards of tarmac disappeared under the nose, and then the Fat Boy felt a sudden lurch as the wheels touched down and locked hot rubber on to hotter tarmac. It was a perfect three-point landing, and in the cabin the terrified passengers cheered their first piece of luck.

The First Officer slammed the protesting engines into reverse thrust for the laid-down time, then pushed the throttles back. A sort of quietness engulfed the aircraft as the brakes were applied and it slowed to taxiing speed and slewed off the runway into a parking-bay before coming to a complete stop.

'Kill engines.'

The American fighters screamed over them, and then there was a magic silence.

The Captain turned his head to the Fat Boy. 'Over to you once again,' he said, and reached for a packet of cigarettes.

'You did a good job,' the Fat Boy said, 'but now we're down don't try to be a hero. Do anything smart and I'll blow your friend's head off.' He pointed the Uzi at the First Officer before releasing his harness and going back into the cabin.

'I'll have one, too,' the First Officer said when they were alone. He found he was shaking and drenched in sweat.

'You gave up.'

'I just started again. Thank God these bloody gauges aren't dead accurate. If I believed them, we ran out of fuel five minutes ago. And by the way, Skipper, that was an ace fucking landing.'

'Yes, to use your own words, it fucking was,' the Captain said, savouring a lungful of injurious tars, in the sure knowledge that, over the past few hours, he had already shortened his life.

*   *   *

239

'Wives are a recurring sickness, like malaria,' Keating said in his most expansive mood. 'One feels perfectly well, and then, suddenly, out of the blue, the temperature rises. We're never safe, old man.'

As Waddington might have guessed, Keating's house complemented the man and was of equal Falstaffian proportions – a large detached mansion set well back from the road in an area noted for its exclusivity. On arrival he had spotted two remote-controlled video-cameras positioned to survey the front gates and garden. There was also an alarm bell bearing the name of Breakproof's main competitor fitted high on the wall.

He had decided to feel his way cautiously where Keating was concerned and for the time being stick to the story that he was the victim of a marital dispute.

'What about your own wife – will she mind me being here?'

'We're in this together, as it happens. Mine has flipped, I think, so we've come to an arrangement to put some air between us for a while. Lots of air. D'you think we ever learn from our turgid mistakes?'

'Probably not.' Certainly not if a Pamela van Norden enters our lives, Waddington thought.

'And it's a bloody fraud to say that "in the dark all cats are grey". If I'm going to exist by a maxim, I prefer good old La Rochefoucauld. Ever read him?'

'No, I confess I haven't.'

'He told it like it is – a few good fucks interspersed with long periods of purgatory, though he tarted it up, of course, in the usual French fashion, but that's what he was talking about. Still, mustn't be too hard on the dear creatures; the occasional fever clears the blood, and they can be delectable in small doses. Now, then, let's get you organized. I've had my man put you in the guest suite. You'll need a house key, and I'll explain how the alarm works – though, I don't suppose that will faze you.'

'It really is very generous of you.'

'Glad of the company. Are you still working for that boring character you told me about?'

'Yes, for the moment, but it's only a matter of time before I jack it in.' Even as he said this his mind moved to Pamela again. My God! I've learnt to love how the other half live quickly enough, he thought, protestations about pimps not-withstanding. I seem to have struck it rich twice in a row. But, given the situation, he would need to sever connections with the wearisome Captain; life at Breakproof could no longer be considered safe. Pamela was a more difficult equation to solve. He was torn between the necessity to take himself out of circulation and the urge to see her again. 'I've been intending to make a move for some time, but I must find something else first before I give the Captain the two-fingered farewell. I sampled the bread-line before, and that isn't too much fun. But obviously I can't abuse your hospitality for any length of time.'

'Don't worry about it; the invitation's open-ended. As it happens, we could help each other out. We might have renewed acquaintance at just the right time. If you hadn't rung me, I was just about to contact you and put a proposition.'

'Really? What was that?'

'Remember I mentioned I dabble in films? Well, I've got too many irons in the fire right now, and it's too much like hard work keeping tabs on all of them. The film industry's an even murkier world than the one we both used to inhabit, and it's been in my mind for some time now to find a reliable partner who can watch the inmates while they run the asylum. Seems to me the time is ripe for you to step into those shoes.'

Listening to this, Waddington wondered was Keating to be believed, or was he the type who invented favours on the spur of the moment merely to show he could?

'Very flattering of you, but I know sweet f— all about films. I'd probably be a disaster.'

'Just another surveillance job, old chap. Piece of cake to somebody like you. You won't be dealing with a bunch of MENSA graduates. From what I've seen so far, the majority of them are just self-employed villains with artistic pre-tensions, out to screw anybody who's fool enough to pick up the tab. They give you a lot of crap about "creative freedom",

241

but all they're really talking about is "creative book-keeping".'

'But surely I'd need some experience. I couldn't just jump in at the deep end.'

'Why not? Most of them do.'

'What sort of film is it?'

'Don't ask me. Here.' He picked up a bound copy of the script from his desk. 'Judge for yourself.'

Waddington glanced at the title page. 'What does this picture of a raven signify?'

'That's the producer's name. Old-time Hollywood who's managed to stay afloat making schlock for schlocks, but his films do well and that's all I'm interested in. I'm told this one is above average for him, and for the first time he's making it away from California. Says the unions are killing him out there.'

'So he's making it here?'

'Yes, the interiors will be shot at Shepperton, and the locations in Europe . . . with one sequence in Russia. At one time he wanted to film the entire thing there, but I squashed that. Too much of an unknown quantity.'

'Russia? That's unusual, isn't it?'

'From what I've heard Raven jumps on every new band-wagon, so he's stolen half the plot of *Ninotchka* and brought it up to date. Western boy meets Russian girl with *glasnost*. Very original. Listen, maybe he's right.'

'Whereabouts will they be shooting in Russia?'

'Leningrad, I think. They tried for Moscow, but didn't grease the right palms or something.'

'Interesting,' Waddington said. 'I'll certainly read the script, and if you're serious about taking me on, then, providing I can make a contribution, I'd like to take you up on it.'

'Just an idea. It's got to be a mite better than playing death of a salesman.'

'Too true. Well, thanks. What can I say?'

'Always more gracious to receive than to give, chum.'

'Is that La Rochefoucauld?'

'No, that's Keating, pure Keating.'

*   *   *

Thirteen hours after it had landed the hijacked jet still stood on the same spot at the end of the runway. Requests to have it towed to another location had been refused by the Fat Boy. His only concessions had been to permit food and water to be brought aboard and to release a mother and her two children, both of whom had become dehydrated by the intense heat: the Turkish military authorities had refused demands for the plane to be refuelled, and there was no air-conditioning. The front exit-door had been opened for short periods, but by now the atmosphere inside the cabin was fetid. The hostages were still strapped in their seats but, as Pamela had predicted, they had been separated into ethnic groups; although she had been isolated at the rear of the cabin, the other seventeen with British passports were in the front section. The only three Israelis had been gagged and bound and grouped close to the midway emergency exit. None of the hostages had any idea where they were, or what was happening outside, the terrorists having pulled the blinds on all the windows. For the hostages there was the feeling that they had all been sealed in a tunnel. From time to time the injured businessman regained consciousness and could be heard moaning.

Beyond the ring of searchlights illuminating the aircraft, the Turkish HRU had set up perimeter security around the entire area and were prepared for an immediate assault should the position deteriorate at any time. Reconnaissance and sniper teams were positioned as close to the plane as possible, armed with AR-15 rifles fitted with laser target-illumination systems. One member of the unit, dressed as a canteen worker, had taken the food and drink out to the plane, but on the Fat Boy's instructions the provisions had been left at the foot of the mobile stairway and had been retrieved by a male hostage while the girl terrorist, wearing a hood, stood to one side of the open door with her gun trained on him. She had been photographed, but no positive identification had been possible. The Zurich HRU team had landed at the island's commercial airport and been rushed to the scene. Their chief negotiator, a psychiatrist, was in the control tower and in contact with the plane, but so far the Fat Boy had refused to talk direct, using the pilot to relay his responses. To stall for time he had been told that the Swiss were flying the three gaoled terrorists to the island. This was untrue. The Turkish authorities had insisted that any rescue attempt would only be carried out by their own commandos. In addition they were adamant that the hijackers' demands would not be met. Urgent, and at times acrimonious, discussions were taking place between the Swiss, Cypriot and Turkish governments, and the British, French and Israelis were being kept fully in the picture. The media had already started converging on the scene.

From the time she and the Fat Boy had come face to face, Pamela had been conscious of the innumerable necessary evils of which her life was made up. In the ordinary course of events she would not have questioned his inalienable right to use terror as a weapon in the world revolution they all sought, but the fact that she was now personally involved presented new and perhaps unsolvable problems. During the long stifling hours since the plane had landed she had had ample time to consider all the probabilities. There was a remote possibility that the hijackers' demands would be met and that she, along with the other hostages, would eventually be released. But attitudes towards such acts of terrorism had hardened in recent years, and she had no doubt that assault plans were in hand and the chance of a bargain being struck was, at best, dubious. Equally, she had no illusions about the Fat Boy; he would not hesitate to kill if the operation went wrong, or if he felt it imperative to regain the initiative. So far, apart from the moment of mutual recognition, he had not approached her. Most of the time he had been in the cockpit, leaving the other two to deal with the passengers and flight crew. From experience she knew that as every hour passed without progress being made their tolerance would be strained. The bogus priest had already demonstrated that he was on a short fuse, and the girl remained an unknown quantity. If forced to abort the mission, they would have allowed for a final solution. They had no faith in anything but death.

244

She was in an aisle seat and by inclining her head an inch at a time obtained a partial view down the cabin. Only the emergency lights were burning, and her line of vision was restricted, but as she looked the cockpit door opened and the Fat Boy was briefly silhouetted against the dying sky. She saw that he was allowing the pilot to use the forward toilet, and while he stood guard the girl went past to take his place in the cockpit. They were obviously working to prearranged silent procedures, as Pamela would have expected. When the pilot emerged and returned to his seat the Fat Boy closed the cockpit door and walked the length of the cabin. He paused by the three Israelis as though selecting them for something in the future; then walked on, coming at last to Pamela.

'You,' he said to her in French, 'unfasten your belt and come with me.'

Pamela did as she was told. The hostages closest to her averted their eyes. She got up and rubbed her cramped legs. The Fat Boy motioned her towards the rear of the cabin with his revolver. There he opened the toilet door and pushed her inside. They stood close together in the cramped space, and he spoke softly in the remembered sibilant voice.

'You've given me an extra problem. One I could have done without.' She caught the scent of garlic on his breath. Like her, he was sweating from the intense heat.

'Yes. It's unfortunate for both of us.'

'Why were you on this particular plane?'

'I was doing a job. I had to make a contact in Marseille.'

'Word was that you'd retired.'

'I was out of it for a time. Now they've decided to use me again.'

He stared at her. 'You know that I can't show you any obvious favours.'

Pamela nodded. The feeling had not yet returned to her legs, and she suddenly sagged towards him.

'Can I just splash my face with water?'

'Go ahead.' He waited until she had finished. 'Did you hear what I said?'

'Yes.'

'If they're prepared to trade, I can make small concessions. That could include you. Could,' he repeated, 'but no guarantees. If they don't . . .' He left the sentence unfinished.

'What are you asking for?' she whispered.

'The release of three comrades held in Switzerland and a safe passage out of here.'

'Where to?'

'You don't have to know that. If you're still alive, you'll read about it.'

'Are they stalling?'

'Of course. What else?'

'I'm sorry,' Pamela said.

'Well, you've been lucky this far. Maybe your luck will hold.'

'Please,' she said, 'before I go back, let me use the john.'

'OK, but be careful what you touch. This place is wired.'

He eased his bulk out of the entrance and allowed her to pull the door closed. When she emerged he ordered her to return to her seat and watched until she had refastened her safety-belt. Again none of the hostages looked at her. The Fat Boy went to take over in the cockpit, pausing midway down the cabin to contemplate the three Israelis.

Once back in the cockpit he called the control tower.

'I'm giving you one more hour to show willing. I have 01.15. In exactly one hour we will shoot a hostage.'

The negotiator's voice remained calm. 'There is no need for that. We're making progress. How are conditions on board? Do you want more food sent out?'

'I want results. You can begin by refuelling the plane. Otherwise you're going to pick up a dead Jew from the tarmac.'

'I give you my word we are doing all we can. The three men flew out from Switzerland ten minutes ago. We expect them to arrive in just over two hours from now. Obviously they can't land here while your plane is blocking the runway.'

'I'll agree to it being moved once it's been refuelled.'

'All right, I'll see what I can do. Please be patient. I am having to consult with more than one authority.'

246

'One hour,' the Fat Boy said before cutting the connection.

In the control tower the negotiator relayed the latest threat. Several alternative plans had been exhaustively deliberated throughout the long day. If all else failed, the Swiss government were prepared to authorize a direct assault on the plane, but only as a last resort. Their scheme was to use a variation of the technique used during the successful rescue of a Lufthansa 737 at Mogadishu. On that occasion a unit of West Germany's Grenzchutzgruppe 9 had started diversionary fires in front of the hijacked aircraft, relying on this distraction to make the terrorists congregate in the cockpit where they could be more easily picked off. The Turkish commander, on the other hand, had put forward a refined and original plan. His scheme was first to show goodwill, by allowing the plane to be refuelled. During this operation key members of his assault team would be left in position below the wings. The second phase would be to tow the plane to another part of the airport where he would have already positioned the remainder of his force. This, he felt, would gain valuable time and convince the terrorists that their other demands would also be met. To convince them further, when the next lot of food was delivered it should also include half the ransom money, with the promise that the remaining half would accompany the released prisoners.

'There is no way we will agree,' the Swiss representative said. 'My government has made that abundantly clear. It is out of the question.'

'Please let me finish,' the Turkish commander shouted. 'I am aware of that. Three of my men, suitably dressed and disguised, will take the place of the prisoners. They will be driven in a bus to within sight of the cockpit and revealed to the terrorists. At that distance and in poor light the terrorists will not be able to tell the difference. Only then will we put our final conditions to them. They are as follows. One: If any of the hostages is harmed in any way, then the prisoners will be shot before their eyes. Two: All the hostages, including the stewardesses, are to be freed; only then will the prisoners be allowed to board. Three: the refuelled plane will be allowed to take off.'

247

'The plan is not feasible,' the Swiss representative remonstrated. 'We cannot allow this.'

'Those are our conditions. I did not say they would all be carried out. During the evacuation of the hostages my assault team will have attached explosive charges to the emergency exit-doors on both sides of the aircraft. Ladders will also be in position. As my three decoy prisoners reach the head of the stairway, the order will be given to explode the charges and force an entry using stun grenades. Provided there have been no prior killings, we will attempt to take them alive. But if necessary we will take them out.'

There was an amazed silence when he had finished. He turned to his Swiss counterpart for a reaction.

The Swiss officer nodded. 'It might work,' he said finally. 'It's never been tried before and it might just work. It's certainly the best we've come up with.'

'Are we agreed, then? We put it into effect, yes?'

The representative of the Swiss government was not to be won over so easily. 'I shall have to refer back to my superiors.'

'Please do. But let us hurry, shall we?' He turned to the negotiator. 'In the meantime, I suggest you keep them talking. Begin by telling them that we believe we have permission to refuel. Every minute gained is valuable. I will start to brief my team.'

Control was not fitted by nature to be a passive player in the game; throughout his career he had always been the instigator of plots, and although the fortuitous circumstances of the hijack could hardly be described as a counter-plot the effect was the same. His concern for Pamela's possible fate was minimal; she would have to take her chances. The all-important factor was to re-establish a safe contact with Moscow and receive instructions. The inexplicable assassination of Mitchell had shaken him badly enough; now this further setback meant that his fresh initiative was stymied. He had to believe that Pamela's presence on that particular flight was pure chance, the joker card dealt at random like the three-card trick employed by pavement hustlers, but he

248

could never dismiss the thought that darker forces had played their part. In the long cruel war he had joined so many years ago, nobody fought cleanly. He detested failure; failure was a weakness, something he pushed to the back of his mind, just as he ignored the evening pain from the arthritic fingers of his left hand.

The irony of it was that until now he had never put a foot wrong. Moscow could not fault the way in which he had shoe-horned Bayldon into Downing Street against all the odds, and the planning of Hillsden's defection had been a masterstroke. That is what made the present situation intolerable. There was something too coincidental about recent events; it had been difficult enough to arrange Pamela's meeting with Abramov – taking a chance which in the normal course of events he would never have contemplated. Moscow had needed a lot of persuasion to agree to it, and if it now proved to have been a waste of time there was no predicting what their reaction would be. Control was aware that they were already losing confidence in his ability to deliver: Bayldon was his man, and Bayldon was not performing as promised, Bayldon had proved a tactical liability. No good telling Moscow Centre that the British system did not operate like the Kremlin, that Prime Ministers could not be overturned easily. Having lost face over Afghanistan, with their African ventures not performing as planned and the Middle East too volatile, the old guard in the Kremlin needed a diversion in order to counter the changes *glasnost* had brought about. No matter what small internal freedoms were being introduced, their sights were still fixed on Fortress Britain. If the Americans could be convinced that the British were unreliable, they would pull out; once that happened, the whole NATO concept would collapse. To bring this about they needed a climate of uncertainty, the very thing Bayldon had been put in office to achieve.

Now the necessary removal of Bayldon was threatened by a hijack engineered by some crackpot group. It really was too galling.

*   *   *

The principal negotiators were almost as exhausted as the hostages in the sweltering plane. After further and often acrimonious exchanges the Swiss had reluctantly given their consent to the Turkish commander's plan, pressure having been brought to bear on them by the Israeli government. The exact procedures having been decided, there had been another dialogue with the Fat Boy, and following a simulated show of reluctance they had agreed to let the plane be refuelled. Stage one began with two crack marksmen from the Turkish unit being taken out to the aircraft on the refuelling tanker, hidden under blankets in the driver's cabin, and exiting from the blind side of the vehicle while the genuine tanker-driver and his assistant connected the hoses. They were now in position under the belly of the aircraft. The Fat Boy had monitored the operation from the cockpit, checking the gauges as each tank was filled.

In the blacked-out cabin, the hostages remained ignorant of what was happening on the tarmac, though Pamela, catching the girl and the bogus priest exchanging a look, guessed that something was developing. Once the refuelling had been completed to the Fat Boy's satisfaction, he again spoke to the chief negotiator and was told that in order for the plane carrying the prisoners to land the hijacked airliner would have to clear the runway. He closely questioned the captain as to the necessity of such a manoeuvre, then insisted that they would taxi under their own power rather than be towed. In addition he gave explicit instructions that the first instalment of the ransom money and extra supplies must be delivered before the aircraft moved. They were to be brought out to the plane on an open truck. This would be driven into position at the forward cabin door with the supplies and money placed halfway up the portable stairway. The driver would then withdraw and two of the hostages would be allowed to retrieve both the food and the ransom.

'Let them know that if these instructions are not carried out exactly', the Fat Boy told the pilot, 'they will be responsible for the consequences.'

He came back into the front cabin and indicated for the girl to put her hood on. Watching through the door window, he waited until the truck had driven off again before opening the door, then moved down the cabin and selected two male passengers at random.

'Get up, both of you.' Now he spoke in English.

They struggled to release their safety-belts with cramped hands. The Fat Boy motioned them towards the exit-door.

'Go outside and fetch the food.'

Both men obeyed, walking unsteadily as the blood returned to their legs, the girl covering them all the way with her automatic. They brought some of the food inside, then went back for the rest. On the second trip the younger of the two suddenly jumped the last half a dozen steps and made a run for it. He had only gone a few yards when the girl opened fire, cutting him down accurately with a spray burst. The bullets spun him around, and he appeared to dance a parody of the sixties Twist, executing a zig-zag pattern before crumpling to the tarmac.

Smoke from the girl's gun drifted back into the cabin, filling the already fetid atmosphere with the smell of explosive. The hostages cowered in their seats. Although none had witnessed the actual killing, they were well aware that something horrendous had happened.

The package containing the ransom money was still on the steps. 'Get it!' the Fat Boy shouted to the other man. 'And don't try what your friend did.' He pushed the terrified man out of the aircraft again. Once he had returned, the exit-door was closed and the Fat Boy took the package from him and went back into the cockpit.

'I warned them,' the Fat Boy said. 'I did warn them.' He opened the package to assure himself that it contained half of the ransom money.

'Is he dead?' the Captain said.

'Who cares?'

'Can I radio for them to go to him?'

'No, not yet. I want them to understand I mean what I say.'

'They'll take you now.' The Captain found the courage to speak out. 'Now you've made sure they'll take you.'

251

'You think so?'

'Unfortunately for the rest of us, yes, I think so.'

'I'm not interested in your opinion.'

He looked out of the cockpit window, but his view was restricted. An icicle of doubt entered his mind. The instincts that had kept him one step ahead of his hunters for over a decade came into play. He had always made it a trademark to act unpredictably and now he took an immediate decision.

'Start your engines and prepare for take-off.'

'Take-off? We're supposed to clear the runway.'

The Fat Boy pushed his revolver against the co-pilot's temple. 'Do as I say or else you'll be flying this plane alone.'

'But take off to where?'

'I'll tell you when we're in the air.'

At first those in the control tower found nothing odd in what was happening, believing that the plane would now move to a parking-bay as agreed. It wasn't until the plane slewed round and the sound of full power reached them that they got an inkling of what was happening. The two marksmen concealed under the belly of the plane were suddenly exposed; they lay spreadeagled and deafened as the plane left them and began its take-off run. The hot blast from the jets rolled them over like pieces of paper caught in a whirlwind. The onlookers in the control tower, powerless to act, could only stand horrified and amazed as the plane lifted off and climbed steeply into the night sky. All airborne military aircraft were immediately warned, and tracking stations throughout the Mediterranean alerted. At that moment nobody, including the pilot, had any idea where the hostage plane was headed.

'What's my flight-plan?' the pilot asked as they levelled off.

'Libya.'

'I'll have to lodge it with air-traffic control.'

'You lodge nothing.'

'It's required procedure under international safety regulations.'

'I make the regulations,' the Fat Boy said. 'Safety doesn't come into it. When I'm ready, I'll speak to Libya. Just set course and keep to it.'

In the control tower violent arguments and counter-arguments were taking place, the Turkish commander remaining adamant that his plan would have worked.

'What about the dead man on the runway? You previously said that if any of the hostages were harmed you would move in immediately.'

'Once all my men were in position. That's what I said. And the crucial factor was the plane supposedly bringing the prisoners. For my plan to succeed all the elements had to come together. I cannot be held responsible for events beyond my control.'

Pressed back in her seat as the plane banked and climbed steeply, Pamela had no illusions: something had gone wrong with the Fat Boy's plans, and she knew him only too well – once denied he was twice as dangerous.

18

It wasn't until he got to Paris and was inside the Russian embassy that Abramov learnt that Pamela was on the stricken plane. With his usual thoroughness he double-checked, telephoning the airline's hot line posing as an anxious relative. Like Control, he had little concern for her welfare; he was angered that the long arm of coincidence had reached out and delayed, possibly wrecked, the timetable Moscow had laid down. His next call was to Geichenko, and he knew what to expect.

'What d'you mean, she was on the fucking plane? How come?'

'I don't know. I wasn't responsible for her travel arrangements, General. Presumably London made them.'

'London! London is useless shit! We can't trust London with anything.'

'It was just pure chance, General.'

'There is no such thing as chance.'

'No, General.'

'Where is the fucking plane now?'

'It took off again and we just had a report it's landed in Libya, General.'

'I want you back here,' Geichenko shouted, and the line to Moscow went dead.

Traffic between Moscow and Libya, on the other hand, was extremely busy during the next few hours.

Until he woke late in yet another strange bed and read the morning papers over breakfast, Waddington was likewise ignorant of Pamela's involvement in the distant drama. Preoccupied with his own problem, he had first scanned the inside pages for any follow-up on Frampton's murder before turning back to the main story. The only photograph accompanying the text was that of the Swiss captain, most of the space being taken up with a fanciful eyewitness account of the way in which he had brought the plane down safely in Cyprus seconds before his fuel ran out. The story also stated that there were a number of Britons on board, and it was while Waddington was idly scanning the passenger-list that Pamela's name sprang out at him. Stunned, he read it twice, hoping his early-morning vagueness had misled him. It seemed unlikely there could be two people with the same unusual name, and Pamela had been in the South of France. The fact that she should have caught a plane originating in Marseille rather than Nice was odd, but not all that odd – the rich moved around. He obtained the emergency number for enquiries for the latest update, and the Swissair spokesman confirmed that a Mrs P. van Norden had been on the passenger-indent.

Bathing and dressing hurriedly, he went downstairs in search of Keating, finding his host at his desk in the panelled library.

'Slept well, I trust?'

'Like a top. Have you seen the papers?'

'I glanced at them. Why?'

'There's been a hijack.'

'That, yes. Now I suppose we're in for a spate of them. Once one succeeds, others imitate.'

'I know somebody who's on the plane.'

'God! How awful. It's my nightmare to be involved in one of those things.'

'Everybody's . . . The point is . . . I can't believe this. My entire world seems to be falling apart recently . . . It happens to be the woman I'm currently having an affair with. Can you believe that? She was just on a holiday in the South of France.'

'You need a drink?'

'No, it's too early. There's nothing one can do; that's the bugger of it.'

'Well, if it's any comfort, statistically the odds are in favour of your lady; they seldom harm women and children – even

255

their twisted minds take some account of public reaction. Once they kill they usually lose out . . . It's not much, but it's something to cling on to. Is this the lady who broke up the marriage?'

Waddington hesitated before replying.

'No, and I haven't been honest with you. It is true my marriage has broken up, but that was some time ago; this particular affair started afterwards . . . Maybe I will have that drink.'

'I'll join you. What time is it? . . . Oh, it's gone eleven . . . A Bloody Mary goes down well at this hour.'

He busied himself expertly at a small bar while Waddington unburdened himself.

'I seem to have become involved at one remove with something from our joint past, and I guess I can't trade on your hospitality without telling you about it.'

'My dear chum, whatever you tell me won't go any further.'

'Well, it might have to. When you've heard it you might change your mind. It concerns Hillsden.'

Keating handed him a beaker of lethal proportions.

'If I've overdone it, I'll add some more tomato juice. You say it's concerned with Hillsden? You don't mean the hijack, do you? What are we talking about?'

'No, that's something else to add to my worries . . . I was sitting at home minding my own business when I got a phone message on my answering machine. No idea who it was; he didn't give a name. Just said he had to deliver something from a friend he'd met abroad, and would I meet him in the food-hall at Harrods. I thought it was a gag at first . . . and then I found out my phone was bugged. That set me thinking.'

'And he didn't give a name?'

'No, nothing. Sounded scared. I was intrigued naturally, adding two and two together. I kept the appointment, went to Harrods as per the arrangement, though I guessed something wasn't quite kosher, so I played it very low profile. Just as well, because a couple of heavies also kept the appointment. You might have read about it. They stabbed one of the

256

Harrods security guards; there was a piece in the papers.'

'That was the same thing?'

'Yes.'

'Did you ever find out who you were supposed to meet?'

'No, he sensibly did a bunk when the trouble started. I got a quick look at him – total stranger – but he did leave something behind which I picked up. A magazine.'

Keating raised an eyebrow.

'Oh, I should have mentioned, he said he'd be carrying a copy of *Country Life*, in order that I could recognize him. He dropped this and – why, I don't know – I picked it up.'

'Significant?' Keating asked.

'Not in itself, but there was a note tucked inside. Sort of shopping-list, which meant nothing at first, but seeing what had happened at Harrods I stayed with it and worked out that the list must be some sort of code . . . well, not a code exactly; it was too amateur for that, the kind of thing you jot down to remind yourself of something you have to do.'

'Did it mention Hillsden?'

'Oh, God, no. Then I got a break. The messenger had stupidly left his name and address on the magazine, and I tracked him down. He lives – lived – the other side of London.'

'Why do you say "lived"?'

Waddington paused and took a choking swig at his Bloody Mary. When he recovered he said: 'The man I eventually came face to face with was called Frampton.'

The name produced no noticeable effect on Keating.

'You obviously don't study the tabloids very closely.'

'I don't take them, and in any case I only read the financial pages.'

'Frampton and his father were taken out. The father had his head blown off, and his son, the one I met, was tortured and mutilated.'

'Jesus Christ!'

'That's why I sought sanctuary with you, and I apologize for that cock-and-bull story about a difficult time with the wife.'

'Don't worry. I understand. Have you told anybody else?'

'Not officially. I contacted an old mate I know at the Yard, somebody I could trust – he was the one who advised me to go to earth for a while.'

'Good advice.' Keating stared at him before speaking again. 'You say you tracked down this Frampton?'

'Yes, I met with him finally. God knows how he got involved, got chosen as a messenger boy, the poor devil was scared shitless.'

'But he'd met Hillsden?'

Waddington nodded. 'In Leningrad, while he was on holiday.'

'And what was the message?'

Perhaps the unaccustomed vodka so early in the day had weakened Waddington's normal caution, or perhaps the added complication of Pamela had thrown him, but having revealed most of it he now went on to complete the story. 'Well, according to this Frampton, Alec' – he slipped easily into the use of Hillsden's Christian name – 'has written his memoirs and wants to get them out. Now, that could bear out what I've always thought – that Alec was set up, that he knew too much, and now he wants to blow it sky high. It holds up in my opinion.'

'Why're you so sure?'

'Somebody out there thinks it's worth killing for. So you see what trouble I've brought into your house. If what he told me is true, I'm back in the game whether I like it or not and bad news as far as you're concerned.'

'Forget that. You came to the right place.'

'If you want I should go – '

'My dear chum, *mia casa* et cetera. It's a problem, but not insurmountable. I'm equally concerned about your girl-friend. What's her name?'

'Pamela. Pamela van Norden.'

'Is she Dutch?'

'No, that was her married name. She's divorced,' Waddington said, wondering if they would ever make love again.

'We must hope for the best.'

There was a smear of tomato juice on Keating's lower lip, and as he pulled himself out of his chair and went to the desk he seemed if anything larger than ever, ballooned within his single-breasted suit, like a fat man drawn by a child. 'You know what I've been thinking?' he said.

'What?'

Keating picked up another copy of the film script and waved it. 'Leningrad, right? Perhaps the unspeakable Mr Raven has done us a favour . . .'

Conjecturing about her future sex life was not one of Pamela's priorities at that moment. Like the rest of the hostages she had scarcely slept for the past forty-eight hours. Fear and fatigue had reduced most of them to crumpled heaps. Apart from a few sandwiches and canned drinks none of them had had much sustenance since the original departure from Marseille, and the food allowed to be brought on board when they had landed in Libya had proved inedible to most. Personal hygiene was a thing of the past, and for most of the hostages disorientation was complete. They could not remember life before the hijack.

In the cockpit the Captain and his co-pilot slept, while the Fat Boy continued his dialogue with the Libyans, for he spoke their language fluently. He argued a dozen scenarios, sometimes screaming in rage when his propositions were rejected. If he was exhausted, he showed little sign. One of the differences which had particularly enraged him was a demand for payment if the plane was again refuelled. The Fat Boy had made a rare slip by telling them he had half the ransom money on board, and this factor more than the fate of the hostages had become the major issue. The Libyans, for their part, were playing a double game and stalling for time, never rejecting his demands outright or agreeing to them. In the past year, faced with a growing crisis in their economy, they had been attempting to repair their image with the West, while at the same time covertly continuing to train and support several terrorist organizations. Basically their policy had not changed; it was merely presented to the world in a different

259

guise. Thus opinion within the governing ranks was sharply divided: one faction favoured giving the Fat Boy every assistance, the other was for storming the plane and thus enhancing their image in the West. There was also a third group pressing for freeing the plane, but allowing the three terrorists to 'escape'. The Colonel remained uncharacteristically passive through all these sessions and had so far not come down in favour of any of the options. His only positive act had been to place all the Libyan armed forces on a war alert in case the American Sixth Fleet mounted a rescue attack. There had been considerable air activity picked up on Libyan radar, and on two occasions Libyan fighters had been scrambled to investigate invasions of their airspace.

Back in Cyprus, with the Turkish plan having been thwarted, the Swiss were urgently considering their own military options. Once they had established the second destination they made use of all available intelligence and studied the feasibility of an Entebbe-type assault, requesting help from Israel's Sayaret Matkal unit which specialized in desert operations. Spy planes from the Sixth Fleet had provided photo-reconnaissance pinpointing the exact location of the hijacked airliner, but the White House had so far refused to be drawn further into the conflict. The new President had only been in office for less than a year and had his own domestic problems; he was not inclined to risk offending the OPEC block and possibly provoke another oil crisis. But he, too, had a problem with the hawks and the doves in his cabinet and was being pressured by the Jewish lobby. The big question-mark all the would-be rescuers faced was the unpredictability of the Libyans and the very real fear that any assault would inevitably put the hostages at risk.

World media sought to make as much capital out of the incident as possible, for it was, sadly, a quirk of human nature to be both fascinated and horrified by such things. Only the families directly involved knew that real anguish was not a spectator sport manufactured to sell newspapers and fill the television screens.

*   *   *

'What this country needs is a kick up the arse,' Pearson said out of the blue.

'The question is whose arse?' Lloyd observed.

'If we knew the answer to that, we would have the secret of semi-eternal life.'

At that moment Pearson's private phone rang. He hesitated before lifting the receiver. Listening, he said: 'Ah! Yes. Will you hold a second? Lloyd get me the Mitchell file, will you?' He waited until Lloyd had left the room before resuming the telephone conversation. 'Waddington, you still there? Or I should say, where are you?'

'As you advised, tucked away out of sight. Any developments?'

'No. All blanks so far. It's being treated as a racist killing.'

'Racist?'

'Yes. Apparently the old man held most of his neighbours in contempt. Made no secret of it. Practically everybody in the street is a possible suspect.'

'Do you believe that?'

'No. But it's keeping the CID boys busy. How's your own situation?'

'Well, I'm living OK at the moment, but obviously it's not a long-term solution.'

'Do you have a number you can give?'

'Yes. Like yours it's not for general circulation.'

'Understood.' Pearson reached for a ballpoint pen, which naturally was dry. 'Hold on. Whatever happened to the old-fashioned fountain pen?' He grabbed a pencil, and the lead immediately broke. 'Shit! Tell it to me and I'll remember.'

Waddington passed the number.

'I'll be in touch the moment anything breaks. I'm following up a few things that might dovetail. Meantime, keep your head down.'

'You don't have any inside gen on the hijack, do you?'

'Only that it's still in Libya. No further killings reported.'

'Thank God for that. I've a particular reason for asking. I know somebody on board, one of the hostages in fact, so I'd be grateful for any news. It'll probably come through to you first.'

261

'That's tough. I'm sorry. Give me his name.'

'Her. It's a Mrs van Norden. Pamela van Norden. She's British; that was her married name.'

'I'll find out what I can.' Pearson hung up and went into the next office, silently repeating the number until he found a usable pen. Returning, he found Lloyd leafing through the Mitchell file.

'Anything new?'

'Not new exactly, but I've just spotted something in his diary we missed before.'

'What?'

'There are two entries a month apart, the last one for the day we found him.' He pointed and handed the file to Pearson. 'Now, on their own they don't mean much.'

Pearson studied the entries. ' "PP"? Could mean anything.' He turned the pages. 'He's got others. Here. "MD" on this page, "TSB" here. People always jot down initials, abbreviations; I do it myself.'

'I agree,' Lloyd said, 'except, if you turn back a few months to January, he's written "Peter Pan".'

'How did you spend your childhood? Didn't you ever go to *Peter Pan*? Traditional Christmas outing, and they always run it into the New Year. All that means is he went to see it.'

'Except,' Lloyd repeated, 'where did they find what remained of him? In Hyde Park, right?'

'Yes.'

'And we know he didn't die there. He was shot and then put there.'

'So?'

'What's just across the park in Kensington Gardens?'

'More grass.'

'The Peter Pan statue.'

'OK, what does that prove, apart from having the same initials?'

'Well, there's a proximity.'

Pearson lit a cigarette, already half switched off. 'Go on.'

'Hypothesis. At certain intervals he met somebody by the statue. And on that last occasion that somebody killed him.'

262

'Brilliant. Why didn't I think of that?'

'Don't take the piss. I'm only trying.'

'You mean he arranged to meet a fellow-transvestite to swap underwear and the other guy didn't like what he brought, so first of all he shot him, then carried him across the park to the Round Pond and planted a sophisticated bomb under him? Who're we looking for, Captain Hook? You're one of the Lost Boys, Alan, living in Never Never Land, or else you've been drinking too much canteen tea. Come on!'

'I wasn't suggesting that.'

'So what were you suggesting?'

'I don't know yet. I just think it's a possible connection.'

'Good. Well, you follow it through. Put on short trousers, take a skipping-rope and stake it out. When they arrest you for child-molesting, don't depend on me to stand bail,' Pearson said.

He walked out of the room.

There was a Russian military mission permanently stationed in Tripoli, mostly composed of GRU personnel, the senior officer of which had conveyed Geichenko's extreme views on the conduct of the hijack. The Colonel had been left in no doubt as to the Kremlin's attitude. It did not suit Moscow's plans for the Middle East to become even more volatile; it was too close to their own borders and ethnic problems.

Even in the face of such pressures, the Colonel still played his usual poker game, disinclined to give something for nothing. He enjoyed horse-trading and was holding out for a badly needed arms deal in return for compliance with their wishes. Equally, the Kremlin had no intention of leaving the field open for the Americans to step in and grab all the glory for a successful rescue. The Russian ambassador to the United Nations had been instructed to put down an emergency resolution in the Security Council condemning all such terrorist acts; in London, Bonn and Paris other diplomatic moves were under way to assure the Western powers that Russia had no intention of taking unilateral action. But, since the game was being played at different levels, at the same time the Kremlin was circulating another version, letting it be known that if the American Sixth Fleet moved, then Russian intervention was inevitable. None of the participants was fooled by such manoeuvres.

These developments suited Bayldon's purpose: he was quite content to let the Russians handle it; Britain still had no diplomatic relations with the Colonel's regime. He made a token statement denouncing the hijack and expressing sympathy for the victims and privately ordered the SAS unit to stand down.

Eventually, having satisfied his own ego, and having reached an understanding regarding the arms deal, the Colonel stated his terms. In return for the terrorists parting with the major share of the ransom money, the Libyans would mount a dummy assault on the plane under cover of darkness and guarantee no serious harm would befall the hostages. The terrorists would then be spirited away and the plane allowed to be flown back to Switzerland. It again demonstrated the Colonel's flair for unpredictable behaviour – cynically presented and cynically agreed to. He would thus show his new humanitarian face to the world while keeping faith with the terrorists and pocketing his share of the spoils. It was generally felt that, in the relief of the rescue operation, the killing of the hostage in Cyprus would soon be forgotten – as, in time, proved correct.

There was one last stall while the Fat Boy held out for a larger slice of the ransom money, but he knew better than irrevocably to antagonize the Colonel, who had long been his principal paymaster.

Elite units of the Libyan army duly mounted the rescue operation, and the full drama was filmed for world consumption; there were few flies on the Colonel. The Libyan task force used stun grenades and dummy ammunition to create the maximum noise and confusion without loss of life. Although a dozen of the hostages received superficial wounds during the scrambled evacuation and two small children suffered damage to their hearing, the bogus mission gave the impression of great daring and efficiency. The Fat Boy and his two companions were shown being taken away, but later bulletins about their subsequent fate were deliberately vague. The Swiss were allowed to bring in a relief flight crew, and once the plane had been certified as airworthy it made the return journey home, again with full media coverage. All in all the Colonel achieved a notable propaganda coup at no cost to himself.

That episode concluded, Geichenko turned his attention to more pressing issues. 'Operation Medusa' targeted on Bayldon's wife had already been set in motion and it was vital that London be kept fully in the picture. Further delays in the long-term strategy could not be tolerated: the fledgling American President was just as hawkish as his predecessor and despite a mounting budget deficit there were no signs that he or Congress intended to cut arms expenditure. A new bomber with a dramatically reduced radar profile, currently beyond the resources of the Russians to counter, had recently been unveiled. It was imperative that Bayldon be toppled so that the disintegration of NATO was hastened. The line of direct communication with London having been broken with the murder of Mitchell, it was vital to mend the link as soon as possible.

Pamela arrived back at Heathrow with the other British hostages to find the airport awash with television crews and reporters, all anxious to reduce a human nightmare to soap-opera proportions. At the first opportunity she dodged into the nearest toilet and remained there until she judged it safe to emerge; she knew the dangers of exposure and had no wish to have her face plastered over the front pages. There was no question of contacting Control; it would be up to him to signal the time and place of their next meeting. She hired a chauffeur-driven car at the airport and drove to her country home, rehearsing a version of the events to relate to Waddington.

Much to her surprise, he was not there to greet her. Instead she was given a message by her staff to say that he had been called away on business and hoped to contact her shortly. He sent love and was overjoyed that she was home safe and sound. Having prepared herself, she was slightly put out by his absence; but, exhausted by the recent ordeal, she took to her bed and slept the clock round.

Watching the television coverage of the hostages' return, Waddington was perturbed not to spot Pamela amongst them. He again telephoned her house and was relieved to be told that she had arrived safely, although not taking any calls. He left word that he had rung, but carefully omitted leaving his own number. He was faced with a delicate situation where Pamela was concerned – anxious to see her again, but not knowing quite how or when, and unwilling to involve her in a dangerous situation.

In Leningrad, denied his own culture and friends, prey to the fear that at any moment the existence of his manuscript would be discovered, Hillsden had convinced himself that Frampton had failed to make contact with Waddington. What had once seemed a reasonably viable scheme now assumed the form of a nightmare.

Normally he and Abramov met on a regular basis once a month when Hillsden delivered his reports on the London traffic. For some reason, which he now regarded as sinister, Abramov had missed a month, so it was in a mood of fearful uncertainty that he took a telephone call from Moscow one morning when Galina was out of the apartment.

'I called you to say goodbye, Alec,' Abramov said. 'We won't be seeing each other for a while.'

'Why is that?' Hillsden kept his voice steady, though a nerve in his right leg went into spasm, and he put a hand on his thigh to try to control it.

'I have been posted to London, and leave tonight.'

'Earlier than you expected.'

'Yes. It's good news.'

'For you.'

'I will send you some of your favourite brand of cigarettes in the diplomatic pouch. Or anything else you think of. Just let my office know and they will forward the request.'

'Thank you.'

'Just one thing you can tell me. Where is the store of Marks and Spencer?'

'*The* store? There's more than one; they're all over London. Your nearest branch would be in Kensington High Street, close to your embassy.'

'I must note this. Say again, please.'

'Kensington High Street.'

'Got it. Well, I shall miss seeing you, Alec.'

'Likewise. Have a good trip.'

'Oh, by the way, I nearly forgot. There was some news from London which concerns you.'

Now it comes, Hillsden thought, and he braced himself for the worst.

'What was that?'

'That man you met here, the English tourist.'

Hillsden's immediate reaction was to jump on it quickly, rather than pretend he had forgotten the name. 'Frampton, you mean?'

'That's right. The strangest thing . . . Apparently he was murdered. Some reports suggest that the father killed him and then took his own life. Very Grand Guignol from all accounts.'

He's playing with me, Hillsden thought; he's concocted that story to trap me. 'Well, I'm told the majority of murders are domestic . . . So my well-intentioned efforts to recruit him proved a waste. Pity. He might have served a useful purpose.'

'It was worth a try, Alec. Everything is worth a try. Anyway, my friend, I thought you'd be interested. Keep well.'

'You, too. Bon voyage.'

Hillsden put down the phone still uncertain as to whether Abramov had been testing him. He searched the apartment for his hoarded copies of *The Times*, hoping he might find more details of the murder, but could find no mention of it. That was not too alarming – *The Times* never devoted much space to crimes of that sort. Only scandals in high places merited its full attention. He sat down in the kitchen and tried to think it through. If Abramov had merely related the truth, it was still too much of a coincidence that Frampton had come to a sticky end so soon after their encounter, and it left the big question mark: had he managed to get word to Waddington before being murdered?

He remained motionless, the virus of doubt coursing through his veins, thinking how everything could be made into a plot. How conveniently they had agreed to his request to live in Leningrad. Hadn't it been Abramov who had suggested enrolling at the University? What if he had instructed Galina to seek him out? Sex was one of the most potent weapons in the armoury of subversion. I used it myself in the past, he thought. I used it on the pathetic Frampton. Then, again, how quickly Abramov had agreed to the blackmail ploy – had it all been too easy, too pat, something he should have allowed for?

Consumed by these dark thoughts, it was with the fear of betrayal uppermost in his mind that he greeted Galina on her return.

'Anything wrong, darling?'

'No.'

She came to him, put her arms round him and kissed him. 'You want to hear some good news?'

'Why not?' He gently disengaged himself from her embrace.

'Remember what you said the other day?'

'Which day was that?'

'When we made love and you felt sorry for yourself.'

'Oh, that day. Don't you mean when we *didn't* make love? What did I say?'

'You blamed yourself.'

He had no idea where the conversation was leading, except that it fed his suspicions.

'You didn't need to,' Galina continued breathlessly, her face flushed with a kind of happiness he had not seen for a long time. 'Because I'm going to have your child. I'm in the third month; the doctor confirmed it today. That's where I've been. I didn't tell you before in case it was a mistake.' She searched his face. 'Are you pleased?'

Hillsden stared back at her, unable to take it in.

'Are you?'

'I'm pleased if that's what you want.'

'You have to want it, too. Don't you want it?'

He answered slowly, 'My dear, it's not a question of want. Want is something you think about beforehand. I never thought of starting a family at my age.'

Her mask of happiness slipped. 'Are you saying you'd rather I got rid of it?' Hillsden paused for too long. 'I could; there's still time. I don't want to make more trouble for you. Is it you feel trapped, is that it? I didn't set out to trap you; it just happened.'

'No, it's not that. I was trapped long before this.' The words were out of his mouth before he could stop them. Seeing disappointment flood into her face, he gathered her to him and kissed her. 'You've never made trouble for me, and I wouldn't let you get rid of a child we'd made. It is good news, very good news. I just have to get used to it.'

'Didn't you ever get a girl pregnant before?'

Hillsden shook his head. 'Believe it or not, no, but I guess it was a matter of luck rather than of good judgement.' An image of Caroline swam before his eyes: Caroline in Austria, in the last days before she went back into Berlin. The reverse blackmail had been constantly in his mind: the man trapping the woman, getting her with child in order to hold her.

'Shall we have a drink?' Galina was asking.

'Should you?'

She burst out laughing, the tension suddenly dispersed. 'How funny you are, you men. Immediately you become protective. Nothing's going to happen because we have a few drinks to celebrate . . . You are truly pleased?'

'Yes,' he said, cradling her face down on his shoulder so that she would not see his expression. 'You see, the trouble is I've only been trained to recognize hate. Love always takes me by surprise.'

19

Bayldon could never walk past the array of portraits of previous occupants lining the staircase of 10 Downing Street without a tremor of satisfaction. Being Prime Minister, surrounded by the hand-picked team of his private office all of whom had a vested interest in keeping him sweet, had proved a heady experience. The times when he gave some thought to the manner in which he had been elevated were spaced further and further apart. Conveniently, he had developed amnesia where that part of his life was concerned.

The mechanics of modern government being so complicated, those at the top of the pyramid are invariably isolated from the truth, hearing and believing only what their conceit wants them to hear and believe. This was certainly the case with Bayldon. There was safety as well as power in having arrived, for one could always evoke the democratic ethos to stifle the small voice of conscience. Yet in recent weeks, beginning with the meeting with Control, even Bayldon had become aware that there were rumblings of discontent within the ranks. A score or so of his backbenchers and one member of the Cabinet had abstained on a vital vote. This had given transient cheer to the demoralized Tory ranks – which in itself did not bother him, but he took the revolt as a direct challenge to his authority. It was no secret that the dissenters had been led by Deacon, who was still smarting at being denied a major ministry. Not that he feared Deacon – the man still did not command sufficient support within the National Executive Council to constitute any real threat – but his arrogance so matched Bayldon's own as to be a constant source of irritation.

'Is there any way', Bayldon asked the Home Secretary, 'we

can find out whether Deacon has been meddling in matters of security?'

'Meddling? How d'you mean?'

'Does he have any contact with Lockfield, for example?' Bayldon asked the question with studied casualness.

'Why Lockfield in particular?'

'I don't know. Just occurred to me that our friend Deacon seems to have an inside track on certain subjects. His intelligence is alarmingly accurate. And the papers always give him so much space.'

'He keeps his ear to the ground, that's for sure, and of course the papers like nothing better than a home-made vendetta.'

'I don't mind admitting, Richard, he's a bloody thorn in my side.'

'Promote him.'

'I did offer him something, as you know, but he had the nerve to turn it down. Said he'd only accept one of three jobs, one of which happened to be yours. Didn't I tell you at the time?'

'No.'

'I thought I did.'

'He had a bloody nerve.'

'Just an eye for the main chance, like us all. Might be worth our while to dig a little around his patch. Perhaps you know of somebody reliable who could keep a closer watch on his activities.'

'Tricky.'

'Why tricky?'

'We could be rumbled.'

'Oh, we mustn't be rumbled. I rely on you to ensure that. Something very discreet. You'll find a way if you put your mind to it. Things are going so smoothly; be a pity if Deacon rocked the boat. He's getting too big for his boots.'

'He's always been an arrogant bastard.'

'Well, see what you can come up with. Never know when it might come in useful. You wanted to see me about something, I believe?'

'Yes.' The Home Secretary hesitated.

'Not about the Militia, I hope. I know you received a deputation from the Chief Constables.'

'No. I dealt with that. I don't quite know how to put this to you. And I don't want you to think that I'm just carrying gossip.'

'I enjoy good gossip, as long as it's not about me,' Bayldon said.

'It doesn't concern you personally, but it is very close to home.'

Again he hesitated, and Bayldon got impatient.

'Tell me, then!'

'I've received a report from MI5 in Belfast that certain rumours are freely circulating about your wife.'

'What sort of rumours?'

'Obviously without foundation, but potentially highly dangerous.'

'Richard, just give it to me straight.'

'The story is that she has secretly donated large sums to the IRA through Noraid.'

'Balls.'

'OK, I agree, no truth in it whatsoever; but, nevertheless, good ammunition to use against you if it got into the wrong hands. They appear to have got some evidence.'

'What evidence could they have?'

'Photostats of cheques with your wife's signature on them.'

'I don't know why you bother to repeat such crap. They couldn't possibly be genuine; they're obviously forgeries.'

'Toby, don't attack me. I didn't invent the story; I'm merely bringing it to your attention.'

'Can you seriously believe that Linda would do such a crazy thing?'

'Of course not. But you wouldn't thank me for ignoring such a report. I have to protect you; that's part of my job. The rumours appear to have originated in New York.'

'That doesn't surprise me. The Yanks are capable of anything.'

272

'Granted the cheques are forgeries, what happens if they surface here?'

'Presumably they're drawn on a bank, yes?'

'Yes.'

'We get the chairman of the bank to issue a sworn statement that they're fakes. End of story. Use your loaf, Richard.'

'Except', the Home Secretary said, 'it's not a British bank. It's in the Cayman Islands.'

'So what's the difference? Get that bank to disown it.'

'You're forgetting something, aren't you? We brought back exchange controls . . . No British subject is allowed to have a foreign account; we've made it a criminal offence.'

'I know that!'

'Mud sticks.'

'Don't fucking well give me that. Linda doesn't have a foreign bank account.'

'Difficult to prove, though. There might be a lot of people who wouldn't give her the benefit of the doubt.'

'Nobody would print it. And, if they did, we'd slap such a fucking writ on them they'd wish they never had.'

'They might accept it. They don't exactly shy away from printing libels, or defending them. Linda would have to go into the dock. Hardly dignified for the Prime Minister's wife. They'd have to throw everything at her.' He met Bayldon's outraged stare without flinching. 'I'm just being devil's advocate, Toby. Whoever started the rumour dotted the *i*'s.'

'What's that supposed to mean?'

'It's been put together very skilfully. Linda's second-generation Irish American. Noraid is one of the main sources of IRA funds. They could make a lot of waves with those two facts, plus the forged cheques.'

Bayldon recovered his composure. 'Has anybody seen the cheques?'

'Not the actual ones. But MI5 have received photostats.'

'How much are they for?'

'Half a million dollars.'

'And the signatures?'

'I'm told they're very good, Toby, not an amateur effort.'

Bayldon paced the room. 'It's a plot.'

'Yes, obviously.'

'Well, get everybody working on it, get the police in on it.'

'Is that wise? I'd suggest we leave it with MI5 for the moment. Right now it's confined to Belfast; there's always a chance it won't cross the water. If we open it up, the possibility of a leak is much stronger.'

'Jesus Christ!'

'The other piece of information I have is that the security forces in Northern Ireland are certain that a large shipment of arms for the IRA has slipped through the net. They got the tip-off from one of their undercover men but, before he could tell them where, he was executed. In the wrong hands, it could all be made to add up.'

'So what do we do?' Bayldon demanded.

'Sit tight for the time being. See what develops.'

'Do I tell Linda?'

'I wouldn't, if I were you. No point, unless events force you to.'

'You're probably right. And there was I thinking that Deacon was my only problem,' Bayldon said, then added, almost as an aside: 'I trust Linda. She wanted this even more than me.'

When the meeting ended the Home Secretary gave more thought to that remark than to anything else they had discussed.

Abramov enjoyed his first weeks in London. He had of course entered the country under a false name. His passport stated he was Oleg Besedin, a director of the State Publishing House in Moscow and a Professor of English at Kiev University. Deliberately, he was not travelling with diplomatic status, Geichenko having decided that the familiar ploy of using trade delegations to mask covert activities had been dangerously overworked. In the more relaxed atmosphere of *glasnost*, reciprocated by Bayldon's government, it was felt that a private citizen with distinguished credentials could move about with more freedom. This notwithstanding, within the

274

embassy he outranked the resident GRU officer and, if required, could avail himself of all the facilities. The calculated risk was thought worth taking.

He arrived ostensibly charged with setting up an Anglo-Soviet publishing house capable of challenging the American and Australian conglomerates. Booked into the Park Lane Hilton, he occupied a carefully chosen corner suite and for the first few days behaved like an average tourist, visiting bookshops and museums and avoiding all contact with the embassy. Then, working to a prearranged plan, he rang the First Secretary and requested an appointment with the Ambassador. This was an elementary test to establish whether his phone calls were being monitored. If he was subsequently tailed, a second plan would be put into operation. He took a taxi for his appointment with the Ambassador and, although he expected his visit to be noted by MI5 or Special Branch, he could detect no sign of undue surveillance. The Ambassador thoroughly briefed him on the current London situation and, in turn, received his own instructions. A series of meetings with leading British publishers had been set up in advance, and Abramov had come armed with genuine commercial proposals to put to them, since his cover was not without substance. The carrot he was empowered to offer was that, if the joint venture became a reality, the Soviet government was prepared to accept what had hitherto always proved a stumbling-block, namely the payment to foreign authors of their royalties in hard currency.

A reception which the Ambassador hosted was given in the embassy. Most of the leading publishers and literary agents attended, together with a number of well-known authors and executives from the Writers' Guild. Some came out of curiosity, thrilled at the chance to step inside the embassy, but the majority went because they welcomed what could possibly be a major breakthrough for their list and their clients. Abramov gave a short speech, addressing himself to the central theme of closer ties between the two literary communities, stressing that if a deal could be consummated there would be no censorship of the material.

275

'Though obviously you should not expect large sales, if the books you send us are hostile,' he told them with great charm, adding, 'except for Stalin – you can write what you like about our great butcher.' His impeccable English relieved the British contingent from the normal boredom of having to listen to everything twice through an interpreter, and he impressed his guests with his grasp of the fundamentals. The evening was accounted a major step forward, and he scored a personal success. Before his guests departed a working party agreed to meet in a few days' time and he received numerous invitations to dine out.

He followed this with a series of meetings with individual publishers and agents, collating all the points discussed and promising to come up with a summary from which the working party could draw up a heads of agreement.

'I shall stay as long as it takes,' he told them. 'I have no wish to go back empty-handed.'

Only when he was confident that his day-to-day movements were not being too closely scrutinized did he set about making contact with Pamela. During one of many meetings with literary agents, he asked if he could use a spare office while drawing up a legitimate publishing contract. He used the occasion to phone Pamela on her unlisted number and to assure her that, despite the hiccup brought about by her delay in reporting back to Control, Medusa was on course, and the second stage primed to go the following week.

Neither she nor Control had any inkling that during the final stages of the hijack Geichenko had revised his strategy; he had struck his own private bargain with the Colonel while negotiating the terms that ended the incident. Medusa had been conceived by Moscow Centre, but he had penetrated the KGB team responsible, subsequently using Abramov's Marseille rendezvous with Pamela to give London the impression that it was his show. He was content to let it run its course; if it worked, all well and good, but at the same time he had set in motion a final solution to the British problem. Abramov had been instructed to play it straight, but to start laying a few traps and to make his own contacts. It was important to establish that the KGB had no real grasp of the situation and ultimately to discredit them. Geichenko was confident that he possessed all the necessary ingredients to bring this about.

In due course Pamela reported their conversation to Control.

'In future he insists we use a dead-letter drop.'

'Did he nominate one?'

'Yes.'

'Which?'

She told him.

'Why there?'

'He said it was conveniently near to the embassy.'

'Well, be extra careful.'

He lit one of his rare cigarettes, a sure sign that he was edgy, then switched the conversation abruptly to Waddington, asking for an update.

'I haven't seen him since I returned.'

'Why not? You told me he'd moved in.'

'He had, but he wasn't there when I got back.'

'So where is he?'

'I've yet to discover, but I'm working on it.'

'And no attempt to contact you?'

'He's phoned, but never leaves a number where I can reach him. I checked with the outfit he worked for, but apparently he handed in his notice and they have no trace of where he went to.'

'How about his house?'

'Empty. He hasn't been near it.'

'Well, don't leave it. I want to know and I want to know soonest.'

'I said I'm working on it. Leave it to me. I'll find him,' Pamela replied with more confidence than she felt. Control scared her.

20

By now Bayldon was in a panic. Although his wife did not have accounts in the Cayman Islands, he was well aware that, relying on her American origins, she had never declared the existence of a Swiss numbered account to anybody but himself. 'I can always plead ignorance if it ever came out,' she told him when the new regulations were put on the statute-book. 'After all, Daddy set it up for me long before your stupid rules were thought of.'

'The laws of the land may be stupid in your opinion, but they're there to be obeyed.'

'Well, there's no way I'm going to close the account, so it's a waste of time talking about it. It's my nest egg.'

Immediately he learnt of the existence of the plot Bayldon had questioned her again.

'You do realize, don't you, that if anything did come out it would reflect very badly on me? The Swiss code of secrecy can be broken these days. It's never admitted, but it has happened with Mafia funds and laundered drug-money. They've been very co-operative lately.'

'Sometimes I think this job has softened your brain, Toby. What has my little savings account got to do with the Mafia and drugs?'

'I'd hardly describe it as little. When we got married your father settled three million dollars on you.'

'You think that's a fortune?'

'To most people, yes.'

'Course, you've never had money; all you've ever had is a talent for spending other people's.'

'Thank you.'

He could not make up his mind to tell her the whole truth.

If, as he prayed, the rumour died a natural death, he would have scared and antagonized her for nothing, and their relationship was delicate enough as it was. Since he had come to power she had made few friends outside her own circle and was quite openly critical of most of his cabinet, describing them as 'the second-rate in pursuit of the third-rate'. On the other hand, should his efforts to stifle the rumour fail, it would be impossible to avoid some very awkward questions. Her gibe about money had gone home: he had always relied heavily on her personal income to fund his ambitions, and she had never forgiven him for choosing the wrong party.

'If you'd only had the sense to join the Tories, we might have been able to lead a normal life.'

'What d'you call "normal"?'

'Well, it certainly isn't playing hostess to a lot of trade union officials and their dowdy wives.'

'Do you imagine I'd have got to Downing Street if I was a Conservative? I'd still be on the back-benches. I thought you Americans were so anti-class. Well, class still counts for everything here, and that's what we're out to correct.'

'Bully for you.'

Thus the argument went back and forth while Bayldon searched for a way in which to warn her of impending events. He derived no comfort when he discussed the situation with Control.

'You're in the firing-line, Toby. You poked your head over the parapet a long time ago; you must expect to draw fire.'

'But this whole thing is a complete fabrication.'

'I believe you, but it would be foolish to expect others to take the same attitude. Many a good man has suffered because his wife shot him in the foot. It's the very stuff that scandal is made of.'

'I don't want to hear that. I want something done. And done quickly.'

'We're working on it night and day, Toby. Everybody has your best interests at heart, but scotching rumours isn't the same as tracing an electrical fault. The wires lead everywhere.

279

I hate to put it this way, but you're quite certain there is no substance to the story?'

'My wife has assured me she does not have an account in the Cayman Islands.'

'Then, you've no worry on that score. And naturally her sympathies are not with the IRA?'

'How could they be?'

'No, of course not. Even so, it might be worth checking through Langley as to whether any of her family has opposite views. The professional Irish in America are often more rabid than the genuine article. If there is any distant connection, we ought to be forewarned. I'm told that in Disneyland on St Patrick's Day they colour everything green. Even the bagels,' he added inconsequentially.

Bayldon swept this piece of folklore aside. 'I don't trust the CIA. For all we know, they set the whole thing up. There's every indication that the thing was first planted at the United Nations.'

'Perhaps we're running ahead,' Control said. 'Allowing ourselves to be panicked for no good cause. Put it this way: were we out to frame somebody, we'd play the same game. Dream up something that's close enough to be possible, add a few trimmings that sound authentic, and sit back to await results.'

'Is that meant to be reassuring? Seems to me you're taking it all very casually on my behalf. I'd remind you that if I'm damaged in the process it will hardly further the cause.'

'Did I give that impression? If I did, it was not intentional. I'm convinced there is no truth in these terrible allegations. After all, I have your word for it, and that's good enough for me. However, I doubt whether you'd thank me if I pushed you into a public denial too soon in the day. One should never deny anything, true or false, until it's absolutely necessary. If political history has proved nothing else, it's proved that time and time again.'

'I've given considerable thought to our problem,' Keating announced over breakfast, helping himself to a generous

280

portion of scrambled eggs and smoked salmon. 'And I think I've refined it.' He reached into the basket of hot toast cut into identical triangles. 'In the beginning was the word. The solution came to me last night. The script, the screenplay.' He paused for effect, and Waddington waited. 'They'll be taking at least forty copies into Russia, when you count all the artists and members of the unit. So it becomes a simple matter of arithmetic.'

'Arithmetic?'

'Yes, forty in and thirty-nine out. D'you follow me? It shouldn't be beyond the wit of yours truly to make a swap: Hillsden's manuscript inside the cover of my script.'

'How d'you mean, *you'll* make the swap?'

'Exactly that.'

'You'll go to Leningrad yourself?'

'I'm entitled, chum. More so than the dreaded Raven. I'm the money man, remember? I foot the bill, and there's nothing your average communist likes better than somebody with the bankroll. Especially when it's hard currency.'

'I never thought of you going.'

'But isn't that the answer?'

'Yes, if you're prepared to risk it.'

'What risk? I've got a valid visa, I've even got a credit as executive producer. No problem.'

'The problem will be making contact with Alec.'

'I've even thought of that. Did you read the script?'

'Yes. I don't pretend to have understood it. Seemed very technical to me.'

'Well, in the Leningrad sequence, we need a certain number of extras to play British tourists. They have to look authentic. Can't have the screen full of Mongolian faces above Berman suits. My location manager will ask the authorities for permission to use the real thing. You've given me Hillsden's address; he'll be put on the list and contacted in the normal fashion.'

'If you say so.'

'It's another world, chum, the film business. I've learnt that. They seem to have amazing chutzpah, these film types, never take no for an answer, barge in where angels fear to tread.'

'OK, I believe you. But, assuming that part of it works, you've still got to bring it out. They could search you.'

'Don't forget I won't be travelling alone, and the rest of the crew will be carrying their copies of the genuine article. There's safety in numbers. In addition, and most important, the local Gestapo will be familiar with it. Before they gave permission and provided the facilities the script had to be submitted and rubber-stamped. That, I thought, was the beauty of it – prior approval, like clearing Customs before you arrive. No, as I see it, the area of risk doesn't lie there. It lies with Hillsden himself.'

'Why with Alec?'

'He's got to be persuaded to part with it, hasn't he?'

'I don't follow you,' Waddington said.

'What's the *Good Housekeeping* guarantee I give him in exchange? Put yourself in his shoes. He sent word to you some months ago. Since when, silence. No way of telling whether or not you ever got the message. Has he been betrayed? Are they just sweating him? By now he's anxious, very anxious, waiting for that knock on the door we all fear. Then I turn up out of the blue. Who am I? Is it a trick? Does he even remember me from the old days? Or, if he does, why should he trust me?' He extracted a sliver of smoked salmon from between his teeth and positioned it carefully on the side of his plate. 'One thing for me to ask for it, quite another for him to admit it exists, or to part with it. I'll need to go armed with something more than my pretty face.'

'Some kind of password, you mean?'

'Exactly. You're not eating a very hearty breakfast.'

'I am for me. Orange juice and a stale bagel are my usual welcome to the day.'

'Oh, I can't function unless I'm stoked up. So what d'you think?'

'It really ought to be one of those trick questions the Resistance used in the war. Like how many runs did Len

282

Hutton score when he slaughtered the Aussies . . . Or . . . something that only I would know, so that it ties in with me.'

'Did he have a pet?'

'What? Sorry, I don't come to very quickly in the mornings.'

'A pet?'

'Yes, yes, he did. He had a cat when he was married to Margot. A neutered tom.'

'What was that called?'

'Wait a tick. He told me he took the name from a favourite book of his . . . MacDonald? No. Mactavish?'

'Macavity?' Keating said.

'Say that again.'

'Macavity.'

'Is that from a book?'

'Yes. Eliot's *Old Possum's Book of Practical Cats*. Macavity was a mystery cat.'

'That's it! I remember now, Alec always used to say "That bloody cat's a mystery". There's your password.'

Keating shook his head. 'Not sufficient in itself. It needs something else, again something personal from you that you could put in a handwritten note. Didn't you and he operate from a bogus wine merchant's at one time?'

'Yes.'

'What sort of stuff did you appear to sell?'

'Piss mostly.'

'Remember any particular brand?'

'There was a Romanian red we used to flog if any genuine customer wandered in by mistake. Cheap and nasty, would rot your guts if you drank more than two glasses of it, called "Castle" – not Château, mind you! – "Castle Draz", but we referred to it as Dracula.'

'That combined with the cat should do it. Give me a note to take.'

Waddington looked dubious. 'Not too sure about the wisdom of that.'

'I think we need it.'

'Wasn't the Firm's motto "Never commit anything to paper"?'

283

'Special circumstances. I'll only have one shot at it, remember? Just something short and sweet but in your own style.'

'OK, if you think so. When do you go?'

'The advance unit's already there. I go with the main group in two days' time. And, by the way, while I'm gone take advantage of my absence, have the girl-friend over. I'm sure you both need to comfort each other.'

'You serious?'

'I'm always serious about sex,' Keating said, taking another helping of buttered toast. 'Sex and food.'

All unknowing of these developments, Hillsden was still coming to terms with Galina's news. The prospect of becoming a father for the first time filled him with both a dread and a kind of wonder. He remembered moments in his past life, with Margot, with Caroline, when the possibility of a child had been skirted but never resolved. Never promiscuous, for certain periods in his life he had been celibate – not always from choice, but because, in the field, he had no choice. Equally, he had been constrained by the chains of romanticism, a romanticism often born of literary associations; for, just as whole lives are shaped by a single childhood experience, his view of women had been taken, rose-hued, from the books he had read in his formative years. There had always been an element of eroticism, never lost, in the descriptions of his favourite heroines: in print they never changed, but could be returned to, or conjured up, during those nights when sleep evaded him. Age could never destroy their beauty; their responses remained constant. Even now, some forty years after first discovering Hemingway's youthful paean, he could not reread the description of Catherine's death in *A Farewell to Arms* without a profound sense of personal loss. Sometimes, as in Caroline's case, the fiction overlapped his own anguish, blurring the reality.

Now, with Galina carrying his child, he was torn between the moral dilemma and the wider issue of his secret manuscript. If the pages hidden within the lining of his overcoat were ever to be made public, then, as his wife, she would inevitably be guilty by association, and he had no illusions as to how she would be treated.

He allowed Galina to see none of this, treating her with new tenderness, becoming oversolicitous in his efforts to conceal his true feelings.

'I'm not ill,' she said. 'I'm just pregnant. I never felt better. Don't worry over me so much.'

'I can't help myself. Does it irritate you, darling?'

'No, but you should see yourself. You're like an old hen.'

'You mean an old cock. Well, that's for sure.'

'The baby's not going suddenly to appear; I've got five months yet. Plenty of time before you have to worry.'

'How d'you mean, worry? What will happen then?'

'Nothing. About getting me to the hospital on time, things like that.'

'Oh, I see.'

He found himself unusually tongue-tied, unable to broach the subject of marriage openly, tackling it obliquely. A lifetime of deceit had not prepared him for honesty in matters of the heart. 'Did you know that Spartan women had a ceremony of spanking unmarried men once a year?'

'Spank?'

'Smack them. They were regarded as undesirables.'

'Really? Why?'

'I suppose because they refused to accept the obligations of marriage, making a home, having children. They were considered traitors to their sex.'

'It sounds very drastic, darling.'

'I wouldn't want to risk you having to go to such lengths,' he said, keeping the joke going. 'To say nothing of the indignity.'

'Is that your real worry?' she said. 'That you have to marry me?'

'I'm an obsolete model. I still believe children shouldn't be born bastards.' Even as he said it, he was conscious that it was not a very elegant proposal. 'And, yes, if you're going to have my child, I want to marry you.'

'Are you sure? I don't want you to feel there is no way out.'

285

He was committed now to whatever happened: the embryo she carried would decide both their futures. He could hardly believe that he had needed to come so far from home to find a kind of love never experienced before, but as he pressed his face against her soft swollen belly a great wave of relief swept over him, and his tears dampened the fabric of her blouse.

'Is that what you want?'

'Yes,' she said.

'It won't be easy, will it? I shall be a very ancient father. There's going to come a time when you'll both be on your own – have you thought of that?'

'Don't talk about that, not now.'

'It has to be faced, though.'

'All I want to know is, are you sure, are you happy?'

'I'm very sure.'

She tasted the salt on his cheeks as they kissed.

'Do you know yet whether it's a boy or a girl? Have they told you?'

'No. What would you like to have?'

'Aren't men supposed to want girls? I don't mind. I'll be happy with whatever you give me.'

'Just so long as it's healthy,' she said, 'with five fingers and five toes. That's what my mother used to say.'

Hillsden frowned. 'What will she think? What d'you suppose your parents will say? Do they know about the baby?'

Galina shook her head.

'Do they even know about us?'

'They know I'm living with you.'

'Will they be angry about the baby, about you marrying somebody like me?'

'Why should they? I love you.'

'But . . .'

'No buts. They'll be happy if I'm happy. And I'm happy. I'm very happy.'

'You'll have to make all the arrangements. I've no idea how one gets married in Russia. I've only seen Russian weddings on films – priests wearing golden crowns, like something out of *Ivan the Terrible* – but I'll go through with it if that's what you want.'

'That's Russian Orthodox. We don't have to have that.'

'We don't?'

'No. We get married, simply, no problem.'

'The sooner the better, then. I'll leave it all to you. Hey! A thought just struck me. Do I have to have a best man?'

'Best man?'

'Yes, in England the bridegroom usually chooses his oldest friend. The best man takes care of the bridesmaids and the ring. I don't have any friends here, except you.'

She kissed him again. 'What a worrier you are. We don't need best friends. We have each other. Isn't that enough?'

'Yes,' he said, 'it's enough for me; more than I deserve.'

21

The second stage of Medusa began with a bomb placed in the Royal Mews at Buckingham Palace, causing extensive damage to the stables housing the state ceremonial carriages, though miraculously there was no loss of life. The explosive device, smuggled into the premises concealed in a bale of hay, had been placed and activated by one of the grooms prior to going off duty. At the time the Queen was boarding an aircraft of the Royal Flight in Newcastle where she had launched a new destroyer. Her plane was ordered to divert to an RAF base in Norfolk where an armed escort was provided for her journey to Sandringham. There, shortly before the royal party arrived, a further and larger explosion was triggered, destroying much of the staff quarters and inflicting numerous injuries. Seven fire brigades were deployed to contain the subsequent blaze. The seriously wounded were ferried by RAF helicopters to hospitals in nearby King's Lynn, and in addition to a massive police presence a company of the SAS was flown in to provide extra security. Despite being advised to divert yet again, the Queen insisted on completing her journey to inspect the damage to one of her favourite homes, and later visited the injured in hospital, before taking another plane to Heathrow and thence to Windsor. The garrison there had been supplemented by a second SAS unit. Bayldon and the Home Secretary were waiting to receive her at Heathrow and accompanied her to the castle. They outlined the measures already taken and obtained her approval for the contingency plans. During this audience news was received that three of the casualties in King's Lynn had died in the operating-theatre. Most of the scheduled television pro- grammes were interrupted and replaced by extended news-bulletins. Police forces throughout the country having been put on full alert, all other royal residences and principal government buildings were now being guarded by troops and tanks. More than the Birmingham pub outrages and the Brighton bomb that had killed members of the Thatcher administration, the incidents provoked widespread and immediate public outrage. Gangs of youths attacked known Irish neighbourhoods in Liverpool and Glasgow, and Molotov cocktails were thrown at the Irish embassy in the capital, mounted riot police being needed to disperse the large crowds. In Northern Ireland, members of the outlawed Ulster Defence Force carried out a number of sectarian murders; the Falls area of Belfast was subjected to a night of retaliatory terror, by the end of which the death-toll had risen to thirty-four, the highest since Bloody Sunday.

The BBC and ITV switchboards were jammed by viewers demanding drastic retribution, the majority calling for a state of war to be declared. The Irish cabinet in Dublin met in emergency session, later issuing a statement expressing their revulsion at these latest terrorist attacks and promising a stringent crackdown on all known IRA suspects. This did little to appease the British public, and when the newspapers appeared the following morning they all carried front-page leading articles strongly critical of Whitehall's security measures, many of them pointing out that it was only by a miracle that the monarch had escaped injury. The *Telegraph*, in a two-page editorial, stated that the Secretary of State for Northern Ireland should resign and be replaced by a military commander empowered to operate a shoot-to-kill policy against the terrorist elements.

Enough is enough, the editorial stated in bold type.
There must be no further hesitation, the gloves must come off. The British people have suffered these outrages with fortitude for too long. These latest outrages against the Royal Family and their servants cannot, and will not, be tolerated by loyal subjects of the Crown. While we must avoid a policy of revenge, the perpetrators of terrorist acts

289

*must be ruthlessly hunted down, and if the authorities are
not prepared to take the necessary measures, then it will
be difficult to contain the anger of the people. Not since
1939 has the country been faced with such a threat to
national security. We did not shrink from the task in those
dark days, and we must not shrink now. England expects
the Government to do its duty.*

Immediately after his return from Windsor, Bayldon presided over a full Cabinet meeting to discuss the crisis. It was with relief as much as with honour that the Northern Ireland Secretary duly tendered his resignation, and it was later announced that he would not be replaced; instead the Prime Minister was to assume direct responsibility for Northern Ireland – all security matters would in future be directed by Downing Street. The armed forces in Northern Ireland were to be increased by an additional 10,000, and a Bill to strengthen the existing provisions of the Prevention of Terrorism Act (1988) was to be rushed through Parliament. This was to include the reintroduction of the death penalty.

Bayldon hoped these draconian decisions would stifle the mounting criticism of his administration, but they played right into Control's hands. Operation Medusa was working as planned. By now Bayldon was aware that photostats of the forged cheques had found their way to Fleet Street. Earlier on the day that the bomb outrages took place he had taken a breakfast meeting with the editors of the national newspapers asking for their voluntary agreement to withhold publication of the story. The Attorney-General had also been present at the meeting. After a heated discussion the editors had reluctantly given an undertaking to sit on the news for a further forty-eight hours on condition that Downing Street issued a full statement from Mrs Bayldon, refuting the allegations and backed up with a full disclosure of her assets.

As soon as the Cabinet dispersed, Bayldon met with the editors again, ostensibly to brief them on the measures he intended to announce in Parliament the following day. As on the previous occasion he took the precaution of having the Attorney-General present.

'You do realize, Prime Minister,' the editor of one of the tabloids interrupted, 'that today's events make it increasingly difficult for us to withhold publication of the other matter.'

'I don't see any connection between the two.'

'The connection, sir, is plain enough. The suspect cheques are made out to Noraid.'

'As I have repeatedly stated, the cheques are forgeries.'

'With respect, sir, that remains to be proved.'

'Are you saying you are not prepared to take my word for it?'

'I'm saying, and my colleagues agree, that the proper place to test that is in the courts. It's our business to print the news, not to conceal it.'

'How can you describe it as news? The news, for God's sake, is yesterday's hideous outrages. We are on the brink of civil war, and all you're worried about is a malicious slur on my wife's character.'

'The trouble is, Prime Minister,' a second editor chimed in, 'the timing appears to be unhappily coincidental. Too coincidental to ignore. In the circumstances a leak is almost inevitable.'

'Is that meant to be a threat, Bob?' Bayldon said, employing his first name in an effort to sound reasonable despite the provocation.

The editor did not back off. 'No, merely a statement of fact, human nature being what it is.'

While they argued the damage, events were overtaking them. The latest issue of *Private Eye* was on the news-stands carrying an item, couched in the magazine's familiar prep-school journalese, that was quickly seized upon and translated by the rest of the media.

Lord Gnome reports that all men (and women for that matter) are not created equal in our egalitarian paradise. There appears to be one law for our masters and mistresses and one for the rest of us. Despite elaborate efforts at the highest level to conceal the matter, friends tell me that the Noraid funds for the brave freedom fighters who are doing

*much to clear the slums in our inner cities have recently
been swelled by a massive contribution from a well-wisher
living not a thousand miles from Downing Street. Our
popular Prime Minister is expected to comment on the
matter in the near future. We await his statement eagerly
and understand that it will be issued from a bank in the
Cayman Islands.*

In Parliament that afternoon a supplementary question was
put to Bayldon by a Tory front-bench spokesman, asking
when the House could expect his statement referred to in a
well-known political journal.

'I would like to assure my Right Honourable Friend, the
Prime Minister, that we on this side of the House feel deeply
for him in this hour of national and personal crisis.' The
emphasis was on the word 'personal'.

All Bayldon could manage when he got to his feet to
respond was: 'I thank my Honourable Friend, the Member
for Slocombe, for his expression of sympathy. I am sure he
speaks for this entire House in supporting the Cabinet's resolve never to submit to terrorism. I shall keep my Right
Honourable Friend, the Leader of the Opposition, fully informed of all developments.'

There was much waving of Order papers and cries of
'Answer' from the Opposition benches, but Bayldon refused
to be drawn further and shortly afterwards left the Commons
to return to Downing Street. Under heavy escort he drove
through the large crowd gathered in Whitehall and was somewhat mollified to find himself being cheered. Control was
waiting for him in the private apartments.

'You've seen *Private Eye*, I take it?'

'Yes. They appear to be well informed,' Control said.

'How?'

'Their sources have always been good.'

'Well, get them to reveal their source.'

'Easier said than done. It means going through the courts.'

'I wasn't suggesting the courts. It surely can't be beyond
your resources to find out by other means.'

'Dangerous. If it went wrong, it would merely strengthen the case against your wife.'

'Don't keep talking as if there *was* a case. There is no case to answer. My wife is entirely innocent.'

'But not above suspicion. Circumstantial evidence has hanged many a man. The most damaging element is the timing. It couldn't have broken at a worse moment. These latest IRA bombings have worked against you. Countries have gone to war for less.'

'You don't have to tell me that. So what do I do?'

'It very much looks as though you'll both have to brazen it out, face the music.'

'That's bloody easy for you to say. You're not in my shoes. I want every available stop pulled out. Get the bloody cheques and destroy them. I don't care how you do it, just do it; that's what you're paid for – to protect me.'

'I can't protect you against rumours. And if the cheques are forgeries, then they can be forged again.'

'So are you saying *nothing* can be done? Next thing you'll be suggesting my wife goes on the Wogan show and does a crying act like Nixon and his dog!' He went to the window and looked down into Downing Street. Television crews stood about in groups. 'What you don't seem to realize is that, although she is totally in the clear as far as this filthy campaign is concerned, there are aspects of her affairs that we don't wish to be aired in public. Once the bloody media scent a scandal they're like stag-hounds; they won't be satisfied until they have a corpse.'

Control used a more conciliatory, almost fatherly tone: 'What other aspects are there? I need to know if I'm to help.'

Bayldon hesitated. 'It's never been a secret that Linda has private means. Her old man left her comfortably off.'

Control waited, betraying nothing on his face.

'Until this business came up, I was in the dark myself about some of her affairs . . . She now tells me that she does have money overseas. Not in the Cayman Islands, I hasten to add.'

'Where?'

293

'The traditional place, Switzerland.' Bayldon bit on the words.

'A numbered account, you mean?'

'Yes. I suppose, being American, she thought our laws didn't apply.'

'Hardly a defence,' Control murmured. 'You see – if I can be devil's advocate for a moment – even if the Swiss thing never surfaces, the rest of the case, although I accept there's no basis for it, is fairly damning from an outsider's viewpoint. We can't ignore that the IRA have tightened it a notch. They've actually attacked the Monarch. They've lit a fuse which won't be snuffed out easily. If you add to that the connection – however tenuous – between your wife and Noraid, you're looking at trouble. Better she'd had an affair with a toy boy in the post room; you could weather that and come out relatively unscathed. But the Queen's life has been threatened; there's real anger outside, you can feel it, and it won't go away easily.'

Bayldon had listened to this without interruption. 'You mean, it could conceivably bring us down?'

'There is that possibility.'

'Well, I've acted swiftly where the IRA is concerned. Apart from going into the Republic itself, I've ordered the gloves off. The next terrorist we arrest is going to hang. Perhaps that will take the heat off.'

'You're confusing two issues.'

'Jesus Christ! You're a big help. What's the point of having a secret service if you can't even solve a simple problem like a forged cheque? I know how the CIA would handle this. They wouldn't hesitate if the President's wife was being framed.'

'Wouldn't they? They didn't save Nixon, and they didn't come clean about Oswald. You have to live in the real world. The name of the game is power.'

'Well, isn't that what we're talking about – staying in power? You sound as though we're on our way out.'

'Not me,' Control said evenly. 'I don't have a wife. It's your neck, not mine.'

*   *   *

'Whose house is this?' Pamela said, looking around Keating's splendid library.

'An old friend's,' Waddington replied casually. 'As you can see, he did rather better for himself than I did.'

'But why are you living here? I got back after my horrendous experience expecting to find you at home, and you were nowhere to be seen. And, if not with me, why not in your own place? Have you gone off me?'

'No, of course not. I would explain, but it might sound too far-fetched. So don't ask me.'

'I don't know that I care for that arrangement.'

'While you were away, I got involved in a situation which I need to sort out.'

'Does that mean your ex-wife is on your tail?'

'You're warm,' Waddington lied. 'I just needed to go to earth for a bit, and I didn't want to involve you.'

'Darling, wives don't bother me. Are you behind with the alimony, is that it? Because, if so, I can bail you out.'

'I told you before, I don't sponge off women.'

'Only men, it seems. You'll have me thinking you're AC/DC if you're not careful. However, if you insist on being a man of mystery I guess I'll have to live with it.'

'I'm much more concerned about you. What a terrifying experience. Come to bed and tell me.'

They went upstairs to Waddington's suite. Pamela examined the paintings while she undressed.

'He has taste as well as money, your friend. Where did he make it?'

'He dabbles in a number of things, all of which pay off. He's investing in a film at the moment.'

'A man of many talents. Who's this?' She pointed to a framed photograph of a woman on the dressing-table. 'This yours or his?'

'His.'

'He's married, then?'

'Several times. You don't give up, do you? Listen, come here.' Pamela walked naked to the bed and threw the Ralph Lauren duvet to one side. Waddington drew her down to him.

295

'If you have to know, his name's Keating. That satisfy you?'

'I'm hoping this will satisfy me,' she said, employing a technique that from past experience she knew he could not resist.

'What did you think of on the plane? Did you think of me at all?'

'I wondered if we'd ever make love again, yes. But most of the time you're just numb, too terrified to move. We were made to stay strapped in. They pistol-whipped the man sitting next to me. Have you ever noticed how slowly time passes when you're flying, even on an ordinary trip? Well, every minute during the hijack seemed like a week.'

'You poor darling. Did they do anything to you?'

His questions stopped as her mouth closed over him again. Waddington lay back and for the next half-hour he forgot Frampton had ever existed. There was a new urgency to Pamela's lovemaking, a kind of frenzy which he took to be a reaction to the events she had passed through. He had never taken any woman so uninhibited; she heightened his own pleasure, goading him on with obscenities, prolonging the final spasm that left them both drained.

'There's something special, isn't there, about doing it in a strange bed?' Pamela said when she returned from the bathroom. 'Hotels do that to me. I always get very randy in hotels; even before I unpack I want to fuck. Do you feel like that?'

'Not the hotels I usually stay in. And I don't usually share rooms with anybody like you.'

She wrapped herself in an enormous bath-robe and snuggled up to him. Waddington slid his hand inside the robe and stroked her breast which was cold from the shower.

'What am I going to do about you?' Pamela said. 'Is this it from now on, me having to come to you?'

'Just for a while, until I get things sorted out.'

'Can't you tell me any of it?'

She thought of how many times she had played the same role, probing in the aftermath of lovemaking when men were at their most vulnerable, using all the tricks in her repertoire, cold-bloodedly picking their brains, while often her feelings were nearer hatred than love. Some were a pushover, others like Waddington knew all the counter-moves and could block her checkmates.

'It's a boring mess I got mixed up in by pure accident.'

'You're not a wanted man, are you?'

'Only by you, I hope. No, nothing as dramatic as that. It's something I have to work out for myself. Maybe when it's over I'll tell you.'

We'll have to know before then, she thought, as he nestled his head in her neck and his eyes closed.

Pearson was somebody else who had not been sleeping in his own bed. Pearson had his hands full. He had not been home in a week. Everybody was on his neck. The latest IRA campaign, his team agreed, was a proper bastard. All leave had been cancelled, and they were working around the clock, snatching a few hours' rest on the premises. Although they had roped in nearly a hundred possible suspects from all over the country, and were holding them under the stringent new laws, nothing material had come to light. The only real lead they had was the missing royal groom. If he and the rest of the Active Service Unit were still in the country, then they had to be found quickly. It had been established that the explosive used was of Czechoslovakian origin, probably part of the huge Libyan shipment Pearson knew had been slipped into Eire some months before. That proved something and nothing as far as he was concerned. In the wake of the two major terrorist attacks there had been the usual spate of hoax calls, all of which had to be investigated. In two cases the Bomb Squad had carried out controlled explosions of suspect parked cars. The SAS had now taken over the responsibility of guarding all members of the royal family. Despite protests from the Palace, Bayldon had prevailed upon the senior members of the House of Windsor to cancel all public engagements until further notice. He had also ordered positive vetting of all staff who had direct access to the Monarch. Again, this had not been received with any enthusiasm. For the first time visas were now required for all Irish citizens before they could enter the British Isles. Supermarkets reported a widespread boycott of all Irish produce, and the large Irish population in the major cities were advised to keep a low profile until the furore died down. The Irish government delivered a strong protest to the British Foreign Office, condemning these measures, and were none too politely told they would have to live with them. Many of the IRA convicted hardliners in Belfast's Maze Prison began a hunger strike, which impressed nobody in Whitehall. Off the record the prison authorities were told to let them starve to death if necessary.

'They'll strike again,' Pearson volunteered to the Police Commissioner.

'You think so.'

'I'm bloody certain. They've been on the front pages of the world for the past week, just what they like. "Breathing the rarefied oxygen of publicity" – isn't that the phrase?'

'What's your guess, then?'

'Well – and it *is* only a guess – the royals are now pretty well sealed off, so they'll try for something equally spectacular, but further afield. My hunch would be a senior member of the Government.'

'All the Cabinet are covered.'

'They still have to move about. A car bomb is the most likely.'

'Who would be the prime target, d'you think?'

'Well, the jackpot would be the Prime Minister. Since he brought back the death penalty he must be number one on their hit-list. I suggest that he uses one of my men to drive his armoured car, plus police and SAS back-up.'

'OK, I'll put that to him at tomorrow's meeting,' the Commissioner said. 'What's your view about the other business, just between these four walls?'

'What's that, sir?'

'The stories going around about his wife?'

'I haven't seen the news or read the papers in days. What stories are those?'

'Well, if you don't know, so much the better.'

When he left the meeting Pearson tackled other members of his unit. 'Tell me what I've missed about Bayldon's wife.'

They told him.

'Has Downing Street reacted?'

'Not really, not so far. There've been questions asked in the House, but so far only *Private Eye* has actually dared to go into print.'

At that moment a report came in that Harrods was being evacuated for the fourth time that week, and Bayldon's dilemma took a back seat. Since no chances were taken any more, the entire Knightsbridge area was sealed off, creating a traffic snarl-up which stretched back to the Heathrow exit on the motorway, causing Keating to miss his flight to Leningrad. Sniffer dogs were sent in, one of them creating a minor crisis when it peed on a rare oriental carpet close to the pet department. A crude incendiary device was eventually discovered and quickly rendered harmless. The search took over two hours, during which time Harrods calculated they lost half a million pounds in sales.

It was while this diversion was taking place that the third bomb Pearson had predicted was exploded. It seemed to typify the IRA's total disregard for the sanctity of innocent lives in the furtherance of their campaign, but in actual fact was carried out by a two-man East German team, both under the age of twenty-three, who had entered the country a week before. They had been supplied with the materials for their mission smuggled into their own embassy many months previously in the diplomatic pouch. Fully aware that by now all the royal residences would be unapproachable, they had targeted Madame Tussaud's waxworks, visited by many thousands of tourists every year and famous not only for its Chamber of Horrors, but also for the replicas of the entire royal family. Knowing that security would be strict and that any shopping-bags would be liable to search, the devices they carried had been ingeniously constructed. The main charge had been concealed in a large hollowed-out guidebook of London, carried quite openly. Two smaller incendiary devices capable of producing intense heat within seconds were hidden inside bizarre cuddly toys such as could be purchased in any tourist gift-shop. These, too, were carried openly and passed the security check without challenge. All three were programmed to be triggered by a radio signal.

Operating from a Hertz car hired at Gatwick Airport, the team parked it legitimately on a meter in the Baker Street area just before 8.30 a.m. They then joined the usual queue which formed before opening-time every day, deliberately distanced from each other and avoiding any eye-contact. When the doors opened they bought tickets and wandered around the exhibition looking for suitable locations. They were working to strict limits, since it was vital that they placed the devices and were off the premises before 10.30 a.m. so that they could return to their car before the permitted parking-time expired. The plan was to drive straight to Heathrow and catch the first available flight to Paris.

In the room housing the royal replicas, the first terrorist bent down to tie a loose shoe-lace, placing the guidebook on the floor so that he had both hands free. Before straightening up he gently pushed the book under a plinth, then walked casually away. Meanwhile his companion had left his cuddly teddy bear in one of the toilets, then left the building. The first man carried his toy, a Mickey Mouse, into the chamber where there were other Disney waxworks. Carefully choosing his moment, he left it propped against one of the exhibits. He then vacated the building to rejoin his companion at the parked car. Only sixteen minutes had elapsed. At approximately 10.19 a small boy discovered the abandoned bear in the toilet and claimed it as his own, carrying it back to his parents. They took it from him and went in search of a member of the staff to hand it in as lost property.

At 10.22 both terrorists were back in the car. Using a specially programmed miniaturized radio, they activated timed detonators on all three devices before speeding off on the West Way.

All three bombs exploded at 10.35. The main charge caused enormous carnage in the royal chamber, which was crowded

300

at the time with a party of old-age pensioners who had travelled down from Liverpool, eighteen of whom were killed outright, with double that number seriously injured. The parents of the small boy were still on their way to hand in the teddy bear when it ignited, and the subsequent fire engulfed the whole family. In the Disney room the second incendiary bomb started another intense blaze. Although the staff made valiant attempts to contain the fires, they swiftly got out of control. There was widespread panic and confusion as acrid smoke blotted out the standby lighting system. Molten wax added to the nightmare as people rushed to escape: many fell and were trampled on by those pushing from behind. Although the London Fire Brigade and the emergency services were on the scene within fifteen minutes, the fires were not contained easily. A score of ambulances ferried the injured to adjacent hospitals where surgical teams battled to save as many lives as possible. Nearby a church was used as a makeshift mortuary, and by mid-afternoon, when the Chief Fire Officer confirmed that all the bodies had been removed, the death-toll had reached fifty-four, including eleven children.

The two terrorists boarded their flight to Paris without hindrance, having returned the Hertz car and disposed of the miniature radio in a waste-bin. This was subsequently retrieved by a female Pakistani cleaner who gave it to her small son. Since it did not function normally, he later swapped it with a friend for a balsa-wood glider.

Stranded, Keating fumed in the gloom of Helsinki airport. He and his small party – one of the featured actresses and the costume designer – having missed the British Airways flight to Leningrad, had been forced to take Finnair and travel Economy. On arrival in Finland the aircraft had been taken out of service because the reverse thrust on the jet engines was faulty. This meant that there was no connecting flight to Leningrad until the following day. Conscious that he ought to live up to his position as financier, he attempted to charter a private jet but without success. There was nothing else for it; they were condemned to spend a night in a hotel. Organizing taxis (he needed two because the actress was travelling with enough luggage for a world cruise), he took them to the Intercontinental Strand, which proved to be a new and curiously anonymous piece of architecture, built round an atrium festooned with pink marble columns that reminded him of not particularly engaging Arabian nights. The lifts were made of glass and climbed inside the atrium for eight floors. They gave him vertigo when he was ushered to his equally bland, anonymous room that was nevertheless functional, with good plumbing and the statutory array of free shampoos, plastic shower-caps and gels which nowadays personified universal hotel life. He raided the mini-bar, poured himself a double gin of dubious parentage, then telephoned his office to let them know of his whereabouts. After taking a bath he went downstairs and met the two girls in the bar connected, open plan, with the only restaurant.

'We can't possibly eat in the hotel,' Keating said, his initial annoyance gradually fading as he consumed his second Martini. 'Let's venture out and explore. I'll ask the desk if there's a decent Russian restaurant in town – get you conditioned for what's in store. What d'you say? Are you both game?'

'Sounds good to me,' Jennifer, the costume designer, replied. She was immensely chic, having decided at an early age that since her looks were unlikely to prove her fortune she would compensate by dressing in a totally individual fashion. She turned to the young actress. 'Yes, Vanessa?'

Vanessa was of a breed that is determined not to be impressed by anything. She had recently made a stir in a West End play, becoming overnight and for a very short period – the play having flopped – a large fish in a small pond. Snapped up by the film company, she now behaved as though at any given moment hordes of photographers would descend and ask her to pose, which was not the case. Little did she know she had not been cast for her histrionic talents, but because the director was a tit man and she happened to be extraordi-

302

narily well endowed. She sipped her glass of white wine with studied boredom, hoping that by being enigmatic she would intrigue Keating. With that predatory cunning that had taken many of her kind to the top, she had an instinct for zeroing in on the money. 'As long as I don't have to eat reindeer. I'm into organic food. Red meat is a turn-off.'

'Does your diet exclude caviare?' Keating said. 'That's as organic as you're going to get in Russia.' He excused himself and went to the desk to enquire and make a reservation.

Jennifer stared after him through her state-of-the-art bifocals. 'As producers go he's rather cosy, don't you think?'

'He's not really the producer; he's just putting up the money.'

'That's producing, honey.'

'Have you worked for our director before?'

'Once.'

'How was he?'

'Well, he's talented, but an evil bastard. Likes to have one whipping boy, or girl, on every film. He totally destroyed Charlotte Baron when we did *Love Feast* last year. Had her in hysterics every day.'

Vanessa's mouth went down at the corners. 'Well, he'd better not try it with me.'

'Haven't you met him yet?'

'Yes, when I auditioned for him, but he was on his best behaviour then, all sweetness and light because they were desperate to have me. I got so many offers after the play and I settled for this because I thought it would be a change of pace.'

'Did you meet our Mr Raven as well?'

'He's the old American, right?'

'Yes.'

'Gross. He breathed stale cigar breath all over me. All he was interested in was whether I'd do the bed scenes nude.'

'And will you?'

'Not unless it's a closed set. I've got no hang-ups about stripping off; it's just that I think all that leg-over acting is terribly old hat. About as sexy as a baby's open grave.'

Keating had been directed to the Troika on the concierge's recommendation. A taxi was summoned and they departed into the damp night.

The Troika proved to have an agreeable atmosphere, somewhat destroyed by the presence of a large party of Japanese who laughed immoderately throughout their meal.

'Oh, gross,' Vanessa exclaimed using her favourite word again as she studied the menu. 'See this? It says: "Bear, when available."'

'Speciality of the house,' Keating said. He selected salted cucumber with honey and yoghurt for his own appetiser, followed by spicy reindeer steak. Jennifer followed his choice.

'How can you?'

'Very tasty.'

Vanessa ordered a plate of vegetables and lectured them both on the toxic qualities of red meat. 'Carnivorous animals have a short bowel, whereas we have yards and yards of it, which means we don't get rid of waste quickly enough.'

'Do we have to discuss that over dinner?' Jennifer asked.

'I'm just telling you. Practically everything we eat is adulterated.' She produced a small vial and swallowed a variety of vitamin capsules with her Russian mineral water which, she complained, tasted of iron. Her vapid and exclusively self-congratulatory chatter throughout the meal, combined with the noisy explosions of the Japanese at the adjoining table, made Keating's head ache.

'You're going to starve in Leningrad,' Keating observed, switching his attention to Jennifer who he had decided to try to make.

'I read somewhere Finland has the highest suicide rate in Europe,' Vanessa continued. 'And I can well understand why. I'd jump off the nearest building if I had to eat bear in semi-darkness all the year. The hotels seem to have been designed with that in mind. Though, curiously enough, legend has it that the statistics soar with the coming of spring rather than during the winter.'

It was with thoughts of her murder rather than of his own suicide that Keating ferried them back to the hotel. It wasn't until he tuned in to the English television news broadcasts that he learnt of the Madame Tussaud attack, now being officially attributed to the IRA, though this had been denied by a Sinn Fein spokesman. Bayldon appeared during the bulletin, speaking directly from Downing Street and promising that the perpetrators would be ruthlessly tracked down. He looked haggard, mouthing the familiar platitudes parrot-fashion and promising swift retribution. This was followed by interviews with relatives of the victims; the reporters revealing, as usual, an appalling lack of sensitivity, posing such questions as 'How do you feel now that you know your sister was one of those who died?', seemingly more concerned with furthering their own personality cults than with any consideration for the feelings of the bereaved. Nowadays, Keating thought, tragedy is a glorious excuse for a media jamboree, a chance to extract the last ounce of human misery. He switched off.

It was dark when the waiter brought his breakfast the next morning, and still dark when they took off on the last leg to Russia. Staring out of the aircraft window, he looked down on snowy wastes below: a landscape of innocence, with the shadow of the jet passing over it, like a huge bird of prey.

The Cabinet, hitherto a placid beast, now showed signs of resisting Bayldon's efforts to manipulate it. In the wake of the hideous slaughter at Madame Tussaud's and with the tide of public opinion turning against the Government, old antagonisms resurfaced. Now they had an underlying menace for him.

It began with the Foreign Secretary saying: 'Toby, I didn't, you didn't, none of us entered Parliament in order to perpetuate an alibi society. Now, we all know that accountability is a bloody nuisance, but it also happens to be a fact of political life. The public – and by the public of course I mean the truffle-hounds in the papers and on television – are demanding answers.'

'I thought we *were* giving them answers, Wilfred,' Bayldon replied. 'Surely the steps we've taken during the past few days

305

are draconian enough to satisfy even the most rabid Tory voter, let alone our own? We have, after all, gone against the wishes of Party Conference – though not against the unions – and brought back hanging for terrorist offences. Are you suggesting we go further and bring back the rack and the Iron Maiden?'

'I don't want this minuted, but you know perfectly what I'm talking about.'

'What *are* you talking about? We're here to discuss the anti-terrorist measures, surely? Isn't that the only item on the agenda, or am I wrong?'

The Foreign Secretary looked around the table for support. 'I think', he said finally, when no one came to his immediate aid, 'I have to employ some verbal brutality, Toby. Your wife's reluctance to deny certain rumours has become a major liability to the credibility of this government.'

Bayldon did not blink.

'I hope we're not going to conduct this meeting on a level of personal abuse. I fail to see what my wife has to do with the present crisis.'

'Well, let somebody else speak up. I'm not going to be made the scapegoat for a view generally held.'

Certain faces around the long table avoided Bayldon's eyes. He settled on the Home Secretary. 'You'd all agree, wouldn't you, Richard, that like all free citizens my wife has a right to privacy? Just because she is my wife she's an obvious target for cranks and fanatics. I take it Wilfred, in his usual diplomatic manner, is referring to certain unsubstantiated items in a magazine that has a long history – for which it has frequently and deservedly paid a high price – of printing libels.'

'Yes. Unfortunately, the particular magazine in question also has a long history of being hideously accurate on many occasions. Of course, if your better half has been libelled, then she has recourse in law.'

'She would hardly stoop to dignify such monstrous lies.'

'She might have no alternative,' the Home Secretary said, shuffling his papers, 'if she's to scotch them once and for all.

The longer they remain unanswered the more it damages your own authority. The events of the past few days make it imperative for her to act.'

'She is already in touch with her legal advisers, and has every intention of issuing a statement.'

'Just a statement?' somebody at the end of the table said. 'Will that be sufficient? Why doesn't she issue a writ?'

'If you must know, my wife is inclined to treat the whole thing as a joke in bad taste. Now, can we move on and discuss the vital business of the day, please. I intend to fly to Dublin tomorrow to hold urgent discussions. At the same time my wife has agreed to visit Belfast, which should go some way to allay the criticism of her and show where her loyalties lie. Personally, I think it's very courageous of her in the circumstances. I shall join her there after Dublin to boost the morale of the security forces. I've arranged full media coverage. No point in making a gesture if it goes unnoticed. Unless I can obtain firm assurances that the Irish government is prepared to co-operate fully, then further and much tougher sanctions will be applied. I've tabled them for you. As you can see, I propose that all imports of dairy produce, meat and manufactured goods will be blocked.'

'And Guinness, presumably?' the Minister for Agriculture chipped in.

Bayldon ignored this. 'The assets of Irish banks and companies in this country will also be frozen, and Irish citizens will no longer be eligible for National Assistance. Does anybody have any problems with these measures?'

Again it was the Foreign Secretary who spoke first. 'We'll have problems with Washington. They can't afford to ignore the Irish lobby. And, in my view, if we really bring the shutters down the collection-boxes will be rattled . . . Noraid' – he dropped his voice on the word – 'will be the main beneficiary. So it's to be hoped that your Dublin mission succeeds.'

'Do you have a better alternative?'

'It might be useful if I flew to New York and addressed the United Nations. I could do some useful buttering-up behind the scenes.'

'No, I don't think so. I want you here minding the shop.' He had no intention of letting the Foreign Secretary steal any of his thunder.

When the meeting broke up several of the senior members of the Cabinet retired next door to Number 11 where, behind closed doors, they voiced their misgivings. It was a guarded exchange, since none of them wanted to reveal his hand too early in the game. If Bayldon was to go and refused to go quietly, then he might have to be pushed. That raised the question of who would replace him. Every man present had ambitions in that direction. Nobody actually mentioned a palace revolution in so many words, but the thought was in everybody's mind.

'Tricky situation,' the Chancellor said. 'We don't want to stir up the Yanks and provoke another run on the pound.'

'There definitely seems to be a cover-up of one sort or another. If she's entirely innocent, she should come out and say so.'

'Especially since the Americans have always had this extraordinary attitude about open government,' the Home Secretary murmured. 'You'd have thought that would have rubbed off on her. They have this mania for baring their breasts in public.'

'Perhaps you should rephrase that in her case, Dick.'

'We know she's got money. After all, she hardly gives the impression she gets her clothes at Oxfam. I've always thought the way she dresses is totally inappropriate for somebody in her position. Remember what she turned up in for the last day of Conference? That didn't go down well with the rank and file. That sort of ostentation provokes envy, and envy loses votes.'

'What's the latest poll?'

'We're holding steady, but Toby's own rating has dropped five points.'

'Well, he should take note. Not that popularity means a bugger. I've never courted popularity,' the Foreign Secretary said. 'One must just do one's duty, as one sees it.'

Nobody commented on that.

308

'Well, we'll just have to wait and see, then. Let's hope Toby doesn't push too hard in Dublin. I've got serious doubts about excluding the Irish. For one thing, half the building sites in the country will grind to a halt.'

'Is there anything we can do?' the Chancellor asked. When nobody else volunteered a solution, he walked to the window overlooking the parade-ground. 'We have to take the long-term view in my opinion. What matters is not personalities, but the party.' He turned back again to face the others. 'Not that I'm advocating a change; I wouldn't like anybody to get that impression. I just think it would be sensible to have a contingency plan . . .' After the briefest of pauses he smiled at the Home Secretary. 'And by the way, Dick, it would be appreciated if you didn't make an entry in the diary we all know you're keeping as insurance for your old age. Give it a miss on this occasion.'

Control was also concerned at the pace of events. Bayldon's refusal to be panicked necessitated a change of plan. Using the safe house he met with Pamela again, instructing her to bring Abramov up to date with recent developments. He then questioned her about Waddington.

'Something happened while I was away – he's no longer living with me, nor at his own home. Instead, he's moved into a friend's house, says he has to lie low.'

'Did he say why?'

'No, he refuses to be drawn. I've tried everything I can without being too obvious.'

'Who's the friend?'

'Somebody called Keating.'

'Keating?'

'Yes.'

'You're sure?'

She nodded. 'Does the name mean anything to you?'

Control's face did not betray him. 'No. Have you met the friend?'

Pamela shook her head. 'He's abroad apparently.'

Cracking his knuckles twice, Control moved around the

309

small room. 'Keep everything normal. When have you next arranged to meet him?'

'Tomorrow night.'

'What time?'

'Eight. I'm having dinner there.'

'Don't keep the appointment.'

'You mean cancel it?'

'No. Let him think you're still coming. Are there staff in the house?'

'A butler and a cook.'

'Any dogs?'

'I haven't seen any. There seems to be a very sophisticated security system.'

'Give me the address.'

Pamela wrote it down and gave it to him. 'What're you going to do?'

'I haven't quite decided yet. But it could well be that your affair is over.'

She knew better than to ask more questions, and shortly afterwards left the house. Control stayed on, waiting for his next visitor.

Owing to staff shortages, there was no restaurant car on the train Deacon boarded on his return from Leicester. He accepted this as yet another of life's miseries, just as he was resigned to the fact that there were no longer any first-class carriages: the Government had recently abolished such divisions, at the same time raising the general level of fares – a political example of what the French, in slang, called *à cheval*: astride the two worlds of socialism and commerce.

The grimed compartment where Deacon finally secured a seat was awash with spent beer-cans and, although it was designated No Smoking, he noticed the floor was littered with butts. He kept his briefcase on his knees. Most of his fellow-passengers shared the appearance of displaced persons, the scene evoking memories of those old movies, so popular immediately after the war, when the hero attempted to cross the frontier into safety. From time to time during the slow

310

journey announcements were made over the loudspeaker system, supposedly to tell passengers the name of the next stop, but the voice was distorted and the information given in what appeared to be an unknown language.

The train finally reached London nearly an hour late. He walked swiftly to the barrier, noting that a group of the Militia were lounging by the closed news-kiosk. They carried short truncheons – a new development, Deacon noted – and he was aware that they recognized him. The length of the queue at the taxi rank suggested he would have a long wait, and he was just about to make for the Underground station when he was approached by a middle-aged man who addressed him with a pronounced Cockney accent.

'Looking for a taxi, governor?'

'Yes, I was, but it seems a forlorn hope.'

'Very few of them about. How far are you going, governor?'

'Holland Park.'

'I could accommodate that,' the man said.

'Are you a taxi-driver?'

'Yes, but at this time of night I pick and choose – look for gents like yourself, don't risk the slag and getting a knife stuck in me ribs at the end of the journey. I'm not on the rank, I'm parked round the corner, so if you'd like to follow me . . .'

Grateful and surprised at his good fortune, Deacon was led away. The man took him to a side-street where an ordinary London taxi was parked. He opened the passenger-door, and Deacon got in. They had only gone a few hundred yards when Deacon noticed that the man had not activated his meter. He leant forward and attempted to slide the glass partition, but it refused to budge. He rapped on it.

'Your meter isn't on.'

The driver made no sign that he had heard. Deacon shouted the same message in a louder voice. Again he got no reaction. It was then that he became aware that they were heading in the wrong direction for Holland Park, going south instead of west. He banged with his signet ring on the glass.

'Where the hell are you taking me? This isn't the right way. I want Holland Park.'

There was no response; if anything, the driver seemed to accelerate, leaving the main roads and taking a back-street route. He finally pulled up inside what appeared to be a builder's yard. They drove straight into a garage. The moment the cab stopped Deacon attempted to get out, but both passenger-doors had been locked automatically. Only now did the driver open the glass partition and speak to him.

'I apologize for that, sir. Please don't be alarmed. Acting under orders.'

'I demand to be let out.'

'You will be, sir. Let me just explain first.'

'You'd better explain. I'll see you lose your licence for this, believe me. I have your number.'

'I doubt that, sir. This cab is a phoney, just used for special purposes.' He produced an identity-card, holding it up so that Deacon could read it. It showed him to be a member of MI6.

'The boss wanted to see you privately, sir. This was considered the best way of doing it. I do apologize once again.'

Only slightly mollified, Deacon said: 'Your boss will have to do more than apologize.'

'We'll see you safe home when you've had your meeting.' He released the locks and got out of the cab, coming round to open Deacon's door. 'If you'll follow me, sir.' He led the way through the rear of the garage into the adjoining house. They passed through a kitchen and a small hallway, then Deacon was ushered into a sitting-room.

'My dear Colin,' Control said, greeting him with a whisky in his hand, 'please forgive my man abducting you like that. These are desperate times and one has to resort to unconventional means. A small peace-offering.' He offered the whisky, but Deacon did not take it.

'What the bloody hell do you think you're playing at, Lockfield?' The use of his surname was deliberately offensive.

'I'm not playing at anything, I assure you. Please take this; I'm sure you can do with it. I also have some ham sandwiches if you're peckish after your journey – I understand there was no restaurant car on the train.'

312

He nodded to the cab-driver to retire. Deacon finally accepted the whisky with ill grace.

'Would you care for a sandwich?'

'I'd like an explanation first of all.'

'Yes, of course. But please sit down.'

Deacon sat, but refused the proffered plate of sandwiches. Control took one for himself, eating it delicately as he continued.

'I know you look upon the activities of my department with a jaundiced eye, and perhaps we do overstep the mark on occasions, but only in the national interest. I can assure you that I have a very valid reason for bringing you here tonight. Perhaps, when you've heard me out, you'll appreciate the reason for secrecy.'

Deacon made no response, but the redness above his collar was beginning to fade.

'You recall that when we last met at Winfield House I said I would contact you at some point. At that time I had certain, but unsubstantiated, evidence of subversion. Since then events have moved somewhat faster than I feared. I believe that I could now produce evidence to prove my case, if you are prepared to listen. I brought you here for that reason, to put you in the picture.'

'Why me?'

'Isn't it obvious? You stand apart from the rest. Because of that, because you haven't been tainted, you command widespread trust and respect.'

'I don't know about "widespread". I have a certain following in the party and in the country,' Deacon answered, unable to resist such flatteries. He now took his first sip of the whisky. 'You say you have evidence?'

'Perhaps not the sort of evidence that would stand up in a court of law but, in the nature of my trade, reliable. I have to consider the significance of every related incident. Isolated, they would not convey much, but when added together they produce an ugly hypothesis. If I'm right, and I believe I am, the time could come when extreme measures might have to be employed to correct a dangerous situation. In which case

313

the country would need a strong man, a man of principle, a man such as yourself, to take over the reins.'

'What you are talking about is sedition.'

'No, I hope not.'

'I think so. However you care to disguise it, the word is *sedition*.'

'I am merely stating that somebody would have to be the instrument to restore a constitutional government.'

'Well, we've always lacked a written constitution, more's the pity; but, leaving that aside, I would remind you that every member of the Commons was properly, democratically elected.'

'It's the current executive I'm concerned with. Correct me if I'm wrong,' Control said, taking a second sandwich, 'but as I understand it Bayldon's Cabinet hardly represents the will of the people. He came to power by default, committed to head a caretaker coalition, did he not?'

'Are we now getting down to personalities, naming names?'

'It is personalities, not governments, that run countries these days, is it not?' Control countered blandly. 'Collective responsibility is merely a public relations palliative, designed to fool us.'

'So what is the "evidence" you have to offer?'

'Some of it must be obvious to you. Your speeches both inside and outside the House make it abundantly clear that you are utterly opposed to much that is going on.'

'I've made no secret of the fact that I consider there has been a betrayal of our socialist revolution.'

'Exactly. So if you became convinced, as I have become convinced, that what you have worked for all your political life is being systematically corrupted, and that if the situation is allowed to continue unchallenged there is a danger of moving towards a fascist state, would you act, or would you remain silent? How would you see your duty?'

'I would still have to act within the democratic process.'

'Yes. Of course, Hitler came to power by the democratic process.'

Control waited.

314

'Do I have your word that this isn't a replay of the Wilson plot drummed up by your outfit?'

'You have my word.'

'Well then, if I was ever totally convinced of the necessity, I would agree to play a role, but there could be no question of a coup,' Deacon said after a pause. His neck was becoming flushed again, but not from anger this time, Control thought. Now he's taken the bait, as I knew he would.

'Understood. We must always vote our masters out of office – unless, of course, circumstances force them to resign.'

'You have something to show me, presumably? Documented evidence.'

'Oh, yes.' Control took out a file from his briefcase. 'For your eyes only. There is no other copy. Read it.' He handed the file to Deacon. 'And for goodness' sake have a sandwich while you're reading. I firmly believe one should never receive bad news on an empty stomach.'

Waddington answered the door himself with a welcoming smile already in place, but it wasn't Pamela who greeted him, just two men he had never seen before. With a skill he just had time to register he was pinioned against the wall by one of them while the second taped his mouth and hands. He was then frog-marched to a waiting car and bundled into the rear compartment. Then he was pushed to the floor and held there by both men. The car immediately pulled away, driving at what Waddington judged to be a steady unhurried speed for some twenty minutes. None of the men spoke during the journey.

When the car stopped he heard the driver get out and open a door. Only then did his other two captors pull him upright and manhandle him out. He was taken through a door set into a wall, and beyond that was a small courtyard. The driver had a further door open to receive him, and within fifteen seconds from leaving the car he was inside, having been given no chance to pinpoint a landmark.

The interior of the building was garish. He got the immediate impression that it had been previously occupied by squat-

315

ters heavily into the drug scene. Makeshift wiring criss-crossed walls painted in psychedelic colours. Facing him in the entrance hall was an enormous home-made birthday-card collage made up of cuttings from magazines across which had been written HAPPY HAPPY BIRTHDAY LUCY WITH THE LOVELY TITS. He was pushed past this into an enormous room that had obviously once been an artist's studio. The only cathedral-sized window had been blacked out. A circle of decaying Victorian armchairs, all sporting wounds of horsehair, was grouped in front of a fireplace that had the charred remains of a stuffed animal in the grate. A bare bulb on a shadeless standard lamp provided scant illumination. Four apple-boxes, scarred with cigarette burns and spilt drinks, served as a coffee-table. But perhaps the most bizarre aspect of this room was the crudely executed imitations of famous paintings that occupied three of the walls: Waddington had time to take in a pseudo-Picasso clown and a Degas nude before he was pushed down on to one of the armchairs, the legs of which immediately gave way under him. The tape-expert now took a jack-knife and slit his suit, dissecting the cloth with the expertise of a chef skinning a rabbit. Flinging the pieces to one side, he then trussed Waddington's hands and feet. He and his silent companion left the room, extinguishing the light and locking the door after them.

Waddington wriggled himself upright, but the broken chair gave way completely and he slid sideways to the floor, as helpless as a chicken in the market. In the darkness, seminaked, he concentrated on stopping his body shaking, but some of the muscles were in spasm. The suddenness and ruthlessness of the abduction had left him in shock. He was conscious that the stale smell of marijuana permeated the room, and he was sure that his first impression had been correct. Wherever he was, the place was semi-derelict, had probably been used by drop-outs until put to its present use as a prison for him. But by whom, and for what? He had no doubt that his captors were professionals: their technique had been too assured for ordinary villains. Now, as he rolled his body backwards and forwards over the rough floor-planks in an effort to keep some circulation flowing, he tried to bring reason into play. He went back over the events of the past two days since Keating had left, checking his every movement.

Apart from Pamela and the staff, who else knew of his whereabouts? He had never left the house, made no phone calls other than to Pearson and Pamela. It was inconceivable that either of them had anything to do with this. Tracing further back, remembering that his home phone had been bugged, reliving the episode with Frampton in Harrods and Frampton's subsequent murder, he realized he had been marked from the start. Whoever was behind his own situation was also looking for the leads back to Hillsden. Did that point to the Firm? Again, he could not bring himself to believe the inconceivable. Am I being too bloody naïve? he thought. Just because Alec and I played it straight, why do I assume that everybody else is straight? Christ! They hack people down in front of the goalmouth and call it a professional foul. People turn a blind eye for a bloody football game; the canker has eaten into the national sport. Why shouldn't it have spread elsewhere? The darkness, the fear and the physical pain now spreading to his limbs intensified his concentration. He willed himself to recall the layout of the room, rolling himself past the apple-boxes in what he hoped was the direction of the electric fire. Twice he blundered into other objects until his cheek touched the cold metal of the fire. Inch by inch he edged himself into position, seeking to get his bound hands against something sharp enough to sever the tape. The effort exhausted him, and he lay still, listening to the thumping of his heart before commencing to rub his wrists against the electric element. He persisted with this for a period, then had a better idea. If he could turn on the fire, maybe he could burn his way through the tape. With his fingertips he found the cord connecting the fire to the wall-point and again slowly jack-knifed his way along it until he touched the plug, only to find it was unconnected. The effort had cost him dear; he was drenched in sweat. After a rest he made another supreme effort and, although managing to lift the plug, he found he did not have sufficient strength to insert it into the wall-point.

317

It was then that he realized he lacked the necessary control to stop himself pissing. For a few seconds the urine warmed his cramped legs, but he was consumed with a spasm of self-disgust, and rolled himself clear of the puddle.

Thus he spent the first night, sleeping fitfully, racked with pain that woke him in the throes of a recurring nightmare. He had no means of telling whether his captors were still in the building, for the only sounds he could discern were distant traffic.

He lay there unable to calculate the passing of the hours, giving himself mental and small physical exercises to try to keep alert, in the sure knowledge that once they felt he had been softened up his captors would return. He recited limericks, then forced himself to remember Beatles song-titles, the stars of old films, anything to pass the time. Somewhat to his surprise, he experienced no hunger pangs, but became increasingly desperate for something to drink. At times during what he took to be the second day he started to hallucinate, sometimes laughing out loud, sometimes crying as he lay in his own filth.

In actual fact his captors left him for over two days before they returned at night. He was semi-conscious when they took him into a squalid bathroom, the mirrors of which were smeared with graffiti and symbols that to Waddington seemed part of the continuing nightmare. He was plunged into alternate hot and cold baths. The cold water seemed an unexpected bonus, for he was past the point where pain had any significance, and he managed to swallow some water before the ordeal was over. They left him in the empty bath and it was only now that they brought him a small quantity of food and fed it to him a mouthful at a time between questions. If he refused to answer, the food was withheld – kept tantalizingly in sight, but withheld. His interrogator sat behind him on the toilet seat, so that Waddington could not see his face, and at first the disembodied voice was gentle and the questions seemingly innocuous. It was standard technique, and he recognized it as such, his mind working in two directions at once.

– Why make things hard on yourself? Just give us the answers and you'll be out of all this.

– What answers?

– You know the answers we want.

– Tell me who you are first.

– You're a smart guy. You know you're here as long as it takes. Why hold out?

– I've been out of the game for years. What could I know?

– You've been in touch with people.

– What people?

– You tell us.

– I don't understand the question.

– Try.

– What people?

– Let me help you. You met a man called Frampton.

– No.

– Oh, yes. Try harder. Why? Why did you meet him?

– I don't know anybody called Frampton.

– What did he tell you?

– I don't know him.

– What did he tell you?

The repetition, drip, drip, like water, the old Manchurian method.

– Do you know what happened to Frampton?

– Who's Frampton?

– Frampton found it difficult to remember your name, too. He had to be persuaded.

– Why would he remember me?

– After persuasion he found his tongue. My friend persuaded him. He's not as gentle as me.

The two men swapped places, always extinguishing the light when they changed over. The second man played it differently; he was the nasty one. Again, standard technique used by security forces the world over, including our own, Waddington thought. He was shivering uncontrollably from the cold long before the end of the first session. There was no more food offered.

– Would you like to know how we made Frampton talk?

319

Why answer? He was going to be told anyway.

– He was a homo. Are you a homo?

The use of such an old-fashioned word dated the man.

– Know how you persuade homos to talk? You stick things up their arses. But not what they're used to. Not sexy things, things that hurt. Afterwards, he told us about your friend Hillsden. The one who ran away.

– Can I have a drink?

– Why should I give you favours when you're not co-operating? Tell me about Hillsden first.

– Nothing to tell.

– Don't make me lose patience with you.

The cold-water tap was turned on. When the water was up to Waddington's neck, a hand came from behind and pushed his head under. He was held there, unable to struggle free, until his lungs felt they were bursting.

– Just a reminder of where you are. Next time I won't let you come up.

The hand put pressure on his head.

– We were talking about Hillsden. He contacted you.

– No.

Again his head was pressed under the water. He was half-conscious when released.

– He contacted you through Frampton. Frampton brought you a message. What was it?

– Just news of an old friend.

– That's better. You're trying now. What news?

Waddington struggled to frame words that would satisfy, but a great tiredness was sweeping over him.

– Come on, try harder. What news?

– Told me Hillsden was in Leningrad.

– We know that. You're stalling again. What else?

The man's voice seemed further and further away, coming to him as though from a tunnel, and even his own voice, weaker now, was disembodied. He wondered who had once told him that drowning was a peaceful death, and was it true? He hoped it was true, that it would bring an end to the ordeal.

Nothing else, he tried to say, his cracked lips moving, but no words coming out.

Then he lost consciousness.

22

'*Tryn-trava,*' Raven said, airing one of the few Russian expressions he had picked up since arriving in Leningrad. He sat opposite Keating in the film's production office, arguing the latest budget. A plate of *zakuski* was between them on the table, for the meeting had been going on for three hours. Nothing, not even mounting annoyance, ever stopped Keating from taking frequent nourishment, and he punctuated his questions between mouthfuls of red and black caviare globbed on to halves of boiled eggs. 'What's that supposed to mean?'

'It makes no difference. Who cares? Why bother?' Raven translated.

'*I* care! I come here expecting to find everything going smoothly, and you tell me this location's going to cost an extra fifteen grand. That makes a hell of a difference in my book.'

'The rate of exchange went against us,' Raven said. 'It was ever thus.' He enjoyed the financial in-fighting that always went with a film; he was on his own ground talking numbers and percentages. The creative decisions confused him – there was always some smartarse director giving him pear-shaped answers that he couldn't challenge.

'What's this item here?'

Raven consulted his own copy of the budget. He knew by heart where all the bodies were buried, having made sure that he was cushioned against everything except acts of God, and the insurance policy would take care of that. He had even taken out insurance against the leading man catching AIDS, since he had a reputation for humping anything that walked.

'What page are you looking at?'

'Thirteen. "Allowance for No Meal Break." What sort of

double-talk is that? We feed them, don't we? You've already got a fortune down for unit catering on the previous page.'

'That's normal.'

'What's normal about it?'

'See, when you call them early, which we have to do because it gets dark early, you're outside their normal hours. So, although you provide breakfast, you also have to give them a No Breakfast Allowance.'

'You mean you have to pay them for a meal they're not supposed to have had when they've just had it?'

'You got it.'

'Jesus!'

'What else bothers you?'

'Everything bothers me.'

'We're getting great stuff on the screen. The dailies are terrific.'

'Listen, I wasn't born yesterday. This reads like a work of fiction to me, and if there's one thing that gets my dander up it's being taken for a ride. I know you're stealing from me, but just don't get too greedy, or I might pull the plug. Leningrad isn't Beverly Hills.'

'You can say that again. How's the hotel? How's your room?'

'It's somewhere to sleep,' Keating said. 'What are you shooting today?'

'Outside the University.'

'I'll go take a look.'

His car and interpreter were waiting for him. He was driven to the location site and stared with grave misgivings at the size of the unit – British, Russian and a sprinkling of Americans – he was payrolling. As with most people who are unfamiliar with the way films get made, he gained the immediate impression that only half a dozen people around the camera seemed to be actually working. Everybody else appeared to be enjoying a holiday: the actors lounging in their canvas chairs, attended by sycophants, and a great mass of anonymous technicians standing about. He felt a sense of isolation, for nobody paid him any attention, money and art seldom being compatible. Only Vanessa, the young actress he had travelled with, made the effort to recognize him, and naturally she had a complaint.

'Oh, I'm so glad to see you. Can you do something about my hotel room?'

'What's wrong with it?'

'I don't have a bathroom.'

'Use mine,' Keating said, thinking: Maybe I can get laid and retrieve something out of this expensive jamboree.

'Oh, I couldn't do that.'

'Why not? Come to my room when you've finished shooting. What's happening here?'

'They're lining up a track shot.'

'How's it going, d'you think?'

'Slow; but then filming's always slow.'

'You can say that again.'

'I was in make-up at six, but they haven't used me yet. Which reminds me, I'd better get my face fixed; I'm in the shot after this.'

'What's wrong with your face? Looks OK to me,' Keating said in what passed for a compliment.

There was a sudden flurry of activity. The First Assistant shouted for quiet, the instruction being repeated several times in Russian by his local counterpart. Two of the actors sauntered to their start mark, followed by a wardrobe assistant and hairdressing. The Continuity Girl approached them, script in hand, and heard their lines. Some fifty feet of metal track had been laid immediately in front of the main entrance to the University and now, after further cries for complete silence, the first request having been ignored by most of the onlookers, the actors took up their positions and proceeded to rehearse. It took six attempts before the bearded director pronounced himself satisfied.

'Final checks,' the First Assistant shouted. 'And get those people further back.' The filming was being watched by a large crowd of spectators, mostly university students.

'Are we ready?'

'Not yet. Hold it. We've lost the sun.' The Cinematographer

324

stared up at the sky through his dark monocle. 'Be another three minutes.'

'Don't relax. Hold your positions. Just waiting for the light,' the First Assistant relayed; but, as far as Keating could see, everybody did relax. The Director went and sat in his chair and put his head in his hands as though suddenly bowed down with grief.

'Fuck the weather,' he groaned. 'Why don't I ever make pictures in fucking Bermuda?'

'Want a cup of tea, governor?' the ever-solicitious Prop Man asked.

'Why not? I suppose a blow-job is out of the question?' This got a dutiful laugh from those around him. 'How long, Harry?'

'Difficult to say,' the Cinematographer replied. He also sat down. 'Take a look. There are about six layers of cloud up there.' He handed over his spy-glass. 'I think the wind's shifted.'

It was during this lull that Hillsden and Galina came out of the university building and lingered with the other spectators, standing on the edge of the crowd close to where the Director was sitting.

'What's happening?' Hillsden asked a fellow-student.

'It's a British film company.'

'British?'

'So I'm told.'

'What're they making?'

'No idea. They don't seem to be making anything at the moment.'

He watched as a portly man walked over to the Director. Something about the man was familiar, although Hillsden could not immediately place him.

'What's the hold-up?' Keating said within earshot.

'Weather. The light's gone dead on us.'

Keating stared up into the sky.

'Doesn't look any different to me.'

'Sun,' the Cinematographer said. 'We started the sequence in full sun. It has to match.'

'Isn't it exciting?' Galina said. 'Find out what sort of film it is.'

Hillsden stopped a passing technician. 'Can you tell us what you're making?'

'A comedy, so I'm told, but I could be wrong,' the man said, intent on an errand.

Hearing an English voice, Keating swivelled in his chair. Before Hillsden walked away their eyes fixed briefly. He and Galina had gone some twenty yards when the First Assistant ran after them.

'Excuse me, sir.'

Hillsden turned.

'Sorry to bother you, but as you can see we're making a film here, a feature film, and we have a sequence coming up which requires some real English tourists. Would I be right in thinking you're English?'

'Yes,' Hillsden said, guardedly.

'My producer over there wondered if you'd be prepared to take part, with payment naturally.'

'No, I don't think so.'

'You wouldn't have to do anything special, just be in the crowd. Only we want it to look authentic, see?'

'Thank you, but no.'

'Well, would you at least have a talk with Mr Keating?'

'Who is Mr Keating?'

'The gentleman sitting over there. He was the one who suggested it. Would you please?'

'Keating, you said?'

'That's right.'

Hillsden hesitated again before turning to Galina. 'Wait here a second, dear. I'll just go and be polite.' Somewhere the name Keating had touched off a memory, a memory he could not immediately place.

Keating rose from the chair to greet him. For once his voice did not boom.

'How kind of you, sorry to be a nuisance. It is Alec, isn't it?'

Hillsden stared at him.

'Alec Hillsden?'

'Yes.'

'Remember me?' He extended a podgy hand, but Hillsden did not take it. 'We worked for the same outfit once. When Dinnsbury was around.'

'Did we?'

'Yes, look, dear fellow, I didn't mean to embarrass you, but when I heard an English voice and recognized you, I felt at the very least I ought to say hello. For old times' sake. Is that the wife with you?'

'Soon to be.'

'She's Russian, is she?'

'Yes.'

'Good-looking girl. So you've settled in here?'

'More or less.'

There was a pause before Keating said: 'Did my man ask you if you'd care to take part?'

'Yes.'

'How d'you feel about that? Might be fun for you, and your wife for that matter.'

'I don't think that would be a good idea. I have a certain amount of leeway in what I'm allowed to do, but they don't encourage me to publicize myself. And it might not do your film any good if I was spotted in the crowd.'

'Understood. Well, would it be wrong for me to ask you to have a drink or a meal?'

Certain details were surfacing for Hillsden. He dimly recalled a slimmer, less aggressively confident Keating from their shared past. They had never been close, though he remembered Dinnsbury had thought well of Keating and had several times mentioned him. For some reason he could not immediately recall, he had the notion that Keating had left the Firm abruptly.

'No, I'm sure a drink would not compromise either of us.'

'I'm being very rude, keeping you from your wife. Why don't you both stay for a while, watch them get this shot? – if they ever get this shot, that is. Please ask her to join us. I'll get you some chairs.'

Hillsden beckoned Galina over and after he had introduced her Keating escorted them to a vantage point and had chairs brought for them.

'Filming, I've discovered to my cost,' Keating said, 'is ninety per cent inertia.'

As he said this a shaft of sunlight appeared and the unit was galvanized into action. The shot got under way but the director wasn't satisfied and announced he wanted to go again. Halfway through the second take the sun went in and the take was aborted.

'Oh, Christ!' the leading actor shouted. 'That was going great.' The hairdresser went to him and brushed a few strands into place.

'Don't relax, nobody relax, we'll go straight away when the currant bun does us a favour.'

'What is currant bun?' Galina whispered.

'Cockney rhyming slang for the sun,' Hillsden told her. Galina appeared none the wiser.

'How long?' the director enquired. He paced up and down, swinging his viewfinder in agitated fashion. The Cinematographer peered up into the turbulent skies.

'Can't say, governor. There might be a short break when that cloud has passed over.'

'I might pass over myself before then.'

During the wait Keating made small talk with a purpose. 'Are you enjoying life here?'

'It has its compensations,' Hillsden said. He took Galina's hand. 'This is the main one. Galina's expecting our first child.'

'Congratulations.'

The exchange was cut short as the First Assistant shouted for quiet once more. The actors and camera crew took up their start positions. This time the leading man fluffed his lines.

'Sorry. Sorry, Zev. It's these bloody long waits between takes. You lose concentration.'

'Some of us don't,' the Director replied, baring his teeth in a parody of a smile. 'OK, first marks, let's go.'

'He needs a touch up,' the make-up man said, advancing

with his box of tricks. When the actor's face had been repaired the shot was attempted yet again, this time with success.

'Make that the print. Check your gate.'

'What are they checking?' Galina asked.

'Something known as "hair-in-the-gate",' Keating told her. 'The gate is part of the camera and for reasons I've been unable to fathom, being of simple mind, hairs get trapped in it with depressing regularity. When that happens they do it all over again, so keep your fingers crossed.' He turned to Hillsden. 'We never really worked together, did we, in the old days? But I seem to remember we had a mutual buddy . . . What was his name? Waddington, was it?'

The sudden mention of Waddington jolted Hillsden. There was something too casual about Keating and his instant friendliness struck a false note.

'I knew Waddington, yes.'

'Funny old world, isn't it, us bumping into each other like this? Who would have believed it? Both our situations have changed since those days. We both got out of the game in different ways.'

This time Hillsden made no response. Hearing Waddington's name had given him a new wariness.

'Would you be free to meet up later at my hotel? Might amuse you to swap a few reminiscences.'

Hillsden looked to Galina.

'You go,' she said. 'I can't because I have to write an essay. But you go. Be a nice change for you.'

'What time?' Hillsden asked.

'Shall we say seven? I'm at the Astoria.'

'Fine. I'll be there.'

'A pleasure to meet you,' Keating said to Galina. 'When is the baby due?'

'In five months.'

'At the rate we're going it'll be born before they finish this film.'

In London the forensic boys established that the house blew up just before one in the afternoon, which, allowing for the

329

time-difference in Leningrad, was roughly the moment when Hillsden and Keating were discussing Waddington and the old days. Because everybody was still jittery and there was a permanent black alert in operation, the Bomb Squad and Pearson's anti-terrorist unit investigated the blast as a matter of routine. After a preliminary examination of the wreckage, which incorporated damage to the two adjoining buildings, Pearson was inclined to the view that the explosion was probably caused by a domestic gas-leak. Officials from the Gas Board confirmed that the installation was prewar and that they had had considerable difficulty in gaining access to the premises while it was occupied by squatters, hence there had been no maintenance for at least two years. According to their records, an ancient hot-water geyser in the bathroom was the most likely suspect.

Pearson was about to leave the site when a police constable reported finding a body in the garden.

'The extraordinary thing is, sir, the body's still in the bath.'

Together with other members of the team Pearson went to investigate.

'Seems to confirm what the chaps from the Gas Board say, Chief.'

Lying on its side amidst other debris was an old-fashioned cast-iron bath. In it was the semi-nude body of a man.

'Bloody lethal, those old geysers,' one of the party remarked. 'My parents used to have one in our house when I was a kid. The wind was always blowing out the pilot light.'

Pearson knelt down on the damp grass to have a closer look. The dead man's head was turned away from him. He got a hand under the corpse to turn it over. The head lolled towards him. He stared, dumbfounded, at Waddington's death-mask.

'Oh, God, no!' he exclaimed.

'What, what is it, governor?' Lloyd said. He, too, peered at the dead man.

'I'll tell you later.'

Pearson straightened up and started issuing instructions. 'I want nothing touched here. Put a twenty-four-hour guard

330

around this whole area, and make bloody sure nobody tramples all over the place. We've probably done enough damage as it is. I'll take a bet with you – the explosion didn't kill him. He was dead before that happened. He was drowned.'

Pamela had made the drop by the Peter Pan statue on the second Tuesday of the month as arranged, choosing the lunch-hour. She had parked her car on a meter in Hyde Park Square before taking a taxi to the Oxford Street branch of Marks & Spencer where she purchased a tuna sandwich and a carton of orange juice. Outside the shop she bought the midday edition of the *Standard*. She then took a bus back to Lancaster Gate and walked the rest of the way to Kensington Gardens. There she sat on a bench a few yards from the drop and ate her sandwich alongside several other office workers taking their break. She saved her crusts and fed them to the sparrows and pigeons that always gathered for the pickings. While drinking her orange juice through the provided straw she opened the newspaper to concentrate on the crossword. From time to time she appeared to use the Marks & Spencer receipt to scribble possible solutions to the clues. At the end of an hour she carefully wiped her mouth on a tissue, then placed the debris, including the receipt, inside the Marks & Spencer bag and dropped it into the litter-basket. She then returned to her car and drove home to Amersham.

Shortly afterwards a member of the embassy staff appeared in the gardens walking a dog. The animal squatted and defacated on the pathway, drawing angry glances from other passers-by. The man went to the litter-basket, extracted some waste paper and gathered up the offending turd. He went back to place the mess in the basket to the satisfaction of the onlookers. While accomplishing this, he skilfully extracted the Marks & Spencer bag, then walked on, making a wide detour before returning to the embassy.

'Unquestionably death by drowning,' Hogg told Pearson. 'And in addition he appears to have been starved.'

331

'Starved?'

'That's what I said. The body was dehydrated and the stomach virtually empty, containing little but bile. Sparse volume of matter in the upper and lower bowels, indicating a period of perhaps a week when no food was eaten.'

'Starved,' Pearson repeated to Lloyd later. 'Hogg was convinced he was starved, poor bugger, though starvation didn't kill him, nor did the explosion. I imagine we were meant to think it was just a domestic accident. Happens frequently – old equipment, a gas-leak and Bob's your uncle. But by a freak the blast must have gone outwards and, being in the bath, that prevented him being blown to pieces. My guess is we weren't supposed to have any remains to identify.'

'Clever, very clever.'

'Except it went wrong.'

'And was it even a gas-leak?'

'Hogg is carrying out further tests. He said he'd expect to find traces of gas in the lungs if that was the case.'

Pearson chewed on a Mars bar, his lunch for the day, and while talking thumbed through the latest batch of contact sheets of photographs taken in Kensington Gardens. The area around the Peter Pan statue had been kept under twenty-four-hour surveillance.

'How long did he think he'd been dead?' asked Lloyd.

'At least two days. What have we found out about the house?'

'It's been empty for eighteen months. The landlord turfed out the last legitimate tenants and has been trying to get planning permission to knock it down and build an office-block. It was occupied by squatters, until they were forcibly evicted after a drugs raid.'

'Well, he'll get his planning permission now,' Pearson said drily. 'We've got to trace Waddington's last movements, and his girl-friend. Get on to the staff at this man Keating's house. See what they can tell us.'

'You don't mind treading on the CID's toes?'

'No.'

He lingered over a set of contact prints.

'Have these blown up.' He ringed three of the shots on the contact sheet.

Lloyd came round to the other side of the desk and examined the print with a magnifying glass. 'Found something?'

'Maybe.'

Lloyd peered at the marked shots. 'Yes, he looks vaguely familiar.'

'Somewhere', Pearson said, 'there's a link to all these incidents. I feel it in my water, or maybe it's just prostate trouble. Never know at my age.'

'Bad as that, is it?'

'Nothing's ever quite what it appears. Mitchell, Frampton, now Waddington. We know there's a link between the last two. Does it join up with Mitchell?'

'Maybe you should take a few extra precautions,' Lloyd said.

'Why?'

'If there is a connection, as you suspect, you could be next in line.'

'Would you say this is a safe place to talk?' Keating asked. 'I'll bow to your superior knowledge on the subject.'

He and Hillsden were sitting in a corner of the Astoria bar. There was a general hum of conversation around them from other imbibers.

'This is safer than your room, but if you don't want to risk it perhaps we should take a walk.'

'Let's have a couple of drinks first. There's no hurry.'

'What got you involved in films?'

'Two things. Another way of making money, and a chance to meet some available young crumpet.'

'I haven't heard that word in a long time.'

Keating looked past him and his expression changed. 'Damn! Some of the actors have just come in. I don't want to get involved and have to listen to their latest gripes. Let's drink up and take that walk.'

He edged by the group at the bar while their backs were turned.

'I think perhaps I ought to come clean with you,' he said when they were safely outside. 'I didn't meet you by chance today. It was chance that you came by at that moment, but if you hadn't I knew where to find you.'

If he had expected some startled reaction from Hillsden, he was disappointed.

'Did the Firm send you?'

'Good God no! No, my set-up here is on the level. I really am payrolling that circus you saw.'

'So who did send you?'

'Waddington. I have a note to you from him, my reference as it were.' He fumbled in a pocket, but Hillsden stopped him.

'Don't show it to me.'

'Don't?'

'No, for all I know we're being tailed. The passing of notes is not a good idea. Just tell me what's in it.'

'You're very trusting.'

'I didn't say I trusted you, I said tell me what's in the note. And let's stop walking close to the traffic.'

'He told me you had something for me to take back to England, but I would need to prove that I came with his blessing. A mystery, like your cat Macavity.' He glanced sideways at Hillsden to see if there was any reaction. 'And that if we had a drink together I should order Castle Dracula.'

'That's your safe conduct pass, is it?'

'Waddington thought it would convince you.'

'How do I know that information wasn't obtained under duress?'

'You're a cautious bastard. I'm here to help.'

'What makes you think I need help?'

'You sent him a message, didn't you? Via some little poof.'

'I see you're fond of the old-fashioned terms – crumpet, poof. Almost as though you're in a time warp.'

'Trust me, Hillsden. I'm your only hope.'

'Trust isn't a word I use too often these days. But let's, for a moment, believe your story, let's pretend I do have

334

something to give you – how would you set about getting it back to Waddington? There's that to consider first.'

'Right now he's staying in my house for his own safety. Your messenger boy was murdered.'

It was only now that Hillsden gave any sign that he was capable of being taken by surprise.

'Name of Frampton, right?' Keating said. 'Well, they were on to him from the start, and they took him out along with his father. Does that go any way to convince you? I know the ropes as well as you. We come from the same stable, remember? – Two of Dinnsbury's thoroughbreds, and we both got the chop. I want to see you get even.'

'You didn't answer my question,' Hillsden said. 'Tell me how.'

'I take it out personally as one of our film scripts.'

They walked on in silence for twenty yards or so before Hillsden finally answered, 'I'll think about it.'

'You don't like it?'

'I'll think about it.'

'D'you have a better idea?'

'What I have is a baby on the way. That changes things. I don't mind signing my own death warrant, but now I have two other people to consider.'

'I'm here for another four days,' Keating said as they crossed the street and started to retrace their steps back to the hotel. 'I have to leave with the rest of the unit if it's to work. There's extra safety in numbers. If you resolve your problem, you know where to find me.'

335

23

Although the police were keeping the file on Waddington's death open, it was not being treated as a murder case. Despite Hogg's findings, and the fact that the dead man had once been an MI6 case officer, they could find no conclusive evidence of foul play. Because he had recently divorced his wife and quit his job for no apparent reason, suicide was the favourite theory, one given added credibility in view of the venue he had chosen. Even so, the CID investigation was thorough; his house was entered and diligently searched. No suicide note was found, but the telephone bug was uncovered, and as a result the police enquiries switched to Century House where, finally, the detective in charge of the case requested a meeting with the Director-General.

'Did he ever give any indication of being unstable, Sir Raymond?'

'I wouldn't go as far as that,' Control said.

'Why was he dismissed from the service?'

'*Dismissed* is too strong a word. We were required to reduce the complement of officers by the Government, and obviously we kept the best we had and let the others go. Waddington was one of those given early retirement.'

'Did that upset him?'

'I've no idea.'

'And you had no contact with him after that?'

'Not personally.'

'We found his phone bugged. Was that on your authority?'

'Superintendent, I don't have such authority. As you must know, only the Home Secretary approves phone-tapping. From time to time we make requests, but the final word is his.'

'I apologize. Put it another way, was there any reason why anybody in this building would request it?'

'Not to my knowledge.'

'Could it have been done without your knowledge?'

'I have to admit that in the past the rules have been bent, but since I've been Director-General any such request has to come through my office. I've been at some pains to avoid a repetition of previous misdemeanours.'

'Then, could you tell me, sir, whether he worked in any particularly sensitive areas before he left the service?'

'I think one could say that everything we deal with is sensitive.'

'I appreciate that.'

'From your line of questioning, Superintendent, am I to take it that this is being treated as a murder inquiry?'

'The death of anybody in unusual circumstances has to take every possibility into account.'

'But what is your own opinion?'

'I don't have opinions, sir. I just go by the evidence. The evidence so far would suggest he took his own life, for reasons we have yet to discover.'

'His marriage had failed, I believe?'

'Yes.'

Control cracked a knuckle. 'Excuse me,' he said as the Superintendent looked up, startled by the noise. 'A very unsocial habit of mine, but I suffer from rheumatism in these fingers. It slightly eases the pain. Yes . . . well, this life, rather like your own, I imagine, is not conducive to a regular home life. The best operatives are usually those without . . . other responsibilities.'

'Occupational hazard, sir.'

'If it was suicide, he chose the classical Greek method, did he not? Death in the bath, like Socrates.'

'Except he didn't open his wrists, sir,' the Superintendent said, scoring a point. There was something in Control's manner that had irritated him from the start. 'From what we've been able to piece together, he relied on a gas-leak to do the job for him.'

337

'A sad end. I hope you get to the bottom of it. We none of us like unsolved mysteries, do we?'

While this was taking place other members of the investigating teams were interviewing everybody at Breakproof, and tracing Waddington's movements during the weeks prior to the tragedy. His ex-wife and Keating's staff were also questioned, but the latter could throw no light on the matter – on the night in question they had been off duty, and since he was a guest of their absent employer they had not thought it their business to report his disappearance. Through them the police learnt of his association with Pamela. She, too, was questioned, but was able to establish that on that particular night she had made up a bridge four with neighbours in Amersham. Keating was down to be interviewed on his return from Russia.

Using his contacts within the CID, Lloyd was made privy to all this information and, operating on his own, paid a visit to Pamela. She gave him the impression she was still genuinely distressed by Waddington's horrific death. In turn, he was impressed by her looks, which distressed him in a different way.

'I can't understand it. We were due to have dinner the following evening.'

'Did he ever mention his previous occupation to you?'

'I knew he worked for a security firm. That's how we first met.'

'I meant when he was a member of MI6.'

'You mean spying?' Her surprise seemed authentic.

'Well, not spying exactly. He was once engaged in counter-espionage.'

'No. I just took him for what he was, what he told me he was.'

'When you last saw him, was he worried about anything?'

She shook her head. 'He had been worried about me. I was caught up in that recent hijacking. But no, nothing else; he seemed quite happy the last time we saw each other.'

'What did he talk about when you were together?'

'Nothing special. Look, we were having an affair; I'm sure

338

you're aware of that. We were both divorced, and we came together because we needed what most people need.'

'What is that?'

'Sex, companionship, a shoulder to cry on if necessary.'

'It was a recent affair, I take it?'

'Yes. It started a month or so ago.'

'And it worked?'

'It worked for me. And it seemed to work for him, too. To save you reading it in the Sunday papers, he was very good in bed.'

I bet you are, too, Lloyd thought. 'So on the face of it there was no reason for him to disappear like that?'

'Not that I know of.'

'You hadn't had a quarrel?'

'No.'

'And he never mentioned his previous life to you?'

'He talked about his marriage. We compared notes about our respective failures.'

'I was referring to something else,' Lloyd said, pressing her. 'When he failed to show up for your dinner date, weren't you alarmed?'

'I thought it odd, yes, but I imagined he had some excuse. We weren't chained to each other.'

'Why d'you think he wasn't living in his own house? Did he give you any reason?'

'He hinted that he had some personal problem. I assumed his ex-wife was chasing him for something. A woman scorned can be vindictive, you know,' Pamela added with a Gioconda smile.

'So I'm told. Just that? He didn't elaborate?'

'No.'

'If I were to tell you that the house he moved to belonged to another ex-member of the security services, would that surprise you?'

'*Are* you telling me that?' she fielded.

'There is a connection, yes.'

'As I said, all I knew is that when we first met he was selling burglar alarms. I knew nothing about his past life.'

339

She took out a handkerchief and dabbed her eyes. 'All this has been a terrible shock, and I've already told all this to the police who came before. We fell in love. That's not so unusual, is it?'

'I'm sorry. I didn't want to upset you, but naturally we're concerned to find out the true circumstances surrounding his death. Why, for instance, he would suddenly leave very comfortable surroundings and, if I may say so, a very attractive woman, and be found days later in the ruins of a derelict house.'

'I don't know why. I wish I did.'

'You would agree, though, that it appears likely that, in the circumstances, he had very little reason to take his own life.'

'Who knows what goes on inside anybody? I had a friend who blew his brains out just before Sunday lunch with the family.'

'Can I ask you one further question? Did he take drugs?'

'I guess like a lot of people he might have tried them, but he wasn't on anything when he was with me. He drank, but not to excess.'

'Well, thank you, you've been most helpful. If you think of anything else, please contact me at this number.' Lloyd handed her a card.

'Quite a looker,' Lloyd said when he next saw Pearson.

'Telling the truth, d'you think?'

'Who knows? A cool bird, if you want my opinion. The sort that might drive a man round the bend. I bet she's red-hot in the sack. Fantastic tits.'

'How old?'

'Difficult to say. I can never tell. Under thirty maybe. She had her war-paint on when I met her.'

They were studying the surveillance photos again.

'We've traced that character,' Pearson pointed to the enlargements he had ordered. 'Russian embassy trade mission.'

'Interesting.'

'Yes, look at those two closely. See what he's doing?'

Lloyd examined the prints. 'Model citizen, picking up dog

340

turds, and depositing offensive material in litter-basket.'

'Now look at this section. I had it computer-enhanced. What d'you see?'

'Like I said, model citizen. An example to us all.'

'Look again, look at his left hand. He puts something in, then takes something out. Or appears to.'

'Do we have one after this in sequence?'

'No, unfortunately. That old man feeding the pigeons blocks him out.'

Lloyd sorted through the entire batch. He suddenly stopped. 'Jesus! I don't believe it.'

'What?'

'There! See that woman sitting on the park bench?' He pointed.

Pearson took a magnifying glass and had a close look. 'What about her?'

'That's her; that's the bird I was talking about. Waddington's bit of stuff. Mrs van Norden.'

'You sure?'

'Bloody positive. Were these all taken on the same day?'

'Yes, they're date-stamped.'

'What order were they taken in?'

'Go by the negative numbers, then you'll get the sequence.'

Lloyd arranged the prints, laying them out in a line. 'Right, that's got them in order. In this one she's just leaving the park bench. Then dumps her trash in the basket and leaves. Seven shots later he appears. That's a bloody coincidence, isn't it? Too much of a coincidence, if you ask me.'

'Coincidence isn't proof.'

'OK, OK. But why would somebody like her take a sandwich lunch on a park bench? Claridge's would be more her style.'

'Agreed, but not conclusive.'

'It sucks.'

'What does that mean? I'm not up on your colloquialisms.'

'Well, I don't know what it means, either; it just sounds good. All I'm saying is that it's bloody odd that our Russian embassy friend and the lady from Amersham just happen to turn up in

341

the same place on the same day and use the same trash-basket. Add to that she was Waddington's girl-friend and I think it's another link in the chain you were talking about.'

'You're absolutely certain she's one and the same?'

'I just spent over an hour with her. I swear it's her.'

Pearson studied the photographs again. 'Maybe you're right. Maybe *link* was the wrong word; perhaps I should have said *web*.'

They lay side by side in bed, Galina asleep, Hillsden awake, his right hand resting on her swollen belly, his thoughts tracing the long journey that had brought him to this moment of truth in an alien city. He was conscious that everything previous in his life seemed to have been a betrayal of one kind or another: now the choice was between self-betrayal and a denial of love. Slowly and gently he removed his hand and slipped from the bed, padding from the darkened room into the kitchen. There he poured himself a whisky and sat, not taking it to his lips, nursing the glass.

When he had commenced writing the manuscript he had accepted that, once it had been smuggled out, his own fate was sealed. At that time, consumed with a desire to get even – the object had been to bring down the whole pack of cards – what eventually happened to him had seemed of little consequence. He had never contemplated somebody like Galina entering his life and, beyond Galina, the child she now carried. Russia had changed, was changing, but he doubted that the minor relaxations of the old order extended to forgiving the wives of traitors.

He went back to the doorway of the bedroom and stood there, watching her as she slept. He had an overwhelming desire to wake her, to take the manuscript from its hiding-place and share the burden with her. I've only ever cared for three women, he thought, and none of them shared my life entirely. There had always been something to hold back – not the ordinary unimportant lies that were part of most intimate relationships, the ones that protected rather than bruised, but the sustained lies that eventually, inevitably corrupted love.

342

It occurred to him how different his marriage to Margot would have been if he had ever found the courage to reveal the truth about himself. He wondered: Would I ever have betrayed her with Caroline if Margot, with no justification, had not already believed me unfaithful? In the end the effort of proclaiming a truth while colouring it with a spectrum of lies had finally worn him down.

Galina turned in the bed; the outline of her belly accused him as he stood watching. He had never made another life before; he had only destroyed lives. Now, forming in her womb, there was a child that he might never live to see. As if suddenly conscious of what he was thinking, Galina sat up in the bed, her eyes wide open.

'What's happened?' she said.

'Nothing. I couldn't sleep.'

'Why are you standing there?'

'Just watching you.'

'You gave me a fright.'

'I didn't mean to. Go back to sleep.'

'Aren't you coming back to bed?'

'In a minute.' He held up the whisky-glass. 'I'm a secret midnight drinker. I'll come when I've finished this.'

'Have you had second thoughts, is that it?'

'What're you talking about?'

'About us?'

'Second and third thoughts, if you must know.'

'About me and the baby?'

Hillsden nodded.

'I know I'm no fun for you at the moment, but the doctor said the sickness will disappear, then we can make love again properly.'

He went and sat on the edge of the bed and stroked her stomach, feeling the warmth of her body through the thin sheet.

'D'you want to know what I was really thinking?' he said. 'I was thinking that we should get married as soon as possible.'

She searched his face. 'You really mean that? You're not saying it because you feel sorry for me?'

343

'My darling, the only thing I'm sorry about is that I didn't meet you thirty years ago when I had something better to offer.'

As he leant down to kiss her amazed vulnerable face he realized that the living rather than the dead had made all the decisions for him.

The bird had flown.

Despite Pearson acting swiftly in conjunction with Special Branch, by the time they reached the house in Amersham Pamela had disappeared without trace. A warrant for her arrest under the Official Secrets Act (1991) was granted, and security forces at all airports and ports were put on the alert. Her aged parents were interviewed, but could offer little but shock and surprise at these developments. They stated that since her divorce from van Norden they had had little contact with her, apart from an occasional visit at Christmas. The Central Police Computer came up with a blank: nothing was known about her; as a student she had never taken part in any sit-ins or protest movements, she belonged to no political party and appeared to have no political associations. Her staff and neighbours in Amersham also gave her a dull clean bill of health. The picture all this built up to was just the average rich divorcee enjoying an affluent life on her alimony. It all seemed too good to be true.

'Nobody's that anonymous,' Pearson observed to Lloyd, sharing a pot of canteen tea strong enough to skate mice across, 'otherwise the tabloids would go out of business. Show me somebody with no skeletons in their cupboard, and I'll show you a skilful liar. When I was with the Met every rapist we ever caught was a mother's boy – shy retiring types, the sort that help old ladies across the street and are kind to dumb animals. We manufacture a particular kind of monster in jolly old England. It suits some people to portray us as gentle, law-abiding, tepid-beer-drinking salts of the earth. In reality there's a hidden beast in a good many of our stalwart citizens, ready to bare its fangs at the slightest provocation. No in-feriority complex in we British, boyo; arrogance is our religion. Forget the wogs begin at Calais, forget tolerance, love your neighbour and all that pious shit; we don't like anybody, not even ourselves. And since we no longer have an empire to push around we've taken the fight to the holiday beaches.'

'Churchill anticipated that, didn't he?' Lloyd remarked.

'Churchill?'

'Yeah. In his speech: "We shall fight them on the beaches." '

'What a mind you have, Lloyd. Always a quote for the occasion.'

'You sound bitter, Chief.'

'Bitter? Of course I'm bitter. Nobody's bringing me arrows of desire any more. That's another quote for you to ponder. You thank your lucky stars you're not still on the beat. When I joined the force way back, there was some respect for the Old Bill. Just a couple of us could take care of a Saturday-night punch-up in the local on our own. No problem. Nowadays you'd have to go in with a riot squad and you'd still be lucky not to get a knife in your back. Mind you, this tea will probably get you in any case.'

'Changing the subject,' Lloyd said, 'I see they've applied to the Home Secretary for a deportation order where that Russian is concerned.'

'Big deal. And next week the Russians will kick one of ours out of Moscow. It's a game, just a game at that level. But I blame myself; I screwed up on this one.'

'How?'

Pearson did not answer immediately. For reasons he could not readily explain even to himself, feelings surfaced that the very nature of his job usually forced him to sublimate. He felt a sense of guilt where Waddington was concerned, a nagging suspicion that if he had acted differently Waddington's life might have been saved.

'Getting old,' he said finally. 'There were signposts all along the way, and I misread them. It means starting again. Get me everything you can on Hillsden. Waddington was convinced Hillsden was framed.'

345

'Framed for the murder of that diplomat?'

'Yes, and the rest. He was on to something, in Waddington's opinion, and they needed to get him out of the way. So see what you can turn up. Let's go out on a limb for this one. We all have to die some time.'

Pearson was edging closer, but not close enough. He was not to know that Pamela's disappearance had been engineered by Control. Immediately after Lloyd had interviewed her she had reported to him, using an unlisted number. She had been swiftly smuggled out of the country.

Again, contact with Abramov had been broken and Control had a desperate need to find an alternative means of communication before it was too late. The confession extracted from Waddington before his death had to be checked and acted upon as soon as possible – there were too many unfriendly ferrets scuttling around for comfort. Equally vital, he had to appease Moscow.

The first necessity was to put Bayldon in the picture, and he requested an urgent meeting. Bayldon's private office fitted him into a gap between a lunch appointment with the Secretary-General of the United Nations and a meeting with the Chiefs of Staff on the defence estimates.

He was greeted with 'I can't spare you very long. I've got a very difficult day.'

'You're going to have a more difficult day when you've heard my news.'

Ever since Bayldon had weathered the engineered crisis surrounding his wife there had been a marked change in his attitude. With a political astuteness that had surprised Control as much as anybody, he had brilliantly defused the situation in one stroke. On his own initiative he and his wife had paid a flying visit to the troops in Northern Ireland where, in one of the most vulnerable border-towns, with full media coverage, she had announced she was setting up a million-dollar trust fund for the widows and children of servicemen killed during the terrorist campaign. 'I am aware of the rumours that have recently been circulating about me, and it is easy to guess where they originated. They were part of a deliberate campaign to discredit my husband through me, and I hope that in setting up this fund I can make it abundantly clear where my true sentiments lie. I may be an American by birth, but my loyalties are with the British people and, like the Prime Minister, I am utterly opposed to any form of terrorism and support his efforts to combat this cancer in our midst.' If Bayldon had a hand in writing her speech, he was not letting on. When loaded questions were put to him concerning her wealth, he made no cover-up: attack, he had decided, was the best defence. 'My wife is well aware that inherited wealth must always pose a moral responsibility, and as a committed socialist she welcomes an opportunity to put it to good use.' His popularity in the polls reached its highest level since he took office.

After this the tabloids dropped the original story and the attempt at a backbench revolt led by Deacon fizzled out since, in the last analysis, ordinary Members were disinclined to rock the boat they sailed in for fear it might capsize and sink them with it. Principles were always on special offer at Westminster.

Bayldon said: 'What is it this time? You have a tendency to panic these days, Raymond. You panicked over the affair of my wife, coming to me with a doom-laden scenario which I quickly proved wrong.'

'It was hardly wrong of me to warn you.'

'But I was the one who found the solution. Money talks in two directions, you know.'

'I'm sure we're all greatly relieved that episode is closed,' Control said acidly, 'but something far more threatening has come up.'

'Really? And you need my help again, is that it?'

'I need you to realize how serious it is. Serious enough to warrant an XPD without delay.'

'Don't talk as though we're solving the *Times* crossword. I haven't a clue what "XPD" means.'

' "Expedient demise." '

Bayldon stared at him. There was a long pause.

347

'I don't want to be involved in anything like that. I don't even want to be told about it.'

'You can't help being involved. You think the journey you took to get to this office kept your hands clean?'

'All right, spare me the sermon. What is it this time?'

'It concerns Hillsden.'

'Hillsden? But he's safely out of the way; that's what you've always told me.'

'Out of the way, maybe, but no longer safe. Circumstances change, and we have to meet them.'

For the first time during the meeting Bayldon faltered. 'What circumstances?'

He listened in silence while Control brought him up to date.

'He should have been dealt with once and for all. I said so at the time. A dead man can't write his memoirs.' He took out a pure lawn handkerchief and wiped his damp fingers. 'So what are you suggesting? That you XPD him by remote control?'

'That's for Moscow to decide as and when I inform them. But it might not stop at that. There might have to be others. It's possible I was too clever last time.'

'I can't believe we're having this conversation. Who are we talking about now?'

'The girl,' Control said, watching Bayldon's face closely. 'Pamela was always a threat to you, remember?'

'There's nothing to connect me to her.'

'Except her mouth. She might open it to save herself.'

Bayldon raised the lid of one of the red boxes on his desk as though expecting to find all the answers inside, but there was no one to brief him on this occasion. When next he spoke he was more placatory. 'Well, we've survived worse and come through. I'm sure you'll do whatever is necessary. The vital element is that I mustn't be implicated in any way . . . Did this man Waddington reveal how Hillsden intended to get his manuscript into the country? And to whom?'

'No. Unfortunately, if I can put it this way, his ability to withstand interrogation was higher than we had allowed for.'

'Well, push him harder.'

'That might be difficult. As far as I know he's sprinkled around the roses in a garden of remembrance,' Control said, enjoying his own ability to shock.

The Fat Boy was on the move again. Having received instructions, he started his journey from Greece, this time travelling on an American passport – the name, Allen Lyndon Witz, and physical details taken from a dead man of his own age and height who had been born in Phoenix, Arizona, profession attorney at law. Provided he did not pass through any United States Immigration check, his papers would stand up in the rest of the world, for he was armed with back-up documentation should he ever be challenged, even to the extent of having a voluminous brief concerning international patents. His wallet contained snapshots of a nonexistent wife and daughter, membership of golf and health clubs in Scottsdale, together with credit cards, driving licence and printed business-cards of a law firm that had folded several years previously. He sported a moustache, and contact lenses that changed the colour of his eyes. As an extra precaution he also wore a corset under a sober, beautifully cut Armani suit. The impression of understated affluence was completed with a button-down Ralph Lauren shirt and a Cartier tank wrist-watch.

Flying first to Nice, he remained in transit awaiting a connection to Rome. Although he took elaborate precautions whenever he ventured into unfriendly territory, he was never overly concerned for his own safety: few countries wanted to apprehend him on their own soil for fear of revenge attacks. He was possibly the most unwanted wanted man on the terrorist-list and never made the mistake of travelling with anything that could tie him into a particular incident. The complete professional, perhaps the only chink in his armour had been his womanizing; but in recent years, growing wiser and more aware that his luck might one day run out between the sheets, if not from betrayal then from AIDS, he had become celibate.

He had not been to Italy since the days when the Red

Brigade had been active. On arrival he found Rome airport disrupted by industrial action: the baggage-handlers were on strike and the Immigration officials were working to rule. Shuffling slowly forward in the long line of disgruntled passengers, he was relieved to find the passport check perfunctory, the Immigration officer hardly glancing at his photograph. Once in his rented Fiat he was amazed by the changes that had taken place since his last visit. It was as if every single car in Italy had swarmed into Rome – metal cholesterol clogging its arteries, they were parked, sometimes three abreast, at every conceivable angle, often mounted on the pavements with a native disregard for regulations that he could only admire. He had the impression that only the ancient ruins looked clean and preserved; the endless incongruous apartment-blocks were stained with neglect, their lower walls defaced with graffiti and posters for pop groups, while those vast edifices marking the Mussolini years had the appearance of an abandoned film-set. Waiting in the inevitable traffic jams he also spotted several swastikas – as though history was about to repeat itself. After taking three wrong turnings he eventually found his way to the Aldrovandi Palace Hotel where a room had been booked for him and paid for in advance. His window overlooked the zoo; he could see half a dozen sad and moth-eaten condors in their giant cage, hunched like lonely old men on the sea-front, and beyond this the white rocks of the polar-bear enclosure.

He helped himself to half a bottle of indifferent champagne from the mini-bar and waited for contact to be made. Despite the failure of the hijack he viewed his coming assignment with confidence: he was anxious to restore his reputation. Despising most of his fellow-terrorists, he thought of them, using de Gaulle's 1968 verdict, as *ce chie-en-lit*, the 'shit-a-beds'. He was only truly happy when he worked alone; then the planning and the risks were solely his to evaluate. His paymasters were invariably generous, and privately he thought of himself as a star soccer player, always prepared to go on the transfer-list and score for any team that could afford him.

The expected phone call came half an hour later while he was lying fully dressed on top of the bed watching the CNN live satellite news beamed from America. He was amused by an item concerning a mass murderer who had just gone to the electric chair: a trio of earnest pundits were debating the morality of capital punishment even when meted out to some sadistic dropout who admitted to killing forty-two women. The sanctity of human life did not rate high on the Fat Boy's list of priorities.

A female voice on the telephone said: 'Mass for the dead is being held in the church at the Piazza Euclide in half an hour. I hope you'll join me to pay your respects.'

'Yes,' he said, 'I will be there.'

He left the hotel immediately and drove to the church. It proved to be a monstrous edifice, its rotunda in architectural conflict with the massive squared-off pillars of the grandiose entrance, where students sat on the steps consuming junk food. Dominating the otherwise characterless piazza, it had been erected not only to the glory of God but also for the greater glory of Benito, even though Benito was a non-believer. The interior, had it been left alone, was in fact simple and could have been impressive, but it had been glitzed-up by some of the grossest paintings the Fat Boy had ever seen. There were some seven or eight private chapels, all vying with each other in banal tastelessness. The first, just to the left of the entrance, featured half a dozen large paintings of nubile angels, executed in flat monotone and resembling centrefolds from a religious version of *Playboy*. Dotted around the perimeter walls were other examples of kitsch, so brightly coloured that one could almost see to shave in them. There was also a model of the nativity which contained a plastic infant Jesus and was surmounted by a disproportion-ately large shooting star picked out in fairground bulbs. None of the altars had candles in front of them; instead there were brass boxes topped with small electric lights that could be activated by the faithful, rather like slot machines. Far from being offended by the vulgarity, the Fat Boy took satisfaction from it: lacking any faith, he was delighted to

351

have his scathing opinion of the Catholic church confirmed.

Even so, he behaved correctly, genuflected in front of the main altar, then sat on a pew at the rear of the church, well away from other penitents, and bowed his head as though in prayer. He remained thus until, perhaps five minutes later, Pamela came and occupied one of the pews in front of him. She did not glance at him or give any sign of recognition but, seeing her again, hatred welled in him – he did not like witnesses to his failures, and the inconclusive hijack still rankled.

He got up to further the charade, placing a coin in one of the brass boxes and switching on one of the fake candles, mocking the Virgin above the garish altar as he mouthed his own prayer: *Holy Mary, bring us chaos.* Then he went and sat close to Pamela.

'I'll do all the talking,' he whispered.

Pamela knelt as though in prayer, her head below the level of the pew in front of her, so that she was partially concealed and able to glance sideways at him.

'Are you sure you were not followed?'

Pamela nodded.

'Do you have a safe place where we can talk?'

She nodded again.

'This is what you do. Turn left when you leave here and follow the road round. Walk slowly until I draw up alongside you, then get into my car quickly. I will leave now.'

He got up, genuflected again in the centre aisle, then exited. Once in his parked car he waited until he saw Pamela come out of the church, then slowly drove after her. He caught up with her a few hundred yards further on. She got in.

'Take me the shortest route,' he said.

After she had given him the first directions, Pamela said: 'Was it a surprise to see me again so soon?'

He made no reply.

'I'll never get over the coincidence that I was on that particular flight. That was scary. I'm sorry it didn't work out as planned for you, but I wasn't sorry when it ended.'

Her condolences angered him, and he lost concentration

and was forced to brake sharply as a Mercedes cut in. He swore in Spanish, another indication that he was rattled.

'They drive like maniacs here,' Pamela said. She reached to attach her safety-belt. 'Turn left at the next lights and follow the autostrada signs.'

'Did you know that Gunther is dead?' she said, breaking the silence and referring to her ex-lover who had first introduced her to the Fat Boy.

'So?'

'Just making conversation. I miss him. He was good.'

'But not good enough to stay alive.'

'He was unlucky.' His attitude forced her to be defensive. 'The explosive he was using was unstable.'

'He was just another amateur, playing at it. What is this place we're going to?'

'One of Control's safe houses that he uses himself.'

'Have you used it before?'

'No, but if you're that uneasy why don't we talk now? I take it you're driving a clean car.'

'Just give the directions.'

They headed out of Rome in the direction of the airport. The traffic thinned as they gained the autostrada, eventually turning off and making for a small village. When she finally pointed out the house, the Fat Boy drove straight past it, continuing for half a mile before he finally pulled in by a small wood.

'What's wrong?' Pamela asked.

'Everything. You call that safe? Two strangers arriving in a village? What d'you take me for? You think you're still dealing with your dead boy-friend?' He drummed his gloved hands on the steering wheel.

'It was the house I was told to use.'

'Fucking amateurs, the lot of you. No wonder London has to call me in every time they want something done properly.'

Pamela reached in her handbag for a cigarette, but before she could light it he tore it out of her mouth.

'Don't you know cigarette butts can hang you? How many of the locals smoke British Dunhills, you stupid cow?'

353

Then, at the sound of a car approaching, he suddenly, alarmingly embraced her, pressing his fat lips to hers, remaining in the clinch until the vehicle had passed.

'Was I supposed to enjoy that?' she said, wiping her mouth.

He did not answer, but put the car into gear and drove on until he came to a small path leading into the wooded area. Once they were out of sight of any passing traffic on the road, he stopped and switched off the engine. He got out and walked around until satisfied that the spot he had chosen was completely safe.

'We'll talk here,' he said, returning to the car. 'Give me the final details.'

'You talk about amateurs. What I've got to tell you could have been said in the church.'

'Don't you know the rules? When in Rome, do it my way.'

His physical presence at such close proximity in the tiny car repulsed her. She could still taste the Cologne he used, and for no reason it reminded her of moments in her childhood when she had shared an apple with her mother and tasted the scent of her lipstick.

She began to outline her instructions, and he let her finish without interruption, only then asking her to repeat one detail. He consulted a small pocket diary.

'The fifteenth is a Saturday.'

'That's right. They always hold the last concert of the season on a Saturday.'

'You're sure you've left nothing out?'

'I'll go over it again if you like.'

'This shop where I get the costume, is it well known?'

'It was just one I chose at random. But there are plenty of others. They're all over London. It's not a costume as such, just a funny hat, or something like that. The ticket will be given to you in London. They're like gold dust.'

He stared straight ahead, appearing to be lost in thought. On Pamela's blind side he extracted something from his jacket pocket and palmed it.

'Does it give you a charge?'

'What?'

354

'Killing.'

He shrugged. 'It pays well.' Then, uncharacteristically, though aware that nothing would be lost, he felt the urge to boast. 'This one especially. I could retire after this one.'

'And will you? Quit while you're ahead? There must come a moment when the luck runs out. The law of averages.'

He turned and smiled. 'It's like roulette. There's no point in playing red or black. The only kick comes when you play *en plein* with a single number. Go for the maximum odds.'

'Gunther felt the same way. Not that I'm comparing you.'

'I'm glad, because there is no comparison. I'm the best,' he said, getting out of the car. 'Just let me check, then we'll go back.' He disappeared from her view, returning after a short interval and seeming to be more relaxed.

'All clear?'

'Yes. Everything's fine.' Again the unexpected softness. 'Do you have a lover now?'

'Not at the moment.'

'What a waste. Perhaps, if I ever retire, you should join me.'

The thought revolted her, but caution framed her response. 'I wouldn't mind getting out of the game. I don't have your confidence about the future.'

'Well, it's something we should both keep in mind. No hard feelings about the hijack?'

'How could there be? It was just kismet.'

'Good.' He leant towards her, and again she had no time to avoid his kiss. The sheer strength of him forced her lips to open to his, and she felt him pass something into her mouth. Then his hands clamped her jaw shut, holding her in a vice-like grip.

'Swallow,' he said. 'Swallow.'

She tried to struggle free, but it was an uneven contest. Her teeth bit into the capsule, and she tasted the acrid powder. The Fat Boy massaged her throat with one gloved thumb, easing the poison down, and the last image she had was his smiling face.

When she was dead he removed anything that might identify

355

her from her handbag, then carried her body into the woods as far from the road as was possible. Then he drove straight to the airport, checked in the hire car, and caught the first available plane to London, where he disposed of her belongings.

24

Keating said: 'Have you reached a decision? We shall be moving out at the end of the week. If it hadn't been for their endless bureaucracy, we'd have finished yesterday. Just to get an extra lamp is like asking for a lock of Lenin's hair. That and the lousy weather.'

Hillsden answered carefully: 'I've been weighing up all the alternatives. But don't think I'm not grateful for the risk you've taken already.'

They were sitting in two folding director's chairs on the fringe of the unit which was shooting a sequence by one of the bridges. He broke off as the Production Manager approached.

'Now what?' Keating asked, seeing the expression on the man's face. He looked mournful at the best of times, the job ensuring that he was regarded as the hatchet man by the crew.

'Slight problem, governor.'

'There is no such thing on this bloody film. So, OK, give me the bad news.'

'Isobel's got the curse.'

Isobel was the female star, a comparative newcomer who possessed that most priceless asset, far removed from any discernible talent, called a *television rating*, which was the only reason she had been cast.

'What difference does that make?'

'She doesn't work when she's got the curse. It's in her contract.'

'I don't believe it. Have you checked?'

The man nodded.

'Offer her more money, anything to get out of this place.'

'She won't budge. She says she looks terrible. Bags under her eyes.'

'Jesus Christ! That's all we need.'

He dragged his bulk out of the canvas chair and waddled over to the camera. There he tackled the Director first.

'I gather we've run out of Tampax, Zev.'

'Actresses,' the Director said, but he didn't appear too disturbed. It suited his purpose; his own contract would shortly go into overage because of the delays.

'Have you talked to her?'

'Sure.'

'And?'

'She does look terrible. And this is meant to be the big love scene when he first gets the hots for her.'

'What about the cameraman? You told me he was a genius when you hired him. Can't he do something? Light out her fucking bags?'

'Possibly, except she refuses to be photographed.'

'I'll sue the bitch.'

'That won't help us right now. Know what the real problem is?'

'There's another one?'

'She isn't getting any.'

Keating stared at him, nonplussed.

'Any what?'

'Cock. The old pork sword. She likes to have a relationship with her leading men. Unfortunately, our leading man hasn't come across.'

'Well, why don't you step into his shoes?'

'There are a lot of things I'll do for this film, but I draw the line there. She's a piranha in spades. I'd rather go down on a Russian roadsweeper.'

'So shoot something else.'

'I haven't got anything else to shoot. She's in every sequence.'

'I won't be screwed like this.'

'You already have been. Listen, I'm sorry, but I understand from Gerry she has it in her contract. When it's Tampax time, the lady is a tramp. But you talk to her by all means; maybe you can charm her. I've tried and got nowhere.'

'Where's Raven?'

'He went back in the hotel with her.'

'So what are we supposed to do in the meantime?'

'Sit it out, I guess.'

'On my money.'

'What can I say? It's bring-on-the-empty-horses time.'

Keating conceded defeat and walked back to Hillsden.

'Trouble?'

'I don't want to talk about it,' Keating said. 'This business is sick.' He stared moodily into space, then took out one of his outsize Havanas and bit off the end. 'You want one?'

'No. I might get to like them.'

With the cigar alight and glowing Keating seemed to recover. 'Alternatives,' he asked abruptly. 'What alternatives?'

'Well, having come this far, I have to trust you. I have to believe that you contacted me with Waddington's blessing. But we're both a long way from home, and there can't be any mistakes. We know things have changed here; there is a degree of – not freedom exactly, not as we understand freedom – call it a loosening of the bonds. The domestic animals have been given an extra length of rope when they're allowed out for a walk; they've let a few more Jews go to Israel; and it's no longer a certain trip to the Gulag to suggest that Joe Stalin wasn't Rebecca of Sunnybrook Farm. But so far they haven't given the KGB *Scouting for Boys* as their standard textbook.'

'I'm listening.'

'In the beginning I didn't care what happened to me. I had precious little to live for here; I just wanted to get even. But since I first tried to contact Waddington my situation has changed. The only alternative I can come up with which protects Galina and my unborn child is to destroy my manuscript and just give you the facts. Assuming I convince you, you can convince Waddington in turn. He'll know what to do with it. I don't know how much he's told you already, or whether in fact he's told you anything.'

359

'He said he believed you'd been framed.'

'That's too tame a word for it. Did he give you names?'

'No.'

'No names at all?'

'Only yours.'

Hillsden was silent for a while. The rich and almost forgotten aroma of Keating's cigar drifted past him, making him reach for a cigarette.

They were interrupted again as the Production Manager hovered nearby.

'Yes, what is it now, Gerry?'

'Should we wrap for the day?'

'Have I got a choice?'

'Not really.'

'So why ask me? Do we know how long she's going to stay in purdah?'

'No, it's never happened to me before.'

'Well, go back to the hotel and tell Raven that if he wants to finish this fucking epic he'd better get that bitch working tomorrow. Otherwise I'll pull the plug on him.'

'Right. I'll tell him. What about the wrap? Shall I dismiss the unit?'

'No, they're getting paid. Why should they enjoy themselves when I'm not?'

Gerry backed away.

'Can you believe this?' he said to Hillsden. 'That stupid little cunt who Raven persuaded me was the difference between profit and loss is refusing to work because she's got the rags on. I don't know why I got mixed up in this in the first place. I need my head examining.'

There was a crudeness to his sudden anger that Hillsden had not seen before.

One of the prop men came up with two glasses of sweet Russian tea. Keating took his without a thank-you. 'Go on, tell me the rest.'

'What if I was able to convince you that all those endless memoirs, articles, thinly disguised works of fiction about the Firm being infiltrated at the top level were true? What if, beyond that, I was also able to convince you that the present occupant of Number Ten was put there and run by Moscow Centre, through Control?'

'Stranger things have happened,' Keating said evenly. 'The Prince of Wales married Wally Simpson. So convince me.'

'First, you have to understand they had Bayldon on ice for years. Patience, as you know, is one of their hallmarks. When I stumbled too close to the truth, they had to set about disposing of me.'

'How did you get close?'

'You have to begin with a murder, the murder of my ex-mistress, a woman called Caroline Oates. At one time she and I and a character named Calder, "Jock" Calder, were all in the Austrian station. Caroline was the bright one of the trio, bright and committed. It wasn't just a job to her; it was something more, much more. She really had a lifelong hatred of the Bolsheviks. She was on to Bayldon first.'

'And told you?'

Hillsden shook his head. 'Nothing as simple as that. I wasn't running her; Control was running her direct from London, using me as the post office when it suited him. And eventually, when he realized his own position was threatened, he betrayed her.'

'How?'

'Oh, he was subtle, very subtle. First of all he made sure I was safely out of the way. We'd played into his hands, you see, broken the house rules by sleeping together. That was strictly *verboten* in Control's book. Fiddling the expenses was allowed, but not fornication. Once I had been shipped home he urged her to follow up her leads and sent her back into East Berlin. It was a one-way ticket; he knew they'd take her there. But what he hadn't allowed for was that Caroline stayed one step ahead. You never met her, did you?'

'No. I knew of her in a roundabout way.'

'She was smart, as well as being the love of my life. And she'd so nearly solved all of the puzzle. To be honest, I don't think she'd slotted in Control at that point, but before Moscow

361

Centre got her and started working her over she managed to get a vital piece of the puzzle back to England.'

'What was that?'

'A photograph, a very incriminating photograph.'

'Of Control?'

'No, I jumped to the same conclusion at first. Not Control. Bayldon with a girl, a KGB plant. In the wrong hands it would have blown fifteen years' preparations. Bayldon had been groomed all that time for his present star role. But he had something in his past that would have crooked their master plan.'

'So how did you discover it?'

'*Discover* is the wrong word. Bear with me. When Moscow Centre had reduced her to a vegetable she was eventually traded, sent across Checkpoint Charlie in a wheelchair. Once home Control with his infinite compassion arranged for her to get the George Medal – not that she would have been able to appreciate the gesture. By then they had tucked her away in a nursing home for terminal cases. They weren't taking any chances. The photograph was there, on her bedside table, just waiting for somebody to spot it.'

'Where you found it?'

Hillsden looked away into the distance where the film crew were gathered in groups, passing the time.

'No, it wasn't like that. I never saw her again.'

'Why not?'

'That's a good question. Maybe it was guilt, maybe it was just plain cowardice, or a combination of both. If I had, things might have been very different. I guess you might say I betrayed her by doing nothing. If I'd ever gone to see her when she came home, she wouldn't be dead, and I wouldn't be here. But somebody else paid a visit, not for old times' sake but to murder her. Somebody from her past, somebody she trusted. He had to murder her, because she knew him.'

'Who was it?'

'Jock. Our old friend Jock. It's possible – anything's possible – that Caroline betrayed him . . . They took her apart, mentally and physically; so, poor darling, she couldn't be blamed

362

for that. The KGB got him, too, but Jock wasn't made of the same material as Caroline; he did a deal, they turned him, orchestrated a phoney death, buried him. Very neat and tidy, right down to a grave in Vienna's Central Cemetery. But favours have to be repaid. When they realized Caroline still had the photograph, they wanted his debt paid; they sent him to England to kill her, which he did most expertly. It's funny how you can live in close proximity with somebody, share their life, and yet not know them at all.'

Keating had listened without expression. Now he said: 'You mean, you never took him for a killer?'

'He was a friend, for Christ's sake! Somebody I trusted. We'd shared so much, the three of us. I cried when I got news he was dead.'

'How did you find out he killed her?'

'I came here as a prize catch. You see, Control devised a really watertight way of neutralizing me. And I fell for it. I suppose if you're going to jump over a cliff you take a run at it, like a lemming; you don't pause on the brink and look back at what you're leaving. Control persuaded me to go back into the field. "Back to where it all began", as he put it. And I went. I jumped. I left my wife, which was no big deal, because our marriage had been a sham for years, and I went to earth. The plan I agreed to was for me to become a dropout, which I did. To make it look kosher, I went up north, got myself arrested, deliberately engineered a prison sentence. Came out, drank myself stupid, until finally I was picked up again and sent to a home that rehabilitated derelicts, a quasi-religious order down in Devon. While I was there, Moscow ran me down, convinced I was ready to defect, as they were meant to, and spirited me out of the country. I played the role to the hilt, though I say so myself. The deal I had been sold was an eventual trade.'

'Quite a story,' Keating commented, and for the first time he seemed impressed.

'Don't tell *me* – I lived it. But as soon as I was out of the country Control closed the trap. I was set up as the prime suspect for the murder of Sir Charles Belfrage. Remember that case?'

'Yes.'

'Dyed-in-the-wool true-blue Tory, Eton and Cambridge, a pillar of the Establishment, but couldn't keep his flies buttoned. An upright cock has no conscience, as an uncle of mine used to say, even in such exalted circles. I knew him, not socially, but because we often liaised on security matters. As a matter of fact we met on the day Caroline was murdered; he came with me to the autopsy. That's by the way; the only important thing is that they pushed his murder on to me.'

'And Jock?'

'They sprang Jock on me halfway through my debriefing. When I got over the initial shock of his resurrection, I was glad of his company. Ostensibly, as the old hand, he was provided as my mentor, to show me the ropes. We were both given apartments in Moscow and for a time I took him at face value. You have to remember, at that time, I had no reason to suspect him, and he accepted that I'd joined his club.'

'So how did you suspect him?'

'Begin to have doubts?' Hillsden answered. He brought his head round and looked Keating in the eyes. 'If you're to believe any part of it, I have to tell you everything, regardless of what you think of me afterwards. Not that my feelings matter. I'm past caring about myself. I wish to God we had a drink.'

'You want to go somewhere else?'

'No, let's finish it now we've got this far. No good leaving it at the end of the second act. While we were in Moscow, Jock was very restless; he couldn't understand why they were keeping him there. Like Belfrage, he was a cocksman, he liked getting his nookie regularly, and Moscow cramped his style; he had a luxury pad in Switzerland he was anxious to get back to. So with Abramov's permission and connivance a party was arranged.'

'Abramov? Who's he?'

'Didn't I mention him before? He's my GRU guru, assigned to me from day one.'

'Sorry, I interrupted you. A party was arranged, you say?'

'Yes. A couple of local girls, some drinks, all of which was very welcome at the time. Pleasant girls, too, not obvious tarts. Hand-picked and knew what the score was. We paired off. I got the blonde – her name was Inga – Jock got the brunette, and we were all set to have a good time. In fact at the start I did have a good time. Not sex: companionship, talk, talk with a woman for a change. Jock had claimed the only bedroom; he didn't waste time . . . And then . . . it turned ugly.' He paused as the memory of what had happened in the locked bedroom crowded back. 'The other thing I didn't know about Jock was that his sexual tastes were . . . twisted. He could only get his rocks off – sorry, that's an Americanism I learnt from him – if he inflicted pain.' His delivery slowed again as he searched for adequate words to describe the events of that evening. 'He used his girl in the same way that destroyed Fatty Arbuckle's career . . . do you know what I'm talking about?'

'Fatty who?'

'He was a big film star way back, but got involved in a bizarre sex scandal that rocked Hollywood at the time. The legend is he killed a girl with the help of a champagne-bottle. Jock wasn't drinking champagne that night, but he killed her in the same hideous way. Do I have to spell it out? It had to be hushed up, and Abramov did the necessary. He was very efficient, I have to give him that. The dead girl was removed before you could say "Molotov". Or maybe she wasn't dead when they took her out. I'm a bit hazy on that, but she died soon after. My girl was told to say nothing, not that she needed to be told.'

'How did he deal with Jock?'

'I'm getting to that. Abramov saw me the next day . . . and asked me to do him a certain favour. It had been decided that Jock had outlived his usefulness . . . Abramov offered me a trade . . . in return for filling in the last pieces of the puzzle . . . giving me the name of Caroline's killer . . . I was to do their job for them . . .' He paused again, watching Keating closely. 'I told you I wouldn't leave anything out.'

'You were to kill Jock?'

'Yes. Don't ever believe they haven't got a sense of humour. A "certain poetic justice" was how Abramov put it.'

'Jesus!'

'It was a kind of Sophie's choice.'

'How d'you mean?'

'Didn't you ever read the book?'

Keating shook his head.

'Well, no matter. I wasn't prepared to accept Abramov's word for it. I had to have proof; I had to have Jock admit it to my face. That was the only way I could even contemplate it. Again, Abramov came up with the answer. He suggested I tricked Jock into believing that I'd got him off the hook where the girl's murder was concerned. And it worked. Gratitude loosens the tongue. Gratitude and a bottle of whisky. He gave me the rest of the story in the end . . . Told me how, if the plot to put Bayldon into Number Ten was to succeed, they had to have a clean sheet: anybody remotely connected had to be eliminated – that was why Caroline, Glanville and Belfrage were murdered. At the same time the country was being systematically destabilized: strikes, racial conflicts fomented, an orchestrated run on the pound – it was all diabolically clever and it worked.'

Keating nodded. 'Yes, it certainly worked.'

'I'd already sussed out a lot of what he told me. After all, I knew *I* hadn't murdered Belfrage or Glanville, and it wasn't that difficult for me to realize that Control had to be the mole, though I had no inkling of his real purpose until much later.'

'Bayldon, you mean?'

'Yes, that came like a bolt out of the blue. But with Jock my only concern was to get at the truth about Caroline. Even when he finally admitted his guilt, I still didn't think I could go through with my side of the bargain . . . Except, it was the way he justified himself. To hear him tell it, killing Caroline was like putting an old dog down, an act of charity. He didn't have any remorse; it was just a job to him.'

'And that made it possible, did it?'

'Yes. I finally found enough hate.'

366

'How? How did you do it?'

'Is that important?'

'I guess not.'

'I said I wouldn't leave anything out. He got drunk, unconscious drunk . . . If he'd ever been aware of me, I might have funked it at the last moment; but, like the expression he used about Caroline – "she wasn't there", he kept saying – he wasn't there, either, he was just an object and I smothered him with a pillow.'

Hillsden took a sip of tea, but it was stone cold.

'He'd been buried once; now they buried him again, for real. Since when I've lived a privileged barren life; that is, until I met Galina. And there you have it, the whole story.'

'Which you committed to paper?'

'Yes.'

'A dangerous gamble,' Keating said.

'I had nothing to lose at the time. I needed to purge it out of me. It's a lot to ask, I know, but if I have convinced you and you're prepared to take the risk, Waddington will know what to do. If the situation in Britain is too hairy, tell him to plant it with the CIA. The Yanks will be more than happy to make use of it; they're always uneasy about Labour governments, and they'll never be completely sold on *glasnost*.'

Keating thought about this, his manicured fingers drumming on the arm of the chair. 'Obviously whatever is done has to be done without directly tying it in to you.'

'That's all I ask, for Galina's sake.'

'Have you destroyed the manuscript already?'

'Not yet. I'll wait until I know you and Waddington have succeeded.'

'How will we get word to you?'

'Use the personal column of *The Times*. Just say: "Caroline arrived home safely." Put it in three weeks running, just in case I miss a delivery.'

That night, when Galina was asleep, he again slipped out of their bed and went into the sitting-room. For the first time in years he thought about the home he and his wife had once

367

shared, comparing her past taste to the furniture he now lived with. Relating his story to Keating had brought the past into focus. Margot had never been able to resist the mail-order bargains, acquiring useless objects, jackdaw-like, to feather what he realized had been a lonely nest: a collection of miniature teapots; reproductions of Impressionist master-pieces 'exquisitely framed', in the words of the brochure; a set of Apostle spoons; the complete works of Beatrix Potter – poor compensation for the children he had never given her. He looked around the room, but everything here was alien; nobody had chosen the décor, even by mail order, the only personal articles the dozen or so books he had managed to scavenge, the small vase of flowers Galina daily put on his work-table.

He poured himself a whisky and went into the kitchen to add water to it. Catching sight of himself in a mirror, he paused and studied his face. How old I've become, he thought, fingering the pepper-and-salt beard. It was as if, in unburden-ing himself to Keating, he had not shed the past, but instead had hastened the ageing process. He was committed now; the secret had been passed on like a baton in a relay race, and now he was relegated to the role of spectator, unable to see the finishing-line.

As he often did these days when unable to sleep, he padded to the doorway of their bedroom and stood looking at Galina. She had one arm thrown across her face – as though warding off a blow, he thought – and he could see the outline of her full breasts beneath the sheet. There was so much he was ignorant of. Would he be equal to the responsibility when the baby came? Would he even be there to see it born? I've never had the care of innocence before, he thought. All I've ever had to protect are the lies that made up my life.

He finished the whisky standing there; then, as quietly as possible, crept back beside her in the bed. Galina stirred but did not wake. He put his hand on her taut stomach, wanting to share the warmth of the unknown life in her womb. He remembered something from his childhood, something his mother had told him: if you whispered to people when they were asleep, the message entered their dreams. He began to whisper to Galina, willing the words to penetrate into her subconscious mind. 'I love you, and we are going to be married tomorrow; then you'll be safe.' But even as he whispered the word 'safe' the doubts returned and the last image he carried into sleep was not of Galina, but of Margot; Margot as a young girl the day of their wedding when brightness, not fear, had fallen from the air.

25

Lloyd posed the question as they took one of their hurried lunches: 'So what are we left with?'

'Something that doesn't fit anywhere,' Pearson said.

'Like the sweater my wife knitted me last Christmas. Do you suffer from home industries?'

'I suffer from fallen arches, an increasingly weak bladder and the delusion that I'm on top of my job. Whereas in fact we're back to square one. Somebody is one step ahead of us every inch of the way. We have a nice line in corpses and a full stop at the end of them. Pass me the ketchup.'

He stared down at his Big Mac.

'Why can't I be like all those laughing happy people in the ads, who come dancing out of McDonald's hand-in-hand with all life's problems solved?' He took a bite and chewed on it slowly. 'Did it ever occur to you that there was a time when crime did not pay? A time when you could eat an egg without fear, when smoking did not give you cancer but attracted the best girl on the block, when the trains ran on time and schoolteachers did not wear crotch-revealing tight jeans?'

Lloyd shook his head. 'You know me, just an innocent abroad.'

'The only thing that hasn't changed is graft in high places. I voted Labour at the end of the war, the first time I'd had a vote. It was the soldiers' vote, you know, that got them in. The rest of the world expected old Winnie to sweep the board – they just couldn't understand it. Nobody knew Attlee, any more than the Yanks knew Truman, but each in his own way changed things irrevocably. Truman gave the go-ahead for Hiroshima, and Attlee brought in the welfare state. Destroy mankind on the one hand, but make sure they have free dentures before they're incinerated.'

'You really think about these things, don't you?'

'No. If I did, I'd top myself. All I think about is retirement. I can't wait to retire to my country estate.'

'You've got a country estate? You never told me.'

'I have about one-eighth of an acre of a foreign field, on the Costa Brava to be exact, which I purchased some years back in the mistaken belief that I would spend the twilight of my years watching the sun go down from my terrace while sipping a jar or two of Fundador, only to find that most of the villains we didn't manage to catch had the same idea.'

'Yes, and if it's not that it's nuclear fallout, isn't it?' Lloyd said inconsequentially. He helped himself to some of Pearson's French fries. 'So where do we go from here?'

'Don't keep repeating yourself. I don't know where we go from here. We've been led up so many blind alleys, and the walls on either side have been whitewashed. Take Waddington's death. Maybe it was a gas-leak that killed him, but what was he doing in that squatters' hovel? Why would he leave the security of a smart address? Then, surprise, surprise, his girl-friend does a moonlight flit, vanishes without trace before we can get to her. That smacks of a tip-off, doesn't it? Almost as if, in the midst of all the other changes this government has brought to our lives, they also found time to create a ministry of fear. Terrific book that, by the way; you should read it.'

'They've actually published a government book?'

'Christ! You're so illiterate. Graham Greene's thriller. No, I was always inclined to believe Waddington's story, though the poor sod can't add anything to it now. He was convinced that everything led back to Hillsden, that Hillsden held all the answers.'

'He was what – MI6?'

'Yes.'

'And last heard of in Leningrad?'

Pearson nodded and pushed the remains of his meal to one side.

'Well, presumably our distinguished friends in Century House still maintain a presence in Leningrad, don't they? Or have they closed shop since *glasnost* came into being? Can't we ask them to do our work for us, contact Hillsden?'

'You've missed the point. Waddington's theory was that Hillsden knows where the bodies are buried in Century House. If he was right, and we go to them, we show our hand. We've already strayed a long way outside our own manor. We're meant to be anti-terrorist, not anti-Establishment.'

'Leave it, then, huh?'

'I can't leave it,' Pearson said. 'I can smell the compost-heap.'

'This bloke whose house Waddington was staying in – what's his name?'

'Keating.'

'Did they come up with anything new on him?'

'Clean. Ex-MI6, but got out years ago, made a pile in various business ventures, buying and selling companies – the usual asset-stripping technique that used to guarantee the City boys a knighthood when knighthood was in flower. Remember when insider trading got them an automatic season ticket to Camelot? I say "clean"; nobody in business is biologically white if I know the Stock Exchange, but he seems to have paid his taxes. Now dabbles in films. He's involved in one at the moment, out of the country; that's why we haven't been able to interview him yet.'

'Yeah, I checked on that with his office. He's in Leningrad.'

'Say again.'

'Leningrad.'

Both men looked at each other.

'Now, isn't that a coincidence!' Pearson said. 'You know something? Occasionally, you're worth your keep.'

The Russian Ambassador to the Court of St James gave his full attention to Abramov's instructions. He was under no illusions as to who was master in his house. London was more to his liking than Rome, his previous posting, where the Italian Communist Party had made his life so tiresome. The

British Communist Party on the other hand were unlikely to bother him, being too occupied with the local class struggle to bother with what the Kremlin dictated. The great thing about England, the Ambassador had quickly discovered, was that to the majority of people, politics generated about as much excitement as the graffiti in a motorway service urinal. Only politicians were habitually held spellbound with the activities of other politicians.

'The changes, when they come,' Abramov was saying, 'will be far-reaching, and you must be ready to capitalize on them.'

They were speaking in the embassy's room within a room, continuously swept for bugs and, as far as modern science could make it, impenetrable. Here, cipher machines encoded and decoded satellite messages: through them flowed details of British and American operations targeted against the Soviet Union. Access to this inner sanctum was restricted to three members of the embassy staff, including the Ambassador, the other two being the resident senior KGB or GRU personnel.

'Moscow is not well pleased with the rate of progress made in the past. Your own position is under review.'

'For what reason?'

'Your social profile is extremely low. You need to be seen more; the name of the game today is how human we are. Most of the people in this building look as though the tailor is still working on their suits. We need to smarten our act. The Politburo is looking for acceleration, an initiative to regain some of the lost ground.'

'Where particularly? I am anxious to be guided.'

'There is still fallow ground to be tilled. We have always had the capacity to seduce British intellectuals and gays. Now we must widen the scope of our activities. We shall still maintain our barrage of disinformation but more subtly, I hope – the Third World is not taken in so easily any longer, and the campaign planting the idea that the Americans deliberately engineered the AIDS epidemic backfired. It was in Africa before America. We will now concentrate our efforts on the technological front, go after the industrialists, the young City computer wizards, because the next stage of the

373

struggle is going to be economic. In this country there is a strong anti-EEC groundswell, helped along by the mistaken enthusiasm for a Channel Tunnel. One can hardly believe the stupidity of the British. For over a thousand years they have relied on that stretch of water to protect them from Europe, and now they build a terrorist paradise. Equally there is no love lost for the Japanese; that smoulders on and could be exploited. We need to gain ten lost years in as many months, and that will be achieved through industrial espionage.'

'Where do you think I can be of greatest assistance?'

'Tell our visa department to cut down the waiting-time for applicants. Show our face to be smiling, get the tourists flowing. We are now an open society. The Intourist department is shortly going to launch an advertising campaign for Aeroflot; we have to convince the public here that we serve something more than bottled water on our flights. They are also recruiting more attractive cabin crews.' He smiled at this, the first time he had allowed the Ambassador to relax.

'What of your own department's activities?' the Ambassador asked, with some courage. 'Are they to change, too?'

'There will still be a subversive presence here, as large as we can get away with, but kept strictly in order. We want no further mass expulsions. In the past there have been too many mistakes. I shall be drafting in a different breed. We will always have the edge in long-term planning; and in the final analysis, should it come to a showdown, conventional forces will be the deciding factor.'

'I am very grateful that you have taken me into your confidence in this manner.'

Abramov deflected the flattery with a nod. 'Be on your toes.'

'Do the changes you envisage also embrace our friends here in high places?'

'There will be certain developments, yes. You'll learn of those in due course. The next stage of the plan has been agreed and will be put into effect shortly. I am only awaiting confirmation that certain elements are in place and then I shall return home. It would be a mistake for me to be in England when it happens, but we shall be monitoring every-thing.'

He led the way out of the room, passing through the sound-baffled double doors into the real world.

It was strange being married again. Hillsden had a sensation of things lost – lost loves, lost youth, lost England; the con-viction that he had finally turned his back on the past, and in so doing had created another wrong, another victim. He wondered whether he had given Galina safety or future sadness. He sat at their wedding-breakfast table, a glass of iced vodka in his hand, listening to Galina's happiness, listening with the concentration one gives to a stranger one meets on a long journey. Why do I have this intense distrust of life? he thought, fingering the simple gold ring she had given him, showing her the face she wanted to see. How does one learn contentment if one is always guilty? Truth, he thought, has never made for real comfort in any human relationship; it's not truth we want but the counterfeit that eases selfdoubt.

'You don't have any regrets, do you?' she asked suddenly. Her healthy cheeks were dotted with two identical bright pink spots. He had been surprised that the old wives' tale about pregnant women 'glowing' had proved accurate.

'Course not. What a thing to ask me, today of all days.'

'You looked worried just then, Alexi.'

'Just my natural look. It comes with age.'

'I'm very happy, and I don't care about your age.'

'I'm glad.' He replenished their drinks, and she dropped juniper berries into their glasses. 'To my husband,' she said in Russian.

He replied in kind: 'To my wife.'

'It takes getting used to, saying "wife" and "husband" . . . Does it?' she asked. Sometimes her excellent English, shamingly superior to his Russian, lapsed slightly.

'I suppose. No, not really.'

'Do they drink vodka at English weddings?'

375

'No, they usually drink very inferior champagne out of stupid glasses that look like eye-baths.'

The red patches on her cheeks grew brighter. He leant across the table and kissed her. 'Why me? Why did you choose me?'

'Because I'm a revolutionary. And drunk.'

'Oh, that's very flattering.'

'No, I meant I'm drunk now. Suddenly.'

'Then, I shall take you home, Mrs Hillsden.'

'Say that again.'

'Which bit?'

'Call me Mrs Hillsden.'

'I think, Mrs Hillsden, that I shall take you both home. Your child has had enough excitement for one day.'

As he helped her out of her chair, and gave her his arm as they left the restaurant, it occurred to him that he no longer knew what he meant by 'home'.

Because of the euphoria Bayldon felt every time he entered 10 Downing Street, it had entirely escaped his notice that a self-important job is invariably one to which, irrationally, importance is attached long after genuinely impressive people have ceased being appointed to it. He had convinced himself that he had turned the corner and that everything was now going his way. The scandal involving his wife had been deflected, the Cabinet was malleable, and despite a media-inspired scare about old-age pensioners being slowly poisoned by sausages – the latest in a long line of food health hazards that had begun in the late eighties – the Government was riding high. The Tories (never a party to take Opposition in their stride, and since the heady days of the Thatcher era ever more convinced that their direct line to God had been temporarily disconnected) were still conducting bitter post-mortems as to the cause of their downfall and feeding on their own scars. Mrs Thatcher had retired from politics and, since there was no longer a House of Lords, had been deprived of a peerage – historically the golden handshake former Prime Ministers awarded themselves. She was now the chairperson of a large chain of supermarkets, and it was her sausages, so her critics claimed, that had been responsible for hastening a few geriatrics' progress to the grave.

Never one to shirk stealing from those he had at one time decried, Bayldon had embraced that all-American need to sell yourself, and gave weekly presidential press-briefings as well as appearing on television at every opportunity. Using his wife's money, he had also employed the services of a top ad agency, instructing them to change his image and find ways of exploiting the up-side of political banalities. In the old days it had been a gentleman's agreement that whenever the Prime Minister was accorded air-time his opposite number would be given right of reply with an equal time-slot. Bayldon had changed all that. He had ensured that his own men occupied all the top administrative posts in the BBC, and the Corporation no longer operated under the umbrella of a Royal Charter but was now controlled by the Ministry of Information. The commercial stations, sold off to the highest bidders in the dying months of the previous government, were subjected to penal taxation and could now only afford to transmit reruns of forty-year-old American sitcoms and Australian soap operas.

As part of the campaign devised for him, Bayldon's image started to appear on gigantic hoardings all over the country, alongside a series of catchphrases: THERE WILL BE NO FALLOUT UNDER THIS GOVERNMENT; THE WORST CRIME IS POVERTY; STATUTORY UNEMPLOYMENT ABOLISHED; LIVE IN PEACE NOT IN PIECES. In addition he made a point of attending football matches whenever they were being televised; he went to the theatre, patronizing fringe productions as well as the popular shows since he was well aware of the value of cultivating the quasi-intellectuals; he lent patronage to the leading AIDS charity and went walkabout (though heavily protected) at the annual Notting Hill Carnival to show solidarity with the ethnic population. Equally he did not neglect the need to be a man for all seasons and classes: he was seen at Ascot, the Oval and the Royal Opera House, and cultivated the City elders. His forward diary included engagements at the Mansion House,

377

the Edinburgh Festival and the last night of the Promenade Concerts.

Concurrent with these calculated moves and sheltered by his private office and numerous acolytes only too anxious to curry favour, he was progressively distancing himself from Control's influence. There was little or nothing Control could do about this without exposing his hand. He was compelled to wait, fine-tuning the elements in his contingency plan, in the sure knowledge that he would have the last word. Prior to leaving London, Abramov had set up a new chain of communication to replace Pamela, activating a sleeper in the Foreign Office who was a member of Control's club.

So, for the moment, both men enjoyed the luxury of believing that time was on their side.

'Do you ever get the feeling', Pearson said, breaking into the radio commercials with his familiar preface, 'that the real purpose of life has passed you by?'

The motorway being under repair, they had just navigated their way through a traffic-jammed Maidstone on their way to the coast. A new type of bomb had been defused in Dover the day before, planted in a department store and thought to be the work of one of the animal rights organizations. Pearson had been ordered to check it out.

'Look around you, Lloyd. This is Kent, once known as "the garden of England". When I was a kid we used to come hop-picking. Now the only thing you could pick up here is the remains of take-away fast food. We've been Americanized without America's vitality.' He killed the radio.

'I expect you're right.'

'But have you?'

'Have I what?'

'Had that feeling?'

'I forget what you asked me. I was listening to the programme. I like phone-in programmes. You get to know what the general public is really thinking about.'

'What you get is confirmation of the general level of stupidity. Everybody is soaked in half-truths, half-baked ideas,

378

pushed at them by fatuous journalists and then spewed out again over the airwaves by idiotic disc-jockeys.'

'You don't like England, do you?'

'I've gone off it. My life seems in every way to have retrogressed.'

'Could be you're not getting it regularly.'

'Ha ha. Chance would be a good thing.'

'I read the other day that even a couple of pints of beer will reduce the sperm count.'

'Good. Maybe with any luck the lager louts won't be able to procreate and the race will die out. The reverse of an endangered species. Let's talk about something more important. That alleged sighting of Rejano, our old friend the Fat Boy – what happened when you questioned the Greek?'

'He insisted he'd seen him in Athens about a month ago, then spotted him again in London.'

'Whereabouts in London?'

'Kensington High Street.'

'How reliable is the Greek?'

'Difficult to say. He's being held on a drugs charge and desperate to get on our right side.'

'Did he give a description?'

'No longer fat, a credit to Weight Watchers apparently, well dressed, every inch the City gent.'

'Has that been circulated?'

'Yes.'

'And nothing further?'

'Not so far.'

Pearson thumped the steering wheel. 'The bugger of it is we've never had a decent photograph of him. The only ones on file are twenty years old. Has the VIP arrivals-list been checked?'

'Yes.'

'Are we expecting anybody he might be interested in?'

'Well, not that I could see . . . There's a state visit of the President of Gambia coming up in two weeks' time, and another Anglo-Irish summit, but on past form neither of those would interest him. Not that you can go by that,' Lloyd added.

'Just a gun for hire, isn't he? First come, first served, and put your money where your mouth is. He's had a long run.'

'Well, tell everybody to keep on top of it, and give the Greek another working-over. If Fatso is here, he hasn't come as a tourist, of that we can be sure.'

Arriving in Dover they went to the main police station where the defused bomb was still being examined by the experts. It proved to be of sophisticated design, a talking teddy bear stuffed with an incendiary device. It had been taken to pieces and laid out for Pearson's inspection. The Bomb Squad major who had handled the delicate task of immobilizing it explained how it worked: 'Any child picking it up and pulling the cord to activate the voice wouldn't have had any more bedtime stories. Bloody diabolical.'

'How was it spotted?'

'Somebody phoned here with the warning,' the local police sergeant answered. 'I took the call as a matter of fact. Not the sort we usually get; that's what makes us suspect a new loony group.'

'What was unusual about it?' Pearson asked.

'Woman's voice for a start. Named the shop but gave no time-limit, then said: "Ask me a riddle and I reply: Cottleston, Cottleston, Cottleston pie." '

'She said *what*?'

'Yes, it fazed me, too, sir. But one of my lads, a young constable quite new to the force, he cracked it. Bloody brilliant, I thought.' He paused, enjoying the moment. '*Winnie the Pooh*. Apparently he reads it to his daughter every night. That's where it comes from.'

'Well, full marks to your lad.'

'Funnily enough, his name's Christopher. Different surname, fortunately – not Robin – otherwise his life wouldn't be worth living now. We evacuated the building and took the dogs straight to the toy department. Happily, they found it without much trouble. My guess is it ties in with one of the animal groups. Woman's voice, teddy bear . . . it adds up.'

Pearson nodded. 'Sounds feasible.'

'Nice types,' the Major said. 'Still, all's well that ends well in this case.'

'Got any leads, Sergeant?'

'No. Wish we had, sir.'

'Well, carry out all the normal forensic checks, then let us have the mortal remains when you've finished. I'd like teddy for our Black Museum.'

'Bit of a waste of time,' Lloyd observed as they set off back to London.

'Stop complaining. You had a day by the sea. It's a bloody funny old world. Save the animals, but kill the kids. Kill anybody who gets in your way.'

Trundling along the motorway just inside the limit they came up behind an Opel.

They stayed on his tail for half a mile, then Pearson observed, 'That joker's only got one brake light and his exhaust muffler's just about to fall off. Pull up alongside and tell him to get it fixed.'

'Still a traffic cop, eh?' Lloyd accelerated and moved over into the centre lane.

'Never leaves you,' Pearson said. Since they were in an unmarked car, he propped a notice saying POLICE against the windscreen then switched on their broadcast system and picked up a hand microphone.

'You, sir, the driver of the Opel . . . This is the police. Would you please pull over on to the hard shoulder and stop your vehicle.'

He got a brief glimpse of the driver, but then the Opel accelerated away from them.

'Oh, we've got a comedian here. Hit your siren and go after him. Did you get the registration number?'

'Yes,' Lloyd said enjoying this unexpected excitement. He gave it to Pearson who passed it to the Central computer to be checked. They kept up with the Opel maintaining, as per regulations, a steady distance between the two cars until word came back on the registration: it was not on the computer.

'What d'you know? We've chanced on a stolen job. Take him.'

381

Lloyd put his foot down and they narrowed the gap, drawing level this time. The Opel swerved into them a couple of times, but then had to straighten up to avoid hitting a large articulated truck. With some practised skill, Lloyd brought the Sierra alongside and hovered there. As he did so the driver of the Opel lowered his offside front window. Lloyd saw the glint of the gun barrel and just had time to shout a warning to Pearson before the bullet caught him on the jaw line just below his right ear, entering at an angle and ricochetting off the collar bone to shatter the rear window of the Sierra. Pearson grabbed the steering wheel as Lloyd slumped on to him. Some instinct made Lloyd take his foot off the accelerator, but even so Pearson could not control the car; it veered off the carriageway, and crashed into the crash barrier, finally coming to a stop facing in the opposite direction. The Opel had speeded on out of sight by the time Pearson recovered from the impact. He radioed emergency calls for assistance and an ambulance.

'Don't take chances, the bastard's armed. He's shot my number two.'

There was a first-aid kit in the Sierra and he held a sterile pad pressed tightly against Lloyd's wound until the ambulance team arrived. By then Lloyd had lost a massive amount of blood. Half a dozen police vehicles blazed to the scene and a police helicopter arrived overhead. Traffic on the motorway was diverted and the area blocked off. Pearson stayed long enough to give the bare details of the incident, then the helicopter landed to lift him back to London. En route he kept in touch with the chase and got a report from the local hospital where Lloyd was undergoing surgery. His chances of survival were not rated very highly.

While Pearson was still in the air, news was relayed to him that the Opel had been found abandoned on the outskirts of Bromley. The driver had vanished without trace.

The sentry at the bottom of St James's Street stamped his feet down with parade-ground precision, momentarily startling Control as he crossed over from Pall Mall on the way to his club, and he remarked how unsuitable the modern rifles were for such ceremonial duties; there had been something brutally pleasing about the old Lee-Enfields, especially when fitted with the long First World War bayonets. Control remembered watching George VI's funeral procession from a balcony in St James's; both pavements had been lined with Guardsmen and, on a distant shouted command, all the heads bowed over reversed rifles in perfect unison, starting at the Palace and continuing up the street to Piccadilly, like a pack of cards slowly falling one by one. It remained one of his most enduring memories. Whatever else the British got wrong, he thought, they had the knack of burying their dead with ceremonial style.

He nodded to the head porter as he entered the building, but was not greeted by name in return: it was an unwritten law that, because of his position, his identity would not be exposed within the marble halls, nor would any of the staff stoop to the vulgarity of asking a member's name.

Depositing his topcoat in the bleak cloakroom that still sported Victorian washbasins and dripping taps immediately associated with the prep school he had attended as a child, he washed his hands and smoothed his hair before proceeding to the smoking-room where certain former glories were enshrined, some of them sleeping in the large leather armchairs that made sounds not far removed from farts when the occupants lifted arthritic limbs from their shiny comfort. His expected companion had not yet arrived, and Control took his usual seat by the bookcase which housed a catholic collection of unreadable donations, the only item of interest being a first edition of *My Secret Life* by the anonymous Walter that had somehow slipped past the Library Committee. There was a smell of wax about the entire building, pungently mingling with stale cigar smoke.

Control had originally joined this particular club on the strength of its wine-cellar, and the fact that it prided itself on being the dullest club in London, though there were many other contenders for this honour. He had wanted a club where the members did not gas too much and where women, when

383

allowed in as guests, were only permitted to occupy the annexe at the back, a room more reminiscent of a ship's bar than of anything remotely feminine. Most of his fellow-members shared his background – public school education, politics and the services – and, although the club had its quota of eccentrics and the inevitable infusion of business types since the sixties, it remained an agreeable oasis. It had seen better days, and every year the fees went up; on one occasion a few years previously it had only been saved from extinction by the calculated generosity of a brash industrialist anxious to buy a knighthood. In the past bedrooms had been offered to members who enjoyed the deadening effect of a London weekend, but this, too, had gone the way of all flesh – rising costs, the impossibility of attracting the right staff, and the fact that the rooms themselves resembled nothing so much as prisons decorated by Viollet-le-Duc. Only on one occasion, temporarily dispossessed of his own flat when the bathroom flooded, had Control stayed a night under the club's roof. The experience had not been one he wished to repeat.

Now, sipping the large gin and it brought by the steward on a silver salver, he studied a copy of *Punch*, leaving each cartoon without a smile until he was suddenly aware that the man he was expecting had entered the room.

Andrew Fonthill, an Oxford Blue who also took a First in Constitutional History, was regarded as a coming man at the Foreign Office. Nothing in his demeanour, dress or accent suggested anything other than an Establishment figure. Perhaps the only external feature that gave rise to comment was the fact that his lips seemed scarcely to move when he spoke. Married, with two somewhat gormless daughters who were often photographed for the society pages of the *Tatler* along with his vapid wife, he exemplified that seemingly inexhaustible stock of courtiers who gravitated around the monarchy and occupied the higher echelons of the Civil Service. Outwardly they appeared to have no knowledge of or interest in anything beyond their immediate circle, but in Fonthill's case the urban façade concealed darker forces at work. His problem had always been a propensity to live beyond his means, and it was this failing, rather than idealism, that had first suggested his potential usefulness to the Russians. In the pre-Falkland War period, when he was First Secretary in Buenos Aires he had become hopelessly entangled with the French wife of a local banker. The demands she made upon him were not only physical, but also monetary, for she had expensive tastes, and he was rapidly plunged into debt. In an effort to extricate himself he had travelled the classic escape route and gambled heavily on the horses. Such ordinary human situations often end in tragedy of one sort or another, but Fonthill's salvation came in the guise of a GRU recruiter. He was persuaded that, in return for immediate solvency and future financial peace, he could render occasional services. Fonthill never thought of it as a betrayal of his country since he was a man of many conceits and felt he owed it to himself to survive. During the remainder of his stay in Argentina he supplied a certain amount of restricted information to his controller, none of which he judged to be of vital national importance. In this he was probably correct since, as the Falklands War demonstrated, Foreign Office know-how was lamentably inaccurate. Long before he finished his tour of duty he eased his way out of his French mistress's bed, bought himself two polo ponies, and returned home to marry his second cousin for no other reason than the fact that she had inherited an estate in Berkshire. Back in London, he settled down to the pursuit of his career and in due course was rewarded with a CBE. Thinking it behind him, he had all but forgotten the Argentina episode when he was phoned late one night and a strange voice told him that Sir Raymond Lockfield wished to meet with him and discuss a highly confidential matter.

Thus he kept the appointment in a disturbed state of mind. He had no idea that he was meeting a fellow-traveller, but assumed that his past was about to be exposed.

The evening began casually; Fonthill could detect nothing in Control's observations on the international scene that gave cause for concern. Over drinks before dinner he gradually relaxed, and by the time they went into the dining-room he had half-convinced himself it was a false alarm.

'What day is it?' Control said, studying the menu.

'Wednesday.'

'Ah, yes. They always have a very good steak-and-kidney pie on Wednesdays. Or would you prefer the duck?'

'No, the pie sounds excellent.'

'You're not into any of these health fads, then? So many people don't eat proper food these days. We have a woman in my office who eats nothing but rabbit fodder. Come to think of it, she's beginning to look like a rabbit. Do you shoot?'

'When I get the chance,' Fonthill said.

'I usually go up to a friend's place in Yorkshire. I must get you invited.'

'Thank you. I'll look forward to that.'

Control wrote out their orders and handed them to the head waiter.

'Burgundy or claret?'

'Whatever you prefer.'

'I think the Burgundy if we're both having the pie. Can't give the old digestion too much to cope with. And half a bottle of Fumé for starters, eh?'

'Fine by me.'

Control selected the wine and broke bread, placing tiny pieces in his mouth with all the delicacy of a spinster taking the wafer.

'What I miss most is not being able to ride any more. Got a gammy hip. Well, that's only part of it. I seem to be riddled with arthritis. You ride, I take it?'

'Yes. I play polo. Keep a couple of ponies.'

'Heady stuff. Where – Windsor?'

'Yes, Smith's Lawn.'

'I used to like to watch it. There was one particular year, I remember, when the Argentines were wiping the floor with us. You were out there, weren't you?'

'Yes, for a period . . . That's where I began to play.' Fonthill's lips were compressed to the point where they almost disappeared.

'Like adultery, not a sport for old men. One of the compensations of getting older – it's no longer necessary to win every race . . . only the last one.'

Their first course was served at that moment. Eating his prawn cocktail, Fonthill was left trying to decide whether Lockfield's last remarks had any significance.

'Well, as you might have gathered, I asked you here for a purpose,' Control said, his face half-concealed by his napkin. 'For some time now I've had you on my shopping-list.'

'That sounds ominous. Is it?' The composure Fonthill had planned faded like a holiday tan on the return flight.

'One is always looking for suitable people whose loyalties are in the right place.' He paused as their empty plates were taken away and the Burgundy brought for his approval. He took another piece of bread before tasting it. When the wine had been poured he raised his glass. Both men savoured the wine.

'Drinkable,' Control said, 'but the whites are not what we excel in here. It's a question of price, of course, like most things in life. The cost of a decent Chablis is ruination. Not that I should be tempted; the acidity goes straight to the old joints.'

It was all too casual for Fonthill's liking.

'The PM said something to me the other day which I think bears repeating. He said: "The lights are coming on all over Europe." You recall the original, of course.'

'Indeed, I did my final paper on the start of the First World War.'

'True, do you think?'

'Well, there's certainly been a thaw; I wouldn't put it any stronger than that. But any relaxation is welcome, don't you agree? I think the next few years are going to be very interesting.'

'Yes, but as with the noble art, if one relaxes, one tends to drop one's guard. And, of course, the noble art is anything but, merely a primeval instinct. Man needs enemies; that is the nature of the beast. So there is always a necessity to maintain vigilance . . . That is why I thought we could use a man of your experience in these matters.'

Fonthill thought: How subtly he is approaching the heart of the matter. He made no immediate response, convinced that his worst fears were about to be realized. The trap was there, baited and ready to be sprung, but he was given a further reprieve as the famed steak-and-kidney pie arrived and the Burgundy was poured. There was a certain irony to the fact that they were eating a patriotic dish while patriotism was under threat.

'Excellent pastry, but parsimonious with the kidneys,' Control observed. 'A note in the complaints-book, I think. One must keep up standards.'

There was a smear of gravy on his chin, and Fonthill wondered whether he should draw attention to it. His wife was fastidious about such things, always admonishing the children. But instead of mentioning it he said: 'I'm not sure what experience we're talking about.'

'Your inside knowledge,' Control answered. 'An invaluable commodity to interested parties. There are so many grey areas in my line of business, nothing is ever black and white, outlines get blurred. In the past that has sometimes led to unfortunate incidents . . . So naturally one is anxious to avoid anything that could lead to a further scandal . . . Much better to turn' – He lingered briefly over the last word – 'possible embarrassments to one's own advantage. A man like yourself, for instance, to use you as an example for the purposes of this little chat, would not be averse to promotion, I imagine.'

'Promotion?'

'Yes. I mentioned your career in the right quarters, and took the liberty of suggesting you are potential ambassador material – a suggestion that was well received.'

'Very flattering, I'm sure.'

'Not at all; you did so well in Buenos Aires, it did not go unrecognized by those who take note of such things. If we could arrive at an accommodation beneficial to our mutual needs, it would be helpful all round.'

'Is that another way of saying you're recruiting me?'

'Oh, don't say I've been that obscure. How tiresome of me. I stupidly imagined you took that for granted when you accepted my invitation. I didn't misjudge the situation, did I? After all, it's a question of exposure or co-operation – and you made such a quick wise choice with the pie I'm sure you'll do the same where your own future is concerned.'

Smiling, Control finally dabbed the gravy from his chin.

26

Since the event the Fat Boy had many times cursed himself for forgetting that the British police now operated unmarked cars on their motorways. Although reasonably certain they could not have got a close look at him, he had taken no further chances: he did not return to his original safe address, but instead journeyed north by train to Bradford and there made contact with a sleeper unit of one of the Libyan factions. They provided him with a refuge while he destroyed all traces of 'Allen Lyndon Witz' and equipped himself with a new identity. In the time still at his disposal he took steps to make small changes to his appearance, dyeing his hair and eyebrows blond. The gun he had used on the motorway also had to be disposed of and replaced; the same with his clothes. His alias was now John Dansie, an accountant.

Every day in hiding he scanned the newspapers for the latest on the shot policeman, anxious that the search for him did not turn into a more intensive murder hunt; he knew only too well that killing a policeman was the worst crime in British eyes. It appeared that, although Lloyd was out of intensive care, and his condition stable, he was still on the critical list. From what the Fat Boy could gather, the enquiries seemed to be concentrated on a gang of armed robbers who had been operating in the Kent area and had already shot a bank clerk. An Identikit image had been issued of one of the robbers, which further reassured him.

'Make yourself comfortable, Alec,' Abramov said. He was wearing his new uniform carrying the insignia of his enhanced rank. There were a few glints of grey in his hair, but he still looked younger than his years.

It was the first time Hillsden had ever been inside any of Abramov's private apartments. These, in Leningrad, were impressive, denoting his rise to power, the furnishings modern and luxurious: Hillsden took in a Japanese television and hi-fi equipment together with a stack of Western LPs, and the overall effect suggested masculine privilege – there were few feminine touches, although Hillsden was aware that Abramov did not live a chaste life. From what Inga had once let slip, he could call upon a pool of compliant girls whenever he wished.

Although the request for the meeting had taken him by surprise, Hillsden had not suspected any ulterior motive, thinking that Abramov was merely keen to talk about his trip to London.

'I thought it would be more pleasant if we talked here. The days when you and I had to meet in underground carparks and have our conversations recorded are over, thank goodness. Which vodka would you prefer?'

'I'd prefer Scotch, if you've got it.'

'Of course. I should have remembered. I have some excellent malt I brought back from London. Fifteen years old, according to the label.'

'Malt would be fine. How was London?'

'A strange city of contrasts, I found. Dirtier than I had imagined. When one thinks that we don't even allow people to smoke in Red Square, I was disgusted at the amount of garbage littering your streets. It is a bad impression to give.'

'But you had a good time?'

'An interesting time.' He handed Hillsden his drink. 'No ice, was that right?'

'Perfect.'

'There are undercurrents in your society that I detected.'

'Really?'

'Yes. I had some fascinating conversations with taxi-drivers.'

'Ah! Well, they always like to air their grievances to tourists. And at least you can understand what they're saying, unlike their counterparts in New York. What undercurrents did they share with you?'

'I got a distinct feeling that not everybody is happy with the number of foreign immigrants that now make up your multi-racial society.'

'That surprised you?'

'I was surprised by the vehemence expressed. You are such a placid race on the outside, but fires smoulder beneath.'

Hillsden shrugged. 'For years now tolerance has been on a short fuse – conveniently ignored by the politicians. It'll be your turn next; you're now experiencing the ethnic revolution from within.'

'You're not religious, are you? No, I asked you that a long time ago. You have no faith.'

'It's difficult enough to have faith in one's own ability to survive without muddying the issue with religion.' If I ever believed in anything, Hillsden thought, it died with Caroline.

'I ate well, that I will admit,' Abramov continued, picking up the threads of his previous observations. After removing his tunic and brushing off some fluff from the epaulettes before placing it on a hanger, he settled down in an easy chair opposite Hillsden. 'I must confess that there London is superior to Moscow. I brought back one of the food guides and I have marked those I visited.' He reached into his bookshelves and extracted the volume in question, thumbing through the pages until he found the right place. 'This one, for example, do you know it?' He handed the book to Hillsden.

'The Firm was never too generous with expenses. I would have had to take out a second mortgage to eat there.'

'But I saw many young people patronizing such places.'

'That's capitalism for you.'

'I also saw many plays while I was there, including one – written by an American, I think – about the differences between our two mentalities. A challenging evening, very well performed by one of your most distinguished old actors, but exposing that no matter how hard the West tries to understand our way of thinking it will never get inside our heads.'

'You don't think so?'

'No. I mean, take you for example, Alec. You have had more opportunities than most, and yet you, too, fall short.'

'In what way? I'm still willing to learn.'

'Are you, Alec? Are you? I hope so.'

There was a certain chill to his smile which to Hillsden mirrored their first encounters.

'Do you recall, Alec, that when you and I became part of each other's life I said that we were going to remake you? Do you remember me saying that?'

'Not exactly, but I'm sure you're right.'

'Slowly, over many weeks, we began to trust each other, did we not?'

Hillsden nodded.

'We operated not as defector and interrogator, but more as two professionals each respecting the other's needs. I look back on that time with great satisfaction. Great satisfaction. Debriefing can be such a painful process sometimes. You impressed me, Alec. I admired the way you stood up to me and of course I will always admire the way in which you passed the most difficult test I put to you. You know, of course, what I am referring to?' Again the conspiratorial thin smile.

'It's not something I'll ever easily forget,' Hillsden replied. He picked up his glass and drained it.

'You wish another?'

'Not for the moment, thank you.' Why bring up Jock's death? he thought. The subject had never been mentioned between them since the event. The recollection brought back powerful images: Abramov's gloved hand tracing Jock's name on the steamed windscreen of the car, Jock's creased drunken face on the pillow and somewhere a clock with a Mickey Mouse dial ticking like his own heartbeat. He remembered how casually the invitation to murder had been put to him: 'If one can resolve two problems at once, there is a certain poetic justice.' As though poetry and justice could ever be married to an execution.

'We were both of us deceived, Alec.'

He waited, but Hillsden did not respond.

393

'Does it surprise you I said "both of us"?'

'You always had the ability to surprise me.'

'But did I always admit to my own failures?'

'No, that's a new one. I fondly imagined that you were a stranger to failure.'

'I think – maybe I said it, or maybe it was one of your more revealing remarks – that life is only significant when it is dangerous. The enigma of pain. The saints are supposed to have unravelled that final mystery of the human condition, but we lesser mortals continually have to struggle to come to terms with it. Not just physical pain, but in our case the pain of betrayal.'

'We're going to have one of our philosophical discussions, are we?'

'In a manner of speaking, yes. Your Oxford dictionary defines a philosopher as one who shows philosophic calmness in trying circumstances. And as you can see I am sitting here calmness itself, even though the circumstances which bring us together on this occasion have tried me. I still admire you, Alec, and I have not yet stopped being your friend. I admire your courage, however misguided. But it saddens me that you felt the need to cling to particles of your past life.'

Hillsden thought: admit nothing, say nothing, let him tell me what he knows.

'Go back to the origins of our relationship. It's useful to remind each other how we came together. Just now I spoke of both of us being deceived. You were deceived by London, and in turn that deceit was passed to me. We got you, not Moscow Centre. That was one up for us, and I was lucky that you became my property. I owe my promotion to that. But why do you think matters were so arranged?'

'I don't know. It puzzled me at the time. When I defected I expected the Third Department to claim me as their own.'

Abramov did not conceal his contempt. 'The Cheka', he said, deliberately using the original name of the KGB, 'would like to think they have the edge on us. But London couldn't risk you falling into their hands. In order for Control's plan

394

to be watertight, we both had to be kept in the dark. It was vital that I accepted you as the genuine article, Alec.'

'What does that mean?'

'So many dark processes condition our lives, Alec, but eventually, inevitably, they are illuminated. We can never say that we will emerge unscathed from the tunnel. You see, somewhat late in the game, I was forced to acknowledge that, although you told me the truths as you knew them, they were not the final truths . . . Is that not so?'

Abramov reached for one of his foul-smelling cheroots, striking the match to light it on the sole of his shoe.

'It's true that when I arrived here', Hillsden said carefully, 'I had no idea of Jock's involvement. I thought he was dead and buried.'

'Alec, I am more concerned with the whole picture rather than with one aspect of it. When you and I formed our friendship – and note I still call it friendship – we were both victims of a conspiracy. The realization came to me later than to you; that is why we have not had this talk before. You were sold a lie and I bought the lie. That has grave implications for us, inherent dangers that we have to resolve.'

'I never lied to you. I avoided certain areas, but I am sure you expected that.'

'Alec, let's not split hairs. Your arrival here was a lie, was it not?'

'I wouldn't say that.'

'You were given certain promises, promises that were immediately broken by Control. Let us consider your good friend Control for a moment. He is, after all, the instigator of our mutual discontent.'

He blew a cloud of acrid smoke in Hillsden's direction, apologized, and waved it away. 'Your glass is empty, and we are both going to need fortifying.'

While he was replenishing both their drinks Hillsden had a brief opportunity to collect his wits. Despite Abramov's protestations of friendship he knew he was being drawn deeper into a minefield.

'You have converted me. I now prefer this to vodka. Let's

drink to a solution, shall we? A solution that satisfies your dilemma and avenges mine. We have both come such a long way, Alec, it would be a pity if, between us, we could not arrange matters amicably. Don't you agree?'

'I'm not sure what I'm being asked to agree.'

'Have I been too subtle? Let me spell it out. You came here under false pretences, though I admit there were mitigating circumstances. I've always known you are a romantic, Alec, and even though I can't share that rosy view of our world I have a certain respect for it. You came because you were driven by love for a cause. That is, after all, the essence of romance. Like that very good American musical I once saw, your cause, your lost Camelot, was a dead woman you once loved. Well, I helped you find the final answer, did I not?'

Hillsden nodded.

'You did us a great favour by the manner in which you disposed of that problem. Perhaps there is no greater test than to be asked to kill a friend, even a friend who has betrayed you. But you did not shirk it, and that is why we are sharing a drink and I am prepared to return the favour – to even the score, as it were.'

Again Hillsden gave no response.

'But let us go back to the beginning. Let's consider the character of Control. Any man who has neither a wife nor a mistress and leads a life which on the surface is above suspicion should always be approached with care. So this man of contradictions, who had the power of life and death over you, whom you did not suspect, was in fact determined to eliminate you. Not in the brutal conventional sense. No, he was cleverer than that. Perhaps there was an element of hatred in the method he chose. You were so blinded, so obsessed, that you allowed your guard to drop. You played his cards for him, if I may mix my metaphors. What did he have to do? Nothing. He had only to suggest a route and you were packed and anxious to go. Stay away from Glanville, he instructed. You ignored the warning. Go back to where it all began, he said. You went willingly. He was ahead of you every step of the way.'

'Yes,' Hillsden said. He took the neat whisky like a convert taking the altar wine for the first time.

'Now you know his motive, the extent of his duplicity. You made a brave decision, Alec, one that I can applaud, and you carried it off brilliantly.' He paused, smiling again. 'But, such is my character, I always retained certain doubts. You gave us very little that we didn't already know, but your arrival in our midst came at a time when we needed a showpiece. If you recall, your defection was just after we had lost a senior officer to the CIA . . . Tell me – I'm interested to know – when did you first realize that you had been tricked?'

Hillsden sensed there was no escape. Abramov was too skilled an interrogator. He was like a Jack Russell; once he had a grip he worked the prey to death. 'I think I realized early on that I had said goodbye to England for ever.'

'Isn't that what you wanted?'

'There have been trade-offs in the past.'

'But not for people like you, Alec. You said "early on". How early?'

'I was still in Austria, waiting to be smuggled out, and I was shown the English newspapers with my face on the front pages, wanted for the murder of that diplomat.'

'Belfrage. Wasn't that his name?'

'Yes.'

'Control making sure the door was securely locked. A spy who recants might possibly be forgiven, but not the murderer of a pillar of society, a member of your Establishment.'

'It was a clever move.'

'Of course, in a sense, if you can see the irony of it, you eventually performed the last task for him. Your friend Jock was the only remaining conspirator. He remained a threat as long as he was alive because, as we know, he had few scruples, he could be bought. That is an irony, don't you agree?'

'It's one way of describing it.'

'The fact that you knew before you arrived here further reflects to your credit. You performed well, Alec, a truly professional job. To be betrayed by one's enemies is painful enough, but to be betrayed as you were betrayed is a living

397

death. You could not endure it, could you, Alec? It burnt into your soul. I understand that. You needed to take your revenge. In your place I would have done the same. Who was it who said "The soul of the spy is the model of us all"?'

'I've no idea.'

'It doesn't matter. The point I am making is that you followed the dictum that the end justifies the means. You struck back at Control from afar, fighting fire with fire.'

'Did I?'

'Yes, you did. With total disregard for your own safety, moreover. Unfortunately, you underestimated me, Alec. That was a mistake. I don't hold it against you; in fact, believe it or not, I am grateful to you.'

He paused again, letting this sink in.

'The written word is a dangerous weapon . . . It can imperil the author as well as bring down tyrants . . . We should use it sparingly, Alec, with enormous caution.'

'What're you getting at?'

'Showing you the errors of your ways. Control might have delivered you, Alec, but he failed to understand your resolve – or call it foolish courage – just as he failed to deliver the rest of the package. What is the expression you British use – "too clever by half"? Once Bayldon had been given the keys of the kingdom, Control was meant to take them back. His role was to be the keeper, but he has proved less than adequate. More important, he took me for a fool . . . So the scenario has to be rewritten . . . Has *been* rewritten . . . Partly by you, Alec, and your contribution was invaluable.'

He stared hard at Hillsden before resuming.

'You see, from the moment you requested a move to Leningrad, I had my suspicions as to what you might be planning. In my place, you would have reacted in the same way. Total trust is never part of our way of life, is it? . . . You didn't always need your winter overcoat by the Black Sea, did you?'

Panic twisted in Hillsden's body like an unborn child, and it required a conscious effort to keep his face composed.

Abramov smiled again: 'Nobody's perfect, not even you,

and you are as good as they come. There was a time, after Inga left, when the house was unattended and I had it searched. A fascinating document, so much detail; you write very well – the journal of an angry man. Well, that's understandable. You have a great deal to be angry about.'

Finding his voice, Hillsden said: 'Why have you waited this long to tell me?'

'We're a patient race, Alec. There is never anything to be gained by haste. My father never ran anywhere, but he always arrived on time. It was an invaluable lesson he taught me.'

'And now what? Now that you have told me?'

'That's a good question, and I could answer it in many ways. You're lucky, Alec, that we have this bond between us. Had the information fallen into other hands, the outcome would have been hideous for you. Since the discovery I have given the matter much thought, examining all the possible alternatives . . . I have to protect myself, as I'm sure you appreciate. My own feelings towards you might not be the same as my superiors'.'

'I realize that. Thank you.'

'But you don't yet know what you're thanking me for. That still has to be decided. However, to move on, I admired the way in which you got word back to your friend in London. The blackmail of that pathetic tourist was a clever ruse; it showed that you had taken the trouble to learn our methods. And it succeeded. Your message was received as you planned. Your friend Waddington made the contact and deciphered your code.'

'If you knew all this, why didn't you move earlier? Why wait until now?'

'Perhaps, Alec, you were doing my work for me. Did that never occur to you?'

'No. Why should it?'

'Why should it indeed? Your manuscript contained a great deal of information that was new to me, much of it of personal interest. It enabled me to fill in certain gaps. As I said earlier, we were both deceived by your sea-green Control. He seems to have overstepped his authority, taken decisions without first clearing them with us. That is always a dangerous route, even at his level. I therefore had to take matters into my own hands. I don't have to tell you that the name of our game is survival. Take your present position: you wish to survive because of your unborn child. But in order to protect ourselves it sometimes becomes necessary to reduce the number of players.'

He paused and flicked an inch of ash from his cheroot.

'What you had no means of telling before you embarked on your literary efforts was that we had already made certain moves. We are patient, as I said, but even our patience wears thin when the desired results fail to materialize. It became necessary to jolt our friend in London out of his complacency.'

'Which friend are we referring to?' Hillsden asked. 'You have more than one in position, surely?'

'The one that matters. The one who by his very title should be in control, guiding the others. We gave him a little fright, something to disturb him. We discovered long ago that the cutting of umbilical cords has a salutary effect. Isolation in any form usually produces the desired results. We took his main contact out of circulation.'

'Permanently?'

'There's no value in temporary measures.'

'Somebody I would know?'

'I doubt it. A nonentity named Mitchell, well situated at your GCHQ, where he had direct responsibility for all our Moscow traffic. One of our sleepers. It was a pity to lose him, but the situation demanded drastic action. It was done most skilfully and intended to seem the handiwork of the IRA, but we hadn't allowed for the expertise of the Anti-Terrorist Squad. They have a Commander Pearson you might know.'

'Pearson? Yes, the name strikes a bell.'

'A man of considerable abilities, though fortunately hamstrung by lack of resources, and the fact that he's compelled to work within the law – such mistaken idealism, don't you agree, if one is pitted against the pitiless? When you are at war you don't equip your army with spears to fight tanks.'

'I suppose', Hillsden said, 'it's known as not descending to the level of your enemy.'

'I would call it suicide. The true order of the world is violence, and violence has always to be met with violence. Why pretend otherwise?'

'Unless one pretends, life would be intolerable.'

'But for the majority life *is* intolerable; that is what makes revolution possible and sustains it . . . However, we have got side-tracked. The good Commander Pearson was getting very close, and that is why I went to London to take charge of events. Of course, I was not actively involved myself – there is no merit in soiling one's own hands when others will do the job for you. Lines of demarcation have to be drawn, Alec, even in friendship. At the first opportunity I concentrated Control's mind, and as a result he felt compelled to dispose of certain liabilities . . . Your gay courier was the obvious first candidate . . . and then it was necessary to deal with your ex-colleague, Waddington.'

Time stopped for Hillsden. It took him several moments to find his voice. 'How did they "deal" with Waddington?'

'He met with an accident.'

'An accident?'

'Yes, something to do with a gas-leak, I was told.'

'Did you believe that?' Hillsden struggled to keep his voice at its normal level.

'Alec, when you decided to contact him you put him in jeopardy. I believe what I want to believe. If I'm told he died as a result of a gas explosion, then that is how it happened. Perhaps your courier betrayed you both – who knows?'

'*You* know.'

'But who started it, Alec? Who set these events in motion? You're not well placed to be outraged. Your friend Waddington died, just as the girl died, because he knew too much. You ensured that.'

'What girl are you talking about?'

'The one Waddington was sleeping with – following your example, if memory serves me. The girl who escorted you on the first leg of your journey here. I can understand why; like

401

you, I met her on one occasion. Had the circumstances been different, I could have fancied her; she was a sexy creature.'

This revelation, coming as it did before he had recovered from the news about Waddington, had the effect of making Hillsden's whole body tremble suddenly. He reached out to put his glass down, but missed the table by the side of his chair and the glass shattered on the stone hearth. He paid no attention; he was hardly conscious of what he had done.

'You mean . . . that same girl? I never knew her real name; she called herself Wendy to me.'

'Pamela, I think. Van Norden was her last name.'

'And Waddington was having an affair with her?'

'Somewhat one-sided, I imagine. She didn't operate for love. She was sicked on to him by Control – isn't that the expression used over there?'

Sharp images flooded Hillsden's memory: a cabin in a cross-Channel ferry, Pamela's naked body in the narrow bunk they had shared for that last journey from England, the answer she had given him when asked what spurred her on – 'It's a game, isn't it? You play it for all it's worth until it ends.' And now he wondered how it had ended for her.

'One has to break all the links in a chain, Alec, if one is to feel secure. Would you like a fresh whisky? You look as though you're in need of one.'

'You enjoyed telling me all that, didn't you?'

'You had to be made aware of the results of your actions, my friend. It's part of your re-education. You see, now that the decks have been cleared, your own future has to be considered. No, I wouldn't say I've enjoyed this conversation . . . In many ways, you've been a great disappointment to me. The only reason we are here sharing these confidences is because all unknowingly, and for quite the wrong motives, you have actually helped to solve a problem for us. Equally, I have personal reasons that enable me to take a lenient view of your betrayal. I'm an ambitious man, Alec, and it wouldn't look good on my record if you were shown to be my failure; it could have a very adverse effect on my career, and I could not risk that. So you and I are going to conceal the truth, something we're both adept at. What I have in mind depends, ultimately, on the success of future events in England. If they work out as I believe they will, you're safe again – not totally safe, but given another chance. The proposition I am offering is this: you will say that the idea of writing your story was mine, that we concocted it together in order to flush out the remaining liabilities in Britain. Such an arrangement will reflect the utmost credit on us both.'

He waited, but Hillsden said nothing.

'Not everybody would be as generous, Alec, but I have always felt we are brothers under the skin.'

'And if things don't work out as you plan?'

'Then, you would have to take your chances. The ground rules in our trade were laid down long ago. It's not what we do, it's whether we are caught doing it. You would be caught – by me – and our arrangement adjusted in my favour.'

'Assuming it all goes smoothly, what is the price-tag for me?'

'A life sentence of silence, Alec. A reasonable price in all the circumstances. You do, after all, have certain added loyalties now. We mustn't forget you have a Russian wife, and a child on the way; it would be a pity for the child to grow up without a father.'

A different, more chilling fear struck Hillsden. He said: 'Did you choose Galina for me, too, like Inga?'

Abramov shook his head. 'I can cause many things to happen to you, Alec, pleasant and unpleasant, but ensuring that a woman falls in love with you is beyond even my capabilities.'

There was some cold comfort in that, yet having finally learnt the cost of survival Hillsden felt compelled to push his luck and ask one more question: 'Just tell me why.'

'Why what?'

'I thought you had it made in England – your Manchurian candidate in Downing Street manipulated by Control. My attempt to destroy that having failed, why disturb the status quo?'

'But your attempt didn't fail; that is why we are here now.

403

Let me put it this way. I read an amusing maxim while I was in England; I think it was said in Parliament by a Tory politician, and possibly he did not mean it to come out as it did. He said: "To sit on the fence is to be on the wrong side of it." We never make that mistake. One must always be quick to adapt to changed circumstances, and we have the great advantage in not having to go through the democratic processes. The beauty of our system is that once the need is there we can start to adapt overnight. The world has moved on since you first arrived here – the world you left and the world you now inhabit. Here, we are going through a process of transition, a further stage in the revolution. We are going to use the West for our own ends; and the time is going to come, perhaps sooner than anybody realizes, when the Western bloc will be glad of our company. You'll see, we will cease to be the enemy; the two superpowers will unite to fight the last great religious war together. It will be religion, not communism, that will bring about Armageddon, and it will start in the Middle East, when our common need for oil leaves the unholy alliance no choice. Forget the war of ideology; the red menace will fade into the background; possession of the black gold is what will determine our fates. The internal combustion engine is a rapacious animal that we can't live without – denied it, we are helpless, our economies destroyed, we would be reduced to the status of savages. It's inevitable, Alec: if one studies history, it's always the unthinkable that eventually comes to pass.'

His tone suggested that their meeting was at an end. Hillsden got up from his chair and started to pick up the pieces of broken glass.

'Don't bother, I have somebody.'

They faced each other.

'I've never asked you this before, Victor' – using his given name for the first time since he had entered the apartment – 'how old are you?'

'How old d'you think?'

'I'm not very good at guessing ages; in the past it's always led me into trouble.'

'Forty.'

Hillsden nodded.

'Will you ever have children, Victor?'

'Perhaps. For the moment I'm wedded to my work.'

'Don't leave it too late, like me. It's taken all this time . . . taken a Russian woman, to make me realize that the worst betrayal is when we betray those we love.'

Leaving Abramov, Hillsden went straight to Keating's hotel to warn him off, but he was too late: the film unit had moved out that morning. He thought briefly of asking for a forwarding address, then the disciplines of a lifetime dictated caution. Despite, or maybe because of, his privileged status, such an enquiry could well arouse suspicion; he knew full well that, even in the more relaxed climate, hotel staff were still the prime source of information about foreigners.

Before returning to his apartment he stopped at the post office to pick up his latest copy of *The Times*. Scanning the headlines before moving off, he read that there had been large-scale riots in London that had spread to other parts of the British Isles. The lead story intimated that the Government had not ruled out the possibility of imposing a curfew in the major cities if the disturbances continued. Naturally he had no means of telling whether the violence heralded the softening-up process for the events Abramov had predicted.

Although there were numerous explanations put forward afterwards, nobody was able to pinpoint the exact flashpoint on the first night of riots in Chelsea. Some said that it began with rival gangs of football fans after a local soccer derby between the home team and Tottenham played under flood-lights. Others blamed units of the Workers' Militia who ignored orders from the senior police officer to withdraw from the scene and fought their own battles. Equally, and predictably, the police riot squads were heavily criticized for over-reacting. But there was little doubt that, whatever sparked it, it was used by many different factions as an opportunity to pay off old scores – some directed at the police, others aimed at the ethnic population.

At the height of the disturbance some two thousand police were deployed, but even so they were outnumbered. Police casualties were heavy, and towards midnight they came under fire from snipers and home-made Molotov cocktails. It was at this point that the Deputy Commissioner authorized the use of CS gas and rubber bullets in an effort to control the major confrontation in the area of World's End. Over sixty cars were set alight, and damage to property, later estimated to run into four million pounds, was extensive. Shopkeepers subsequently reported widespread looting. In all the police made nearly two hundred arrests and the neighbouring hospitals treated as many casualties. The final tally was one hundred and eighty injured and fourteen fatalities, including five policemen. The situation was only brought under control in the early hours of the following morning, and by daylight King's Road and its surrounds presented a scene reminiscent of the Blitz. Until the streets were cleared of debris and opened again, traffic jams built up throughout the capital, disrupting the state visit of a Third World dictator.

The Home Secretary, accompanied by the Commissioner, toured the area and later issued the usual statement that such violence would not be tolerated in a civilized society. This was of little comfort to those whose belief that they existed in a civilized society had already been irrevocably shattered.

'There is no doubt in my opinion, backed up by the reports of my senior officers on the spot, that the whole thing was deliberately engineered and orchestrated,' the Commissioner told the Home Secretary.

'I can't accept that without firm evidence. As you know, we have announced we are immediately setting up a committee of inquiry.'

'Whether you accept it or not, sir, I must hold to that view. Many of those arrested came from far afield.'

'But that's normal at a football match, isn't it? Since they're barred from Europe, they're bound to seek other outlets for their violence.'

'These were two London teams playing. Equally, one cannot use the excuse that this was a ghetto riot such as have happened in the past. This is an affluent area with no previous racist incidents of any consequence. The speed with which it escalated points to a planned operation.'

'I think that, as with some of your men last night, you're over-reacting, Commissioner.'

'Sir, I have five men dead, and sixty-eight injured, many of them seriously injured. I don't know how you under-react when a Molotov cocktail sets you alight, but I imagine there is a government pamphlet on the subject setting out guidelines.'

'This conversation is not helpful,' the Home Secretary said, making for his car and police escort.

Pearson felt his life was like the tangled weeping pear in his suburban garden that bore no fruit. He blamed himself for the shooting of Lloyd; if he had not started that schoolboy chase, it would not have happened. Every day he contacted the CID to find out if they had any further leads, and made time to visit Lloyd in hospital. The stolen Opel had proved to be the property of a butcher in Newcastle-upon-Tyne, who was quickly dismissed from any connection with the case. Although it had been taken apart, it was clean of fingerprints and surrendered no other evidence.

Despite his personal involvement in this particular incident, the apprehension of armed robbers was not his concern: he had other, more pressing, demands on his time. Militants in the animal rights movement had stepped up their campaign: a research laboratory belonging to one of the largest cosmetics houses had been fire-bombed, and letter bombs had been sent to half a dozen doctors concerned with animal experiments, though all but one of these had been intercepted by vigilant post office staff and rendered harmless. The remaining one had slipped through the net, and the doctor's secretary had lost a hand. Tracking down the perpetrators was more difficult than dealing with the IRA for the simple reason that, when and if they were caught, they invariably proved to be ordinary citizens with no previous criminal history, often operating alone.

In Lloyd's absence, Pearson took over the interrogation of

the Greek drug-dealer who was being held on remand. If the Fat Boy was loose, this took precedence over everything else.

'You saw him in Athens, you say?'

'Yes,' the Greek said.

'How come you recognized him?'

'I've told your people already.'

'You haven't told me,' Pearson said.

'What's it worth to me?'

'Right now it's worth nothing.'

'I was promised a deal.'

'If you convince me, if it leads to anything, then maybe you'll get seven years instead of life,' Pearson answered, speaking off the top of his head. 'Heroin-smugglers aren't exactly favoured visitors. So I'll ask you again. How come you recognized him when a dozen police forces have drawn a blank?'

'I knew him before.'

'How?'

'About a year ago I had dealings in Libya.'

'Dealings?'

The Greek shrugged. 'Drugs – what else?'

'I don't buy that. He doesn't meddle with drugs; he doesn't need to, and he's too smart. Try again.'

'It's true, I tell you. I was in Tripoli and I met with him at the house of a friend. And you're wrong. He may not deal, but he uses coke. Who doesn't?'

'I don't for one. How did you know it was him?'

'My friend told me afterwards.'

'OK, assuming I buy that part of it, then you saw him in Athens. When was that?'

'Three weeks ago.'

Pearson consulted the transcript of previous interrogations.

'When my colleague questioned you, you said a month.'

'Three weeks, a month, who's counting?'

'I want exact dates.'

'Look at my passport. It was two days before I left.'

'Where did you see him?'

'At the airport.'

'Did you talk to him?'

'No. I'm not crazy.'

'Do you know what flight he took?'

The Greek shook his head.

'Had he changed his appearance since Tripoli?'

'He was thinner. I've given the description.'

'Then you saw him here, just before we arrested you?'

'Yes.'

'Where?'

'Kensington. It's all there in your papers.'

'You said you were coming out of the Underground station and he passed you on the way down?' Pearson read from the previous notes. 'Did he see you?'

'I don't think so.'

'You hope not anyway. And he was well dressed and clean-shaven, right?'

'Like I said.'

'Take a good look at this photograph and think hard before you say anything. Is this the same man? Not a very good shot, but it's the most up-to-date one we've got.' He turned it over. 'Taken in Beirut, five years ago. Look carefully, then tell me how much he's changed since then. Take your time, and don't box clever. I don't want guesses. Mark any differences on this blank. Here, use this pencil.'

The Greek studied the picture.

'He's changed a lot since this was taken.'

'Haven't we all?'

'He has dark hair now, and his chin is not like this.'

'How does he wear his hair? Show me.'

The Greek marked the blank outline of a face.

'And you're sure that's how it was when you spotted him in Kensington?'

'I'm sure.'

'You know he doesn't travel anywhere for pleasure. So think carefully. Have you any idea why he might be in England?'

'I told you, killing people is not my scene.'

'Heroin doesn't kill, is that what you're telling me? You're

409

two of a kind, and I don't know who I hate most. Answer the question.'

'No, how could I?'

'Somebody knows. Why shouldn't it be you? After all, you've admitted a connection. If we add terrorism to the other charges, you're never going to perform Zorba's dance ever again.'

'I swear to you!'

'Well, have a good think. If you get any flashes of inspiration – I won't say *conscience*, because scum like you don't have one – ask to see me again. But only me, understood?'

'I co-operated, right? I've given you good help.'

'We'll see,' Pearson said. He rapped on the cell door to be allowed out.

When he got back to his office, and after making sure the new description was immediately circulated, he went through his various lists yet again, looking for possible targets. He had stated the truth to the Greek: the Fat Boy never travelled without a purpose. In the past his favourite victims had been Jews, though on his last known visit to England he had bungled the assassination of a prominent Jewish businessman – one of his rare failures. On that occasion they had discovered a notebook, left behind when he fled his hideout in haste. That had contained a hit-list of a number of people in the public eye, including show-business personalities, Gentiles as well as Jews, seemingly selected at random. Pearson had often puzzled over that.

Going over the same ground once again, he compared the old list with the latest ones he had compiled, looking for duplications. He studied the forthcoming public engagements of the royal family, then the schedules for members of the Cabinet, noting possible danger areas. He then wrote a series of reports, putting his recommendations to the Palace, the Prime Minister's private office and the Commissioner of Police and MI5. He stressed that, because of the possible presence of the Fat Boy, security should be intensified and members of the SAS should be employed on those occasions he considered particularly vulnerable. Later, he tracked down his SAS chum, Hugh Woodley, who was at home on leave, having just finished another tour in Belfast, giving him such details as he had.

'I'm not like you bods,' Woodley said when he had heard the story. 'I can't act unless I'm ordered to.'

'Don't bullshit me. You have your own sources.'

'Mostly concerned with the Irish situation, though.'

'Well, you never know. Do me a favour, keep your ears peeled. I'm stymied right now. Everything I try to follow through ends in death. Remember the last occasion we met and discussed that MI6 defector, Hillsden? An ex-colleague of Hillsden's, a man called Waddington, had just contacted me with a strange story. Are you with me?'

Woodley nodded. 'Something about Hillsden having written an explosive book he was trying to get smuggled out.'

'That's right. Hillsden got word of its existence to Waddington using some tourist, and Waddington convinced me there was a case to answer. Well, the tourist, Frampton, was murdered along with his father. Waddington, poor sod, was found dead in very dodgy circumstances – my conviction is he, too, was murdered – and finally his girl-friend vanished without trace.'

'Jesus!'

'An added factor is we established a connection between the girl-friend and that KGB man who was recently deported.'

'Did the manuscript ever surface here?'

'No, not that I know of. But from the start Waddington was definitely the object of somebody's attentions. They bugged his house, and after Frampton's murder we felt it was too coincidental for comfort, so I encouraged him to go into hiding. Somehow he was flushed out – they eventually discovered his body in some squat.'

'And you've come up with nothing?'

'Hugh, I got involved early on, but I'm not a bloody detective. You know how sensitive the CID boys are if anybody poaches on their manor. I can't force the issue because I don't have any real evidence. The ones who could back me up are all dead.'

'What about MI6 themselves – aren't they interested?'

'No way. As far as they're concerned Hillsden was a traitor. The last thing this government wants is to re-open the case. They remember the pig's dinner the Thatcher mob made of *Spycatcher*.'

Woodley rolled a cigarette and licked the paper carefully before sealing the rough tube. 'It's difficult to see how I can help.'

'I realize that,' Pearson said, 'but I don't have anybody else to confide in.'

'Originally, you thought the trail could lead right back to Downing Street. Has anything that's happened since hardened that view?'

'Listen, I don't rule out anything any more. It seems to me that anything's possible these days. If you look at the record, why should we believe otherwise? Read some of the memoirs that have been published. All those ex-ministers who apparently spent most of their time rushing home to write "Dear Diary, how I stuck the knife in my best friend" – putting down their fucking squalid versions of events. And all the time they were in office conning us, making pious statements about the responsibility of power, then the moment they got slung out they reveal what really went on behind the scenes. Remember Wilson's motheaten old bloodhound, the good Colonel – sorry, Lord – Wigg? That holier-than-thou walking Gestapo. He was the one who fingered Profumo, but in the twilight of his non-career he got nabbed kerb-crawling for tarts. Don't talk to me about politicians; I'd rather lie down with panthers. What can I do, one man on my own? At my age all I need is to find myself up shit creek without a paddle.'

'I get the drift,' Woodley said.

'The awful thing is – and it's a terrible admission – I don't want simple justice any more; I'm tired of being manipulated, I want revenge. Do you ever feel like that?'

'Two weeks ago I was in the land of bigotry. We had a patrol out on the border, breaking in some young soldiers, showing them the ropes. Except some of them never finished the first lesson. They walked right into a booby-trap and got blown to smithereens. A remote-control job, set off on the other side. I was lucky; I was in the leading group and just missed it. All that happened to me is I had to get a new uniform; my old one was covered in brains . . . It got a mention on the news that night, sandwiched in between another Stock Exchange scandal and the marriage of a pop singer. So, yes, to answer you, I could do with some revenge myself.'

Poor Waddington, poor old Wadders, he deserved better from me, Hillsden thought, as guilt crept up on him like a whipped cur. For the first time since a child, when for a few weeks he had believed in the Pre-Raphaelite Jesus of the Sunday-school postcards, he wished he had some sort of blind faith to turn to. But even that early short-lived conversion had had more to do with an unrequited passion for a small girl his own age than with any belief in a merciful God. A sudden memory of those halcyon days when love had meant sharing a bag of boiled sweets in St Saviour's dusty church hall, the innocents sitting in a circle listening without comprehension to the doctrines of an inexplicable God of wrath. Not that his weekly attendance had sprung from any true revelation: long after, he realized he had been shunted towards God in order that his parents could have the house to themselves for the ritual of sex on a Sunday afternoon, equally incomprehensible in childhood. His passport to the country of the blind had been a penny for the collection, and that had been his first betrayal, denying the missionaries half of it so that he could buy a kind of love with the gift of sweets. Now he could not conjure the little girl's name, though he recalled the image of her puzzled eyes before other betrayals crowded his memory. There had never been a Saviour to give him absolution from a lifetime of deceit. He would carry Waddington's death to his own grave like a penitent's cross, continuing the long journey that had begun in the old Austrian station – the choice had been made then, all those years ago: the choice between the risk of betrayal and the risk of love, and betrayal was a demanding god needing to be satisfied with

413

a regular halfpenny bag of sweets by thieving children.

Time and time again he cursed his simplicity. How could he have overlooked Abramov's cleverness? The trade of spying was not conducted like a driving test; the inspectors did not give advance warning of an emergency stop. To have allowed for everything else, and yet to have missed that, he deserved to be caught. The final hideous irony being, of course, that all those deaths could have been avoided – Waddington, Frampton, the girl. Writing my memoirs, he thought, I was so bloody sure, believing I was throwing double sixes every time in a game I had to win. But there was never any end to the particular game he and Abramov played, and now the dice had been passed.

At night, ever sleepless, he would look at Galina, drawing from her the only comfort left – the realization that whatever happened he could at last love somebody without demanding a price.

27

Crushed between two jolly female Promenaders on the packed floor of the Albert Hall – that 'great Victorian cake', as it was sometimes called – Pearson sang himself hoarse during the sea-shanties, for he was well aware that nobody went to the last night of the Proms to be seen and not heard. Equally, the sound of his voice was not his prime concern. Like the other members of his team stationed around the arena, he felt slightly foolish wearing fancy dress even though it attracted no undue attention. The perennial Promenaders, young and old, were likewise decked out for the occasion, many of them dressed like vintage *Punch* cartoons of John Bull with waistcoats fashioned out of Union Jacks, wearing funny hats and false noses, blowing paper whistles that unfurled like snake's tongues, or else waving flags and banners. It was vital, he had told his unit, for them to merge into the crowd and act like the genuine article.

His report on the possible sighting of the Fat Boy had been acted upon, and the presence of the Prime Minister and his party this evening had meant a top alert. Ensuring total security in such a building as the Albert Hall was a nightmare for all concerned. Bayldon had insisted on occupying the royal box where he was in full view of the majority of the house. The building had been swept for explosives before the audience was let in, members of the orchestra and choir had been vetted and careful checks made on the occupants of the boxes on the opposite side of the arena. Tickets for the last night were always at a premium and, since it was inevitably oversubscribed, entry to the floor of the hall for the true Promenaders was allocated by lottery. All handbags had been scrutinized, but Downing Street had insisted that body searches would ruin the festive atmosphere and antagonize what was known to be a dedicated audience. In addition to Pearson's men, members of the Met's elite C7 unit were positioned at various high vantage-points around the arena.

Several times during the course of the evening it had occurred to Pearson that he would never understand his own countrymen. Most comments about the youth of England emphasized loutish degeneracy, yet here he found himself amongst a cross-section not only prepared to stand for hours listening to classical music in reverent silence, but also capable of responding to blatant jingoism, as though their once vaunted empire still existed and the entire audience had been transported back to the swansong of the Edwardian era. The hard core of dedicated Promenaders were contentedly squashed together; he could not detect any drug-induced hysteria – rather, the good-humoured enthusiasm for the set proceedings seemed to stem from a true love of the occasion that needed no additional stimulus, the whole mass swaying to the familiar tunes that every year formed the second half of the hallowed ritual.

It was traditional for the Promenaders to enter into a good-humoured race with the orchestra as the conductor gradually quickened the tempo; then, at the conclusion, a great roar of applause went up and those closest to the podium threw streamers and flowers towards the orchestra, so that very soon the platform was inches deep in coloured paper and blossoms.

There was another man on the floor of the arena who was also amazed by the atmosphere. Despite having studied and memorized the hallowed ritual of the last night from a cassette, the actual performance had nevertheless startled the Fat Boy. Like Pearson he also thought how paradoxical it was that the same nation that exported the most violent tourists and football fans could also produce a capacity audience of docile music-lovers.

Now expectancy hung in the air as the faithful waited for the highlight of the evening: the playing of Elgar's 'Pomp and Circumstance March No 1 in D Major' – perhaps one of the

416

most stunning tunes ever written and by virtue of the verses subsequently given to it, for many transformed into an alternative national anthem. The emotion it generated when sung by a large crowd was a throwback to a land when perhaps there had been the prospect of hope and the realization of glory. But, although the trench life of the First World War had made a mockery of those sentiments, the music itself still had the power to convert all but the most cynical. Succeeding generations sang it with fervour, perhaps harbouring a subconscious nostalgia for an era they had never known and which would never come again. As with Blake's 'Jerusalem' the winged chariots would be absent from their lives, the arrows of desire blunted, but it was inherent in the British character never to acknowledge that their influence had waned. The Promenade audience sang for an England they would never see again.

Elgar's great march begins quietly: it was part of his genius to make his listeners wait for the splendour to come; he was rich enough in invention to afford to squander the first theme, giving no hint of what lies ahead – that sudden starburst of majestic melody that soars into the musical firmament.

Now, as the conductor raised his baton, waiting for the hall to become silent, the faces around the Fat Boy happily anticipated their coming role in the proceedings. There was a moment of total silence, then the baton descended and the first notes swelled into the hushed arena.

The Fat Boy was aware that the audience invariably demanded and were given two encores. He knew he must wait for the climax of the second encore when the volume of sound would be at its height. He wore a comic top-hat banded with a Union Jack and white gloves that gave him the appearance of an old-time minstrel. Now, as he joined in the singing of the verse, he removed it, allowing the gun concealed inside to slip into his hand.

   . . . *Mother of the Free* . . .

He had loaded the gun with special ammunition designed to spread on impact, and had fixed a small flag to hang down from the barrel.

. . . How shall we extol thee . . .

He had a good view of the royal box from his position. Bayldon and the rest of his party singing for dear life.

. . . Who are born of thee? . . .

The Fat Boy's gloved fingers massaged the safety-catch. Another glance up at the royal box, calculating the angle.

. . . Wider still and wider . . .

The first time around the words were sung with muted fervour since the habituals knew they had to save their greatest efforts for the encores. Nobody wanted to run out of steam too early.

. . . God who made thee mighty . . . make thee mightier yet.

A solid roar of applause greeted the end of the first rendering, and the sweating conductor of the BBC Symphony Orchestra left the podium to disappear through the tunnel towards the dressing-rooms. It was part of the ritual to clap him back and force a repeat, and the applause now took on a deliberate rhythm. After a calculated interval the conductor reappeared and the noise swelled momentarily until he once again raised his baton and brought in the brass. The great sound swelled again, percussion and trumpets building to a new climax and bringing the entire house to its feet. The Promenaders swayed like one amorphous mass, and to the Fat Boy's amazement he saw that several of those close to him actually had tears running down their cheeks. Looking up, he saw that Bayldon, too, was standing, giving him a larger target.

At the end of the first encore the audience refused to let go, demanding one final emotional splurge. Their insistence was rewarded; again the baton was raised and the build-up began again.

The Fat Boy released the safety-catch. All eyes were on the orchestra as he brought the gun up to aim. With the flag it had the appearance of another party toy.

. . . God who made thee mighty . . .

Now his trigger finger took the first gentle pressure.

. . . Make . . . thee . . . migh-tier . . . yet . . .

The cacophony at the finale exceeded anything that had gone before: streamers arced through the air, balloons were exploded. And it was at this moment that he took aim in one swift movement, squeezing the trigger three times in quick succession. The first bullet struck Bayldon in the shoulder; then, as he twisted, his mouth gaping in an unheard cry, the second and third bullets tore most of his face away. Blood spattered his wife and other members of his party. The force of the impacts jerked him backwards, and he fell against one of his guests before slumping like a broken marionette on the velvet rim of the box.

Few in the audience were looking in his direction, but one of the police marksmen on the other side of the arena grasped what was happening and gave the alarm to the master control over his walkie-talkie.

Sheltered in the still riotous and unaware crowd, the Fat Boy secreted the gun in his hat. He had predetermined the position of a waste-bin by the nearest exit where he would get rid of the weapon. As the conductor began his customary speech of thanks, the Fat Boy started slowly to edge his way out, calmly excusing himself through the ranks like several others intent on beating the rush to the cloakrooms, but he had only gone part of the way to the nearest exit when the noise suddenly died.

On the podium the conductor had faltered in the middle of his speech, suddenly aware of the commotion in the royal box. An official in evening dress hurried to him and said something. The conductor nodded and gave way for the official to take his place.

'Ladies and gentlemen,' the official announced, 'I regret to inform you that an attempt has been made on the Prime Minister's life.' As he gave the news a single balloon exploded and a girl screamed. All eyes immediately went to the royal box, now crowded with security forces.

'Will you all remain where you are – for your own safety and in order not to hamper the police and medical services. Do not leave your seats or make your way to the exits. It is

419

believed that the assassin is still within the building. I ask everybody to remain calm.'

Now the entire orchestra was on its feet, the carnival atmosphere snuffed out. Most people just stood in shock, some crying, unable to comprehend the enormity of what had happened. Bayldon's body had been gently lifted from the edge of the box and was no longer visible.

Immediately he became aware of what had taken place, Pearson had ordered all exits covered. Emergency services had been sent for as well as police reinforcements, and outside the road was being blocked to traffic. A police marksman elbowed his way through the crowd to Pearson's side.

'The shots could only have come from the floor, sir.'

'Did you see it?'

'No, but I was watching the PM at the exact moment, and from the angle, the way it took him, the gunman must have fired from here.'

'Well, we've got all exits blocked. If he's here, we'll get him.'

By now armed policemen had ringed the arena, and the sight of their weapons induced a wave of panic. Some of the audience crouched down as though at any moment firing would commence. Shouted commands added to the sense of impending violence. Most of the occupants of the boxes had ducked out of sight, giving the impression that the hall had suddenly half-emptied.

Experience dictated that the Fat Boy feign fear like the majority. Following the example of those nearest to him, he lay on the debris-strewn floor, the hat with the gun in it crushed beneath him. He was within sight of the exit he had chosen, but all escape routes were blocked by armed police. Although he could not believe they would risk opening fire in such a situation, he was under no illusions: his chances were nil unless he disposed of the gun.

Pearson arrived at the conductor's podium and addressed the entire house through a loud-hailer.

'Ladies and gentlemen, your attention, please. The building is now secure. Will you kindly obey the instructions I am about to give in an orderly manner? We intend to evacuate the building in stages and take every precaution to ensure your safety. I must ask you to obey the orders given to you by my uniformed officers quickly and calmly. For the moment, all those in the tiers are to remain where they are. I repeat, remain where you are. Those of you here on the floor of the hall will be directed to leave first, six at a time, when my officers give the word. Once you have been cleared, other officers outside will ask you to identify yourselves and give your names and addresses. Once that has been done you are free to leave the area; and, again, for your own safety, do this as soon as possible without panic. Families should leave together and of course ensure that any children in the audience are always accompanied by an adult. Are those instructions quite clear?'

Nobody answered, though the sound of a child crying could be heard.

Immediately Pearson finished speaking, the police began the orderly evacuation, indicating six at a time who were then body-searched as they passed through the exit-doors. Although many were understandably fearful and shocked, the evacuation proceeded smoothly. Six at a time the audience was filtered out through the numerous exits.

The moment came when the Fat Boy was amongst the next batch to leave. He got to his feet, leaving the crushed hat on the floor, and was body-searched. Cleared, he was halfway through the exit-door when a young girl in the following group immediately behind shouted after him.

'Sir! Mister! You dropped your hat.'

For one second his composure faltered and he made an involuntary turn of the head. At that moment the gun fell out of the proffered hat and dropped at the feet of one of the policemen. Before anybody had a chance to react, the Fat Boy savagely chopped the nearest man in the side of the throat, the force of the blow toppling him into his companion and opening up a narrow escape-route. There were too many people milling about in the circular passageway for easy pursuit, nor did the Fat Boy present an immediate target

421

for the police guns. He ran through the screaming crowd, cannoning into and scattering anybody in his path, desperately seeking an exit. Alerted by radio, at least a dozen armed police gave chase, converging on him from both directions as he raced around the rotunda. Because of the geography of the building and the fact that Pearson had sealed off all the stairways and exits, he had nowhere to go. Inexorably, the gap between his pursuers narrowed. There was a moment when he considered taking a hostage, but realized it could only be a delaying tactic before the inevitable end. He backed into one of the deserted bars only to find it was windowless. Cornered he turned to face the guns just as Pearson arrived on the scene. 'Fuck you!' he screamed. 'Fuck you all!' slipping the capsule between his fat lips and biting on it.

'Take him,' Pearson said, but as four armed police advanced into the room the Fat Boy slumped behind the bar counter, falling sideways into a pool of spilt Coke which seeped from under him like blood. He was unconscious by the time they reached him and dead before they could remove his body from the room.

28

The Right Honourable Toby Bayldon lingered seven hours beyond the moment when the lethal capsule ended his assassin's notorious career. Despite the combined and dedicated efforts of the surgical team at the Hammersmith Hospital, it proved impossible to save him. His wife and other members of the Cabinet who had been summoned to the scene, including the Deputy Prime Minister, were present when death was pronounced. A short bulletin was issued to the waiting press and news media assembled outside. Scheduled radio and television programmes had played solemn music following the first newsflash, and now all stations carried tributes. After conferring with the Commissioner of Police and being told that all the available evidence pointed to the assassination being the work of a lone gunman, the Deputy Prime Minister first went to Buckingham Palace for a short audience with the Monarch, and from there to the studios of BBC and ITN to make a statement. He was an indifferent speaker and uneasy in front of the cameras, which was possibly one of the reasons Bayldon had chosen him to be his number two.

Although shocked by such an outrage, the country as a whole took the news stoically, and there was actually a letter to *The Times* complaining of the desecration done to the memory of the founder of the Proms, Sir Henry Wood. The obituaries were complimentary but not overly fulsome, most of them stating that Bayldon had proved a stabilizing influence, coming to power as he did at a time of widespread disillusion. Others gave him the benefit of the doubt, saying that his murder would prevent history from recording whether he would have been successful in carrying through his major policy reforms. All of them praised his integrity and parliamentary skills. There was talk of a state funeral, but the Palace felt that this would set an embarrassing precedent and the idea was shelved. Much of the editorial comment immediately switched to the question of his successor. It was none too tactfully hinted that the Deputy lacked the necessary qualities to reunite the country in the aftermath of such a tragedy, and that what was needed was a strong man who would tackle the rising tide of violence and corruption at all levels of society.

Three days after the assassination Bayldon's name disappeared from the front pages, the headlines being given over to an appalling air crash which realized everybody's nightmare: a fully loaded 747 caught fire shortly after take-off from Manchester Ringway airport and crashed into a densely populated suburb of the city. All but five passengers out of nearly four hundred perished, and the death-toll on the ground added another one hundred and seventy-six, including fifty-two children in a kindergarten. One whole street was virtually written off the map, and the emergency services took over a week to bring out the last body from under the mountain of debris. Few of the victims could be positively identified and, while sabotage was not ruled out, the most widely accepted cause of the crash was structural fatigue. It was the worst domestic airline tragedy ever, and the Archbishop of Canterbury called for a national day of mourning on the day of Bayldon's funeral. At the express wish of his widow a disaster fund in Bayldon's name was set up for the victims of the Manchester crash. As might have been expected, the ordinary public were far more moved by the deaths of the small schoolchildren than by the departure from their midst of the Prime Minister.

Having observed the minimum period of neutrality that decency demanded, the Opposition parties went on the attack, clamouring for Parliament to be dissolved and a General Election called. On this, as on other historical occasions, they completely misjudged the mood of the electorate. In the public's mind the twin tragedies were inter-related, so that some of the sympathy felt for the victims of the air crash also

424

passed to Bayldon; in death he was accorded a greater degree of popularity than he had ever achieved while alive. Within the inner power-circle of Bayldon's party various soundings from around the country confirmed this view, and the question of who should lead the party into the election became a matter of some urgency. After much in-fighting and clandestine meetings in back rooms, three names were put forward as the front runners. Deacon's was not amongst them. When the first ballot was counted no outright winner emerged. None of the three would concede, and it went to a second vote which again ended in stalemate. Judging the moment with some of his old skills, Deacon canvassed support from the backbenchers and – not without some bogus hesitation – allowed his name to be added to the vote. He had timed his intervention well since the procedures had attracted widespread derision from the Opposition and a great deal of acrimony within the party. On the third ballot he was returned with an overwhelming majority, a verdict greeted with relief. The following day he went to the Palace: Parliament was dissolved and a General Election was called.

With memories of the assassination and plane crash still fresh in everybody's mind the short period of electioneering that distinguishes the British system from the American was refreshingly free of dirty tricks. Deacon proved to be an able performer on television, statesmanlike, giving the impression of being removed from the battle in the manner of de Gaulle, and his promises were few. Instead he appealed to the electorate to vote for a period of stability and reconstruction, a sentiment that went down well and cut across class barriers. The middle parties being in their usual state of confusion, the election became a straight fight between the Tories and Labour, and since in the post-Thatcher years, the former had never fully recovered from the shock of being thrust from office, the polls gave Deacon a healthy lead which, on the day, proved accurate. On a below-average turnout, Labour was returned to office with an overall majority of forty-six, more than sufficient to ensure a full term. The electorate relaxed back into its customary stupor, the media allowed

Deacon his honeymoon period and outwardly very little changed.

Deacon spent two thoughtful weeks before finalizing his Cabinet choices, bringing in several young backbenchers as junior ministers, and in general appointing only those he believed he could trust. In his post-election address to the nation he promised to tackle the burning problem of inner-city violence and the plight of old-age pensioners – two very popular issues.

Behind the scenes he prepared to pay off old scores and settle old debts. He had waited a long period in the wings, and now was determined to enjoy playing the star role. Always a skilful debater in the House, he was less concerned with the day-to-day parliamentary scene than with consolidating his position in those areas where he knew he had to protect himself.

He invited Control to be his house guest the first weekend he spent at Chequers – the unprepossessing Cromwellian pile that serves as a grace-and-favour dwelling for the Prime Minister of the day. It was there, after a dinner that could hardly be described as gourmet fare (Deacon always ate frugally), that the first of these old scores was settled.

'I think', Control said, raising a glass of port laid down by Churchill, 'that modest congratulations are in order.'

They were alone in the long gallery.

'You fought a brilliant campaign, and perhaps you will allow that I played my own small part in bringing it about.'

Deacon accepted the toast. 'Though we should never forget the tragic circumstances that prompted the election.'

'Indeed not.'

'Naturally, I would have wished it otherwise.'

'Wouldn't we all?'

'Not wishing to speak ill of the dead, it did seem to me that in certain respects Bayldon invited his own untimely end.'

'Really? You think so? In what way?'

'It's always dangerous not to be the master in one's own house.'

There was something about his tone – a note of overfriendliness – that gave Control a twinge.

426

'I always got the feeling that he was being manipulated. Again, one doesn't want to malign a man who can no longer defend himself, but the impression gained was that of a puppet.'

'You mean his wife exercised undue influence?'

'Possibly that was a factor. But I was thinking of more sinister influences.'

'They were never brought to my attention,' Control said. 'What excellent port this is. May I help myself?'

'Please. You surprise me,' Deacon continued relentlessly, spotting the ploy. 'The fact that you say you were unaware of outside pressures where Bayldon was concerned.'

'There are always rumours, of course. I dare say that before long they'll rear their heads in your direction; it's a hazard of high office. My main function is to sort the wheat from the chaff.'

At that moment their discussion was interrupted by a member of the staff.

'Your other guest has arrived, Prime Minister.'

'Oh, right. Ask him to be good enough to wait a few minutes, will you? Offer him a drink. I'll ring down when I'm ready.'

'Am I in the way?' Control asked.

'Not at all. You were saying about your main function . . .'

'Yes. Looking after the security of the realm is always a balancing act. If one has a secret service, then it has to be secretive. People, especially Members of Parliament if I may say so, feel that every aspect of confidentiality should be made public except that which concerns them personally. Is that a very cynical observation?'

Deacon did not give a direct answer. 'Wouldn't you also say that also applies to the holders, past and present, of your position?' He lingered momentarily over the word 'present'. 'We all need to recall Caesar's wife.' He leant to pick up the decanter and replenish his own glass. 'A period in the wilderness has certain advantages. One has the time, employing one's own sources, and using your own metaphor, to sort the wheat from the chaff with a degree of objectivity – sources,

427

I might add, that appear to have a more reliable perspective on things than yourself. Tell me,' he continued evenly before Control could react, 'that case a few years back about your man Hillsden . . . As I studied it, there was an element of mystery that was never fully explained.'

'The facts spoke for themselves. He was a rotten egg, like too many others before him. But I think we can now say with confidence that our stables are clean.'

'Clean, but perhaps not spotless,' Deacon said.

'What does that mean?'

'Hillsden, it appears, like that other wretched case that surfaced some years back, had an urge to write his memoirs from afar. By sheer good fortune they found their way to me, and I must say they make fascinating reading. Unpublishable, of course, but of consuming interest to stable-cleaners.'

Control just managed to keep his face composed. He took a sip of port. 'Can one ask how they found their way to you?'

'Yes, of course. Excuse me.' He pressed a button on the house phone. 'Charles, show my guest up.'

He turned back to Control. 'I thought the most useful way of dealing with such a sensitive matter was to ask your successor here to explain matters. After all, we none of us want another tawdry scandal, do we? And I'm sure that once you've heard what he has to say you'll take the right course.'

He stood up as a door was opened halfway down the gallery and a man entered the room and advanced towards them.

'I believe you know each other from way back,' Deacon said, as Keating joined them.

29

Just before dawn on a November morning, a firing squad drawn at random from units of the SAS took up their position in an isolated field close to the permanent army encampments at Aldershot.

In front of them three members of the Workers' Militia stood bound to gun-carriage wheels secured by stakes driven into the damp soil. Each wore a uniform stripped of all insignia. Tried in camera, they had been found guilty of treason and the torture and murder of the ex-member of one of Her Majesty's security services, to wit William Charles Waddington.

The scene was witnessed by high-ranking officers from all three services, together with a small group of civilians, the Deputy Commissioner of the Metropolitan Police and a judge, together with an Army Medical Corps major, a Catholic priest and a Church of England padre. Two army ambulances waited on an adjacent roadway.

The officer commanding the firing squad, Lieutenant-Colonel Hugh Woodley, attended by his Regimental Sergeant-Major, walked to the three men and made a final inspection of the bonds securing them. When satisfied, he and the RSM withdrew as the judge came forward to read the authority for the execution in a voice that failed to carry to the onlookers.

'Pursuant to the Suppression of Terrorism Act 1991, you have been found guilty of treason against the Crown and the elected government of the United Kingdom, for which the sentence is death. I am charged hereby to inform you that, all the due processes of law having been exhausted, Her Majesty's Principal Secretary for Home Affairs could find no grounds for commuting the sentences and that therefore the verdicts of the court of execution by firing squad will be carried out forthwith. And may God have mercy on your souls.'

The three men listened without expression, staring past the judge as though trying to identify the faces of the firing squad. Once the judge had retired the two clergymen came forward, passing along the line to intone the last rites. When they had finished Woodley offered the condemned men blindfolds. Two accepted. He and the RSM then came to attention in front of the three men, both turning to the left without command and marching away some thirty paces. Halting, they did a parade-ground about-turn and, still at attention, Woodley gave the order to take aim.

The twelve men in the firing squad brought their automatic rifles to the ready. As was customary, only eleven of the weapons were loaded with live ammunition and had been scrambled before being issued.

Some of the official observers looked down at their feet in the wet grass as the sound of twelve safety-catches being released broke the silence. There was a moment's pause, then Woodley dropped his hand. Each soldier in the squad fired three rounds rapid. As the reports died away a great gathering of rooks rose screaming from a nearby copse, the massed fluttering of their wings conjuring up, for some of those present, childhood images of the angels of death.

The three men had sagged against their bonds, their shoulders distorted in the same way that the shoulders of cripples are distorted by crutches. Now Woodley marched forward again and removed his revolver from the side-holster. Stepping close to each man, he administered the *coup de grâce*. Then it was the turn of the medical officer to examine all three and pronounce that life had been extinguished. This done, Woodley handed over to the RSM who brought the firing squad to attention before giving the order for dismissal. They marched in somewhat ragged fashion, for they were all young, as the ambulances drove across the field to remove the bodies.

The official party made their way to the officers' mess where they were served a hot breakfast, the two clergymen saying grace before they ate. The Home Secretary put through a personal call to Deacon informing him that the verdict of the court had been duly carried out without hitch. No statement concerning the trial or execution was ever issued.

It was the first such execution since the end of the Second World War.

POSTSCRIPT

Shortly before the birth of his daughter, Hillsden noticed a small item on the inside pages of *The Times* that he had missed at first reading. Headed DEATH OF A DIPLOMAT, it stated that Sir Raymond Lockfield, who for many years had served in the Foreign Office, had been found dead in his car with a rubber hosepipe connected to the exhaust. At the inquest evidence was given that he had been suffering from depression and a verdict of suicide was recorded.

When next they met he not unnaturally questioned Abramov for further details.

'I know as much as you, Alec. But don't worry about it. He's at peace. That's what we're all looking for. Peace, the world over. Look at your splendid daughter; she's peaceful enough. We must neither of us have regrets. "The past is a foreign country" – isn't that what you once quoted to me?'

'There's another half to the quotation: "They do things differently there." Who will replace him?'

Abramov looked up from admiring the new baby.

'Who can tell? Anything's possible in a democracy, isn't it?'

'Yes,' Hillsden said as Galina joined them, 'even the impossible.'